Somehow he got to his feet and began to run. A foot tripped him and his temple smacked against the wired glass, cracking it across. He kicked out, swung into a crouch and blundered through the first pair of doors, within his reach the exit, the steps, the street. His legs went from under him and the side of his face hit the floor with a slap. Through the muffled sound of traffic, he could hear his attacker breathing hard. Not wanting to, he forced himself to turn his head. Through blood he saw black sweater, balaclava, black gloves. Movement. Fletcher screamed and on his hands and knees he tried to crawl away. The blade cut into his thigh and began to slice towards the knee.

Cutting Edge is the third of John Harvey's Resnick novels, which have met with great critical acclaim and been translated into more than a dozen languages. He has adapted two of the novels for television and is currently adapting them for radio. His other television and radio work includes dramatisations of Arnold Bennett, A.S. Byatt and Bobbie Ann Mason. Since 1977 his Slow Dancer Press has published many contemporary English and American poets and a selected poems, *Ghosts of a Chance*, was published in 1992. After living for several years in Nottingham he now lives in London.

Also by John Harvey

Lonely Hearts*
Rough Treatment*
Off Minor*
Wasted Years*
Cold Light*
Living Proof*
Easy Meat

Ghosts of a Chance (Poetry)

**available in Mandarin*

JOHN HARVEY

Cutting Edge

Mandarin

The lines on page 101 are from *Monkey Links: a love poem*, by David Kresh, published in *SLOW DANCER 21* (Slow Dancer Press, 1988) and used with the author's permission.

A Mandarin Paperback
CUTTING EDGE

First published in Great Britain 1991
by Viking
This edition published 1996
by Mandarin Paperbacks
an imprint of Reed International Books Ltd
Michelin House, 81 Fulham Road, London SW3 6RB
and Auckland, Melbourne, Singapore and Toronto

Although this novel is set in a real city, it is a work of fiction and its events and characters exist only on its pages and in the author's imagination

A CIP catalogue record for this title
is available from the British Library

Typeset by Deltatype Ltd, Ellesmere Port, Cheshire
Printed and bound in Great Britain by
Cox & Wyman Ltd, Reading, Berkshire

One

The first time she had taken off her clothes for him, he had told her she was perfect: not meaning to, not able to stop the word escaping. Perfect. He had met her at a dance two months before and now he pictured her not far from the hospital, occasionally glancing at her watch as she drank a second glass of wine, waiting.

Perfect.

'You look more dead than alive.' The words snapped him back to where he was, the staff nurse facing him, one hand pulling at her uniform where it had bunched above her belt.

'Thanks,' Fletcher said.

Sarah Leonard smiled. 'The new admission . . .' she began.

Fletcher blinked, willing himself to concentrate. He had slept three hours out of the last twenty-four, eleven from the past seventy-two and he thought he might be delirious.

'Probably a stroke,' Sarah was saying. 'Neighbour alerted the police. He'd been on his kitchen floor for two days.'

'How old?'

'Seventy?'

'I'll clerk him in the morning.'

'He's going to need fluids. You'll have to put in a Venflon tonight.'

'You could do that yourself.'

'You know as well as I do it's against policy.'

Fletcher smiled. 'I won't tell.'

She gave him the smile back a little with her eyes. Somewhere along the ward, a patient was breaking one hacking cough upon the back of another. Nearby, a youth with stitches latticed across his face was silently crying. Calls of 'Nurse!' rose and fell like a litany.

'Very well, staff,' said Fletcher with mock solemnity.

'Thank you, doctor.' She waited for him to move then fell into step beside him.

The patient lived alone on the twelfth floor of a tower block and it had taken two ambulance men and one police officer to get him down the stairs after the lift had jammed. Now he lay on his back beneath blankets, his face grey, legs and ankles swollen. He had to weigh close to seventeen stone.

Fletcher slapped the inside of the man's forearm with the back of his own fingers, searching for a vein. It wasn't only the excessive fat that was a problem: there were hypothermia, shock.

'He's peripherally shut down,' Fletcher said, turning over the arm.

Sarah nodded, watching the needle, waiting to apply the necessary pressure higher up.

'I'll try the back of the hand,' Fletcher said.

He opened his eyes wide and then narrowed them, focusing down. The point of the needle punctured the edge of the vein and passed through.

'Shit!'

He steadied himself and prepared to try again. Behind them, the screaming that had started several minutes ago showed no signs of stopping.

'Can you manage?' Sarah asked.

'Does it look like it?'

Quickly, she applied a tourniquet and left him to it. Fletcher succeeded in finding the vein this time, but was slow in releasing the tourniquet and blood jumped back before he could close off the end of the cylinder. A fine spray speckled his hands and the front of his white jacket and now a puddle was seeping through the top blanket.

He passed Sarah on her way back to the bed. 'A thousand ml of natural saline over twenty-four hours,' he said, not breaking his stride.

'Where are you going?' Sarah asked over her shoulder.

'Off duty.'

She picked up the bloodied needle from where he had let it fall beside the patient's arm and, shaking her head, deposited it in the *sharps* disposal. The blankets were slowly staining a deeper red and would need changing. Without seeming hurried, Sarah finished setting up the drip.

Fletcher bent low over the sink and splashed cold water up into his face. In the mirror he looked like someone who habitually spent long hours underground. He knew that if he didn't shave, his stubble would score Karen's skin raw but it seemed more important to get there before she grew tired of waiting. He would phone as he left the hospital and tell her that he was on his way.

He cupped his hands beneath the tap a final time, combed his fingers through his tangle of dark hair and pulled on a padded blue anorak over his doctor's coat.

For a change the telephone near the exit wasn't already in use, but in Karen's shared house nobody was picking up and answering. After a dozen rings he gave up and hurried up the stairs towards the upper level, fitting the headphones from his Walkman over his ears as he climbed. He pushed through the first set of double doors on to the pedestrian bridge as the duet from the final act of *Manon* was beginning. The bridge arched over the ring road midway between the underpass and the flyover, linking the hospital with the university and the residential areas that closed around it.

Fletcher immediately identified the familiar smell of

rubber that rose from the floor, although the personal stereo, turned up high, kept out the squeak of his shoes as he walked. The air was always stale, the warmth trapped in at either end, no matter the outside temperature.

He walked unsteadily, hands jammed down into his pockets, weaving slightly like someone the worse for drink. The lights of cars moving fast down hill, south from the city, blistered through the wired glass. Here and there, the sides had been flyposted, advertising social events, political meetings, a pram race along the canal.

Fletcher sang along with the music, suddenly energetic and off-key. If things worked out with Karen, he'd get tickets for Opera North next month and bribe himself a couple of evenings off. If things worked out . . . Unobserved, the door giving access to the steps up from the street swung open at his back.

Fifteen yards from the far side and he had still not heard the accelerated tread of soft-soled shoes in his wake. Strange that he was thinking, not of Karen, but of Staff Nurse Sarah Leonard's half-smiling, half-accusing eyes, when finally he realized he was not alone. A quick reflection glimpsed in the glass door before him and Fletcher turned his head in time for the downward sweep of the blade, illuminated in a fast curve of orange light.

The blow sent him stumbling backwards, losing his footing as he cannoned against the centre of the doors and pitched forward, thinking before the belated sear of pain that he had been punched, not cut. The headphones had fallen from his face and Massenet poured tinnily out. Fletcher raised an open hand to ward off his attacker and the blade sank deep into his palm before swerving clear.

Somehow he got to his feet and began to run. A foot tripped him and his temple smacked against the wired glass, cracking it across. He kicked out, swung into a crouch and blundered through the first pair of doors, within his reach the exit, the steps, the street. His legs went from under him and the side of his face hit the floor with a slap. Through the muffled sound of traffic, he could hear his attacker breathing hard. Not wanting to, he forced himself to turn his head. Through blood he saw black sweater, balaclava, black gloves. Movement. Fletcher screamed and on his hands and knees he tried to crawl away. The blade cut into his thigh and began to slice towards the knee.

Karen Archer upended the empty bottle into the waste bin in the corner of her room and fingered the portable TV set off. By the time she had got downstairs to the phone, whoever had been calling had rung off. It could have been Tim, wanting to tell her he was on his way, apologizing yet again for being delayed.

'Go out with a houseman,' one of her medical student friends had said, 'and that's what you get.'

'What?'

'Not a lot.' Laugh. Except that it wasn't.

The last time Tim Fletcher had been round he had been fast asleep within ten minutes; she had pulled off the rest of his clothes, tucked the duvet round and sat cross-legged beside him, wearing two extra sweaters and reading Eliot. He hadn't been a lot of fun either.

Karen took a pack of cigarettes from the back of her underwear drawer, failed to find a box of matches and put the pack back again. She didn't need one. If that had been Tim on the phone, he might be on his way.

She pulled on her ankle-length suede boots and took down from behind the door the camel coat her aunt had thoughtfully found in an Oxfam shop in Richmond. Pocketing her keys, she headed down the stairs, automatically stepping over the one with the missing tread. If she walked in the direction of the bridge, more than likely she would meet him.

Two

'Another, Charlie?'

'Better not.' Resnick shook his head. 'Time I was making a move.'

'Right. Right.' Frank Delaney nodded understandingly, reached over the bar and poured a fresh Guinness into the detective inspector's glass.

'Some of us start earlier than others,' Resnick said. The clock to the left of the small stage showed the wrong side of midnight.

'Sure you do,' Delaney winked. 'Sure you do. And after tomorrow I needn't be getting up at all.' He raised his own glass towards Resnick's face and smiled. 'A toast, Charlie. Early retirement.'

The glasses clinked and both men drank, Resnick sparingly.

'How long is it for you, Charlie?'

'Retirement?'

'Can't be long now.'

'Long enough.'

It lay ahead of him like some unwelcome sea, something to be swum through every morning, no matter the weather; the same aimless movements, made simply to be doing something, an illusion: either that or you trod water until one day you drowned.

'Tomorrow morning,' Frank Delaney said, 'eleven o'clock. I shall be in the bank in my best suit, shaking hands. Someone will give me a fountain pen with a 24-carat gold nib and not so many minutes later I'll be walking out of there with a cheque for a million pounds. Not bad, eh, Charlie, for an ignorant son of a bitch like me? Left school at fourteen with the arse hanging out of his trousers. Not bad.'

Resnick sipped at his Guinness and glanced around the room. When Frank Delaney had bought the place – what? Ten years back? More? – it had been little more than four walls and space on the floor for the drunks to fall safely. Frank had brought in carpets and couch seats with dark upholstery, chandeliers and a mishmash of mostly fake Victoriana. At the weekends, he'd instituted Old Time Music Hall and with a little persuasion would get up at the mike himself and lead the patrons through choruses of 'You Made Me Love You', 'Who's Sorry Now?'

In the week the doors were opened to other things: country and western, poetry and jazz. By this week's end the developers would be tearing out the inside, stripping it all away. Another office block in the making.

'We've had some good nights here, Charlie.'

Resnick nodded. 'We have.'

On that stage he had heard some of the best music of his life: David Murray, Stan Tracey – on a cold March evening, Red Rodney, who'd played trumpet with Charlie Parker when little more than a kid, had brought tears of pleasure to Resnick's eyes and goose pimples to his skin.

'Have I told you what folk said when I bought this place, Charlie?'

Only a dozen times.

'They said I'd go bust within a six-month. Bankrupt.'

Delaney laughed and opened another bottle of Newcastle Brown. 'I've shown 'em. Eh?'

Resnick covered his own glass with his hand and stood up. 'No regrets, then, Frank?'

Delaney gave him a long look across the rim of his glass. 'A million pound? From nothing, more or less. What have I got to be regretful about?' He got to his feet and shook

Resnick's hand. 'Anything else, that's sentimentality. Won't even pay the rent.'

Resnick walked through the partly-darkened room towards the door. Sliding back the bolt, turning the heavy key, he let himself out on to the street. Fletcher Gate. Directly across from him a youth wearing baggy jeans and with his shirt sleeves rolled high was vomiting chicken biriani against the brick of the car-park wall. A black and white cab rose up the hill from the station and Resnick thought about hailing it, but realized he was in no great hurry to get home after all.

'Hey, you!' the youth opposite called out at him belligerently. 'Hey, you!'

Resnick slotted his hands into his overcoat pockets and crossed the road at a steep angle, head slightly bowed.

When Resnick had first been a beat copper, walking these streets in uniform, himself and Ben Riley, the winos, the down-and-outs, the homeless had looked away as they passed. A scattering of old men who sat around their bottles of cider, VP wine. Now there were kids who hung around the soup kitchens, the shelters, young enough to have been Resnick's own. And these thrust out a hand, looked you in the eye.

Eighteen to twenty-six. Smack in the trap. Too many reasons for not living at home, too few jobs, precious little from the state: now they shared Slab Square with the pigeons, sprawled or hunched before the pillars of the Council House, the ornate mosaic of the city's coat of arms, the pair of polished limousines waiting to carry civic dignitaries to this important function or that.

The more you descended Goose Gate, the less prestigious the shops became. Two sets of lights and you were in the wholesale market, broken crates and discarded dark blue tissue, and beyond that Sneinton, where gentrification was still a word best left to crosswords. Fourteen Across: A process of changing the character of the inner-city.

Before the first of those traffic lights the pavement broadened out and Resnick slowed his step. There were a dozen or more people between the telephone kiosk and the entrance to Aloysius House. Two were in the kiosk itself, keeping warm with the aid of a quarter-bottle of navy rum. *This is a dry house* read the sign by the entrance. A middle-aged man, wearing the upper half of a grey pin-striped suit and with dark trousers that gaped over pale flanks, leaned back against the wall as he drained a can of Special Brew, shaking the last drops into his mouth.

'Locked out?' Resnick asked the nearest of the men.

'Fuck you!' the man replied.

Resnick moved closer to the door, brushing against a couple who declined to step aside.

'Wondered how long it'd be before they sent for you,' one of them said accusingly.

Resnick's head turned instinctively from the cheap alcohol on his breath.

'Sodding copper!' he explained to his companion.

The second man stared at Resnick, cleared his throat and spat on to the pavement, close between Resnick's shoes.

'Need a bloody sight more than you to sort this out,' called someone. 'Bastard's in there with a bastard axe!'

Resnick knocked on the glass of the hostel door. There were two men in the small lobby, one of them sitting on the floor. Resnick took out his warrant card and held it against the glass, motioning for them to let him in.

Inside the dimly lit main room, bodies shifted and snored in the darkness. Here and there Resnick saw the dim glow of a cigarette. From one of the chairs, knees tucked into his chest, someone cried out in a dream.

The woman who had charge of the night shift came towards Resnick from the foot of the stairs. She was wearing a cream-coloured sweater over dark sweatpants,

Resnick couldn't be certain of the colour in that light. Her hair had been pulled up at the sides and sat a little awkwardly, secured by a pair of broad combs, white plastic. She was in her late twenties, early thirties and her name was Jean, Joan, Jeanie, something close. He had been introduced to her once at Central Station, he couldn't remember exactly when.

'Inspector Resnick?'

He nodded.

'Jane Wesley.'

That was it. He thought she was about to offer him her hand, but she thought better of it. She was a well-built woman, tall, five nine or ten, and she had the nervousness in her voice pretty much under control.

'I didn't send for you.'

'I was passing. Quite a crowd you've got outside.'

'They're all waiting to see what happens before they come back in.'

'What is going to happen?'

She glanced towards the stairs. 'That depends.'

'On what?'

When she grinned, the dimples at the edges of her mouth made her seem much younger, more carefree; the way she was before she got into social sciences and Christianity. 'On what he does with the meat axe,' Jane said.

'What seems to be his plan?'

'The last I heard, he was threatening to chop his foot off.'

'Unless?'

'Unless I stayed on this side of the door.'

'Which is what you've done?'

'So far.'

'Sounds reasonable.'

Jane frowned; the dimples were a long time gone. 'He's not on his own. There are two others in with him.'

'Friends?'

She shook her head. 'Not as far as I know.'

'Has he threatened to harm them?'

'Not yet.'

Resnick looked at his watch. It was a quarter to one. 'Why didn't you call the station?'

'I was about to. I think. With the best will in the world, every time somebody steps in here in uniform, we lose somebody else's trust.'

'Better than their foot,' Resnick suggested.

'Yes.'

'Besides, I'm not in uniform.'

'You don't need to be.'

'Will you shut up,' bellowed a voice from the corner, 'and let me get some sleep!'

Resnick went towards the stairs. 'Which room?' he asked.

'Straight ahead,' Jane answered. 'The reading room.'

Resnick depressed the switch for the landing light, but it remained stubbornly off. He knocked on the door and waited: nothing. Knocking again, he identified himself. No response. If there were three people inside and all three of them still alive, they were exhibiting more than usual control. It occurred to him that the excitement might have exhausted them to the point where they had all fallen asleep.

He tried the handle and it turned.

'All right,' he called. 'I'm coming in.'

'No!' The muffled voice stretched the word into two syllables.

'Stand well back,' Resnick warned.

'Open that door and I'll use this fucking thing! Don't think I'm fucking kidding!'

Resnick went in fast. Several piles of books had been strewn across the floor, mostly discarded paperback westerns and old copies of *Reader's Digest* donated by well-wishers. More books, dog-eared, sat on shelves to one side: Leon Uris, Wilbur Smith. Of the three people inside the room, however, none was showing the least interest in reading.

One man, his feet bare within open leather sandals, sat on the floor, a soiled grey blanket with red stitching at the hem, covering his head and shoulders. Another, eyes closed and aimed at the ceiling, sat on a straightbacked chair, hand inside his open fly, thoughtfully masturbating.

The third, narrow-cheeked, grey-haired and bespectacled, stood clutching a butcher's cleaver threateningly above one foot, from which, as if in preparation, he had pulled off both shoe and sock.

For some moments he didn't look up at Resnick and then he did.

'Just heard a kid who thought he'd rediscovered bebop singlehanded,' Resnick said. The man's eyes flickered. 'Bit like hearing somebody fluent in a language they don't understand.'

The eyes flickered again but aside from that the man didn't move.

'Time was,' Resnick said, 'you'd have blown him off the stand.'

'Aye, I daresay.'

'How about the cleaver?' Resnick asked, one cautious step closer.

The grey-haired man looked at the blunted blade, then at his foot. 'Charlie, I think I'll fucking do it this time. I think I will.'

Three

'She's a lovely woman, that.'

'Jane?'

'Lovely.'

They were in a cab skirting the Lace Market, passing Ritzy's on their right. The purple sign still shone above the door, although by now it was all locked up and the last dancers had made their way home. My place or yours? Resnick had been there on a few early, bachelor Saturday nights when it had been, simply, the Palais, and there were still couples quickstepping their way between the jivers. He remembered the women standing alone and sad-eyed at the end of the evening; men who prowled with something close to desperation, anxious to pull someone on to the floor before the last number faded.

'How old d'you think she is, Charlie? Tell me that.'

'Around thirty.'

'Too young for me, then, d'you think?'

Resnick looked at Ed Silver, leaning half against the window, half against the cab's worn upholstery. His grey hair straggled thinly across his scalp and bunched in snagged folds around his ears, like the wool of an old sheep; one lens of his glasses was cracked and the frames bent where they had been trodden on and twisted not quite straight. His eyes were hooded and watery and refused to focus.

'No,' Resnick said. 'Not a bit of it.'

Ed Silver eased himself further back and smiled.

When Resnick had talked Silver into handing him the butcher's cleaver and walking peacefully downstairs, Jane Wesley had been grateful and surprised.

'You know him, don't you?' she asked, spooning instant coffee into chipped mugs.

Resnick nodded.

'But before you went in there? There's no way you could have known who he was.'

Resnick shook his head, gestured no to milk.

'I don't know if I can let him stay. I mean, here, tonight.'

'He can come home with me.'

Her eyes widened; they were pale blue and seemed the wrong colour for her face. 'Are you sure?'

Resnick sighed. 'Just for a bit. While he sorts himself out.' It wasn't as if he didn't see the dangers.

Jane Wesley sipped at her coffee thoughtfully. 'That might take longer than you think.'

'Well,' said Resnick, 'maybe he's worth a little time.' He glanced over to where Silver was sitting in the near dark, fingering the air as if he could turn it into music. 'Runner up in the *Melody Maker* poll three years running. Alto sax.'

Resnick put down his mug of coffee, almost untouched, and turned away.

'When was that?' said Jane Wesley to his back.

The cab pulled over by a stone wall, a black gate that was in need of fresh paint. Lights showed from one of the upstairs rooms and through the stained glass above the front door, an exercise to deter burglars. Resnick leaned down to the cab window and gave the young Asian driver a five-pound note, waiting for the change. The radio was turned low, an almost endless stream of what the Radio Trent DJ would probably call smooth late-night listening for night-owls.

Ed Silver was steadying himself against the wall, while a

large black cat arched its back and fixed him with slanted, yellow eyes.

'This yours?' Silver asked.

'The house or the cat?'

'Either.'

'Both.'

'Huh.' Silver stood away from the wall and offered a hand towards the cat, who hissed and spat.

'Dizzy!' said Resnick reproachfully, opening the gate.

'There's one thing I can't stomach,' Ed Silver mumbled, following him along the twist of slabbed path, 'it's cats.'

Great! said Resnick to himself, turning the key in the lock.

Dizzy slid between his legs and raced for the kitchen. Miles came down the stairs from where he had doubtless been sleeping on Resnick's bed and purred hopefully. Bud, skinny and timid, backed away at the sight of a stranger, until only the white smudge beside his nose could be seen in the furthest corner of the hall.

'Christ, Charlie! You've got three of the little buggers!'

'Four,' Resnick corrected. Somewhere, paw blissfully blindfolding his eyes, Pepper would be curled inside something, anything, sleeping.

'If I'd known that, I'd never have left the cleaver.'

He made up a bed in the room at the top of the house. It smelt damp, but no worse, Resnick was sure, than his guest had become used to. Even so, he fetched up a small electric fan heater and set it working in one corner. By the time he got back downstairs, Silver had swung his legs up on to the sofa in the living room and seemed sound asleep. Resnick went back and found a blanket, draping it over him, smelling the rancid, sickly-sweet smell of his clothing. Urine and rough red wine. Carefully, Resnick removed Silver's glasses and set them down on the carpet, where

Miles sniffed at them curiously to see if somehow they might be food.

By now it was past two and Resnick was wondering whether he would get any sleep himself at all. In the kitchen he ground coffee beans, shiny and dark, doled out food into the cats' four coloured bowls, examined the contents of the fridge for the makings of a sandwich.

The last time he had seen Ed Silver he had not long been wearing his sergeant's stripes. Uniform to CID then back to uniform again: forging a career, following a plan. Silver had been guesting at a short-lived club near the top of Carlton Hill, so far out of the city that few people had found it. When Ed Silver had walked in, instrument cases under both arms, he'd looked around and scowled and called the place a morgue.

The first tune he'd tapped in a tempo that had the house drummer and bassist staring at each other, mouths open. Silver had manoeuvred his alto through the changes of 'I've Got Rhythm' at breakneck speed, but when he realized the locals were capable of keeping up, he'd let his shoulders sag a little, relaxed and enjoyed himself.

Chatting to Resnick afterwards, rolling cubes of ice around inside a tall glass of ginger ale, he'd talked of his first recording contract in seven years, a tour, later that year, of Sweden and Norway.

'See,' he'd said, stretching out both hands. 'No shakes.'

Then he'd laughed and set the glass on the back of one hand and after a few seconds the ice cubes ceased to chink against the inside.

'See!' he'd boasted. 'What'd I tell you?'

Resnick heard nothing more of him for over a year. There was a paragraph in one of the magazines, suggesting that he'd recorded in Oslo with Warne Marsh, but he never saw the album reviewed, or any announcement of its release. What he did read, near the foot of page two on a slow Saturday in the *Guardian*, was that Ed Silver had fallen face first from the stage at the Nuffield Theatre, Southampton, suffering concussion and a nose broken in two places.

Someone had done a good job on the nose, Resnick thought, finishing his sandwich, looking over at Ed Silver, fast out on his sofa. It looked to be the part of his face in the best shape.

He went quietly to the stereo and set Art Pepper on the turntable. Midway through 'Straight Life', he thought he saw Ed Silver's sleeping face twist into a smile. As the tune ended, Silver suddenly pushed himself up on to one arm and, eyes still closed tight, said, 'Charlie? Didn't you used to have a wife?' Without waiting for an answer, he lowered himself back down and resumed his sleep.

Four

Karen Archer found Tim Fletcher at around the time Resnick was beginning his walk down through the Lace Market towards Aloysius House. That is, she found something sprawled across the top of the metal steps which led up from the university grounds to the pedestrian walkway; something dark, wedged half-in, half-out of the first set of doors. An old bundle of discarded clothing, bin-liners stuffed with rubbish and dumped. It wasn't until she was almost at the head of the steps that she realized what was lying there was a person and at first she took it to be a drunk. What told her otherwise was the tubing of a stethoscope protruding from beneath it.

Karen held herself steady against the railing, staring down at the surface of the ring road, rainbowed lightly with petrol. The chipped metal was cold against the palms of her hands, cold on her forehead when she lowered her face against it. When the worst of her panic had passed, when her breathing had finally steadied, only then did she go back to the body. Get closer. Possibly three minutes, four.

She held the door open with her hip and dragged, then pulled, Fletcher inside. No part of him seemed to be moving, other than what she moved for him. As best she could, Karen turned him on to his back and lowered her face until it was close to his; her fingers fidgeted at his wrists, searching for a pulse. She tried not to look at his wounds, along which dark knots of blood had begun to coagulate.

'Tim!' She shouted his name as if the force of the cry might waken him. 'Tim!'

With a soft swoosh an articulated lorry moved beneath the bridge, its lights catching Karen's face as she stood. Fletcher's Walkman lay close by the inner door and, irrationally, she stooped to make sure it was in the *off* position, the battery not wasting.

She hurried through to the hospital, willing her legs to run but getting no response, the squeak, squeak of her trainers on the hard, grooved rubber following her across. She didn't know whether she was leaving Tim Fletcher alive or dead.

It took several moments for Karen to make clear what had happened, but from there all was quiet speed and efficiency. If the casualty officer who spoke to Karen was surprised, he did nothing to betray it. All she saw of Tim were blankets, a stretcher being wheeled between curtains. All she heard were the same quiet voices. Transfusion. Consciousness. Surgery. They sat her in a corner and gave her, eventually, tea, sweet and not quite warm, in a ribbed and coloured plastic cup.

'Is he all right?'

'Try not to worry.'

'Will he be all right?'

Unhurried footsteps, walking away.

'God!' Tim Fletcher had exclaimed, that first time in her room. 'God!' Staring at her face, her breasts. 'You're perfect!'

'Miss?'

Karen's fingers tightened around the cup, glancing up. The police officer had gingery hair and a face that reminded her of her younger brother; he held his helmet against his knee, tapping it lightly, arhythmically, against the blue of his uniform.

'I was wondering,' he said, 'if you might answer a few questions?'

Karen's chest tightened beneath her purple jumper and she began to cry.

The officer glanced around, embarrassed.

'Miss . . .'

The crying wasn't going to stop. He squatted down in front of her, took the cup from her hands and rested it on the floor beside his helmet. In the three months he'd been on the force, Paul Houghton had stepped between four youths squaring up with bottles after closing; he had lifted a panicking three-year-old from a second-floor window and out on to a ladder; close to the end of one shift, he'd followed screams and curses to an alley back of a pub and found a middle-aged man on all fours, the dart that his girlfriend had hurled at his face still embedded, an inch below the eye. In each case, he'd acted, never really stopped to think. Now he didn't know what to do.

'It's okay,' he said, uncertain, reaching out to pat her hand. She grabbed hold of his fingers and squeezed them hard.

'Maybe you'd like another cup of tea?' he suggested.

When she shook her head, Karen's breath caught and the tears became sobs. Inconsolable. Bubbles appeared at both nostrils and, with his free hand, Paul Houghton fished into his pocket and found a tissue, already matted with use.

'Here,' he said, dabbing gingerly.

Heads were turned, staring.

'Rotten bugger!' a woman shouted. 'Leave the girl alone.'

'Stick 'em in a uniform,' commented another, 'and they think they can do as they bloody like!'

'I'm sorry,' breathed Karen, using the soiled tissue to wipe round her eyes, finally to blow her nose.

'S'all right.'

He wasn't like her brother, Karen thought, looking at

him through blurred lashes, he was younger. She felt sorry for him then, beyond the mere platitude, meaning it.

Karen handed him back his scrappy tissue and he stuffed it out of sight, standing. The backs of his legs ached and he wanted to rub them, but didn't. He took his notebook from his breast pocket.

'I shall have to ask you some questions,' he said, blushing.

Resnick had finally got to bed at four and found himself unable to sleep. Miles and Bud were a weight at the bottom of the covers and Ed Silver's broken snoring filtered up from the floor below, nudging him where he didn't want to go.

Didn't you used to have a wife, Charlie?

No cats then and every penny counted. DC's pay. Elaine had kept the house well, having been the one to see it first, boxed advert in the paper, *must be viewed to be appreciated.* Walking him round from room to room, hand in his or beneath the arm, guiding. *That fireplace, Charlie. Look. Isn't it wonderful?* The mortgage had stretched them fine, his salary and hers; evenings of repapering and painting; front and back garden some nights till dark. *Just as well I'm working, Charlie. Without that, I don't know where we'd be.*

Back in Lenton, Resnick's answer, unspoken, St Anne's or Sneinton, a two-bedroom terraced with a bricked-in yard and a front lawn you could clip in fifteen minutes with a pair of shears.

Time a-plenty for moving, he might have said. When we need the room.

All that early interest in real estate, it prepared Elaine for the man she was to go off with, eventually, when the tacky weeks of subterfuge were at an end. That Tuesday afternoon when Resnick had driven through Woodthorpe, not his usual route at all, cutting down from Mapperley

Plains, he had seen the dark blue Volvo first, parked with its near-side wheels on the kerb, close to the For Sale sign at the gate. A man in a three-piece suit, not tall, keys in hand, walking towards it. And a pace behind him, buttoning up the tailored jacket that she wore for work, Elaine. Still smiling.

How many other empty properties she had visited with her lover, how many evenings she had passed in his Volvo, discreetly parked, Resnick had not wanted to know. Later, all out in the open, in court, nothing left to lose, Elaine had made sure that he did.

Knowing hadn't meant that he understood. Not exactly, not quite. The mystery of living with someone for so long and never really knowing them, little more than how they like their tea, the wrist on which they wore a watch, which angle they prefer to lie in bed.

Not long ago there had been three letters: the first two close together, the third after a gap of several months. There had been no mistaking the writing and by the time the last arrived, curiosity had got the better of him. He had read the first sentences quickly, the first communication from Elaine in almost ten years; glanced at the end, where she had written, *Love.* After tearing it, he had taken it into the kitchen and burned it.

Ed Silver had stopped snoring; the cats were curled into each other and still. Without meaning to, Resnick slept.

'How'd it go at the hospital, Ginge? Waste of time?'

Paul Houghton fidgeted with a collar that was always too tight. 'Not exactly, sarge.'

'Let's be having it, then.'

Only a brief way into Houghton's verbal report, the sergeant interrupted him, picked up the phone and dialled the uniformed inspector on night duty.

'If you've a minute, sir, you might care to come through . . . Right, sir. Yes.'

He set the receiver down and looked across at Paul Houghton with a half-grin. 'Making a bit of a habit of this, aren't you? Darts, sharp implements.'

Houghton shrugged. 'Suppose so, sarge.'

'Girl as found him, all right, was she?'

'Upset, sarge, naturally, but . . .'

'No, I mean was she *all right*?'

He could feel the red rising up his neck. 'I didn't really . . .'

'Held her hand, did you? You know, make her feel better.'

Paul Houghton was blushing so strongly that the backs of his eyes had begun to water.

Five

Season of mists and bollocking fruitfulness! Okay, it meant, with any luck, he'd be back in the First XV, a few jugs after the match, but that apart, what was it? Grey mornings when your car wouldn't start on account of the tossing damp and alternate Saturdays when, instead of playing a proper game, you were on overtime babysitting a bunch of pissed-up morons with shit for brains and arseholes where their mouths were supposed to be. Christ! Mark Divine thought, if there was one thing that summed autumn up for him, that was it. Hanging around the railway station waiting for some excursion special so you could crocodile a mob from Manchester or Liverpool or Chelsea (they were the worst, Chelsea, the ones for whom he saved his real loathing, no doubt about it) across the river to trade insults and worse with the Forest fans massed at the Trent End.

That was autumn, not the poncey crap Yeats or Keats or whoever reckoned it to be. And he'd seen that other soft bastard, not Keats or Yeats, six foot under the pair of them, dead from the neck down now as well as up, not them but Quentin, that bloody teacher, the one who had them all learning that gobbledegook, standing up and reading it out. Clearly, clearly, what are you mumbling into your boots for? That's it, Mark, you read it for us. Good and strong. Wonderful, Divine! Smirking at his own stupid joke, rest of the kids sniggering and making faces, bending their hands at him like he was some kind of poofter. As if it wasn't hard enough, going through school with a name like

Divine, without some clever-clever bastard taking the piss out of him in front of everyone.

Still, he'd seen him, Quentin, just the other week, standing in line at the post office, waiting to get his old-age pension most likely, poor old sod with one leg locked like he had bad arthritis and dandruff spread over the back of his jacket as though someone had been at his scalp with a cheese grater. Given Divine a lot of satisfaction that had, thinking about him shuffling off home to read some crap about getting old, dying.

It still brought a smile to his face now, signalling right going round Canning Circus, weather forecast on the radio, five to seven driving into the station for the early shift.

Divine spun the wheel hard, loosening his grip as it swung back, straightening before turning again, left this time, across the pavement and into the car park. One good thing about coming in at this time, always plenty of room. He grabbed his jacket from the rear seat and locked the car door. The only good thing, just about. The night's files to sort through, prisoners in and out, messages to be arranged into two sets, national and local, all of that so that the DI didn't stand there with his mouth gaping open when he took the briefing at eight.

Like as not there'd been the usual rash of burglaries in the small hours and that would account for the best part of his day, his responsibility, trying to have patience with some stupid cow who left the kitchen window open to let the air circulate and didn't reckon on her new video and CD player being put back into circulation at the same time.

And – pushing open the door past the custody sergeant's office, the corridor leading to the cells – on top of all that, he had to make the sodding tea!

Not this particular morning.

'I've mashed already.'

Bloody hell! What was he doing here? Hadn't noticed his car downstairs. Resnick sitting at one of the desks in the middle of the CID room, not even in his own office, chair pushed back on two legs and reading the paper. He wasn't supposed to be here for half an hour yet.

'You can pour us a mug if you like. Milk, not too much, no sugar. Couple of juicy break-ins waiting for you, by the look of it. Just carry on as if I wasn't here.'

Resnick turned another page of the *Independent*, dreading the obituaries these days, always another film star you'd lusted over in your youth, another musician you'd heard and now would never get to see. DC Divine walked past him, draped his jacket over the back of his chair and turned the corner to where the teapot was waiting.

Well short of nine the CID briefing was over and Resnick was back in his office, a partitioned rectangle with rotas pinned behind the desk and filing cabinets alongside. A number of the other officers were at their desks, finishing up paperwork before setting off. Mark Divine was already out knocking on doors, ringing bells, examining broken catches, faulty locks, standing straight-faced as homeowners practised on him the exaggerated claims they would foist on their insurance companies by first-class post. Diptak Patel, thermos flask, telephoto lens, Milky Ways and binoculars, was behind the wheel of a stationary Fiesta, watching a clothing warehouse on the Glaisdale Park Industrial Estate. His highlighted copy of Benyon's *A Tale of Failure: Race and Policing* was in the glove compartment for when this, the third successive day of obs, became too boring.

Lynn Kellogg, hair cut newly short and sporting a certain amount of shine from a henna rinse, was allowing Karen Archer an extra half-hour's rest before calling to ask questions about last night. Kevin Naylor stood at the back of the lift making its way up to the ward where Tim Fletcher was now a patient; the last time he'd been in the hospital had been when Debbie had been giving birth and if he were silent enough, he could still hear her voice as she screamed for Entonox, an epidural, anything to stop the pain.

Resnick's DS, Graham Millington, knocked on his door before leaving for a liaison meeting with officers from the West Midlands. A spate of organized thefts of cigarettes and liquor, lorries hijacked or broken into at service areas where they had been parked, had spread from the West Midlands to the East and back again.

'If this takes as long as it might, sir, OK if I nip straight home? Wife's got her Spanish class, starting tonight.'

'Thought it was Russian, Graham?' said Resnick, looking up.

'New term, sir. Thought she'd have a go at something different.'

Resnick nodded. 'Right. Ring in if that's what you're going to do. You can fill me in in the morning.'

He watched through the glass of the door as Graham Millington automatically adjusted his tie and gave a quick downward tug at the front of his jacket. If he wasn't necessarily going to be the brightest over at Walsall, at least he could be the best pressed. Cleanliness and godliness: a drawer full of perfectly folded shirts and seven pairs of well-buffed shoes set you right on the road to heaven. Millington's father had worked all his life for Horne Brothers and at weekends been a lay preacher for the Wesleyan Methodists.

Resnick checked his watch and collected his files. If he failed to knock on the superintendent's door by a minute short of nine Jack Skelton would count him as late.

'Charlie. Maurice.'

Skelton nodded at Resnick and the uniformed inspector in charge, Maurice Wainwright, recently down from Rotherham and still with a little coal dust behind the ears.

'Have a seat.'

While Wainwright was making his report, Resnick kept

his attention on the superintendent's face. Since Skelton's daughter had run wild not so many months back, shoplifting, truanting, acquiring a taste for Ecstasy, the lines around his eyes had bitten tighter, the eyes themselves more ready to flinch. A man who no longer knew where the next blow was coming from. Resnick had wanted to talk to him about it, allow the senior man the chance to unburden himself, if that were what he wanted. But Jack Skelton kept offers of help and friendship at a careful arm's length; his response to the rupture of a life that had seemed so symmetrical was to withdraw further, redraw the parameters so that they seemed even more precise, more perfect.

'How's the house-hunting coming along, Maurice?' Skelton asked, the inspector's report over.

'Couple of possibles, sir. Wife's coming down for a look at weekend.'

Skelton pressed together the tips of his spread fingers. 'Sort it soon, Maurice. Down here with you, that's where they should be.'

Wainwright glanced across at Resnick. 'Yes, sir,' he said.

'So, Charlie,' said Skelton, replacing one sheet of paper square on his blotter with another. 'This business at the hospital, doesn't look like your ordinary mugging?'

'Had nigh on fifty pounds on him, small wallet in his back pocket. One of those personal stereos. Credit cards. None of it taken.'

'Lads out for a spot of bother, then, drunk. Lord knows they need little enough reason, nowadays. Wrong place at the wrong time, wrong face, that's enough.'

'Possible, sir. You do get them using the bridge on the way back from the city. Anyone who'd tried a couple of clubs after the pubs'd chucked out and found themselves turned away, they might have ended up there around that time.'

'No reports?'

'Nothing obvious, sir. I'm getting it double-checked.'

'We know there was more than one assailant?' asked Wainwright.

Skelton shook his head. 'We know nothing. Except that he was badly cut, lost a lot of blood. Blow or blows to the head. More than one looks the most likely, either that or someone pretty strong and fit.'

'And presumably not pissed out of his socks,' Wainwright said.

'Someone with a reason, then, Charlie,' said Skelton. 'Motivation other than robbery, if we can leave that aside.' The superintendent uncapped his fountain pen, made a quick, neat notation and screwed the top back into place.

'Hopefully we'll be able to talk to the victim this morning, sir. Any luck, he'll be able to tell us something. And we're having a word with the girl who found him.'

'Chance, was that?'

'Girlfriend, sir. On her way to meet him, apparently.'

'Funny time of night.'

'Funny hours.'

'Worse than ours,' said Wainwright.

'It would be useful if we found the weapon,' said Skelton. 'Attack like that, especially not premeditated, likely to have thrown it.'

'Maurice has sent a couple of men out,' said Resnick, with a nod of acknowledgement in Wainwright's direction. 'Pretty wide verges either side of the bridge, front of the hospital to one side and all that warren of university buildings on the other. A lot to search.'

Skelton relaxed his frown sufficiently to sigh. 'As you say, Charlie, the poor bugger on the receiving end, he's our best hope.'

A more superstitious man than Resnick would have been crossing his fingers; touching wood.

Since being carried into the hospital in the middle of the

previous night, Tim Fletcher had encountered a considerable amount of hospital practice from the receiving end. After some cutting away of clothing, preliminary cleaning of the worst affected areas – right leg, left arm, face and neck, both hands – pressure bandages had been applied in an attempt to staunch further bleeding. A drip had been set up to replace the lost blood with plasma expanders. Those were the essential emergency procedures: the ones which kept him alive.

The casualty officer injected lignocaine into the wounds before beginning the careful, laborious process of stitching them up. Outside, in the corridor, sitting in wheelchairs, chairs, slumped over crutches or girlfriends' shoulders, stretched across the floor, the procession of those waiting for surgery grew. Traffic accidents, disco brawls, teenage bravado, domestic misunderstandings. The casualty officer, conscious of this, took his time nevertheless. As a fellow doctor, Tim Fletcher merited his best attentions – and trained professionals were not so thick upon the ground their potential could be easily wasted. The officer took especial care with Fletcher's hands.

After crossmatching his blood, the plasma was followed up by two units of packed cells. Fletcher, who seemed to have been shifting uneasily in and out of consciousness for hours, was given injections of intramuscular pethidine to help control his pain.

When Kevin Naylor stepped, somewhat self-consciously, on to the ward, Fletcher was lying in a side room, a single bed with its attendant drip attached to the back of his arm. One sleeve of the pyjama jacket he had been given had been cut to allow for bandages, which also swathed his hands and partially masked his face. When Naylor leaned over him, one of Tim Fletcher's eyelids twitched sharply, as if in response to something dreamed or remembered.

'Are you a relative?'

The nurse looked West Indian, though her accent was

local enough, Midlands born and bred. Her hat was pinned none too securely to thickly curled hair and the blue of her uniform lent a gleam to her skin.

'Relative, are you?'

Naylor realized that he hadn't answered. 'Kevin Naylor,' he said. 'CID.'

'Sister know you're here?'

Naylor shook his head. 'I phoned from the station, make sure it was okay to come. Not sure who I spoke to.'

The nurse moved alongside him, glancing down. 'I don't know how much sense you'll get out of him, sedated to the eyeballs. Still, he'll have to be woken soon for his obs. Every half hour.'

Turning back, she saw a smile crossing Naylor's face. 'What're you laughing at?'

'Obs.'

'Observation. What about it?'

'We call it that as well.'

'Same thing, is it then?'

'Similar.'

The nurse grinned: 'If you want to know your temperature, ask a policeman.'

Naylor looked back towards the bed; maybe he'd be better leaving, trying again later.

'I'll let sister know you're here,' the nurse said, heading back on to the main ward.

Tim Fletcher had been aware of various bodies around him during the preceding eight hours; pale faces, white or blue uniforms. Voices that were hushed to hide their urgency. In the midst of it all a single shout, sharp and clear. At one point he had been certain that Sarah Leonard had been standing there in her staff nurse's uniform, smiling down at him, telling him to rest, be assured it would be all right. But when he had tried to speak her name she had disappeared. And Karen. He had not seen Karen, awake or sleeping.

This time there was a young man, twenty-three or -four, wearing a pale blue shirt, a dark check jacket, dark blue tie. Brown hair that didn't seem to be obeying any rules. Doctor? No, he didn't think he was a doctor.

'Detective Constable Naylor,' said the man, younger than Fletcher himself though not looking it – except now, except today. 'I'd like to ask you some questions.'

Fletcher would have loved to have answers. The why and the who of it. Especially the who. All he knew for certain, it had been sudden, unexpected; he had been frightened, hurt. He remembered a black sweater, gloves, a balaclava that covered all of the head save for the eyes and mouth.

'What colour?'

'Black.'

'The eyes?'

'Balaclava.'

'And the eyes?'

Fletcher thought about it, tried to formulate a picture. Identikit, isn't that what they call them? 'Blue,' he said, almost as much a question as an answer.

'You're not sure?'

Fletcher shook his head; just a little. It hurt.

'It could be important.'

'Blue.'

'For certain?'

'No.'

'But . . .'

'As far as I know, as far as I can remember . . . blue.'

'Dr Fletcher,' said the nurse, 'if I can just put this under your arm?'

Naylor watched as the nurse slid the thermometer into the pit of Fletcher's bandaged arm and wrapped a cuff about the other, inflating it prior to checking his blood pressure.

'Go ahead,' she said to Naylor. 'Don't mind me.'

'The weapon,' Naylor asked, glancing at his notebook, 'did you see what it was?'

'I felt it,' Fletcher answered.

The nurse continued to pump up the rubber balloon, inflating the cuff.

'Then you didn't see it?' Naylor persisted.

Downward sweep of the blade, illuminated in a fast curve of orange light.

'Not clearly.'

'Was it a knife?'

'It could have been.'

'An open blade?'

Flinching, Fletcher nodded.

'Can you remember how long?'

'No, I . . . No, I can't be certain.'

'This long?' Naylor held his Biro before Fletcher's face, tight between the tip of his middle finger and the ball of his thumb.

'Blood pressure's fine.'

Fletcher closed his eyes.

The nurse eased the thermometer out from beneath his arm and held it against the light. 'Well?' she said, glancing down towards Naylor with a half-grin.

'Well, what?'

'Temperature, what d'you think?'

'Look,' said Naylor, a touch of exasperation.

'Thirty-seven point eight.'

'Smaller,' said Fletcher weakly, opening his eyes.

'You're doing fine,' the nurse said, touching his shoulder lightly, almost a squeeze. 'Soon be up and about. Dancing.' She looked at Naylor. 'The doctor here, he's a great dancer.'

'It was smaller,' Fletcher said again, an effort to breathe now, an effort to talk. 'Smaller. Like a scalpel.'

Six

Lynnie love, I know your job keeps you awful busy, but it do seem such a long time since your dad and me seen you. Try and come home, even if it's just for a couple of days. That'd mean a lot to your dad specially. I worry about him, Lynnie, I do. More and more into himself he's getting. Depressed. Sometimes it's all I can do to get him to talk, sit down to his supper. Make an effort, there's a love.

Her mother's words jostled inside Lynn Kellogg's head as she crossed University Boulevard, dark green of the rhododendron bushes at her back. Ahead of her was the brighter green of the Science Park, technology disguised as an oversized child's toy. Lynn had a friend she'd gone through school with, bright, but not much more intelligent than Lynn herself. 'My God! You can't be serious? The police? Whatever d'you want to throw your life away like that for?' The friend had gone to Cambridge Poly, got interested in computers, now she was earning thirty thousand a year plus, living with a zoologist in a converted windmill outside Ely.

Thrown her life away, is that what Lynn had done? She didn't think so, glad most of the time that she was in the job, enjoying it, something more worthwhile maybe than writing software programmes to record the fertility and sexing of Rhode Island Reds. What did it matter, what other people thought? The neighbours in her block of housing association flats, who only spoke to her if someone had been tampering with their locks, trying to break into their parked car. Patients in the surgery, where Lynn was waiting for her check-up and a new supply of pills; nudging one another, staring, know what she is, don't you? The way most men she spoke to in a bar or pub would evaporate at the mention of what she did, as if by magic.

Lynnie, no! You aren't serious?

The job.

She checked the address in her notebook and looked up at the front of the house. Mid-terraced, the one to its right was a prime example of seventies stone-cladding, that to the left sported a shiny new door, complete with brass knocker and mail box.

Twenty-seven.

Two curtains had been draped unevenly across the downstairs window, probably held up by pins. Among the half-dozen bottles clustered on the step was one ripe with yellowing, crusted milk. At least, thought Lynn, she didn't live like this.

The girl who finally came to the door was a couple of inches taller than herself, even in woolly socks. She had near-black hair to her shoulders, unbrushed so that it made a ragged frame around the almost perfect oval of her face. She was slender in tapered black jeans, with a good figure that two jumpers – purple and green – failed to disguise. Her eyes were raw from lack of sleep or tears or both. Looking like that, she'd get the sympathy vote as well.

'Karen Archer?'

The girl nodded, stepping back to let Lynn enter. She scarcely glanced at Lynn's warrant card, motioning her past the hall table with its telephone almost hidden beneath free papers, free offers, handouts from Chinese restaurants and taxi firms. A succession of tenants had etched numbers on to the wallpaper in a rising arc, some of them scored heavily through.

'Mind the fourth step,' Karen warned, following Lynn closely.

There was a poster stuck to the door of Karen's room, two lovers kissing in a city street.

'Go on in,' Karen said.

It had originally been a back bedroom, a view from the square of window down over a succession of back yards, old outhouses, an alley pushing narrowly in between. Cats and rusted prams and washing lines.

The interior was a mixture of arranged and untidy: neatly stacked books alongside music cassettes, each labelled in a clear, strong hand; earrings hanging from cotton threads, red, yellow, blue; on the bed a duvet bundled to one side, as though Karen had been lying beneath it when Lynn had rung the bell: tights in many colours dangling down from the mantelpiece and the top of the opened wardrobe door, drying.

'Sit down.'

The choice was between the bed and a black canvas chair with pale wooden arms and Lynn took the latter.

The room smelled of cigarette smoke and good perfume.

'Would you like some coffee?'

There were five used mugs, one on the scarred table, three close together on the floor beside the bed, the last standing on the chest of drawers, in front of a mirror with photographs jutting at all angles from its frame. 'No, thanks,' Lynn said with a quick smile. She was wondering which of the men in the photos was Fletcher.

'What d'you want to know?' Karen said.

They went through the worst first, the discovery of the houseman on the bridge, the fears that he might die, be already dead; then their arrangements for that evening, the phone call which might have been from Fletcher yet might as easily not.

'You haven't known him all that long then?'

Karen shook her head. 'Two months.' She lifted her head to see that Lynn was still looking at her, encouraging her to continue. 'I went to this Medics Ball, I don't know.'

She gestured vaguely with her hand, the one not holding a cigarette. 'I'd been going around with these medical students, I don't know how that started really, except most of the people on my course are a bunch of deadheads. Either that or posers of the first order.'

'Your course?'

'English. Drama subsid. If he didn't die before the Second World War, he didn't exist. That's English anyway. Drama's not so bad.'

'Are they all men, then, the people you study?'

'Sorry?'

'Writers. You said, he.'

Karen stared at her. What the fuck? A feminist policewoman? 'Figure of speech,' she said.

Lynn Kellogg nodded. 'The medical students you mentioned, were they male?'

'Mostly. To be honest, I think women are pretty boring, don't you?'

'No,' said Lynn. 'No, I don't.'

She could see the shifting look in Karen Archer's distressed eyes, the word forming silently behind them – dyke!

'Anyway,' asked Karen, 'what does it matter?'

Lynn sidestepped the question. 'Before you began going out with Dr Fletcher, you did have another boyfriend?'

'Yes.'

'One or several?'

'What's that got to do with you?'

'I mean, this relationship, the earlier one, was it serious?'

Karen dropped the end of her cigarette into a quarter-inch of cold coffee. 'I suppose so.'

'And the man?'

'What about him?'

'Was he serious?'

'Ian?' Karen laughed. 'Only things he gets serious about are anatomy and *Blackadder*.'

'Is he over here?' Lynn went to the mirror, Karen almost grudgingly following. 'One of these?'

'There.'

Karen pointed to a figure in a skimpy swimming costume, lots of body hair, posing at the edge of a pool with a champagne bottle in one hand and a pint glass in the other. There were three other pictures: Ian in a formal dinner jacket but wearing a red nose; Ian flourishing a stethoscope; Ian as Mr Universe.

Wow! thought Lynn. What a guy!

'He looks a lot of fun,' she said. 'Why did you stop going out with him?'

'Is that any of your business?'

'No.'

Karen shrugged and wandered over to the kettle, shaking it to make certain there was enough water before switching it on. 'Sure you don't want one?' she asked, opening the jar of Maxwell House.

'Thanks, no,' said Lynn. 'What's Ian's last name?'

'Carew.'

'And he's still a student here?'

'A medical student, yes. He's in his second year.'

'But you haven't seen him?'

'Not since I started seeing Tim.'

'Not at all?'

'I don't know. Once, maybe.'

'How did he feel about you and Dr Fletcher? I mean . . .'

Karen was laughing, shaking her head, reaching for another cigarette, all at the same time. 'I know what you *mean*. Poor old Ian was so heartbroken at being chucked, he couldn't cope. Especially when the other man was a qualified doctor and he was only a student. So he waited for him one night and tried to kill him: jealousy and revenge.'

The kettle had begun to boil and Karen did nothing to

switch it off. Lynn reached down past her and flicked up the switch, removing the plug safely, the way her mother had taught her.

'It's the sort of thing you see on a bad film on television,' Karen said, 'late at night.'

'Yes,' said Lynn. 'Isn't it?'

She turned back towards the mirror. Right across the top were the pictures of the man she assumed to be Fletcher. Young, young for a doctor, Polaroids that had been taken there, in that room, those strange reflections from the flash sparkling at the centre of his eyes. Bottom left was a strip from a photo booth, one they had sat in together, goofy faces, weird expressions, only in the last were they serious, kissing.

'Have you been to see him?'

'No. I phoned. They said this afternoon.' She glanced at her watch. 'After two.' She spooned milk substitute into the mug of coffee and went back to the bed, stirring carefully. 'I'm a bit frightened to see him, I suppose. After what's happened to him.' She sipped, then drank. 'What he'll look like.'

Does it matter? thought Lynn. And then, of course it does.

'You didn't notice anybody?' she asked. 'Walking to meet him. Hanging around by the bridge.'

'No one. Traffic. No one walking. Not that I saw.'

'You're sure?'

'Sure.'

'This Ian,' Lynn said, nodding over towards the photographs as she stood, 'someone will most likely talk to him.'

'That's ridiculous.'

'Maybe. But I expect it will be done.' Lynn hesitated at the door. 'If you do think of anything that might be important, give me a call.' She placed a card on the corner of the pillow. 'Thank you for your time, I'll see myself out.'

Karen stood up but made no move towards the door.

Lynn hurried down the stairs, remembering which step to beware, wondering why she had felt so hostile, offered the girl so little support. What combination had it been, she wondered, walking briskly up the street, that had made her withhold her sympathy? Why had she felt jealous and superior, the feelings hand in hand?

Seven

Mid-morning. Graham Millington was sitting in a smoke-wreathed room in Walsall, watching a DI write names and dates on a white board, using his coloured markers with a definite flourish. A detective sergeant stuck flags into a map of the Midlands at appropriate points and offered commentary in a flat Black Country accent. What was it the wife wanted me to pick up from the shops, Millington was thinking, mushrooms or aubergines? Millington had never been quite clear what it was you did with an aubergine. He copied information down into his notebook, glanced about him. Nine out of eleven smoking away as if their lives depended upon it. He tried to remember what he had heard on the radio earlier that week, research some Americans had been doing into passive inhalation of nicotine. God, he thought, if this goes on beyond twelve that's likely as not another six months off my lifetime . . . or was it six minutes?

Patel pushed his tongue up against the back of his teeth, trying to ease away the last remnants of Milky Way. You could sit for just so long watching cream-coloured breeze-block without going into a trance. Meditation. Hadn't he been toying for ages with the idea of taking it up? He could hear them in the canteen if ever they found out. Yeah, great, Diptak, what comes next? Swallowing fire? Sleeping on nails? Except that they never called him Diptak. Or much else. To his face, anyway. He picked up his camera as two men in blue overalls came out of the nearest building and almost immediately set it down again. The men settled themselves up against the wall, facing what sun there was, unpacked their sandwiches, unscrewed their flasks. Patel wondered how long he could go before opening the empty orange juice container under the seat to take a pee.

'I think they must have got in through here.'

'Yes,' murmured Divine, 'most likely.'

He stood at the window of what estate agents liked to call a utility room, looking out over a quarter-acre of lawns, fruit bushes, shrubs with unpronounceable Latin names and flowers fading down into wooden barrels. Beyond that, on a lower level, was a full-sized tennis court, complete with green wire surround and floodlights. He wondered where they kept the swimming pool. Probably down in the basement, along with the steam room and the jacuzzi.

'You will do your best to catch them?'

Daft cow, standing there in some sort of silk dressing-gown, rings down her fingers enough to open a branch of Ratners and a bit of tangerine cloth round her head like she's thinking about joining a very select order of nuns.

'Yes,' said Divine, choking back the word 'madam'. 'We'll do what we can. You'll let us have a full list of what's missing, of course?'

The doorbell chimed four bars of Andrew Lloyd Webber.

'Excuse me,' she turned smoothly away, 'that must be the cleaning woman.'

Oh, yes, thought Divine, coming in the front door too, must have had good references. He was glad he'd forgotten to wipe his feet on the way in.

Lynn saw Kevin Naylor sitting on his own at the far side of the canteen and wasn't sure whether to go and sit with him or not. Up until recently she would have had no hesitation, but lately Kevin had been short with her, abrupt and eager to keep his distance. She knew there were problems at home with Debbie, with the baby. There had been an evening when they might have talked about it, Kevin and herself, almost had. Tired, he had come back to her flat for coffee, but instead of talking he had fallen asleep. Waking, he had only hurried away, half-guilty. Lynn recalled from that evening her hand momentarily against Kevin's upper arm. What had that been about? And asking him back – coffee? Come back for coffee? She thought about Karen Archer saying that to Fletcher after the Medics Ball, that or something like it. What had he understood by that?

There had been a film they'd shown on the TV, a year or so before, between the adverts. A young woman moving around her flat, making sure the bedroom door was open, clear view of the bed; the camera on the man's face then, suggesting what he was thinking, condoms, AIDS, wouldn't you like to stay the night? Was that what Kevin had been afraid of? She doubted it. She took her cup of tea and pulled out the chair opposite him. If he didn't want to talk to her, he could get up and move away.

'How did it go at the hospital?' she asked.

'It's your wife, sir,' called someone as Resnick left his office.

'What?'

'Your wife.' A young DC leaned back from his desk, holding a receiver aloft.

'Don't be so bloody daft!'

Resnick shouldered his way through the door and hurried down the stairs. He was already late for his appointment with the DCI. He wondered whether Ed Silver had woken and, if so, if he were still in the house. Remembering his remark about the cleaver, Resnick felt a twinge of apprehension on behalf of his cats. No, he thought, stepping out on to the street, if he tries anything funny Dizzy'll soon sort him out.

Ignoring his car, Resnick crossed in front of the traffic at an ungainly trot and set off downhill past the new Malaysian restaurant, raincoat flapping awkwardly around him.

'Kevin,' said Lynn, unable to lift the testiness from her voice.

'What?'

'We've been sitting here for almost twenty minutes and you've either said nothing or gone on about some nurse you reckon fancied you.'

'So?'

'So I thought we were supposed to be comparing notes, seeing if we're any closer to understanding why that doctor was attacked.'

'Funny. I thought we were having a tea break. Bit of relaxation. Besides, I never asked you to sit here.'

'Maybe you'd prefer me back in uniform – just a different kind.'

'Maybe I would.'

When she stood up, Lynn scraped her chair back loudly enough for several others to turn around. 'If you're thinking of going over the side,' she said, 'I should keep it to yourself.'

'What's the matter, Lynn?' said Naylor. 'Jealous?'

'You bastard!'

She pushed her way between the close-set tables, the backs of jutting chairs, her normally ruddy cheeks redder still.

'What's up?' said Mark Divine, all mouth and mock concern. 'Getting your period?'

Lynn Kellogg rocked back on her heels, swivelling to face him. Divine standing there with his tray balanced over one arm, the rest of the canteen watching.

'Yes,' she said, 'matter of fact, I am.'

Once before, in the CID room, she'd struck out at him, smack across the face, marks from her fingers that hadn't soon faded. She moved a half pace towards him now and his arm went up instinctively for protection. There was a large glass of milk on the tray, a cream cake, pie and chips.

Lynn reached out and took a chip. 'Thanks, Mark. Nice of you to be so concerned.'

The roar from the rest of the canteen cowboys was still loud around Divine as he found a seat, echoes of it following Lynn all the way back along the corridor.

'Espresso?'

'Large.'

Resnick looked at the girl as she turned away. Short hair like bleached gold at the tips, mud at the roots. Two silver rings in her left ear and a fake diamond stud at the side of her nose. He hadn't seen her before and he wasn't too surprised. Mario would take on a girl, teach her to work the machine and then she'd leave.

'Thanks,' he said as she set down the small cup and saucer, brown and white. He gave her one pound thirty and she looked surprised. 'Half's for the next one,' Resnick explained.

'Tomorrow?'

'Ten minutes.'

There had been a period of almost six weeks when the stall had closed down and Resnick had felt bereft. Usually, when he went to the indoor market near the Central police station and shopped at either of the Polish delicatessens, or bought fresh vegetables, fish, he would stop off at the Italian coffee stall for two espressos. Sometimes – the luxury of half an hour to kill, more than usual to read the paper in – he would have three and spend the rest of the day tasting them, strong and bitter, at the back of his throat. Then, suddenly, no warning: it was closed.

Resnick had asked around. He was, after all, a detective. There were rumours of grand changes, expansion, everything from toasted ham and cheese to microwaved lasagne. One morning, local paper under one arm, half a pound of pickled gherkins, soused herring and a dark rye with caraway in a carrier bag, it was open again, Mario himself behind the counter. There were new covers on the stools, fresh red and green paint on the counter, the cappuccino machine had been moved from one side to the other. Everything else seemed the same. Resnick had greeted Mario like a long-lost brother, a material witness he had never thought would show up at the trial.

'Coffee? Wonderful coffee!' sang Mario, as though he had never seen Resnick before. 'Best coffee you can buy!'

'What's happened?' Resnick asked. 'What's been happening?'

'The wife,' Mario said, 'she had a baby.' Explaining nothing.

Then, as now, Resnick drank one espresso and slid his cup back across the counter for another.

Across from him a mother and daughter, similar hair styles, identical expressions, listened to Mario declaring undying love to the pair of them and were pleased. A serious young man who had strolled in from the Poly refolded his *Guardian* as he spooned chocolatey froth from the top of his cappuccino. No more than eighteen, a woman prised the dummy from her three-year-old's mouth so that he could drink his banana milk shake. Along to Resnick's right, a man with check cap and a hump glanced around before slipping his false teeth into his handkerchief, the better to deal with his sausage roll.

'Inspector.'

'Ms Olds.' Resnick recognized the voice and didn't turn his head. He waited until Suzanne Olds had climbed on to the stool alongside him, careful to smooth down the skirt of her light grey suit, the hem settling several inches short of the knee. She lifted a small leather bag into her lap and snapped it open; its matching satchel, containing court notes and papers, rested by her feet.

'Ah!' cried Mario. '*Bellissima!*'

'Stuff it, Mario!' she said, enunciating beautifully. 'Or I'll have this man arrest you for sexual harassment.'

Resnick walked through the Centre with her, a tall woman in her mid-thirties, slender, an inch or two under six foot. Standing on the escalator, passing between the Early Learning Centre and Thornton's Chocolates, Suzanne Olds made him feel shabby, she made him feel good. She was talking about a case she was in the middle of defending, three black youths who had been stopped by a police car on the edge of the Forest, two in the morning. Illegal substances, backchat, a charge of resisting arrest.

'Why do it?' she asked, buses pulling away behind her, turning right into Trinity Square. 'When there are real crimes to be solved.'

'Hospital doctor attacked!' called the paper seller. 'Slasher at large!'

'Enjoy your say in court,' Resnick said, already moving.

'Next time the coffee's on me,' she called after him, but Resnick failed to hear her, her voice drowned in the sound of traffic as he hurried away, fists punched deep into his pockets.

Eight

'Ah, Tom.'

'Tim.'

'How're we today? Feeling better?'

'A little.'

'Good. That's the spirit.'

Tim Fletcher felt like shit. He winced trying to lever himself up in the bed; with one arm covered in bandages and the other attached to a drip it wasn't easy.

The consultant stood near the end of the bed, white coat open over a pair of ox blood brogues, beige trousers, a grey tailored shirt with a white collar and silk tie in red and navy diagonal stripes. His face was full around the jaw, more than a little flushed below pouched eyes; the pupils themselves were unclouded and alert. He took the file containing Fletcher's notes from one of the junior doctors, gave it a peripheral glance and handed it back.

'If you cut us, do we not bleed?' Laughing, the consultant took hold of Fletcher's toes through the blanket and gave them an encouraging shake. 'Gave the lie to that one, eh, Tom? Those buggers who think we're made of stone.'

He lifted his head for the approval which his entourage duly gave.

'Well,' he said, 'young chap like you, should heal quickly. Soon be ready for a spot of physio . . . Physio, yes, sister?'

'Yes, Mr Salt.'

'Soon have you back on your feet again.'

'Arsehole!' murmured Fletcher, as soon as the consultant and his party were out of earshot. And don't tell me, he thought, that I'm ever going to end up like that, parading around at the head of some royal procession.

He leaned back against the pillows and let his head fall sideways and that was when he saw Karen, hovering uncertainly, brown paper bags of pears and grapes clasped against her waist, a dozen roses, red and white, resting lightly against her perfect breasts.

Resnick opened the door and went in. A woman with greying hair and a pair of red-framed glasses looked away from her desk, fingers continuing to peck at the keyboard of her computer.

'Any chance of seeing Mr Salt?'

His secretary looked doubtful.

'It's to do with Fletcher, the houseman . . .'

'Such a dreadful business.'

'I understand Mr Salt was responsible?'

She blinked behind her lenses, wide, oval frames.

'He took charge himself,' Resnick said.

'Mr Salt went straight into theatre the instant he heard, insisted. One of our own.' She looked down at the warrant card Resnick was holding open. 'He's finishing his rounds.'

'Should I wait or go and find him?'

For a moment, the secretary glanced at the green monitor of the display unit. 'He sees his private patients in the afternoon.'

Resnick slipped his card back into his pocket. 'I'll go and see him now – before I have to pay for the privilege.'

Bernard Salt stood inside Sister Minton's office, hands behind his back, feet apart in the at ease position, giving a lie to the way he was feeling. He could feel the sweat dampening today's collar at the back of his neck, insinuating itself into the hair beneath his arms and at his crotch. He hoped to God she couldn't smell it. The last thing he wanted was for her to realize he was rattled, even a little frightened.

Helen Minton was aware of her own breathing; forcing herself to sit back in her chair, she closed her eyes. 'How many more times are we going to have to go through this?' she asked.

There was a single knock at the door and both started, but neither spoke; other than that, neither of them moved until Helen Minton opened her eyes and Salt was looking at his watch.

Two knocks at the door, followed close by two more.

'Come in,' Helen Minton said.

The first thing Resnick noticed was the rawness at the corner of her eyes; the second was the relief on the consultant's face.

'Sorry to interrupt,' Resnick said, introducing himself. 'I wondered' – looking at Salt – 'if I could have a word about Tim Fletcher?'

'Of course, inspector.' And then, 'Helen, would it be all right if we made use of your office? I shouldn't think we'll be many minutes.'

The sister held Salt's gaze until the consultant had to look away. Then she picked up the diary from the desk, the sheets on which she had been working out the next ward rota, and left them to it.

Bernard Salt closed the door lightly behind her. 'Now, inspector . . .' he began, moving across to sit in the sister's chair.

Bernard Salt, Resnick came away thinking, was a powerful man with powerfully held views; it had come as no surprise to learn that he had played rugby as a young man, swum butterfly and breast stroke; now golf three times a week and occasionally allowed himself to be badgered into an evening of bridge. More importantly, Resnick had gained a keener understanding of the wounds Tim Fletcher had sustained.

Those to the face were untidy but superficial; in time their scars would lend him a more interesting appearance than he might otherwise have grown into. The cuts to his upper arm had drawn a good deal of blood, but were less serious than the injuries to his hand. What interested Resnick, however, had been the consultant's description of the damage that had been done to the houseman's leg.

The blade had entered high in the thigh, having been driven with some considerable force into the gluteus maximus and subsequently drawn sharply through the remaining gluteal muscles and from there into the hamstring muscles at the back of the thigh; here pressure seemed to have been reapplied before the blade was forced through the gastrocnemius, running the length of the calf between ankle and knee.

Without the use of those muscles, Fletcher would be unable to flex either knee or ankle joints; unless they repaired themselves healthily, he would experience, at best, difficulty in walking or otherwise using the damaged leg.

'At worst?' Resnick had asked.

Salt had simply stared back at him without expression.

'The wounds to the leg, then?' Resnick had said. 'Quite a different nature to the rest?'

'More serious,' Salt had agreed. 'Potentially.'

'More deliberate?'

Salt had swivelled in the sister's chair, shaken his head and allowed a smile at the corners of his mouth. 'I cannot speculate.'

'But they could suggest an attacker who knew what he was about?'

'Possibly.'

'One with a knowledge of anatomy, physiology?'

'A member of the St John Ambulance Brigade, inspector? Anyone, I should have thought, with basic knowledge of how the body works.'

'And without wishing you to speculate, Mr Salt . . .'

'Please, inspector.'

'You wouldn't have formed any opinion as to the kind of weapon that was used in the attack?'

'Fine.' The same smile narrow at the edges of the consultant's full mouth. 'Sharp. Other than that, no, I'm afraid not.'

Resnick had thanked him and left the room, taking with him one further piece of knowledge that Tim Fletcher had yet to learn: the injuries to the tendons of his hand were unlikely to heal completely; the chances of him furthering his career in surgery or some similarly deft area of medicine were slight.

Fletcher was sleeping, Karen Archer's hand trapped beneath his bandaged arm. The roses beside the bed were already beginning to wilt. Resnick couldn't tell if the girl were bored or tired, sitting motionless in the centrally heated air. He wondered why Lynn Kellogg had felt about her as she did, the antagonism evident even in her verbal report. Half a mind to go over and talk to her, Resnick turned away instead, back into the main ward, reasoning that Fletcher needed all the rest he could get.

He sidestepped the drugs trolley and nearly bumped into a student nurse wearing a uniform that resembled a large J-Cloth with poppers and a belt. Just before the door he turned and there was the sister, looking at him from the nurses' station in the middle of the ward. Resnick hesitated, wondering if there were something she wanted to say to him, but she glanced away.

Resnick ignored the lift and took the stairs, no lover of hospitals. There was a queue of cars at the entrance to the multi-storey car park as he drove out. If whoever attacked Tim Fletcher had found his victim by more than chance, if he had sought him out . . . He? Resnick took the exit from the roundabout that would take him along Derby Road, back to the station. He was thinking about the medical student who had been Karen Archer's previous boyfriend: somebody with motivation to cause hurt, maim. Knowledge. The long trajectory from hip to knee and beyond. Resnick shuddered, realized that his own hand was touching his leg, as if to make sure it was still sound. He had to brake hard so as not to run the light by the Three Wheatsheaves, swerving into the left lane around a Metro which had belatedly signalled its intention to go right.

Ian Carew.

He would find out where he was living, pay a visit. Because something seemed obvious, that didn't have to mean it was wrong.

Nine

'Debbie!'

Kevin Naylor pushed the front door to, slipped his keys into his coat pocket and listened. Only the hum of the freezer from the kitchen. Faint, the sound of early evening television from next door. Walls of new estates like these, you need never feel you were all alone. Perfect for the first-time buyer, one point off your mortgage for the first year, wait until you'd painted, roses in the garden, turf for the lawn, something more than money invested before they hit you with the full rate, fifteen and a half and rising. A couple across the crescent, one kid and another on the way, they'd had their place repossessed last month, moved in with her parents, Jesus!

'Debbie?'

There were dishes in the bowl, more stacked haphazardly alongside the sink. In a red plastic bucket, tea towels soaking in bleach. Kevin flipped down the top of the rubbish bin and then lifted it away; the wrapping from packets of biscuits lying there, thin coils of coloured Cellophane pushed down between torn cardboard, treacle tart, deep-dish apple pie. He knew that if he checked in the freezer the tubs of supermarket ice-cream would be close to empty.

The neighbour switched channels and began to watch the evening news.

The baby's room was neat, neater than the rest; creams and talc on the table near the window, a carton of disposable nappies with its top bent back. A mobile of brightly coloured planets that Lynn had bought at the baby's birth dangled above the empty cot, suns and moons and stars.

'Where's the baby?'

Debbie was a shape beneath the striped duvet, fingers of one hand showing, her wrist, a wedding ring. Light brown hair lifelessly spread upon the pillow. Kevin sat on the edge of the bed and she flinched; her hand, clenching, disappeared.

'Deb?'

'What?'

'Where's the baby?'

'Who cares?'

He grabbed at her, grabbed at the quilt, pulling at it hard, tugging it from her hands; she pushed her hands down between her knees, curling in upon herself, eyes closed tight.

'Debbie!'

Kneeling on the bed, Kevin struggled to turn her over and she kicked out, flailing her arms until he had backed away, allowing her to seize the duvet again and pull it against her, sitting at the centre of the bed, eyes, for the first time, open. She loathed him. He could see it, read it in those eyes. Loathed him.

'Where is she?'

'At my mother's.'

Kevin Naylor sighed and looked away.

'Is that wrong? Is it? Well? What's wrong with that, Kevin? What's so terrible about that?'

He got up and crossed the room, opening drawers, closing them.

'Well?'

'What's wrong,' he said, facing her, fighting to keep his voice calm, 'is that's where she was this morning, yesterday, the day before.'

'So?'

Kevin made a sound somewhere between a snort and a harsh, humourless laugh.

'She is my mother, Kevin. She is the baby's grandmother. It's only natural . . .'

'That she should look after her all the time?'

'It isn't all the time.'

'Good as.'

'She's helping . . .'

'Helping!'

'Kevin, please! I get tired. You know I get tired. I can't help it. I . . .'

He stood at the end of the bed, staring down at her in disgust, waiting for the tears to start. There. 'If I want to see my own child,' he said, 'I have to make a phone call, make sure she isn't sleeping, get back into the car and drive halfway across the fucking city!'

He slammed the door so that it shook against its hinges. Switched on the radio so that he couldn't hear the sound of her sobbing. On either side of them, television sets were turned up in direct retaliation. At least, Kevin thought, when their kids cry I can sodding hear them.

There were tins of baked beans in the cupboard, packets of soup, chicken and leek, chicken and asparagus, plain chicken; four or five slices of white bread inside the wrapper but outside the bread bin. Eggs. Always too many of those. He could send out for a pizza, drive off for a takeaway, curry or Chinese.

On the radio someone was pontificating about mad cow disease, the effects it might have on children, force-fed beefburgers for school dinners. Kevin switched it off and instantly he could hear Debbie, bawling. He switched back on, changed stations. Del Shannon. Gem-AM. Poor sod who shot himself. Well . . .

There was one can of lager left in the back of the fridge and he opened it, tossing the ring pull on to the side and taking the can into the living room. If Debbie's mother were there, she'd be tut-tutting, Kevin, you're not going to drink that without a glass, surely? But she wasn't there, was she? Back in her own little semi in Basford, caravan outside the front window and his bloody kid asleep in her spare room.

He scooped the remote control from beside the armchair and pressed Channel Three. Might as well have the whole street watching together, synchronized bloody viewing. Nothing on he wanted till the football at half past ten, bit of boxing.

Thinking of going over the side, Lynn had said in the canteen. Maybe, he thought, over the side and never coming back.

When Tim Fletcher woke he saw the roses and then he saw Sarah Leonard and he knew something wasn't right. She was standing at an angle to the bed; her staff nurse's uniform had been exchanged for a long, beige cotton coat, broad belt loosely tied and high epaulettes. Maybe she was still wearing the uniform underneath, but he didn't think so.

'Karen . . .' he said.

'She went a long time ago.'

Fletcher nodded.

'Girls her age,' Sarah said, 'they get restless. Haven't the patience.'

She was, Fletcher thought, what, all of twenty-seven herself, twenty-eight.

'I just popped in,' she said, 'to see how you were getting on.'

'How am I?'

She smiled. 'You're the doctor.'

He glanced down at his pillows. 'You couldn't . . .'

'Prop you up a bit? I expect so.'

She leaned him forward against her shoulder as she plumped and patted the pillows, the inside of his arm pressing against her breast. 'Overtime, this.' Her face was close and he could feel her breath. Sarah leaned him back into the pillows and stood back.

'Thanks.'

'There's nothing else you want?'

Fully awake now, the pain was back in his leg, not sharp the way he might have imagined, but dull, persistent, throbbing. A nerve twitched suddenly in his hand and he winced, twice, biting down into his bottom lip. At least there was still a nerve there to twitch. 'No,' he said. 'I'm fine.'

She raised her head. 'I'll look in tomorrow.' She was almost out of earshot when his voice brought her back.

'You off home now?'

'Soon.'

'Walking?'

'Yes.'

'Be careful.'

Resnick arrived home to find the front door open on the latch and Miles pressing his nose against it while Pepper nervously kept watch. His immediate thought was that the house had been burgled, but a quick check proved this not to be so. Bud was lying on the top step of the stairs, ready for flight. Dizzy and Ed Silver were neither of them to be seen, off about their business, hard into the night.

Ed's note was propped against the edge of the frying pan, *Out for a quick one, back soon.* He had washed the plate but not the knife and fork, rinsed out his cup and left the tea stewing dark and cold inside the pot. Three tea bags. The bacon and the sausage he had found in Resnick's fridge, the oven chips he would have had to fetch from the grocer's on the main road. Also, the half-bottle of cheap Greek brandy, empty between the cats' bowls.

Resnick picked up Bud and nuzzled him, conscious of the animal's ribs like something made from a kit, balsa wood and glue. He dropped his coat over the back of a chair and, carrying the cat with him, pulled an Ellington album from the shelf. 'Jack the Bear', 'Take the A Train', 'Ko-Ko'. His friend, Ben Riley, twelve years in the job before he left for America, had sent him a card from New York. *Charlie – Finally got to take the 'A' train. Head-to-toe graffiti, inside and out, and anyone white gets off below 110th Street. Stay home. Stick to the music.* Ben, he'd stayed there: Resnick hadn't heard from him in more than two years, four.

Ed Silver had scorned the Czech Budweiser and Resnick opened a bottle and slowly drank it as he sliced a small onion carefully into rounds and overlapped them along two slices of dark rye bread. He covered these with Polish ham, then cut slivers of Jarlsberg cheese. Backtracking to the fridge, he found one solitary pickled cucumber, set rounds of this on the ham, then added the cheese.

The grill was gathering heat when he stood the sandwiches, open-faced, beneath it and finished the first beer, rolling his hand across his stomach as he reached for another.

When the cheese was brown and bubbling, he forked some coleslaw on to a plate, used a slice to lift up the sandwiches and set them down next to the coleslaw, balanced two jars of mustard, Dijon and mixed grain, on the rim, pushed his index finger down into the neck of the Budweiser bottle and headed back for the living room.

Ben Webster was just beginning his solo on 'Cotton Tail', rolling that phrase over the rhythm section, springy and strong from Blanton's bass, round and round and rich, like rolling it round a barrel of treacle. Just when it seemed to have become stuck, sharp little phrases from the brass digging it out, and then the saxophone lifting itself with more and more urgency, up, up and into the next chorus.

Resnick wondered what it must be like, being able to do anything with such force, such grace. Would he see Ed

Silver that evening or the next and in what state? You spent half a lifetime striving to reach a point of perfection and then one night, one day, for no reason that any onlooker could see, you opened your fingers and watched as it all slipped away.

In their two-bedroom, two-storey house, Debbie Naylor had fallen back to sleep, mouth open, lightly snoring. Kevin still sat in the chair before the television, watching, soundlessly, as two boxers moved around the square ring, feinting, parrying, never quite connecting.

Tim Fletcher lay on his back, awake in the half-light, counting stitches, trying to sleep.

Like a metronome, the even click of Sarah Leonard's low heels, along the pavement leading from the bridge.

Ten

Debbie Naylor stood looking down at her sleeping husband, alone save for the blue hum of the TV. The first time she had seen him, a friend had pointed him out, standing at the edge of half-a-dozen men at the bar, neither quite one of them nor alone. It hadn't been until he was driving her home, oh, three weeks later, home where she still lived with her parents, Basford, that he had told her what he did.

'You're kidding.'

'No. Why?'

'You just are.'

She had learned, some of it soon enough, the rest later. After the lunchtime meetings, Sunday afternoons with her family, Kevin embarrassed, wanting to leave; after the jokes from her friends at the office, the wedding with all of Kevin's friends, tall and shorthaired and already three-parts drunk, lining up to kiss her open-mouthed; not above, some of them, trying to cop a feel through the brocade of her wedding dress. Posing for the photographer, one of the bridesmaids had jumped in front of them, slipped a pair of handcuffs over their wrists.

After the honeymoon, the collision of late nights and early mornings; evenings with dinner in the oven and drying out, dreading the phone call that would, almost inevitably, come. Just a quick half. Wind down. With the lads. You know how it is.

She knew.

When Kevin had been accepted for CID it got better and

then it got worse. Put your foot down, her mother had said, else he'll walk all over you.

Better, Debbie had thought, than walking out.

She stood there, gazing down at him, asleep in the chair, looking little different at three and twenty than he had at nineteen. She couldn't believe that after all that had happened in the past four years, he was still the same. When she was so different.

'I'm sorry,' she said softly. 'I'm sorry.'

Kevin didn't hear her. She wanted to go down, carefully, to her knees and feel the side of her face against the warmth of his neck. Instead she left the room, pulling the door to but not closing it, not wanting to disturb him.

Alone, Kevin stirred and, waking, heard the soft thunk of the freezer door; Debbie, he thought, sneaking out for another pigging midnight feast.

The cats heard the phone moments before Resnick himself, jumping down from the bed and scuttling towards the bedroom door. Resnick blinked and groaned, lifting the receiver at only the second attempt.

'Yes?' he said, scarcely recognizing his own voice. 'What is it?'

He listened for less than a minute then set down the receiver. He had sat up for too long, hoping that Ed Silver might return, chasing the Budweiser with shots of vodka brought back by a friend from Cracow, the real thing. Setting his feet to the floor gingerly, he pushed himself up and padded to the kitchen. Miles and Bud had beaten him to it and were sniffing at their empty bowls expectantly. Pepper, who had taken to sleeping in an old plastic colander, yawned a greeting and reclosed his eyes, forgetting to put the red tip of his tongue back inside his mouth.

Knowing he was unlikely to get back to sleep, Resnick made coffee, drank half and put the remainder into a flask which he carried out to the car. Overhead lights shone a dull orange along the empty street. He went straight across the lights at the Forest, keeping the cemetery to his right. One last prostitute lingered against the wall near the next junction, shifting her weight from one foot to the other, face pale in the glow of her last cigarette.

When he began driving Resnick hadn't known for certain where he was going, but now he did.

Large blocks of brick and glass, by day the hospital didn't have enough character to be ugly. By night, most of its lights extinguished, some of them burning here and there, it was more inviting, mysterious. Resnick went slowly around the one-way system and parked fifty yards short of the medical school entrance.

A few swallows of black coffee and he took a torch from the compartment alongside the dash, locked the car and started to walk towards the bridge. It was a good hour later than the time Fletcher had been attacked, the flow of traffic was sporadic, there was no one else on foot. A short avenue of bushes and trees separated the hospital from the road. He flicked the torch on and shone it up the metal spiral before beginning to climb. Whoever had followed the houseman had either come directly after him from the hospital, or taken this route up from the road. This way, Resnick reasoned, pausing as his head came level with the glass above. Less likely to create suspicion, loitering about; easier to wait for your victim, pick him out.

The door at the top could have been locked, likely would have been if someone had not removed the bolt. Wonder, thought Resnick, exactly when that was done.

He pushed the door open and stepped through, turning left so that the hospital lay behind him, the bridge stretching out ahead. The occasional vehicle now, head-lights sliding down the glass panels as they sped along the ring road, north or south. Resnick stood quite still, listening to the muted thrum of engines, concentrating on the double doors at the far end, the bridge spanning six lanes of highway, those doors a long way off.

Do people feel unhappy only during office hours? Black print on white paper, Blu-tacked to the wired glass. *Phone NITELINE 7 p. m. to 8 a.m.* Resnick tried to imagine being trapped in there, terrified, desperate to escape. He began to walk, slowly, towards the other side, the smell of rubber clearer with every step.

Whoever had seen Fletcher, followed him, what had determined his choice? Being there, now, the middle of the night, Resnick found it difficult to believe in a chance attack. Whoever had stalked the exhausted houseman almost the length of the bridge had done so for a reason. Resnick needed to believe it had been personal. He hesitated for a moment, staring down. He had to believe that, cling to it, knowing that if it were not true, there was somebody still out there, somewhere in the city, who had wreaked terrible havoc on Tim Fletcher's body for reasons that only a psychologist might ever understand. And who might do the same again.

City Life, read the poster facing Resnick as he went through the double doors. A bicycle had been left chained to the railings on the broad platform, two-thirds of the way down the steps. The air that touched Resnick's hands and face was surprisingly cold, driving up from the flyover. Something caught his attention, low by the wall of the first building and he brought up the torch.

It was only boxes, crammed with computer printouts: metallurgy, something close. Resnick switched off the torch and stood there, feeling the adrenalin in his body. Seek and you shall find. He crossed back over the ring road, stepping easily over the metal safety barriers at the centre.

Sitting in the car, he dribbled the last of the coffee into the plastic cup. There had been no mistaking his ex-wife's voice on the phone, nor, in those few not-quite-coherent sentences, the mixture of resentment and pleading he had thought forgotten.

Eleven

He had the kind of profile that could have been selling aftershave; thick hair, naturally curly and dark, a hunk wearing a black vest and loose-fitting sweatpants with a draw-string waist. He was wearing a pair of running shoes that had cost him close to eighty pounds, but that didn't mean he was running. He had walked down the street and now he stood outside Number 27 and rang the bell. When nothing seemed to happen, he hit the door with the flat of his hand, enough to make it shake. Pushing back the letter flap, Ian Carew called Karen's name.

A couple of minutes and he saw her through the couple of inches of door: salmon socks, double-knit and large and folding loosely back down her calves; hem of a white T-shirt bouncing as she came down the stairs, enough to give him a glimpse of expensive underwear, beige lace and broderie anglaise. There was a large Snoopy in relief on the front of the shirt. Carew let the flap snap into place and stood back.

Not far.

'What . . . ?'

He stepped in without speaking, anger in his face, forcing her back along the threadbare carpet at the other side of the mat.

She looked at him and shook her head and for a moment he thought she was going to bite down into her lower lip, like a child. Her hair was tied back in a loose pony tail and there was sleep in the corner of her eyes.

A woman walked past on the opposite side of the street,

Asian, wearing a purple and gold sari and pushing a pram, twins. Karen didn't think she'd ever noticed Asian twins before.

Carew moved forward, blocking her view.

'Good at it, aren't you?'

'I don't understand.'

'Natural. Comes natural. Something mummy fed you along with the milk.'

'Now you're being stupid.'

'And don't do that!' His hand was on her face before she could move, fingers squeezing against the sides of her jaw, forcing her mouth slightly open so that she could no longer bite the soft flesh inside her lip.

'Lying,' he said. 'That's what you're good at. Lying. "No, Ian, there isn't anything wrong. I'm not seeing anybody else, of course I'm not seeing anybody else." Weeks until I found out.'

Karen turned her head aside, laughed dismissively. 'Is that what this is all about?'

'What do you think?'

'Tim.'

'Gets himself mugged and you send the police round after me.'

'Oh, Ian.'

'Oh, Ian, what?'

She didn't want this conversation, didn't want this to be happening. She might have guessed that cow of a policewoman would put two and two together and come up with the wrong answer. Probably she should have warned him, but she hadn't. Now he was there in the house, angry, and she didn't think she could make him leave against his will, not by herself. She didn't think there was anybody else in the house.

'Look,' Karen said, 'let me get dressed. It won't take a minute.'

Carew didn't move.

Shrugging, she turned and went back upstairs, conscious that he was following her, looking at her legs.

'Mind the . . .'

'I remember.'

The room was much as he'd remembered it as well, clutter and last night's cigarette smoke. It had almost been enough to put him off her, the way, after a meal, after the cinema, after sex, she would automatically light up. Cheap. Expensive to look at but cheap underneath. He watched as she pulled on a pair of faded blue jeans and exchanged her socks for a pair of sports shoes, white with a pink trim.

She picked up the kettle. 'Tea?'

'When did I ever drink tea in the mornings?'

Karen spooned instant coffee into mugs, relieved that he seemed to have calmed down, feeling safer now that he was almost friendly, wanting to keep him that way, only not too much. Carew watched her as the water boiled, lounging with one of his bare elbows against the wall, posing.

'I should be really pissed off with you,' he said, as she spooned sugar into her own mug, ready.

'You mean you're not?'

'I ought to be.' Not leaning any more now, standing close as she lifted the kettle, almost touching her, touching her. 'Desperate without you, that what you reckoned? Thought of someone else in there with you, in bed, picture of it driving me insane?' His knee was resting against the back of her thigh, knuckles sliding gently up and down her arm.

Karen moved away, turning back towards him at arm's length, offering him the coffee.

'Thanks,' smiling through the faintest shimmer of steam.

Smug bastard! Karen thought. 'It was the police who asked me about you,' she said. 'I didn't mention your name.'

'I have been thinking about you, you know.'

'I doubt it.'

'It's true.'

'It's because you're here. If you weren't here, you'd be thinking about running, getting drunk, lectures, somebody else.'

'Well,' he said, reaching for her, hands up under the sleeves of her T-shirt, alternately pushing and stroking, someone who read an article on massage once but became distracted midway through the third paragraph. 'Well, I'm here now.'

Somebody along the street shouted at a dog, a cat or a child and slammed their back door so forcefully that Karen's window, despite folds of yellowing newspaper, rattled in its frame.

'Look,' said Karen, pushing his hands away, moving across the narrow room, picking up things and putting them down, trying to seem businesslike, 'I'm sorry about the police. Really. But now I've got to go. I'm already late for a lecture.'

'What?'

Hand on hip, she looked at him. Unmade, the bed was between them, a tatty stuffed animal poking out from beneath the rumpled duvet.

'What lecture?'

'It doesn't matter.'

'Then don't go.'

'I mean it doesn't matter to you, what does it matter, what bloody lecture I have to go to?'

'Hey, Karen. Calm down.' Oh, God! Trying the smile, giving his teeth their best shot. Don't bother! She opened the door to the room and left it open, wide to the stairs.

He didn't move.

Neither of them moved.

Karen prayed for the communal phone to ring, someone to come to the door, postman, milkman, double-glazing salesman, anyone, one of her fellow-tenants to return. She considered leaving him there and taking off down the stairs, but knew he would come after her and catch her, haul her back before throwing her down on the bed. It had happened like that several times before but then it had been different, she had enjoyed it, they'd been going together.

'What I can't understand,' Carew said, 'is why you'd prefer someone like that anyway.'

'Someone like what?' Karen said, knowing as soon as the words were out of her mouth that she shouldn't.

'Oh, you know . . .' He gestured with his hands. 'Small.'

Karen shook her head. 'You don't know the first thing about him.'

'I've seen him in the hospital. Scurrying around with those headphones on, like whatever, the white mouse, white rabbit.' He started around the bed. 'What's he listening to all the time anyway? Special little tapes you make for him?' He patted the duvet, patted the mattress, caught hold of the toy animal and tossed it to the floor. 'Little fantasies. Used to be good at those, I remember. Train carriage fantasy. Swimming pool fantasy.' Close again, voice low in his throat and that look in his eyes: she knew that look. 'Burglar fantasies.'

Karen turned and ran, swung herself round by the banister rail and jumped the first four steps, stumbled the rest. He caught hold of her before she reached the bottom, hip thrust into her side, a hand fast in her hair.

'All right, Karen,' he said, 'just like the old days. Like it used to be.'

'Someone with something against him, this Fletcher? That what you think, Charlie? Someone with a grudge?'

Resnick nodded.

'Professional or personal?'

'I don't know, sir.'

'But if you had to guess.'

'Fletcher's at the bottom of the heap. Starting out. I

shouldn't have thought he'd have stepped on the wrong toes, become involved in rivalries ... not enough to warrant this.'

'Personal, then?'

Again, Resnick nodded.

'This ...' Skelton glanced at the notes before him. '... Carew.'

'Claims to have been at the Irish Centre ...'

'Doesn't sound Irish.'

'He's not, sir. Claims he was there till one-thirty, quarter to two. Back home quarter past. Straight off to sleep.'

'Fletcher was attacked when?'

'Went off duty a few minutes after two. Staff nurse in charge of the ward where Fletcher was working is pretty certain of that. Quick trip to the Gents, find his coat, he'd be on the bridge in five minutes, ten at the outside. Anxious to get away, see his girlfriend.'

'That time of the morning?'

'Promised to wait up for him. Fletcher'd been talking to the staff nurse about it, earlier.'

'And the girlfriend, she found him?'

'Yes, sir.'

'How old?'

'Nineteen.'

Skelton's eyes flicked in the direction of the framed photographs, his daughter Kate. 'Carew alibied for the time he was at this ...'

'Irish Centre.'

'That's it.'

'Went on his own, left the same way. Claims to have seen several people there he knows.'

'Checked out?'

'Doesn't know all of them by name, not surname, anyway. We've spoken to two of the rest.'

'And?'

'One, another medical student, thinks he may have seen

Carew there, but he isn't positive. Place gets packed after eleven-thirty, twelve, and it isn't what you'd call well lit. The other one, however, postgraduate student in psychology, she's definite. Didn't see him all evening.'

There was a knock at the superintendent's door, discreet, and Skelton ignored it.

'You bringing him in?' Skelton asked.

'Thought we should give it a little time, finish checking him out,' said Resnick. 'Haul him in too soon, we might end up having to let him go.'

'No chance he's going to do a runner?'

Resnick shook his head. 'Naylor's down there, keeping an eye. Anything out of the usual, he'll stop him.'

Skelton inclined his head upwards, pressed the tips of his fingers together, outsides of the index fingers resting against the centre of his upper lip. There was a time, Resnick remembered, when the super used to have a neat little moustache.

'Keep me informed, Charlie.'

'Yes, sir.'

When Resnick was almost at the door, Skelton spoke again. 'Your eyes, Charlie, looking tired. Should try for a few early nights.' Resnick turned and looked at him. 'Single man your age, shouldn't be too difficult.'

Resnick liked to let Lynn Kellogg drive: it enabled him to set aside any charges of being hierarchical or chauvinist in one fell swoop and besides, it gave him time to think. Ian Carew was living with three other medical students in a house in Lenton, easy walking distance from the medical school, the hospital, the bridge. Naylor was sitting in a Ford Fiesta just around the corner from the Boulevard, there at the end of a short street of Victorian houses, the last on the right being Carew's. Lynn pulled up in front of him and Naylor got out of his car and walked towards theirs. He looked about as happy as he usually did, these days.

'Went out almost two hours ago, sir. Not been back since.'

Resnick glared.

'Had his running gear on, I thought, you know, just off for a jog. Couldn't exactly start chasing after him, sir. Not like this. Besides, I thought he'd be back in a bit. Shower and that. Sir.'

'Perhaps he's gone for a long run, sir,' suggested Lynn.

'Half-marathon, you mean?'

'Possible, sir.'

Resnick looked across at her. 'Any other ideas?'

After a moment, she said, 'Yes, sir. I might have.'

Resnick nodded. 'Good.' To Naylor he said, 'Hang on here, in case he comes back.'

Naylor was climbing forlornly back into the Fiesta as Lynn Kellogg was signalling left, filtering into the stream of traffic heading south along the Boulevard.

Carew had finally fallen asleep and Karen had lain underneath him, pinioned by his heavy leg, an arm, settling herself, moving as slowly as she could across the mattress; the last thing she wanted to do was to wake him. She was just sliding her arm free when the doorbell rang. Carew stirred and she pulled herself clear and hurried from the room, closing the door behind her, but not locking it.

There were two people at the door, man and a woman, and she wondered if they were Jehovah's Witnesses, travelling in pairs; then she recognized the policewoman from the previous day.

'Detective Inspector Resnick,' said the man, showing her his card.

'Hello, Karen,' said Lynn, no mistaking the way she was staring at her, at her face.

Karen touched high on her left cheek and winced; she couldn't see the bruising, only imagine it. Her mouth was swollen and now that she thought about it, she realized it felt numb. The Snoopy T-shirt was torn at one shoulder.

'Can we come in?' Lynn asked, Karen moving back from the door to allow them, Lynn going in first, Resnick, tall, bulky, careful to keep well behind her.

The door to Karen's room opened and closed and all three of them turned to face the stairs. Carew had pulled on his sweatpants and stood there barefooted, not quite focusing, someone who has just woken from a deep sleep.

'This is Ian,' Karen said, pointing, pointing him out to Lynn in particular. 'This is Ian Carew.'

Twelve

They made a disparate couple, sitting there, mid-morning, in the front of Resnick's car, not looking at each other, looking out. Resnick's jacket had become hunched up at the collar when he sat, the knot of his tie had gradually twisted as the day had worn on and the top button of his once-white shirt was either missing or undone. Alongside him, Ian Carew was showing good posture, smooth shoulders highlighted against the broad black straps of his vest. For minutes at a time, his expression wouldn't change. It was only his fingers that fidgeted slightly, smoothing the grey material of his sweatpants, toying with the slack string bow at the waist, nails pushing hard at the soft skin inside the first digits of each hand.

Resnick made himself wait, the watch on his left wrist just visible below his frayed cuff. Just because Carew had chosen not to go running, didn't mean he shouldn't sweat.

It was Lynn Kellogg who made the tea, straight in the mug, lifting the bag clear with a spoon before setting the mug into Karen's hands. Karen was sitting on the very edge of the bed, dangerously close to overbalancing. Lynn made tea for herself and sat carefully alongside her.

'If you want to talk about it,' Lynn said.

Karen brought the mug to her mouth but didn't drink.

'What happened,' Lynn continued.

The numbness in Karen's bottom lip caused her to misjudge and hot tea splashed on her bare leg, the white and black rug. Lynn reached over and steadied the girl's hands with her own.

'Tell me,' she said, before letting go.

Instead Karen began to cry and Lynn took the tea away from her, resting it on the floor, holding her then, Karen's face warm on Lynn's white blouse, sleek black hair caught across the corners of Lynn's mouth.

'It's all right,' Lynn whispered. 'It's all right,' down into her hair, Karen's sobs growing and part of Lynn thinking how strange, to be sitting there on that strange bed, holding that hurt and beautiful girl.

'It's all right.'

Karen stopped crying almost as abruptly as she had begun. She wiped the hair from her face, careful round her cheekbone where the bruising was beginning to deepen, change colour.

'He didn't do it,' Karen said. 'He couldn't.'

'Didn't do what?'

'Tim. The other night. He wouldn't do that.'

'That's not what I'm concerned about,' Lynn said. 'Not now.'

Karen reached towards the mug of tea but changed her mind. Head up again, close to Lynn, less than a foot away, she bit down gently into her swollen lip.

'You've got to tell me what happened,' Lynn said.

Karen shook her head.

'Your face – how did that happen?'

'It doesn't matter.'

'It does. He hit you. Carew, he hit you, didn't he?'

'He didn't mean it.'

Lynn looked at where the flawless skin was hardening yellow, shading into purple: the cut mouth. 'Are you saying all that was an accident?'

'He didn't mean to hurt me.'

'No?' said Lynn. 'What did he mean to do?'

A few occasions, when Resnick had been young enough to think there were things you did because you should, because they would do you good, he had been to orchestral concerts, the Philharmonia, the Hallé. The Albert Hall it had been then, dodgy acoustics and a balcony that ran round three sides, red seats in fading plush that played havoc with your knees, a listed organ only heard by the Methodists on Sundays. It had taken him four or five visits and a little more self-confidence to admit that once the overture was over and the second movement of the concerto was underway, he was bored. Shitless. The ones who thought they understood jazz were the worst: Gershwin, Milhaud, Dvořák – that dreadful *From the New World*, its ponderous rhythms and emasculation of black gospel.

He had been reminded, on those rare, early visits, of Friday evenings when he was a kid, Sunday afternoons. TV off – Had they had a television then? He wasn't sure – radio on. 'For God's sake,' his father would say, 'sit still and stop the endless fidgeting.' George Melachrino, Semprini: old ones, new ones, loved ones, neglected ones. His mother, who sang around the house each and every day, old songs from her own country, hers and his father's, songs she had herself learned as a child, needed no warnings. In this, it seemed now to Resnick, as in all other things, she sensed what his father required of her and obeyed. She never sang in his presence. Listening to the radio or gramophone, she would darn socks and stockings, rarely speak. It was his father who switched on the set, controlled the volume, lowered the needle into place. Black shellacked 78s. *The Warsaw Concerto*, *Cornish Rhapsody*, Tchaikovsky's Piano Concerto No. 1, only the first movement. His father would tilt his head towards the ceiling, close his eyes. During *The Warsaw Concerto* his mother would cry, stifling the tears with her embroidered handkerchief, lest she be dismissed from the room.

To Resnick, all three pieces sounded alike; his mind would dovetail between football and sex, Notts County and Denise Crampton's knickers. 'What is the matter with you?' his father would demand. 'All that stupid wriggling.' His fellow patrons had shot him similar looks on those evenings when he had tried in vain to find a more comfortable position for his legs and struggled to be more sympathetic to composers who thought that jazz was something you could play from written scores with banks of musicians, the whole enterprise weighed down by such seriousness of purpose that it suffered from elephantiasis of the spirit.

Older, a man, though younger than now, his thoughts had skittered and soared and settled, finally, on those perennial mysteries, soccer and sex: when County got around to scoring would the earth move?

Sitting there in that side road beside Ian Carew, he thought about Ed Silver, slumped somewhere over an empty bottle of cider or wine, about where Carew had been between one forty-five and two-fifteen two nights ago; he wondered what his wife might have said into the telephone had he allowed her the time.

'Are you charging me?' Carew asked.

Resnick turned to face him. 'What with?'

'He had sex with you, didn't he?'

'What?'

'Did he have sex with you? Ian? Carew?'

'So what if he did?'

'Intercourse?'

'Yes.'

'This morning?'

'Yes.'

'Did you want him to?'

'Look, what difference . . . ?

'Did you want him to have sex, make love to you?'

'What?'
'Did you want it to happen?'
'No.'
'Did you tell him that?'
'That I didn't want him?'
'Yes.'
'Yes.'
'What did he say?'
'He laughed.'
'That was all?'
'He said he didn't believe me.'
'And?'
'Said I was dying for it.'
'And?'
'And he hit me.'
'He forced you.'
'He grabbed me on the stairs . . .'
'On the stairs?'
'I was trying to run away, I don't know, into the street. He caught hold of me and dragged me back here and dumped me on the bed.'
'You were still struggling?'
'I was screaming. I kicked him. As hard as I could, I kicked him.'
'What did he do?'
'Hit me again.'
'And then?'
'He had sex with me.'
'He forced you.'
'Yes.'
'He raped you.'
She started to cry again, soundlessly this time, her body still and not shaking; Lynn leaned over to comfort her but Karen shook her away. After several moments, Lynn stood up and went to the window. A large cat, pale ginger, sat

perched on a fence post, catching the autumn sun where it fell between the houses.

She knelt in front of Karen and held her hand, both her hands. She said, 'You'll have to come to the station, see a doctor.'

Karen's eyelids, violet-veined, trembled. 'Have to?'

'Please,' Lynn said. 'Please.'

'You've got an alibi,' Resnick was saying, 'like a string vest.'

'I don't need an alibi,' said Carew. What the hell did he think he was doing, bastard, breathing garlic all over him!

'That's good to hear, if a little inaccurate.'

'And if you intend to keep me here any longer, I insist on seeing a solicitor.' Pompous now, Resnick thought. Practising his bedside manner. Breeding coming out of him under stress. Likely he was Hampshire or Surrey; looks like those, he didn't come from Bolsover.

'D'you know any solicitors?'

'My family does.'

'I'll bet they do.'

Carew sneered. 'What's that supposed to mean?'

'Probably not a lot.'

The sneer grew into a snort and Resnick's irrational impulse to punch Carew in the mouth was frustrated by Lynn Kellogg's tap at the car window. Resnick wound it down, responding to Lynn's expression by getting out on to the pavement. Behind her, the door to the house was open. Here and there, up and down the street, neighbours were beginning to take an interest.

Resnick listened and when he glanced round at the car, Carew had shifted over in his seat and was checking his hair in the rearview mirror. Resnick radioed for Naylor to collect Lynn and the girl, take them to the station. 'I'll go on ahead,' he said. 'With him. Make sure they're ready for you.'

Lynn was staring at Ian Carew, who had resumed his former position and was staring straight ahead. A woman came out of one of the houses opposite, dyed hair, man's overcoat open over shirt and jeans. Carew's eyes followed her automatically, mouth ready to smile.

'How's the girl?' Resnick asked.

Lynn shook her head. 'As good as can be expected. Better, probably.'

Resnick nodded and climbed back into the car.

'What now?' said Carew, midway between bored and angry.

Without answering, Resnick fired the engine, slipped the car into gear, executed a three-point turn and headed back towards the centre of the city.

Thirteen

Ever since the problems with his daughter had come to a particularly nasty head, Skelton had abandoned his early morning runs. Now he ran most lunchtimes instead. In the mornings he would try and spend time with Kate, toying with a slice of toast as, absent-mindedly, she spooned her way through a morass of Weetabix and Shreddies, warm milk soaking in until what was left resembled Trent sludge. Skelton asked about her school work, teachers, school friends, anything but what he wanted most to know – where had she been the evening before, who had she been with? He sat and listened to her halting, half-hearted replies, scraping Flora across his toast and wondering how much she drank, if she were back on drugs? Sixteen and a half: what were the chances that she was still a virgin?

Skelton was on his way out of the station as Resnick drew up, opening the door so that Carew could get out. Two men in running gear and Resnick between them with trousers that were too loose above the ankles, too tight at the hips, a jacket on which he could do up one button with ease but rarely two. Moments like this could induce paranoia: the certainty that at some point of each day, at some time within the twenty-four hours, everyone else goes running, jogs, works out, lifts weights. Everyone.

'Charlie.' Skelton beckoned him to one side. 'This Carew?'

'Yes, sir.'

'You've not charged him?'

'Here of his own volition, sir. Happy to answer any questions that might help us with our inquiries.'

Skelton glanced over at Carew. 'Happy?'

Resnick shook his head. 'Cocky enough.'

'Don't blow it, Charlie. Technicalities.'

Resnick changed position, shifting so that more of his back was towards Carew. 'Just might be something else, sir. Went to the girl's place this morning, pushed his way in, could be he raped her.'

Skelton's face was stone.

'Lynn's with the girl now, she's agreed to be examined. Take it from there.'

'Ex-boyfriend, isn't he?'

Resnick nodded.

'Difficult. Cases like that. Difficult to prove.'

Resnick turned towards Carew, motioned for him to go up the steps to the station.

'I'll not be gone long,' said Skelton, moving around on the spot, warming up. 'Make it a short one today.'

Oh, good, thought Resnick, following Carew towards the doors, just a quick four miles. Must remember when I get back tonight, fit in a few push-ups while I'm waiting for the omelette to cook.

A youth with gelled green hair and a gold ring through his left nostril was sitting opposite the inquiry window, dribbling blood and snot into his hands. At the window a middle-aged man in a suit, navy blue pinstripe, was explaining to the officer on duty exactly where he had left his car, exactly why he'd been stupid enough to leave his briefcase on the back seat. Inside the next set of doors, a uniformed constable was squatting down beside a girl of nine or ten, trying to get her to spell out her address.

The custody sergeant was in a heated argument with one of the detainees about the exact dimensions of the man's cell and whether or not they contravened the Geneva

Convention. Somebody was crying. Somebody else was singing the *Red Flag*. Not, Resnick assumed, someone on the Force. 'You wouldn't fucking believe it,' Mark Divine was saying on his way downstairs. 'The whole place covered in brown sauce. Not just the kitchen, the living room, everywhere. Before they'd left they'd emptied half-a-dozen tins of baked beans into the bath.' The young DC he was with didn't know whether to be sceptical or impressed. 'Packet soup in one of them things you sit on.'

'The toilet?' suggested the DC.

'No! One of those women things with taps on.'

'A bidet,' said Resnick, going past.

'Probably. Yes, sir. Thanks.'

'Up there,' Resnick said to Carew, pointing ahead.

'What the fuck they want one of those for?' Divine said to the DC as they left. 'Not as if they haven't got a bath.'

'We can talk in here,' said Resnick, showing Carew into his office and offering him a chair. 'Tea? Coffee?'

Carew shook his head. 'I hope this isn't going to take long.'

'Shouldn't think so,' said Resnick. 'If you hang on, I'll organize some tea for myself.'

He closed the door on Carew and moved out of sight, picking up the nearest unused phone and dialling the number of the woman officer detailed to deal with cases of reported rape.

Maureen Madden had passed her sergeant's exam almost a year to the day before she got her stripes. Twenty-nine and married, wanting to have a baby, not exactly eager for it, but suspecting, half-knowing that the further she turned past thirty, the more pressing that need would become. Let me get my promotion, she'd kept telling her husband, get a year in the job behind me, then we'll see. They kept offering her things she didn't want – traffic, community liaison. Then the rape suite. Women's things. Soft issues.

The times she'd arrived at a pub, fight going down, bottles flying, you hang on here, her male colleagues had said, no sense you going in there, you wait outside.

As if she were afraid. As if she couldn't handle herself.

She had gone in on her own once, up on the Alfreton Road, just short of closing, case of having to. Bloke had come out on his hands and knees, most of one ear left behind inside. She'd stepped in between three of these fellers squaring up, two on to one, broken pint glasses in their hands. If she'd been a man they'd have set on her, the lot of them, she was certain. As it was, they'd grinned like great kids, there'd been a lot of backslapping and some language, and they'd helped the injured man look for his ear while Maureen had radioed for an ambulance.

She knew she'd been lucky.

Until the night she'd run across to the Asian shop, been watching a video with her husband and got this sudden craving for custard. Tinned custard. Two youths had grabbed her from behind and had her on the floor in seconds, right there on the pavement. Not yet ten-thirty. She'd struggled and fought, kicked and screamed, still they'd torn her tights, kicked her face, left, one of them, a bruise the size of a fist below her breast. One white, one black, Maureen had been unable to identify them, they had never been caught.

All right, Maureen had said, I'll run the rape suite. All right.

'Hello,' she said to Karen when Lynn Kellogg brought her in. 'I'm Maureen. Maureen Madden. You must be Karen. Come over here and have a seat. The doctor won't be long.'

'I can leave any time I choose?' Carew asked, seeking confirmation.

'Absolutely,' Resnick said.

'Get up and walk out of your office?'

Resnick nodded.

'Right out of the station and no one will lift a finger to try and stop me?'

'Not a finger.'

'Right,' Carew said, making no attempt to move.

'Now,' said the doctor, adjusting her glasses, 'just one more swab and we're through.'

'I'd have thought,' Resnick said, 'that might be a bit of an understatement, pretty pissed off. Dropping you like that.'

Carew shrugged well-rounded shoulders. 'Happens, doesn't it?'

'Does it?'

'Don't tell me it's never happened to you.'

Resnick leaned sideways a little in his chair, made no reply.

'Happily married then, are we?' grinned Carew.

Cocky little shit! thought Resnick. Getting more sure of himself by the minute. 'Not any more,' he said. 'As it happens.'

'Then you must know what I mean,' Carew said. 'Unless it was you that left her.'

What is it about you, Carew, Resnick thought, makes me want to behave the way all those kids selling *Socialist Worker* outside Marks imagine I behave all the time?

'What did you want to do to him?' Carew asked, reading Resnick's silence correctly.

Resnick saw him, Elaine's estate agent, walking away from that empty house where he and Elaine had just made love, the suit, the Volvo and the keys. 'Hit him,' Resnick said.

'And did you?'

'No.'

'Not ever?'

'Never.'

Carew smiled. 'I bet you wish you had.'

Resnick smiled back. 'Satisfying, is it?'

Ian Carew's smile faltered.

Resnick leaned his weight in the opposite direction. His stomach made a low, groaning noise and he remembered he had had nothing for lunch.

'And Karen?'

'What about her?'

'You must have felt like hitting her. Lying. Seeing this man behind your back.'

Carew shook his head. 'I don't think you understand, inspector.'

'What's that?'

'I don't hit women.'

Maureen Madden was sitting to one side of Karen, Lynn Kellogg to the other. Both women were looking at her and Karen was looking at the pattern in the carpet, noticing a scattering of small burn marks. Cigarettes, she thought. She had that minute stubbed one out herself in the ashtray; now she lit another, waited till the first swathes of light grey smoke were rising to the ceiling. 'I'm not going to press charges,' she said.

Lynn and Maureen Madden exchanged glances over her head.

'We'll help you,' Maureen said gently. 'Every step of the way.'

'I'm sure,' Karen said.

'What's worrying you?' Maureen asked. 'Is it the court, giving evidence?'

Karen shook her head.

'Ian,' suggested Lynn, 'are you frightened he might come after you?'

'I'm not frightened.'

'Then what is it?'

Smoke veiled the brightness of her eyes. 'It's over. It's happened. That's an end to it.'

'No,' Lynn said too sharply, a warning look from Maureen.

'You agreed to come in,' Maureen reminded her.

'I was upset. I wasn't thinking.'

'Look at your face,' said Lynn.

'It's not only your face,' said Maureen. 'Remember what he did.'

'Oh,' said Karen, turning for the first time towards her, 'you don't have to worry about that. I was the one it happened to.'

'Then stop it happening again.'

'How do I do that?'

'Help us put him away.'

Karen lowered her eyes, shook her head.

'If he gets away with this . . .' Lynn began.

'Then don't let him.'

'Without you, without your evidence,' said Maureen, 'we wouldn't stand a chance. It probably wouldn't even come to court.'

'He'll get off scot-free,' Lynn said. 'He can do it again.'

'Think of other women,' said Maureen.

Karen squashed her cigarette into the ashtray as she got to her feet. 'You! You think of other bloody women. It's your job, not mine.' She reached past the two police officers for her coat. The corners of her eyes were red and blurred with tears.

Lynn moved towards the door, as if to prevent Karen leaving, but Maureen Madden shook her head. 'If you'll wait a few minutes,' Maureen said, 'I'll arrange for you to be driven back.'

'It doesn't matter.'

'I'll take you back,' said Lynn.

'I'll walk.'

Thanks, Lynn thought. Thanks for that. Thanks a whole lot! She opened the door and stood aside.

Resnick had the phone in his hand at the first ring. He listened and set the receiver back down, standing up. 'Excuse me a minute,' he said to Carew. 'Something's come up.'

'I'll go,' Carew said, beginning to stand himself.

'No,' said Resnick. 'Wait. Five minutes, that's all I'll be. At most.'

Ian Carew waited until Resnick had left the office before sitting back down. Patel was sitting near one of the windows in the CID room, typing up his report. 'If he tries to leave,' Resnick said, nodding his head back towards his office door, 'stall him.'

'I'll try, sir.'

'Do better than that.' He glanced down at what Patel was typing, trying to read it upside down. 'Anywhere with the clothing thing?'

'No, sir.'

Resnick hurried from the room. Lynn Kellogg and Maureen Madden were already in the superintendent's office and the expressions on all of their faces told Resnick what he didn't want to know.

'No chance she'll change her mind?' asked Resnick.

'She might,' said Lynn. 'A couple of hours later she'll have changed it back again.'

'How about the other business?' asked Skelton. 'It is the more serious charge.' He carried on, intercepting Maureen Madden's fierce look and ignoring it. 'GBH at least, attempted murder.'

'More serious than rape, sir?' said Maureen regardless.

'No time to ride the hobby horse,' said Skelton sharply. 'I treat rape every bit as seriously as you do.'

'Really, sir?'

'Well, Charlie?' Skelton said.

'Possible motivation, sir. Dodgy alibi. Now we know he's capable of violence. But, no, nothing to link him in directly. Not as yet.'

'So we let him go.'

'Sir,' said Lynn, cheeks flushed, 'he beat up that girl and raped her.'

'Who says? I mean, according to which account?'

'The medical evidence . . .' Maureen Madden began.

'Intercourse had taken place, cuts and bruising to the face and body – without the girl's sworn word, what does that prove? No worse than what goes on between couples all over the city every Saturday night. Consenting adults. What's to prevent him getting up and saying, well, it was how she liked it? Hard and rough.'

'Jesus!' Maureen Madden breathed quietly.

Lynn Kellogg stared at the floor.

'We can warn him,' Skelton continued. 'Even though she won't press charges, we can officially warn him, let him know that warning will be registered, documented. On that matter, that's all we can do and it will be done. For the rest – watch and wait.'

There was only the flat click of the wall clock, the sounds of four people breathing. Outside, along the corridor, officers and clerical staff walking, talking, getting about their business. The greedy persistence of telephones, like starlings.

'All right, Lynn?' Skelton said. 'Maureen?'

'Yes, sir.' Overlapping, subdued.

'All right, Charlie?'

'Yes, sir.'

Resnick's office was empty. Anxiety hovered around Patel's dark eyes. 'He walked out, sir. Insisted upon leaving. He said he had the right. I didn't think I could try and prevent him.'

'Don't worry,' Resnick said. 'Dig out Naylor and go and

pick him up again. No charge, no caution, get him back here just the same.'

'Yes, sir.'

Resnick's stomach gave another empty lurch. Time enough to cross to the island at the middle of the circus, have them make up a couple of sandwiches, smoked ham and Emmental, breast of turkey with wholegrain mustard, pickled cucumber and mayonnaise. He would have a quiet word with Lynn on his way out, perhaps she'd like to be present while he was giving Carew a good bollocking.

Fourteen

When Karl Dougherty had told his mother he was going to be a nurse, she had pointed through the kitchen window at the way the chrysanthemums were leaning over and blamed the rain. When he had told his father, the look in the older man's eyes had made it clear he thought his son was telling him he was gay. Not that Dougherty would have called it that: nancy boy, shirt-lifter, plain old-fashioned poof – those were the expressions that would have come to mind.

'You can't,' his mother had said after the third time of telling.

'Why ever not?'

Karl watched as she placed six pounds of oranges on the Formica work top and began to slice them with a knife. The copper jam-pot she had bought at auction was waiting on the stove. Soon the kitchen would be studded with glass jars, scrubbed and recycled, labelled in her almost indecipherable hand. Quite frequently at breakfast one of the family had spooned gooseberry chutney on to their toast by mistake.

'Why can't I?'

'Because you've got a degree.' His mother had looked at him as if that were the most obvious reason in the world and she couldn't understand why he hadn't thought of it for himself.

He had shown her the letter, accepting him for a place at the Derbyshire Royal Infirmary as a student nurse.

'There you are,' she said. 'You're not a student. You're

a BA, a good upper second. They've got it wrong.' She smiled up from the last of the oranges. 'There's been a mistake.'

Karl had found his father in the cellar, planing a length of beech. 'We can't support you,' his father said. 'Not again. We've been through all that.'

'I shall be paid,' Karl explained. 'Not very much, but a wage.'

'And living? Where will you live?'

Karl looked at the woodworking tools, arranged on and around the shelves in neat order, each wiped and cleaned after use. 'There's a place in the nurses' home. If I want it.'

'Good.'

When Karl was at the steps, his father said, 'I never wanted you to go to that bloody university in the first place, you know.'

'I know.'

'Waste of bloody time and money.'

'Maybe.'

'And you know one thing – this'll do for your mother. She'll not begin to understand.'

A few nights later, Karl had been in his room to the rear of the upstairs, writing a letter. His father had come in with a half-bottle of Scotch and two glasses, tumblers that had been given away with so many gallons of petrol.

'Here,' sitting on the bottom of Karl's bed and handing him one of the glasses, pouring a generous measure into them both. He had seen his father drink bottled beer on Sunday afternoons, port and the occasional sherry at Christmas; he had never known him to drink whisky.

They sat there for close on three-quarters of an hour, drinking, never speaking. Finally, his father tipped what remained into Karl's glass and stood up to leave.

'Was there something you wanted to say to me?' his father asked.

Karl shook his head. 'I don't think so.'

'I thought there might have been something you wanted to tell me.'

'No.'

The incident was never referred to again by either of them, but for some time, whenever they met, Karl's father would avoid looking him in the eye.

There was scarcely a week went by during Karl's training, he didn't consider throwing it in. Neither was there a week when something took place – usually an interchange with one of the patients – which didn't confirm for him the rightness of his decision. For the first time since he could remember, his life had a purpose: he felt he was of use.

'This is my son, Karl,' his mother said, introducing him to friends when he made an unannounced visit home. 'He's training to be a doctor.'

'A nurse,' Karl corrected her.

She smiled at her guests. 'There's been a mistake.'

The evening after Karl received notification that he had qualified, he called his father and arranged to meet him for a drink. They went to a pub on the old road from Eastwood to Nottingham and sat with halves of bitter while youths in leather jackets played darts and Elvis on the juke box. 'You think I'm gay, don't you?' Karl asked. 'Homosexual.'

His father sucked in air and closed his eyes as if a heavy foot had been pressed down on his chest.

'Well, I'm not. I just don't like women very much. I mean, only as friends. Okay?'

When his father opened his eyes, Karl reached out a hand towards him and his father pulled his own hand, sharply, away.

After his registration, Karl did a couple of years of general nursing before specializing; he worked on a genito-urinary ward for three years, not bothering to tell either of his parents the day-to-day focus for his skills. He spent two years nursing in the States, Boston and San Francisco, well paid and, he felt, under-used. Patients paying for their private rooms thought it was okay to summon him to fetch their newspaper from across the room, reposition the TV set away from the sun. Before he could do as much as issue an aspirin or clip a toenail, he had to call a doctor and obtain permission.

Back in Britain, he clung to his short haircut and the habit of wearing coloured T-shirts under lightweight suits, at least until the weather beat him down. For months there was a touch of a transatlantic accent to his speech and he wore a watch on either wrist, one of them set to West Coast time. After two years of general surgical work, he was appointed senior staff nurse, with the expectation of being promoted to charge nurse within the next eighteen months.

Karl Dougherty had been a qualified nurse for nine years; aside from Christmas and his mother's birthday, he had not visited his parents more than half-a-dozen times in the last four. Soon after returning from the States, he had breezed in wearing an off-white suit, a short-sleeved green T-shirt with a breast pocket and yellow shoes. He had a box of Thornton's special assortment in one hand, a vast bouquet of flowers in his arms.

'Oh, no,' his mother had exclaimed. 'There's been a mistake.'

'Hello, Karl,' one of the patients called. 'How was your night off?'

'About as exciting as yours.'

'Hi, Karl,' said a nurse, swinging the bedpan she was carrying out of his path.

'Is that accidental,' said Karl, 'or are you just not pleased to see me?'

Karl liked to get on to the ward a little early, have a sniff round before handover, things he might notice and want to ask questions about that might otherwise go unremarked.

'Where's sister?' he asked.

A student nurse glanced up from the care plan she was adding to and pointed her Biro towards the closed door. 'Hasn't shown herself for the best part of an hour.'

Oh, God! thought Karl, moving on, in there wrestling with the menopause again!

He turned into the side ward and found Sarah Leonard sitting on Tim Fletcher's bed, holding his hand.

'This isn't what you think,' Sarah said.

'You mean you're not taking his pulse.'

'Absolutely not. This is therapy.'

Karl raised an eyebrow.

'Comfort and consolation,' Sarah smiled. 'Tim's feeling forlorn today. His girlfriend failed to pay him a visit.'

'There's a singularly ugly man with halitosis and very little bowel control, back down the ward; he hasn't had a visitor in three weeks. Perhaps you'd like to hold his hand as well.'

Sarah Leonard poked out her tongue and got to her feet. 'I'd better go, before Karl here asserts his authority.' She gave Fletcher a smile, Karl a toss of her head and hurried away.

'Impressive!'

Tim Fletcher nodded agreement.

'How are you feeling?' Karl asked. 'Apart from horny.'

'Sore.'

'No more than that?'

Fletcher shrugged. 'I'm okay.'

'You don't want anything for the pain?'

'Thanks. I'll be all right.'

Karl patted his leg. 'I'll check with you later.'

Helen Minton came out of her office just ahead of Karl as he walked back down the ward, making a slight nod of acknowledgement in his direction and nothing more. Karl didn't think it was that she felt threatened by him, not that alone. She spent her days on duty as if everything around her might explode or evaporate unless she held it together by sheer force of will.

Poor woman! Karl thought. He had stumbled across her late one evening, standing with Bernard Salt beside the consultant's BMW. Whatever they had been talking about, Karl didn't think it was hospital business.

'Sister,' he said breezily, catching her up. 'Another fifteen minutes and you'll be finished. A free woman.'

The look she gave him was not brimming with gratitude.

Naylor and Patel had found Ian Carew sitting in the small yard at the back of his rented house, drinking pineapple juice and reading about ventricular tumours. For several moments, it seemed as if he might tell the two plain-clothes men to go and play with themselves; he might even have been tempted to take a swing at them, Naylor in particular. But then he grunted something about being left in peace, something else about people who could have been making better use of time and resources, grabbed an Aran sweater and followed them along the narrow alley at the side of the house.

'I don't have to put up with this,' Carew said as soon as he was in Resnick's office. 'This is harassment.'

Resnick was careful to keep his hands down by his sides. 'Coming from someone who not so many hours ago beat up a young woman in her own home and . . .'

'That's a lie!'

'. . . and forced her to have sex with him . . .'

'You've got no right . . .'

'. . . that comes over as a bit rich.'

'You can't *say* that.'

'What?'

Carew looked at the inspector, standing behind his desk, at Lynn Kellogg, in a white blouse and a mid-length pleated skirt standing off to his right. 'I want a solicitor,' Carew said. 'Now. Before I say another word.'

'You don't have to say anything,' Resnick said. 'And you don't need a solicitor. Just listen.'

Carew opened his mouth to say something more but thought better of it.

'In accordance with Home Office instructions,' said Resnick, 'I am issuing you with a warning about your future behaviour, in so far as it concerns Karen Archer. Although, up to the present, she has declined to press charges, there is little doubt from what she has alleged, backed up by medical examination of her injuries, that you have been guilty of an assault upon her person.'

'What assault?'

'Shut it!'

'What . . . ?'

'Shut it and listen!'

Carew retreated the half-step he had taken towards Resnick's desk.

'That girl,' said Resnick, 'was elbowed in the face, she was punched in the mouth, she was struck in the body. You're a big man, you're strong and my guess is you're used to having your own way.'

'That's bullshit!'

Resnick was around the desk more quickly than either Lynn or Carew would have given him credit. He didn't stop until his chest was all but touching Carew's, face almost as close as it could be.

'We've got photographs of her injuries, Polaroids of the bruises and they're going on file. Your file. I hope for your sake I never have to refer to them again. Stay away from her, that's my advice. A wide berth. She doesn't want anything to do with you. That's over. Leave it.'

Resnick moved his head aside, rapidly swung it back, so that Carew blinked. 'Word you've got to learn: no. Doesn't mean, yes. Doesn't mean, maybe. Girlfriend, wife, whatever. No means no. Understand it any other way and you're for it.'

Resnick stepped back: not far. He stared at Carew for ten seconds more. 'Now get out,' he said quietly.

Carew had to walk around Resnick to get to the door, which he left open behind him, anxious to leave the building as fast as he could. Lynn Kellogg wanted to go over to her inspector and say well done, she wanted to give him a hug; she settled for offering him a cup of tea.

Before Resnick could accept or decline, his phone rang.

'Yes?'

'Someone down here asking for you, sir,' said the officer on duty. And then, before Resnick could ask further, 'Think it's personal, sir. Should I . . . ?'

'I'll be down,' said Resnick. 'The tea,' he said to Lynn. 'Some other time.'

All the way down the stairs, Resnick's insides danced themselves into a knot. He knew what he would see, when he pushed his way through into reception: Elaine standing there, that distraught expression on her face, impatient, *who do you think you are, keeping me waiting* – what was it? – *ten years?*

'Charlie!'

Ed Silver was sitting with his back to the wall, meagre grey hair resting below a poster asking for information about a thirteen-year-old girl, last seen in Louth three months ago. Something matted and dark clung to the front of his jacket.

'Charlie,' he repeated, rising unsteadily to his feet. 'Lost my glasses. Didn't know where you were.'

Resnick looked at his watch. 'Half an hour,' he said. 'Three-quarters at most. I'll take you home.'

Fifteen

'N'cha got no real food, Charlie?'

'Such as?'

'You know, bangers, bacon, nice pork chop.'

Resnick shook his head. 'I can fix you a sandwich.'

Ed Silver made a face and tried the refrigerator again, unable to believe his bad luck.

'How about an omelette?'

'All right,' Silver said grudgingly, and Resnick began to chop an onion up small, half a red pepper, a handful of French beans he'd braised a few days before in butter and garlic.

'Vegetarian now, are you?'

Another shake of the head. 'Just can't bring myself to buy meat. Not red meat. Not often. I think it's the smell.'

'That beer you got in there,' Silver asked, pointing back at the fridge. 'You keeping it for something special?'

Resnick opened his last two bottles of Czech Budweiser and lifted glasses down from the shelf. 'No,' Silver said, reaching across. 'Have mine as it comes. Won't do to get too used to creature comforts; never know when you might pitch me out on me arse.'

He wandered off into the living room and several minutes later, as the butter was beginning to bubble up round the edges of the pan, Resnick heard a few bars of off-centre piano and then, instantly recognizable, the sound of a trumpet, burnished, like brown paper crackling; the soloist stepping into the tune with short, soft steps, deceptive. Clifford Brown. The notes lengthening, sharp blue smoke, rising. The *Memorial* album. Resnick doubted if he had pulled the record from the shelf in eighteen months, yet he could picture its cover.

a photograph of a playground, a trumpet
lying on a swing, over there
the slides, the splintery line
of benches, chaotic segments of
chain link fence, hazy
apartment buildings beyond.
Perfect.

He continued to listen, tilting the pan so that the egg mixture rolled round the curved sides and down, forking in the onion, seconds later the pepper and the beans. He left it on the flame long enough to cut slices of bread, dark rye, gave the pan a shake and folded the omelette in two. Before Brownie had finished 'Lover Come Back to Me', it would be ready.

'They're all dying, Charlie.'

'Who?'

'Every bugger!'

Resnick handed him a plate, set his own down on a copy of *Police Review*, went back for forks and black pepper, started the LP again at the first track.

'Know how old he was when he copped it?' Ed asked.

'Twenty-six?'

'Five. Twenty-five.'

Less than half your age, Ed, Resnick thought, and you're still going – in a manner of speaking.

'Nineteen,' Silver said, 'he was in a car crash nearly finished him. Almost a year in hospital. Enough to kill you in itself, way some of those butchers wade in when they've got you strapped down. Anyway . . .' He pushed a piece of omelette on to a corner of the bread and lifted it to his mouth. '. . . got over that, started playing again, made it big and *wham*! Another sodding road accident. Dead.'

'Mm,' said Resnick.

'Twenty-five.'

'Yes.'

'Poor bastard!'

'Amen.'

'Stockholm Sweetnin' ' became ' 'Scuse These Blues'. Resnick took the plates into the kitchen and dumped them in the sink. He thought the last thing he should do was let Ed Silver catch sight of his bottle of Lemon Grass vodka, but the last stray gleams of light were striking the room at just the right angle and, whatever the risks, it seemed the proper thing to do.

'Cheers,' said Resnick.

'To Brownie,' said Ed Silver.

'God bless.'

They drank a little and then they drank a little more. There was a moment when Ed Silver's wispy grey hair and scarred scalp were outlined against deep orange light. Resnick looked at Silver's knuckles, cracked and swollen, and wondered when those hands had last held a saxophone; he wanted to ask him if he thought he might ever play again. Of course, he didn't. They drank a little more. Dizzy sneaked out of the half-dark and lay across Silver's lap, sniffing from time to time at whatever was matted thick on his jacket.

'They're all dead, Charlie.'

'Who?'

'Clifford, Sandy, Pete, Lawrence, Vernon, Marshall, Tom. All the fucking Browns. Gone.'

Muted, but jaunty, Clifford Brown was playing 'Theme of No Repeat'.

There had to be better places to spend the evening, Millington was thinking, than a lay-by close to Burton-on-Trent. Heavy lorries yammering cross-country between Derby and West Bromwich, bits of lads in tuned-up Fiestas driving as if they were on Donnington race track. Three nights before, a truck loaded with cartons of Embassy, packets of twenty, had pulled in here so that the driver could rest. He had been hoping for a cup of tea, something warm to eat, but the man who ran the stall had closed early and gone home. The driver had stood by the field edge to take a leak and someone had hit him from behind with a wrench and taken his keys. When he came to, surprise, surprise, the truck was gone.

It had been found early the following morning, abandoned and empty, close to the motorway. The police also discovered the driver to have two previous convictions for theft and one, when he was a youngster, for TDA. Which didn't mean that he had whacked himself round the head, nor agreed beforehand that somebody else should do it, but it did mean officers were keeping a keen eye on who he contacted and watching for tell-tale signs of unsuspected wealth, anything from a spanking new fifty-one centimetre flat-screen TV with a Nicam stereo decoder to a holiday for two in Tenerife.

Either of which Millington would have been pleased to receive. He stopped trying to figure out exactly what the couple in the car behind were up to by careful use of his rear-view mirror and got out to stretch his legs. The tea stall was actually an old caravan now devoid of wheels and painted all over in a bizarre tartan. Its proprietor was a Glaswegian with one glass eye and a five-inch scar down his cheek along which you could clearly see the stitch marks. Millington reckoned he'd been sewn up on a back-parlour table with a domestic needle and thread and a bottle of Glenlivet for anaesthetic.

'Tea, is it?'

Millington fished in his trouser pocket for the money.

'How about a steak and kidney pie? Keep away the cold. If you don't fancy eating it, you can always set it under your feet, like one of they old stone jobbies your grannie used to have.'

'That the best you can offer?' Millington asked.

'I've a hot dog or two in here somewhere,' the man said, lifting the lid from a metal pan and swishing away with a pair of tongs. 'Maybe a burger?'

'Yes.'

'A burger?'

'Yes.'

'You're certain?'

'Great salesman, aren't you?'

'Onions or without?'

'Onions,' Millington said. 'With.'

He tipped sugar into his tea and stirred it with a spoon that was attached to the counter by a length of chain. Three motor bikes throttled down and swung in off the road, stopping between the caravan and Millington's car. One of the riders was skinny and tall, totally bald beneath his helmet when he took it off; his companions were overweight and stocky, one of them sporting a belly that hung over his studded belt like a pregnancy about to come to term. All three wore boots and leathers and were old enough to have seen *Easy Rider* and *The Wild One* when they were first released. The girls riding with them were none of them more than seventeen, pale, pretty faces, sharp features drawn sharper by hours staring into the wind.

They ignored Millington and joked with the Scot behind the counter, old friends. Millington took his burger, added some watered-down ketchup and walked back towards his car to eat it. The couple parked behind him had forsaken the front seat for the back. The burger was grey and greasy, pitted with white gristle; two bites and Millington tossed it into the surrounding dark. He thought about his wife, sitting on the settee with her legs curled beneath her skirt, chuckling over Mary Wesley. 'I don't know how she can even think about sex at her age,' she'd said, 'never mind write about it.' Millington had grunted non-committally and waited for her to change the subject: he knew that thinking about it was never the problem.

'Debbie?'

Kevin Naylor lay facing his wife's back, early night for once, both of them hoping against hope the baby would sleep right through.

'Deb?'

He touched the nape of her neck, above the collar of her nightdress, and felt her flinch.

'Debbie.'

'What?'

'We can't carry on like this.'

Not for the first time, Karl Dougherty was wondering why there were only fifteen minutes in which to hand over to the night staff; never enough, especially when they'd had two unexpected admissions, which had been the case tonight. The administrators who closed wards for financial reasons didn't seem to understand there were others who failed to respond to budgetary shortfalls: the sick and the dying.

'Now then,' Karl said to one of the nurses as she stood waiting for the lift, 'off home to a cold bed and an improving book, I hope.'

'Oh, yes!' she grinned. 'And the rest!'

As Karl walked towards the main road and the buses, he caught sight of Sarah Leonard in her beige coat ahead of him. Hurrying, he drew level with her at the entrance to the subway.

'Catching the bus?'

Sarah smiled and shook her head. 'Walking clears my head. Besides, by the time you've waited, you could be indoors with your feet up.'

'Well, I'd walk with you, only I promised to meet a friend in town for a drink.'

They came up from the subway at the far side of the street, side by side. 'Think of me,' Sarah said, 'settling down to a good-night bowl of cornflakes.'

Karl laughed. 'I'll be having mine later, don't you worry. Only with me it's Shredded Wheat. I keep thinking if I eat three at a time, it'll make a man of me.'

Sarah raised a hand as she started to walk. 'So much for advertising,' she said.

Karl was still at the bus stop, five minutes later, when Ian Carew drove past. Approaching the railway bridge short of Lenton Recreation Ground, he slowed down, the better to look at the tall woman he was passing, stepping out briskly in a long raincoat, definitely someone who knew where she was going. Even so, Carew thought, no harm in pulling over, offering a lift.

Graham Millington had read the *Mail* from cover to cover, back to front and front to back. All that was left was to try it upside down. The couple behind had come to a similar conclusion twenty minutes earlier, wiped two circles of steam from the windows and driven off to their respective spouses. Talking to the Scot in the caravan and trying to get some useful information had been like searching for the sea on Southport beach.

'Sod this for a game of soldiers,' Millington said to no one. 'I'm off home.'

Kevin and Debbie Naylor lay back to back, their bodies close but not quite touching, each assuming the other was asleep. Very soon, the baby would wake and start crying.

Karl Dougherty came up the stairs from Manhattan's and looked to see if there was a cab on the rank near the Victorian Hotel. Never when you want one, he thought, when you don't they're all over you like crabs. He crossed the street towards Trinity Square, thinking of cutting through towards the centre, pick one up there. Seeing that the light outside the Gents was still on, he realized that he needed to go again. Never mind it hadn't been more than ten minutes. Anything above two lagers and it went through him like a tap.

Ah! He stood at the centre of a deserted line of urinals and unfastened his fly. Better off if he'd said no to his appointment, hurried home like Sarah Leonard and got stuck into some cereal, lots of sugar, warm milk.

He fumbled with his buttons, thinking how inconvenient it was that zips had gone out of fashion. Laughing at his own joke, he failed to hear the bolt on the closet door behind him sliding back.

Sixteen

There must be some people, Resnick thought, for whom a telephone ringing in the middle of the night doesn't spell bad news. There he was, ear to the receiver, the clock across the room stranded between three and four. 'Yes,' he said, tucking in his shirt. 'Yes,' fastening his belt. 'Yes,' reaching for his shoes. 'I'll be there.'

Sheets of white paper, smeared with ketchup or curry sauce, littered the pavements; crushed cartons still holding cold gravy, mushy peas. Patel was standing on the street corner, concern on his face clear in the overhead lighting; he took his hands from his raincoat pockets as Resnick approached. One police car was parked outside the entrance to the toilets, another around by the fast-food pasta place, facing up the slope of Trinity Square. A uniformed officer stood at a kind of attention, doing his best not to look tired or bored.

'I wasn't sure, sir, if I should call you or not.'

Resnick nodded. 'Let's see.'

Patel and a DC from Central had been forming the token CID presence, overnight. The first report had only mentioned a male, white, late twenties to early thirties; it hadn't been till later that his profession had been referred to. When Resnick walked into the Gents, Patel behind him, DI Cossall was already there, taking a leak at the end urinal. Between them, the scene of crime team had finished dusting for prints and were firing off a few more Polaroids for posterity.

Across the floor, the thick chalk mark showed where the

body had fallen; rather, the position it had finally crawled into. One chalk toe damp at the foot of the urinal, a hand reaching towards the closet door, it looked less like the outline of a body than abstract art.

'Your young DC, there,' Cossall nodded towards Patel, 'could've let you get a few more hours' beauty sleep.'

Resnick was looking at the chalk lines on the floor. 'He *is* from the hospital?'

'So it appears.'

'Attacked with a knife, some kind of blade?'

'Yes.'

'Then Patel here did right. Anything less he'd have got a bollocking.'

Cossall pointed downwards. 'Pretty much like this sorry bastard, then. Sounds as if whoever went for him, tried to chop his balls off.'

A quick shudder ran through Resnick and, despite himself, he cupped one hand towards his legs, like a footballer lining up against a free kick. 'Let's get outside,' he said. 'The stink in here's getting up my nose.'

Cossall and Resnick were more or less contemporaries; their movements between uniform and CID ran parallel, the dates of their promotions approximately matched. Cossall had transferred outside the local force at one point, but nine months as a detective sergeant in Norfolk had been more than enough. 'The only place,' he'd once confided in Resnick over a drink, 'where the stories on the wall in the blokes' bog are about shagging sheep.'

'Trouble was,' Cossall was saying now, 'he lay there so long. Lost so much blood. Looks as if youths were coming in and out, stepping round him to take a piss. Likely thought he'd passed out, drunk.'

'What about the blood?'

'Figured he'd fallen, smacked his head, if they noticed at

all. It's a wonder some bugger didn't throw up over him into the bargain.'

'Where is he now?' Resnick asked.

Cossall shook his head. 'Somewhere between intensive care and the morgue, I should reckon.'

'And family?' Resnick said. 'They've been informed?'

'Ah,' said Cossall, looking away towards the light flashing intermittently from the roof of the nearest police car, 'I knew there was something.'

Resnick turned right alongside the Fletcher Gate car park and came to a halt outside the Lace Market Theatre. He switched off his headlights and let the engine idle. The only situation in which he was glad he'd never had children was this: the only part of the job he hated to do alone. Not so long back, he remembered, it had been Rachel he had woken with a phone call in the middle of the night. Come with me. A skilled social worker, she had been the perfect choice. There's a woman I have to talk to, I need your help. A woman, already crippled with pain, who had to be told her daughter was dead. Of course, he hadn't only wanted Rachel there for her expertise – when to speak, when to be silent, the right word, the touch at the proper time – however unconsciously he had been drawing her into his life. Sucking her in. So deep that before it was over she had nearly been killed herself.

Rachel.

The scrape of a shoe against the uneven pavement made Resnick turn. A woman stepping forward out of the shadow, collar of her dark raincoat eased up, hair that framed her pale face short and dark. Resnick reached across and unlocked the near side door.

'Sorry to haul you out,' Resnick said.

'S'all right, sir,' said Lynn Kellogg, 'I've done the same to you before now.'

Resnick switched back to main beam, slid the car into gear. 'I'll fill you in on the way,' he said.

Wollaton was the place that time forgot. An inner-city suburb of bungalows and crescents and neat detached houses with crazy paving and front gardens fit for gnomes. A light shone in the porch of the Dougherty house, dull orange. Resnick pressed the bell a second time and stepped back. Another light appeared, filtered through the curtains of the upstairs front. Cautious footsteps on the stairs.

'Who is it?'

'Detective Inspector Resnick. CID.'

Through the square of frosted glass set into the door, Resnick could see a figure, shoulders hunched, hesitating.

'It's the police, Mr Dougherty,' Resnick said, not wanting to raise his voice too loud and wake the neighbours. Wanting it to be over: done.

The figure came forward; there was a slow sliding back of bolts, top and bottom, a latch pushed up, a key being turned: finally, the door was inched back on a chain.

Resnick identified himself, holding his warrant card towards the edge of the door and stepping to one side so that Dougherty could see him.

'This is Detective Constable Kellogg,' Resnick said, pointing behind him. 'If we could come in.'

'Can't it wait? What's so important that it can't wait?'

'Your son,' Resnick said. 'It's about your son.'

'Karl?'

'Yes, Karl.'

The door was pushed closed, but only to free the chain. Dougherty stood in tartan slippers on a mat that said *Welcome* in dark tufts of bristle. His ankles were bony beneath the hem of striped pyjama trousers, the skin marbled with broken blue veins. The belt of his dark green dressing-gown had been tied in a tight bow. His hair tufted up at angles from the sides of his head.

'What about Karl?' he asked. 'What's happened to him?'

But the expression in his eyes showed that he already knew.

Not exactly, of course. That came a little later, in the small living room, the only light from a standard lamp in one corner, the three of them sitting on furniture that had been built to last and had done exactly that.

All the while Resnick had been speaking, Dougherty's eyes had flickered from the cocktail cabinet to the light oak table, from the empty vase they had brought back from Holland fifteen years ago to the small framed photographs on the mantelpiece above the variflame gas fire.

In the silence that followed, Dougherty's eyes were still. His fingers plucked at the ends of his green wool belt. Resnick wondered how much, how clearly he'd understood.

'Would you like us to take you to the hospital?' Resnick asked. 'You and your wife?'

'My wife . . .' Dougherty began, alarmed.

'We could take you,' Resnick repeated. 'To see Karl.'

'My wife can't go,' Dougherty said.

'She is here?' Resnick asked.

'I told you, upstairs. She can't go, she mustn't know, she can't . . .'

'She'll have to be told, Mr Dougherty,' Resnick said.

'No.'

'Would you like me to speak to her?' Lynn offered.

'She can't know.'

'What?' said Pauline Dougherty from the doorway. 'What is it, William? Who are these people? I woke up and you weren't there. That was when I heard voices. Your voice, William. I thought it was Karl. You know, one of his little visits. To surprise us.'

'What visits?' said Dougherty, staring at her.

'You know, his little . . .'

'He doesn't make visits,' getting to his feet. 'One year's end to the next, he scarcely comes near us.'

'He does, William. Oh, he does. You forget.'

William Dougherty closed his eyes and his wife stood close in front of him, recently permed hair held tight in a net, a dressing-gown of quilted pink and fluffy pink slippers without heels.

'William,' she said and he opened his eyes.

'Karl's dead,' Dougherty said.

'No,' Resnick said quickly, half out of his chair.

'He's dead,' Dougherty repeated.

'No,' said Resnick quietly. 'Mr Dougherty, that isn't what I said.'

'There you are,' Pauline Dougherty turned her head towards the inspector and then back towards her husband, reaching for his hand. 'There you are,' almost beaming. 'You see, there's been a mistake.'

The sky was lightening and the milk-float was only two streets away. Lynn Kellogg had spoken to Pauline Dougherty's sister in Harrogate, who would catch the first train down via York. One of the neighbours would be across to sit with her within the half hour, and meanwhile Lynn herself sat in the kitchen holding Mrs Dougherty's hands, watching the birds land for a moment on the cotoneaster bush and then fly off again. Going to the hospital meant acknowledging the truth of what had happened and Pauline Dougherty was not ready for that yet; Lynn wondered if she ever would be.

Meanwhile Resnick phoned the hospital, the station, the hospital once more. A uniformed officer came to take William Dougherty to see his son. Karl was in surgery and fighting for his life, struggling, unknowingly, to prove his father wrong.

Resnick and Lynn Kellogg went to the café near the

Dunkirk flyover and ate sausage baps with HP sauce and drank strong, sweet tea. Looking out through the steamed-over window at the blur of early morning traffic, neither of them said a word.

Seventeen

By eight that morning, Karl Dougherty was under constant observation in intensive care. He had come round for several minutes close to six o'clock; again, an hour later. His father had been sitting at the foot of his bed, but if Karl recognized him, he gave no sign. The cuts and lacerations to his face and forearms had been straightforwardly treated; wounds to his lower chest and abdomen had been more severe and required more careful surgery. Hard as he tried, the surgeon had been unable to save one of Karl's testicles.

Resnick drove Lynn Kellogg back to her flat, easing into the flow of early morning traffic. The first report on Radio Trent spoke of a man attacked in the city centre, detained in hospital in a serious condition. 'Think he'll pull through, sir?' Lynn asked. Resnick didn't know: just that if he didn't, if the incident changed to one of murder, a whole different set of procedures would fall into place. Fletcher, he was thinking, swinging left past the Broad Marsh, Fletcher and Dougherty – how much of that was coincidence? He shifted across to the centre of the road, indicating right; braked beside the Lace Market Theatre, back where they had started not so many hours earlier. 'Cup of tea, sir?' Lynn asked, car door open. 'Thanks,' said Resnick, shaking his head, 'any more, folk'll think I've got problems with the prostate.' He watched her walk from sight before reversing away. A few more like her in the Force wouldn't do any harm at all.

William Dougherty got up from his son's bed, told the nurse he'd be right back, took the lift to the ground floor and stood for several minutes, outside the main entrance, smoking a cigarette. It tasted old, stale, God knows how long it had been in his coat pocket, months. Ever since Pauline had taken to complaining if he smoked in the house, he had been cutting back. One in the garden on a Sunday, trimming back the hedges, straightening up the lawn. When they had first moved to Wollaton, Karl had been little more than a baby. Barely able to keep his feet as he followed his father around. 'Pay ball! Pay ball! Pay ball!' 'William, be careful of the flowers!' Dougherty put out the cigarette with forefinger and thumb and blew on the tip before dropping the nub end back in his pocket. Waste not, want not. Waste. *I never wanted you to go to university in the first place, you know. Waste of bloody time and money*. Now he looked like a robot, lying there, unreal. Something from science fiction, an astronaut. For a while that's what he'd wanted to be. Dan Dare. Thunderbirds. Something like that. Now he'd be lucky to be anything. Machines controlled the flow of his blood, the air from his lungs. Not that Dougherty understood, not exactly, but there was no avoiding the apparatus, the tubes, wires, digits on the faces of all those machines. Nurses who smiled at him deftly before reading off the figures like mechanics, noting them down. Not dead, the police inspector had said, not dead. What did he know? What was this? Instead of going back inside the hospital, he started walking away.

Resnick was not altogether surprised to see Reg Cossall queueing up for a second breakfast in the canteen, his sergeant, Derek Fenby, alongside him.

'What's up, Reg?' Resnick said. 'Don't they feed you enough down there?'

Cossall poked a finger into Resnick's stomach. 'Not as well as they do up here.'

'DCI,' Fenby said, his voice a natural growl, 'wanted us to report to your super.'

Cossall winked. 'Politics, Charlie. Argue till he's blue in the face, Jack Skelton, keep both cases up here. While since you lot had anything tasty.'

'Happy for you to handle this one,' said Fenby. 'Eh, boss?'

'Late-night emasculation,' said Cossall with a cock-eyed grin. 'Not our style.'

'Handy for some, though,' said Fenby, 'saves on the vasectomy.'

Jesus, thought Resnick, they're enjoying this. Keeping their knees clenched and thinking there but for the grace of God . . .

'Hey up!' said Cossall loudly at the woman behind the counter. 'Call that thing a sausage? I've seen better between our dog's legs.'

Jack Skelton's suit jacket was on its hanger behind his office door and all was right with the world. For now. The notebook and blotter on his desk were the regulation inch and a quarter apart, his fountain pens facing magnetic north. Only the photograph of Kate as a young girl had disappeared from its frame, replaced by another, a family group in which the background was unclear, the faces were blurred.

'What do you think, Charlie? Pull Patel off this jeans business? Be light-handed otherwise.'

'He'd be pleased, no mistaking that.'

'Let's have him out to the hospital then. Need someone with a bit of tact.'

'I was wondering about Graham Millington . . .'

Skelton was quick to shake his head. 'Put in a lot of work on those hijacks already. Be good to see a result. And it doesn't hurt us any, let them see over there we're not poor cousins.' He smoothed his hand across his upper lip, stroking the moustache that was no longer there. 'Reg Cossall'd be happy to lend us Fenby.'

'I'll bet he would.'

'Nothing wrong with Fenby, Charlie. Good old-fashioned copper.'

'Exactly.'

'Just the job for something like this, lots of double-checking, knocking on doors. Wind him up and let him go.'

Resnick stood up and shuffled a few paces back towards the door, not quite certain he was through.

'Long day already, Charlie,' Skelton said, midway through dialling. 'Once you've got them going, get yourself home. Snatch an hour.' The superintendent's face slumped into a frown. 'This is going to get a sight worse before it gets better.'

When William Dougherty finally arrived home his shoes were damp and flecked with mud, but he had no clear sense of where he had been walking or for how long.

One of the neighbours sat in the kitchen, brooding over a pot of tea, too long mashed to be drinkable. Seeing Dougherty, she looked away and then, with a slow shake of her head, pointed towards the rear window.

Pauline was standing close to a pink rose bush, most of its petals blown. Her dressing-gown had become unfastened at the front and there was nothing on her feet.

'She won't come in,' the neighbour said. 'I asked her, but she won't.'

Dougherty nodded and let himself out through the side door. The sounds of birdsong seemed unnaturally loud, calls and responses laid over the dull hum of traffic.

'Pauline.'

Turning at the familiar voice, she smiled. 'William, the roses, we have to be careful . . .'

She forgot what it was they had to be careful about.

Gently, Dougherty took the watering can from her hand

and set it on the path before leading her back towards the house.

Without his helmet, the constable who escorted Sarah Leonard up to CID was scarcely the taller. He led her through the main door, knocked on the window to Resnick's office and left her. Glancing up, Resnick saw a woman with dark hair, lightly curled, a strong nose and a full mouth, dark eyes that fixed upon him and didn't let him go. For the first time in some little while, he thought of Rachel, shaking the thought free as he got to his feet and beckoned her to enter.

'Inspector?'

Resnick held out his hand. 'Have a seat.'

'Sarah Leonard,' she said. 'I work at the hospital.'

'You're a doctor?'

'I'm a nurse. Staff nurse.'

'And you work with Karl?'

Sarah nodded.

Resnick relaxed back into his chair, allowing his shoulders to slump just a little.

'We finished at the same time yesterday, nine o'clock, more or less. We went through the subway together. Karl doesn't live all that far from me, sometimes we walk part of the way together – last night he was catching the bus into the city. Said he was meeting someone for a drink.'

There was sweat forming lightly in the palms of Resnick's hands.

'Did he say who?' Resnick asked.

Sarah shook her head. 'Just a friend.'

'Nothing more?'

A slight tightening of the mouth and she shook her head again.

'You don't know if this friend was female? Male?'

The merest hesitations before Sarah said no.

'How about where they were meeting?'

'No, but . . .'

But, echoed Resnick inwardly. But . . .

'I know Karl used to go to this place near the Victoria Centre . . .'

'A pub?'

'More of . . . I don't know . . . not a wine bar exactly . . . a club.'

'Have you been there?'

'Once, yes, I think it was Karl's birthday. We . . .'

'Downstairs, is it? Underground?'

She nodded emphatically. 'Yes.'

'Manhattan's.'

'Yes.'

Resnick wiped his hands along his trouser legs. 'And you think that's where he was off to last night? Nine o'clock?'

'Nearer a quarter past.'

'But there?'

'I don't know. I think so. Yes. I looked back before the turn in the road and he was still standing there, the bus stop.' She leaned forward across Resnick's desk. 'If it was there, that Karl was going . . . It's close to where they found him, isn't it?'

'Yes,' said Resnick slowly. 'Yes, it is.'

Sarah stared at him hard. 'Whoever it was. Did this. He wants locking away.'

For several moments Resnick didn't say anything. And then he found a smile and thanked her for coming in so promptly. 'One of the officers will take your statement,' he said, escorting her through the door.

Rachel, he thought, would never have talked of locking the person who did this away; she would have spoken of safety, providing help and care. He remembered the consultant giving his description of Tim Fletcher's wounds, the sight of Dougherty, unconscious in his own blood. He didn't know who needed caring for the most.

Eighteen

'Borrowed one of your shirts, Charlie. Hope you don't mind.'

Ed Silver had dragged a stool close to the stove and was spreading peanut butter on the nub end of a rye loaf. Several tea bags oozed orangey-brown from where they had been dumped on a corner of the chopping board. Silver had also found a pair of Resnick's older grey trousers while rummaging through his wardrobe and wore those now, held at the waist by a red-and-grey striped tie. Resnick wasn't sure whether the socks were his or not. Without doubt the cat was. Dizzy, stalker of the night and the least susceptible to human advances, had found in Ed Silver a fellow spirit.

All these years, Resnick thought, and he'd misjudged him. Poor, blackhearted Dizzy. Not a football fan at all, a lager lout – in his soul Dizzy was something more serious, more tragic, an artist, an alcoholic *manqué*.

'Nearly out of this,' Silver said, tapping the peanut-butter jar with the blade of the knife.

Resnick was more worried about his vodka.

'You had a phone call,' Silver said, chewing earnestly.

'Message?'

'Said she'd ring back.'

'She?'

'Don't know how you do it, Charlie,' Ed Silver cackled. 'Pulling birds at your age.'

Resnick glanced at his watch. There wasn't time, but he wanted to shower. The smell of stale urine still clung to him, the memory of the wavering chalk line that had marked Dougherty's body. The expression on Pauline Dougherty's face, smiling: *You see, there's been a mistake.* Parents like that, those situations, the ones whose children had been buried high on cold ground or laid waste between the brick ginnels of blackened cities, what did they ever understand? What beyond the numbness and after the pain?

He dropped his clothing on the bathroom floor and switched the shower to full. Eyes closed, needle jets of water washed his body. Resnick turned up the temperature, turned his face towards the stream.

Patel sat outside intensive care, staring at his shoes. Better, at least, than surveillance outside another anonymous warehouse or factory, cold on the trail of 36 gross pairs of wide-fitting mislabelled jeans. Here one of the domestics would push a cup of tea into his hands, a biscuit; from time to time a nurse would slip him a sidelong smile.

Through a double set of glass-panelled doors he could see the apparatus around Dougherty's bed, observe, as if through water, the ritual observations of blood pressure, temperature, vital signs. The watchers watched.

Two doctors passed quickly through, white coats flapping around well-cut dark trousers, talking in hushed, conspiratorial tones. Consultants, registrars, housemen – Patel knew the names, didn't know the difference. His father had wanted him to become a doctor, had preached long nights about it, the honour, the prestige. Eighteen hours in a corner shop his father worked, seven days a week, every day except Christmas, all to make things easier for his children, easier than they had been for him, arriving in England with little more than names written on the back of an envelope. Welcome to Bradford. See, Diptak, you will receive an education, your brothers also. You will be a professional man. I will be proud of you.

After his degree, Patel had applied to join the police and at first his father had been less than proud. His friends, some of them, had ostracized him, cut him dead. *Traitor!* The word had dogged his footsteps along the streets where he had grown up, assaulted him from the walls; one evening, serving in the family shop, his best friend had spat in his face. The vehemence of it had been unsuspected and the hurt clung to him still, worse by far than the racist jokes his fellow officers would repeat to his face without a second thought, the calls of 'Paki bastard!' he had to ignore most days of his life, most nights in the city.

'Excuse me.' Patel got to his feet as the two doctors walked back through the doors. 'Excuse me, but Mr Dougherty, is there any change?'

They looked at him as if he could only be there in error.

'Is there any change in his condition?' Patel asked.

'No,' one of the doctors said, walking away.

'What do you think?' said the other. 'A jar before squash or after?'

No hats or trainers read the notice taped to the door. *Sorry no jeans.* No hats, thought Resnick, pushing his way through, must be some kind of code.

A short staircase wound down to the centre, a curve of seats and small tables off to the left, the DJ's decks to the right, more steps led down to the main floor and the facing bar. Knees resting on a rubber pad, a blonde-haired woman was polishing away at the wooden dance floor.

A pair of lights shone dully from beneath the glass shelves at the back of the bar. Alongside the Labatt's and Grolsch in the cold cabinet, Resnick spotted some bottles of Czech Budweiser and his admiration rose several notches.

'Anyone around?' he asked.

'Too early,' said the woman on the dance floor, not bothering to turn around. 'Come back in an hour.'

'You're the only one here, then?'

'Didn't I tell you?' she said, with a touch of put-on weariness. 'Are you thick or what?'

Hands to her hips, she arched her back and swivelled her head. 'Oh, it's you,' she said. 'I didn't recognize your voice.'

'Hello, Rosie,' Resnick said.

The last time she had heard his voice had been in court, Resnick giving evidence against two of her sons, the pair of them arrested and charged with offences under Sections 47 and 38, causing aggravated bodily harm and using force to resist arrest. They'd be back out any time now, but probably not for long.

'How's the girl?' Resnick asked. Rosie's daughter had been born with a severe disability to the spine that had kept her shuffling in and out of hospital for years.

'What the hell do you care?' Rosie said.

A door to the side of the bar opened and she picked up her polishing cloth and went back to her work. 'We're not open yet,' said a man in a loose white shirt and a maroon bow tie, hair gelled upwards in short, fashionable spikes. 'Come back in . . .'

'I know,' Resnick said, 'an hour.' He pushed his warrant card along the bar.

'What can I do for you, inspector?' the man asked.

'Are you the owner?' Resnick asked. 'Manager?'

'Derek Griffin. I'm the manager.'

'Here last night?'

'Most of the time, why?'

Resnick looked over towards the nearest table. 'Let's sit down.'

Resnick leaned against the padded backrest; Griffin perched himself uneasily on a stool, reminding Resnick of a cockatoo from the aviary in the Arboretum, likely to fly off at any moment.

'Can I get you something, inspector?' Griffin asked, glancing towards the bar.

'How many staff here with you?'

'Last night?'

Resnick nodded.

'Three behind the bar, bouncer on the door. Four.'

'That all?'

'Unless you count the DJ.'

'Five, then.'

'All right, five.'

'Names and addresses.'

'Look, what's this about?'

'You don't know?'

'No. Should I?'

'A man was attacked.'

'In here?'

'Outside. Between eleven and one.'

'Whereabouts outside?'

'He's in critical condition.'

'Where did it happen?'

'Toilet across the street.'

Griffin relaxed a little on his stool. 'Not here then, is it. I mean, it's nothing to do with us. It didn't happen in here.'

'We think there's a good chance he'd been in just before, for a drink.'

'Somebody see him?'

'You tell me.' The photograph of Karl Dougherty had been supplied by his parents and photocopied. It had been taken five years earlier and showed a half-way good-looking young man smiling into a friend's camera. There were palm trees in the background and Karl was wearing a T-shirt and a pair of shorts that finished just above his knees. It was the most recent picture they had. Griffin lifted it towards his face, stared at it for several seconds and set it back down. 'No,' he said.

On the level above them, Rosie was polishing tables.

'No, you didn't see him last night, or no, you don't know him at all?'

'Either. Both.'

'You're sure?'

'Certain.'

'Don't tell him a thing,' Rosie said, 'it'll get twisted arse-uppards and used against you. Though you're lucky, you got me as a witness.'

'How many d'you reckon were in here yesterday?' Resnick asked. 'Give or take.'

'Three hundred, maybe more. Not all at one time, of course.'

'None of them wearing hats.'

'What?'

'Skip it.'

'This bloke,' Griffin said. 'What happened to him? I mean, exactly.'

Resnick told him briefly, not quite exactly. It was still enough to make Griffin cross his legs and for sweat marks to dampen his shirt. If his bow-tie could have drooped, probably it would.

'The staff on last night,' Resnick said. 'Any of them in today? Lunchtime?'

'Maura. None of the others.'

'Tonight?'

'All except one.'

'Better get me the list,' Resnick said. 'Mark on it when they're here, days and times. Home numbers if you know them. We'll need to talk to them as soon as we can.'

Griffin nodded and crossed towards the bar. 'The customers,' he said, turning back towards Resnick. 'You're not going to be in here, bothering them as well?'

'Oh, yes,' said Resnick. 'I should think so. But don't worry, anyone I send, I'll make sure they're properly dressed.'

Once or twice, when he'd been younger, fifteen, sixteen, Kevin Naylor had been beset by panic: once in the middle of a crowded street, another time in the Broad Marsh Centre, Saturday afternoon. Everyone hurrying around him, scurrying past, purposeful, busy, knowing exactly what they were looking for, where they were going. Naylor had stood where he was, quite still, scared, unable to move, and they had continued to stream past him, these people, not seeing him, not even knocking into him: as if he weren't there.

He had experienced much the same sensation at training college, a large role-play exercise, civil unrest, riot shields and batons. Other trainee officers in jeans and jumpers, pretending to be students, strikers, loving it. The chance to scream and yell and charge. So easy to pretend emotion, feign feelings, hate. Call slogans till you were red in the face.

Wearing protective clothing, engaged in strategic retreat, Naylor had become separated, targeted. Stranded amidst all that simulated anger, faces, limbs and bodies flying past. Shatter of glass on the tarmacked ground. Flash of flame. He had stood exactly as he was while the fire sought to claim him. Awake and asleep: immovable till they had dragged him clear.

There had been a session with a counsellor after that, talk of nervous failure, unsuitability; only the diligence of his written work had prevented him from being back-classed.

Nothing as dramatic had recurred since then. Out on the job, first in uniform and now plain clothes, in most situations you simply responded, did what it was clear you had to do. Only occasionally did events threaten to overwhelm him and the possibility of panic return; rarely for more than moments at a time. There had been a cup match at Forest with several thousand United supporters locked out; eighty or so youths racing down the Forest towards Hyson Green in the half-light; now.

Two sets of nurses were moving between shifts, handing over; shouts for assistance, trolleys, bells; screens pulled around one, then another; at the nurses' station the telephone that never seemed to stop ringing and never seemed to be answered. Underpinning all of this, Naylor was aware of the near-mute chatter from a dozen television screens, the same banalities being mouthed, adultery and another slice of cake between the commercial breaks.

He had to check with the sister that it was okay to begin interviewing staff on duty; Lynn Kellogg was waiting to see those going off as they left. Helen Minton took hold of him firmly by the elbow and propelled him towards her office. 'I know this is important,' she said, 'but I'd appreciate it if this takes as little time as possible. What we're doing is important too.'

Vainly waiting for the chance to question Dougherty, Patel had found a copy of yesterday's *Mail* and was stuck on 13 Across: Vital to sustain life (9). He was still struggling over it when Karl Dougherty's blood pressure sank to 90/40 and they decided that a further transfusion would not be enough. Chances are he was bleeding internally. Patel sat there and watched as they wheeled Dougherty towards the theatre for more surgery.

Lifeblood.

He filled in the squares and thought about the next clue.

Nineteen

No more than a couple of hundred yards to Central Station, Resnick slid the Manhattan's staff list across to Fenby, five names, all of them needing to be checked.

'This one,' Resnick said. 'Maura Tranter. She's working this lunch time. I'll nip back over, see her myself.'

Fenby nodded slowly, the same speed at which he did everything. A Lincolnshire man with thick hair and a ruddy complexion, Fenby had grown up boot-deep in mud, face to face with the easterlies that came scudding in off the North Sea and cut through the Wolds like a rusty scythe.

'Report direct to you, then?' Fenby said.

Sir, Resnick thought. 'Yes,' he said.

Divine, with the help of two uniforms, was checking out any taxi drivers using the rank near where the incident had occurred, staff who would have been working at the other clubs and pubs in the area, restaurants and car parks, the toilets themselves.

NURSE FIGHTS FOR LIFE was the headline in the local paper. *Victim of an apparently motiveless attack*. . . It could have been worse. The last thing Resnick wanted to read were panic stories about some Midlands Slasher, intent upon carving up the NHS more speedily than Kenneth Clarke.

He took the escalator up beside Miss Selfridge and entered the market via the meat and fish. No time for an espresso, he paused at the first of the Polish delicatessens and allowed himself a small treat, deciding between the three kinds of cheesecake always a problem.

'This business last night,' said the man running the stall, 'that's for you to sort out?'

Pointing at the middle tray, Resnick nodded.

'I'm surprised you've time even to think of eating.'

Resnick lifted the white paper bag from the glass counter and hurried between the flower stalls, heading for the far exit, the second escalator that would carry him down again, landing him close to the entrance to Manhattan's.

It was busy already, plenty of people with time to drink as well as eat, the money to make it possible. There was a spare stool towards the end of the bar and Resnick manoeuvred towards it and sat down. He was always surprised when he went into a place like this, especially in the middle of the day, how many men and women under thirty could afford, not simply to be there but to be in fashion, able to pay the rising cost of keeping up appearances.

Haves and have-nots: trouble with his job was, likely you spent so much time with the have-nots, it was easy to see them as the norm, be surprised when you found yourself surrounded by those for whom the system, supposedly, worked.

'What's that?' said the young woman behind the bar, pointing at the bag Resnick had set on the counter.

'Cheesecake,' said Resnick. 'Cherry topping.'

'Can't eat your own food in here.'

'I'm not eating it.'

'That's what I said.'

She had an open face, cheeks a hungry squirrel could have hoarded nuts in; her hair was in a lavish disarray it had taken ages to arrange. Her accent placed her east of Kimberley, but north of Ilkeston.

'Are you Maura?' Resnick asked.

'Tuesdays, Thursdays, Fridays, Sunday afternoons. The rest of the week I'm Leslie.'

Resnick thought it best not to inquire why. 'Maybe your manager told you to expect me?'

'You're not the detective?'

'Mondays, Tuesdays, Wednesdays, Thursdays, Fridays, Saturdays.'

'What happens Sundays?'

'I rest.'

When she smiled, Maura's cheeks puffed out still further, for all the world like Dizzy Gillespie playing trumpet. 'According to Derek, you're fat and fifty and dressed like something out of the ark.'

Sooner that, thought Resnick, than someone who looked as if he should be inside it. 'No wonder you didn't recognize me,' he said.

'Right, you're not so fat.'

'Thanks.'

'Not like some we get in here: half a hundredweight of cholesterol on feet.'

'Hey, Maura . . .' called somebody along the bar.

'I'm busy,' she called back.

'This is the man.' Resnick unfolded the photocopy of Karl Dougherty and turned it towards her.

'Four halves of lager, pint lager shandy, orange juice, pineapple, tomato juice with Worcester sauce and a Cinzano and lemonade – if you can tear yourself away.'

'What about you?' Maura was looking at Resnick, not the photograph. 'Fancy anything?'

'Budweiser. Thanks.'

'For Christ's sake, Maura . . . !'

She sighed and swore not quite below her breath.

'Is there a problem here?' Derek Griffin appeared at Resnick's shoulder sporting a different tie and a piqued expression.

'No problem,' Maura said brightly.

'No problem,' said Resnick.

'You do get paid to work here, you know,' said Griffin.

Maura raised an eyebrow theatrically. 'Just,' she said.

Griffin turned away. Maura set a bottle and an empty glass at Resnick's elbow, opened the bottle, tapped the picture of Dougherty with a false finger nail and said, 'I'll be back.'

'Now,' she said, moving along the bar, 'what was it? Four small lagers . . .'

Resnick retreated and found another seat amongst the other lunchtime drinkers: well-groomed young salespeople from River Island, grey men in lean grey suits from Jessops talking earnestly about the partnership, bank clerks of both sexes from Barclays and NatWest. Dougherty had been here not so many hours before, enjoying a drink like these, maybe laughing, maybe not. He glanced over at the toilet sign, midway along the side wall. Was there anything strange in leaving here and going straight into the public lavatory across the road? If he did go straight there, that is? And besides, Resnick could remember, with embarrassment now and not pleasure, evenings when negotiating a path home via every toilet in the city centre had still not been adequate to prevent him slipping into an alley, urinating against the wall.

'Hi!' Maura pulled over a stool and sat close beside him, orange lipstick on the rim of her glass like a kiss, on the filter tip of the cigarette she held in her other hand.

'Sure this is okay?' Resnick asked.

'Don't fret.'

'I don't want to get you into trouble.'

'That's what the last one said.' Laughing.

'No, I mean it.'

'So did he. So he said. But then they all do. Try it on, lie. You expect it. Funny thing was . . .' She angled her mouth away to release a small stream of smoke, eyes staying on him. '. . . he said he was one of your lot, a copper.'

'And he wasn't?'

'Milkman. Dale Farms. Hardly the same, is it?'

Resnick grinned.

''Bout the only thing that interested me, really. The policeman bit.' She leaned back and moved her head so that her hair shook. 'Got a thing about authority, you know?'

'Tell that to your boss.'

'Derek? No, I mean the real thing. Not some little tosser spends half his time trying to push you around and the rest round the back, jerking off in front of the mirror.' She drank some gin and tonic. 'You need something to push against, you know? Otherwise where's the fun. Anyway, this bloke, the milkman. I thought he might be it.' She laughed loudly enough to make several people break off their conversations and stare. 'Till I went back to his place and talked him into putting on his uniform.'

'Maura!' came the shout from the bar.

'All right, all right.' She finished her drink in a swallow and stood up, leaning down until her hair covered her face. 'Yes,' she said, tapping the picture of Dougherty, 'he was in here, last hour before closing. Him and another guy, comes in quite a bit. Peter, Paul, one of those names. Don't know if they were having a row or what, but they were getting loud, I remember that.'

'You didn't hear what they were saying?'

Maura shook her head.

'You think any of the other staff might have?'

She shrugged. 'Possible. Ask.'

'I will.'

'Maura!'

'Got to go.'

Resnick pushed himself up. 'Right. Thanks for your help.'

Maura started to move away, then stopped. 'The other feller. Paul, Peter. I think he must work round here. Comes in lunchtimes, three or four days a week.'

'You sure he's working?'

'He wears a suit.' She grinned. 'Wouldn't use it as a floorcloth myself, but to him it's a suit.'

'Anything else special about him? Except for bad taste?' Standing there, Resnick was conscious of the creases in his bagged trousers, the stain on his jacket lapel.

'Hair.'

'What about it?'

'Not a lot of it. For someone his age.'

'Maura!'

'All right!'

Resnick picked up the photocopy and the now sweaty bag, dark where the fat from the cheesecake had run through.

'Look in again some time,' Maura said. 'When it's not so busy.' A toss of the head and she was heading back towards the bar. Outside it had started to drizzle and a thin film of water was collecting across the grey pavements. Breaking into an awkward trot to avoid a double-decker turning up into the square, Resnick sensed the bottom of the bag begin to break. A vain grab failed to prevent the cheesecake from falling, squashed, into the gutter, leaving Resnick licking cherry topping from his fingers on the corner of the street.

Twenty

It had taken William Dougherty the best part of two hours to calm down his wife, stop the persistent tremble in her hands, persuade her to focus on his words. Pauline listened and nodded and said something William couldn't catch. Before he knew what she was doing, her hands were under the sink, fumbling for the scouring powder, cream cleanser and cloths. He watched while she lifted the hard plastic bowl from the sink and set it on the draining board, upside down; slowly she began to rub at the already spotless metal; painstakingly, she twisted a thin strip between the links of the chain that held the plug.

'Did you understand what I said?' he asked. 'Any of it?'

Her permed hair, not so much as a comb through since morning, sat lopsided, like an ill-fitting wig. 'Yes, William. Of course I did.'

As she went back to her cleaning, Dougherty left the house. Asking the neighbour across the way to call in again and sit with Pauline, he caught a bus to the hospital. Without entering the unit he could see Karl's bed was empty and his knees buckled beneath him. Had Patel still been waiting, likely he would have reached Dougherty in time to steady him before he fell. As it was, Patel had left a note of where he could be contacted and returned to the station and it was a good ten minutes before one of the porters found William Dougherty slumped against the wall.

Nurses helped him to his feet and sat him down with a hasty mug of tea.

'Now then, Mr Dougherty,' one of the nurses said as she took his pulse, 'we can't have this. We don't want the whole family in here, sure we don't.'

'Karl . . .'

'Oh, we just had to pop him back into theatre. Don't you fret now. He's in recovery, doing fine. He'll be back on the ward in a while and then you can see him. All right now? I'll leave you to finish your tea.'

He sat there, one hand to his head, staring at the floor, uncertain whether he should be more worried about his wife or son.

Kevin Naylor tried Debbie a third time and still there was no reply. Probably round at her mum's but he wasn't going to phone there, he'd be buggered if he was.

'Okay?' Lynn Kellogg was standing further along the corridor, near the doors, arms folded across her chest.

'Yes. Why shouldn't I be?'

'Thought you looked a bit worried, that's all.'

'I'm fine.' Heading past her, hoping she wouldn't follow.

'Kevin . . .'

Naylor stopped short, breathed in slowly, then turned to face her.

'It's not Debbie, is it?'

'It's nothing.'

'Only . . .'

'Do us a favour, Lynn.'

'Yes?'

Naylor jabbed a finger at her like a hammer, like nails. 'Go out and get a bloke of your own. Then you won't spend so much time fussing round me.'

She flinched like she'd been hit. Naylor glared and walked away and Lynn watched him – whatever it was between us, she thought, now it's gone. Just another man who didn't like what he was feeling: choke it down until you're not feeling anything at all. Her notebook was in the bag that hung from her shoulder, all of the staff she'd talked to had known Karl Dougherty, thought he was wonderful – efficient, funny, caring: an outstanding nurse. The impression she was left with was that none of them knew him at all.

She would go and talk to Tim Fletcher before leaving; see if there wasn't something he could add.

Fletcher was sitting in an easy chair beside his bed, learning Italian care of his Walkman, eyes gently closed as he repeated the phrases over and over: *'C'è una mappa con le cose da vedere?' 'C'è una mappa con le cose da vedere?' 'C'è . . .'* He broke off, aware of someone's presence.

'Sounds really impressive,' Lynn said.

Tim Fletcher smiled. 'It could *sound* like *La Traviata*, I'm afraid I still wouldn't understand it. Most of it, anyhow.'

Lynn introduced herself and sat on the edge of the bed. After several minutes' polite conversation about his injuries, she asked him if he'd heard about Karl Dougherty and then how well he'd known him.

'Hardly at all.'

'You haven't worked together, then? I mean, on the same ward or anything?'

Fletcher shook his head. 'Not for any length of time. Not that I recall.'

'Wouldn't you remember something like that?'

'The way it's organized, I'm attached to a consultant, Mr Salt as it happens. Now it's likely the bulk of his patients will be in one or two wards, but, especially with the bed situation the way it is, the others might be just about anywhere.' For several moments he stared at her, vaguely aware that beneath his bandages there was an irritation waiting to be scratched. 'You don't think there's a connection, something more than coincidence, what happened to the two of us?'

'Oh,' said Lynn, 'I really don't know. Except, well, it is a bit of a coincidence, isn't it? If that's what it is.'

Fletcher didn't want to talk about it, not any more. Bad enough being reminded of what had happened every time you tried to turn over in the bed, each faltering move you made under the physio's eye. In the waste of night, his senses recreated for him the hot smell of hard rubber from the bridge floor with uncanny accuracy.

'All these flowers,' Lynn said, seeking a polite note on which to leave, 'from Karen, I suppose?'

'Not all of them.'

'They're lovely.' She got up from the bed and moved in front of Fletcher's chair. 'How is she? Karen.'

'I don't know.'

'I thought . . .'

'I haven't seen her.'

'Oh?'

'She called, left a message with the sister. Bit off-colour.' He glanced round at the bedside cupboard. 'She sent a card, lots of cards. I'm sure she'll be in tomorrow.'

'Yes,' Lynn said, 'I'm sure.'

Last thing she was likely to do, Lynn thought as she walked back through the ward, show herself with her face looking like a relief map of somewhere Wainwright might have hiked. Probably she was hiding in her room, waiting for the bruising to subside. No reason to think it was any more than that. Taking the stairs instead of the lift, Lynn glanced at her watch. It wouldn't be far out of her way and if nothing else it would set her mind at rest.

For what was still the middle of the day, the street seemed unnaturally quiet. The rain had stopped, leaving grey cloud overhanging the sky like a warning. The bottle of unclaimed milk on the doorstep was a crusted yellow beyond cream. Lynn had lived in shared houses and understood the tendency never to see what didn't immediately concern you; once you started taking out the garbage, you were saddled with it until you left. Holding her breath as best she could, Lynn rang the bell, then knocked. Through the letter box she could see the same pile of unwanted mail on the low table, the telephone. She had feared it might prove a wasted journey and the silence inside the house told her she had been right. Oh, well . . .

As she was turning away, Lynn heard a door opening inside.

She knocked again and eventually a man appeared, blinking at the dull light. He was in his early twenties, wearing a V-neck sweater over jeans with horizontal tears across both knees. Several days' stubble on a blotchy face. A student or out of work, guessed Lynn, she found it difficult to tell the difference.

She told him who she was and showed him her warrant card, but he was already shambling back along the narrow hall.

'Karen Archer,' Lynn said, stepping inside. 'Is she . . . ?'

The man mumbled something she failed to catch and pointed upwards. Closing the front door behind her, Lynn climbed the stairs, almost forgetting the broken tread but not quite. The picture of kissing lovers had gone from the door to Karen's room and the catch that had once held a small padlock stood open. There was a sudden burst of music, loud from below, and the top half of her body jerked. *The door to the garden had not quite been open.* Almost two years now, still whenever she went through a door, uncertain of what she might find, the same images came silently slipping down. *Stray ends of cloud moved grey across the moon. A bicycle without a rear wheel leaned against the wall. Her toe touched against something and she bent to pick it up.* Mary Sheppard had taken her two children to her mother's and gone out to meet a man; invited him home. What? Coffee? Mary Sheppard: the first body Lynn had found. *Dark lines like ribbons drawn through her hair*. Come on, Lynn. She turned the handle and stepped inside.

Stripped: stripped and gone. The box mattress, slightly stained and sagging at its centre, the veneered dressing table were the only furniture left in the room. Screwed-up tissues, pale blue, yellow and pink, clustered near one corner. A single sock, purple and green shapes that had begun to run into one another, lay in the space between window and bed. Looking down over the back yards, Lynn saw short lines of washing, a baby asleep in a pram, geraniums; on the end of a square wooden post, a white and grey cat sat immobile, ears pricked. In one of the dressing-table drawers Lynn found an old receipt from the launderette, in another an empty box of tampons. Curling already at the ends, the Polaroid strip had fallen behind and, easing the dressing table from the wall, she lifted it out. Karen Archer and Tim Fletcher making funny faces with the photo-booth curtain as backdrop; no matter how distorted Karen tried to make her features, it was impossible to disguise her beauty. Or, now she looked at the photos closely, Fletcher's hopefulness. There was a print mark on the bottom picture, the one in which they kissed. Lynn opened her shoulder bag and, carefully, placed the strip inside her notebook.

Downstairs in the communal kitchen the young man who'd let Lynn in was pouring warm baked beans over cold mashed potato.

'When did she leave?'

'Who?'

'Karen.'

'Dunno.'

Lynn wanted to force his head under the cold tap, wake some life into him. 'Think.'

He struck the underside of the sauce bottle with the flat of his hand and a gout of tomato sauce flopped out, most of it on the plate. 'Might have been yesterday. Must've been. Supposed to give us notice, four weeks. Now we've got to go tarting round for someone else.'

Lynn's heart bled for him. 'Any idea where she's gone?'

He looked up at her disparagingly. 'Home to mummy.'

'She's giving up her course?'

He shrugged and stirred the beans and potato together.

'Have you got an address for her?' Lynn asked.

'Somewhere.'

It was all she could do to stop herself from pushing his face down into his plate. She contented herself by plucking the fork from his hand, waiting till she had his attention firmly on her face. 'Get it,' she said. 'Wherever it is, the address, get it now.'

He didn't like it but he did as he was told.

During all of this, Resnick had been doing more than his share of window-shopping: anywhere with male assistants wearing suits. In succession, he had feigned a passing interest in bicycles, fourteen-day trips to the Yugoslavian coast, all-in, a new sports jacket, a signet ring, a char-grilled burger with fries and a 90-Day Extra Savings account; he had considered the possibilities of walking boots, cricket bats, Filofaxes, framed posters of James Dean, Marilyn Monroe and Elvis Presley, separately or together; now he was standing between broad rolls of carpet, listening to a disquisition on the virtues (or otherwise) of underlay, when he noticed one of the salesmen leading a couple towards a central table to confirm the details of a sale.

As the salesman filled in the form, pausing at intervals to ask a question, once to laugh, several times to smile, Resnick watched him. Twenty-five or -six, but already thinning on top, hair combed from either side towards the centre of his head in a vain attempt at disguise. He was wearing a double-breasted light grey suit that would have fitted somebody perfectly, but not him. Resnick waited until the final handshakes, the nod of the head, promise of delivery, beginnings of an accompanying walk towards the door. Don't go all the way, don't waste time, there is commission to be earned.

'Excuse me,' Resnick said evenly, approaching from behind.

The salesman blinked as he turned, moving half a pace back so as to get Resnick properly in focus. Family man, not about to spend a fortune, with any luck a three-bedroom semi in need of recarpeting throughout.

'Yes, sir.' Cheerily.

'Peter . . .' tried Resnick.

'Paul, as it happens. I . . .'

'You know a Karl Dougherty, by any chance?'

Paul Groves shot a glance towards the door and instinctively Resnick moved across to cover any attempt to escape. But: 'Is it still raining?' Groves asked. 'Wondered if I'd need a coat.'

Twenty-one

Resnick watched Groves all the way back to the station, alongside him in the back of the summoned car, one of his elbows resting against the window, not staring, not making it too obvious. Just the fifteen feet across the pavement from the shop doorway to the kerb had been enough to destroy the loose thatch of Groves's hair, one side falling past his left ear, the other sticking out like a mistake, pale scalp exposed clearly between. Even so, he didn't look too disturbed, now and again glancing out, interested, as if being driven through a city he only remembered. Sure, his fingers tugged at the slack of his suit trousers once in a while and the collar beneath his blue-and-silver striped tie was getting a touch too tight, but underneath he seemed unconcerned. As if, at base, he knew nothing could really get to him; he was safe. Resnick wondered.

Outside the CID room he told Groves to hang on and put his head round the door, beckoning Patel from the desk where he was diligently making his way through his paperwork.

'News from the hospital?' he asked quietly, as they turned into the corridor.

'Back in intensive care. Apparently stable.'

Resnick nodded and directed Groves into the nearest interview room, with a view across the sloping car park towards four-storey houses where two-bedroom flats were still fetching in excess of a hundred thousand. He pointed to a chair and waited for Groves to sit down, taking the chair opposite for himself, leaving Patel room to make notes at the end of the table.

'I knew you'd want to talk to me,' Paul Groves said. 'After what happened.'

Resnick didn't respond, not directly. 'You're here of your own volition to make a statement and can leave at any time. You understand that?'

Groves nodded.

'Why don't you tell us about last night?'

Groves loosened his tie a little, then tightened it again, holding the knot between the thumb and first two fingers of his left hand while he pulled on the short end with his right. No matter how easily they come to water, Resnick thought, rare that they rush to drink.

'Karl and I had arranged to meet for a drink,' Groves began. 'Half nine and he was late, but then he always was.' Resnick noted the always but let it go. Questions later. 'I suppose it was nearly ten by the time he arrived. We stayed there till closing, talking, as much as you can over the music, two or three drinks, that's all. We're not what you'd call drinkers, either of us.'

He paused and looked at Resnick directly, the first time since he'd begun talking.

'That's Manhattan's. That's where we were. But I suppose you know that?'

'Go on,' Resnick said.

'There's not a lot more, really. Karl left a bit before me, not long. I went home. I assumed he'd done the same. Until this morning when I heard the news. Local. They didn't give many details at first, not even a name. Went through the back of my mind it might have been Karl, but why should it have been? I mean, really? Why would it?' His arms were resting on the edge of the table, several inches back from the wrist; the more he spoke, the more he gesticulated with his hands. Now they closed into fists and were still. 'Then they said who it was.'

It crossed Resnick's mind that Groves had been practising this, rehearsing the shifts in tone, the moves.

'I called the hospital,' Groves said, 'wouldn't say a lot over the phone, but they did tell me how he was.' A quick glance up. 'I was going in to see him, tonight, after work. I mean, I would have taken time off, only with Karl being like he is . . .'

'Like he is?'

'Not conscious, not really conscious and in intensive care. They said they might have to operate again . . .'

'They did.'

Now the response was real, concern jumping across his eyes.

'Whatever they did,' Resnick said, 'seems to have been successful. The last we heard he was resting. Not out of the wood, but . . .' Resnick spread his hands, suggesting, with luck, everything would turn out all right.

'Is this going to take much longer?' Groves asked.

'There's just a couple of things . . .'

'Yes?'

'You say Karl left first?'

'Yes.'

'Why was that?'

Groves looked at him sharply.

'You met for a drink, spend – what? – an hour together, more, normal thing, I would have thought, you'd have left at the same time.'

'Karl was worried about getting home.'

'Oh?'

'He was on an early. Next day, today.'

'Arrived late, left early.'

'Yes.'

'One of the penalties, going out with a nurse.'

'Sorry?' Just a touch sharper, arms away from the desk, but not still, stretching away from his sides.

'Same with the police. Shift work. Plays havoc with

your social life. Police and nurses. Earlies and lates.' Resnick leaned his chair back on to its rear legs, relaxed. 'That's all there was to it, then? His leaving before you?'

'That's what I said.'

'Yes,' Resnick nodded. 'So you did.'

He smiled at Groves helpfully, waiting for more. Revisions of revisions. Groves fidgeted, the tie, the table, creases in his trousers, the tie again. 'I can't think of any other reason.'

Resnick could: several. 'It's not true there was an argument, then? No truth in that?'

'What argument?'

'I don't know, it's only a suggestion.'

'Whose suggestion?'

'Probably nothing to it.'

'That's right.'

'There's nothing to it?'

'No.'

'Karl and yourself, you didn't argue?'

'No.'

'No raised voices?'

'No.'

Resnick lowered the front legs of his chair carefully to the floor. He leaned forward across the table and, instinctively, Paul Groves leaned back. Of the two, Resnick was by far the bigger man. 'Like I said, it was pretty noisy, the music. Quite a few dancing. Almost had to shout to make ourselves heard.'

'I expect that's what it was, then.'

Groves shrugged.

'Not a row at all.'

Groves looked at him. 'What would we have to row about?'

Resnick gave him another encouraging smile. 'You tell me.'

Three shots out of four, Divine could get the paper into the waste bin without it touching the sides. Mind you, that was after twenty minutes of concerted practice. The boss was in the interview room, safely out of the way, everyone else God knows where, and he was writing up another report. A couple of hours of sitting in taxis down round the square, all very well for them to have those NO SMOKING stickers in the front, came out of the cabs smelling like an Indian restaurant. Anyway, there's this bloke comes prancing by in that purple sports gear they all seem to fancy just now, brand-new ghetto-blaster in one hand and an Adidas sports bag in the other. All Divine had done was go across and talk to him, by the numbers, warrant card, name and rank, station. 'I have reason to believe . . .' Now the guy was threatening official complaint, witnesses, racial harassment. In the court just the other week, some clever-bollocks of a barrister trying to make him look like a lifelong supporter of the National Front. 'Why did you stop the accused, constable? Had my client been white, would you have acted in the same way?' If the bastard had been white, he'd have been a sight less likely to be walking home at two in the morning with half an ounce of crack and his wallet thick with dirty tenners he'd just ponced off the girls he pimped for on Waverley Street.

Racial harassment, it choked him up. If they didn't want to get harassed, why didn't they clean up their act? Go straight, get a job. Instead it's sponging off the State one minute and calling it for every evil, repressive pigging thing the next. If harassing the buggers didn't make for an improvement in the crime statistics, it would stop soon enough. Not his fault if it was like shooting fish in a barrel. Asking for it and when they got it crying foul.

He cursed and screwed up another piece of paper, lobbing it through a high arc, into the bin in one.

Same with the bollocking IRA, they were another bunch of two-faced bastards. Over here, over in Europe, up to their armpits in Semtex and sub-machine-guns, blowing women and kids to kingdom-bloody-come, someone from the SAS sticks a gun up against their heads and pulls the trigger. Smack through the brain pan, that'll do nicely, thank you, they start squawking about illegal acts, overstepping the mark, operating outside the rule of law. What the fuck were they doing, if it wasn't operating outside the rule of law?

No.

Either they fuck off back to their own country, the lot of them, go back to growing potatoes or whatever it was they did over there, else give up running behind the skirts of some Human Rights Commission and accept the consequences.

Over here, looking for trouble, IRA or any other bloody terrorist, *whap!* Have them up against the wall fast and let the rest see what they're up against. That'd soon put a stop to it, no mistake.

And in the mean time, don't let anyone waste their breath telling him he was prejudiced. Not anyone. He swivelled in the chair, arm raised, going for something more fancy, in-off, side of the desk on to the wall, down into the bin, when the door opened and Patel came into the office.

'Bollocks!'

The ball of paper rebounded from the wall and skittered across the floor.

'Paul Groves,' Patel said, handing Divine a page from his notebook with the address, 'the boss says can you check him through records?'

'When I've got time.'

'I rather think he meant now.'

Divine waited until Patel had left the room. 'What's wrong with doing it yourself, Diptak? Too busy rimming the old man's arse to find the time?'

'You haven't any ideas yet then,' Paul Groves was saying, 'who might have done it?'

'Oh, yes,' Resnick said. 'We've always got ideas.'

He stood up and held out his hand. After only the slightest of hesitations, Grove shook it, looking Resnick in the eye, but likely, Resnick thought, having to force himself to do so. Knowing it was the right thing to do.

'There's nothing else, then?' Groves asked.

Resnick smiled. 'Not for the present.'

Patel opened the door.

'DC Patel will show you out.'

Divine didn't know what Resnick had expected him to come up with, maybe nothing, but the way Groves was shaping up he was ripe for something. Two and a bit years back, he'd been charged with gross indecency; that had been lowered to behaviour likely to harass, alarm or distress, before being dropped altogether. Nine months after that he had received a warning for remaining in a public lavatory longer than was reasonable for the purpose.

Not for his purpose, Divine said to himself, little bugger spends his lunch-hours out cottaging.

Resnick was standing just outside the CID room, chatting to one of the other DCs about soccer.

'If I were you, sir,' the DC was saying, 'I'd give County the elbow. Better off going up the Chesterfield and watching John Chedozie.'

'Maybe you're right.'

Divine came across and handed Resnick the details. 'Won't pay to turn your back on this one, sir,' said Divine. 'He's a bloody poof!'

Twenty-two

Calvin heard his father's footsteps overhead and leaned on to his left side, wondering if he was about to come downstairs. But the steps carried on towards the kitchen and Calvin relaxed and made himself comfortable again on the bed, drawing down hard on the spindly roll-up to keep it alight. Trouble with dope, especially stuff as good as that, the lingering sweetness of the smell; one move of his father's towards the stairs and Calvin would have been across to the door that opened out into the garden, wafting in air, spraying aftershave around like it was going out of style. 'One thing,' his father had said, 'and one thing only. You bring home girls, I don't want you bringing them down to your room. And I won't have you smoking dope. Not in this house.' Calvin had nodded, agreed, not pointing out to him that was two things. What did it matter? It was like school, you said yes and carried on doing what you liked. Calvin had reasons to remember school: endless afternoons of woodwork and skiving cross-country runs, and kids who'd yell at him across the playground: 'What's the matter with you, Calvin? Not got the balls to be a real nigger!' Real niggers were black. Calvin, son of a Bermudan father and a Nottinghamshire mother, was a shade of light coffee. 'Hey!' the black kids would shout. 'You ain't one of us!'

They were right. Calvin wasn't one of anybody.

Closing his eyes, resting his head back, he could see his room as clearly as if his eyes were still open. Three of the four walls were painted matt black, the fourth, the one with the window, deep purple; the ceiling was dark blue, the colour of the night; when all of the lights were extinguished he could lie on his back and stare up at the formations of stars and planets he had stuck there, iridescent and sparkling. The cupboard and the chest he had painted in white-and-black diagonal stripes; a black metal trolley held his stereo tape deck, record deck, amp and tuner. The cover draped over the bed was shiny black, fake silk. He had bought it in the market with the money his father had given him the day he was accepted for City College. He hadn't given him anything the day he'd quit. Not even a good shouting. When that had happened there had been other things on his father's mind.

There were no pictures on the walls, no posters. Only, in white letters he'd cut out himself, high above his bed, the name: Calvin Ridgemount.

The tape came to an end and clicked off. Calvin stubbed the last quarter inch out into a tobacco tin and slid it beneath the bed. Any minute his father would call down, asking him if he wanted anything to eat. He slid off the bed and straightened the cover; one thing you couldn't say about his room, you couldn't say it wasn't neat.

One of the differences Calvin had noticed in his father since it had happened, his father had taken to cooking. All the while they'd been together, a family, the only times he'd as much as entered the kitchen had been to fetch a cold can of Red Stripe from the fridge. He hadn't even carried out the plates after eating, not since Calvin had been big enough to do the job for him, Calvin or Marjorie. Marjorie was Calvin's sister, four years younger. It had seemed a long time before she had been able to manage more than the water glasses, Calvin having to take the remainder on his own.

Now, twice a day, three times on a Sunday, his father would fetch proper meals to the table. Nothing fancy, experimental, but none of that ready-to-serve, chill-cooked, out of a packet, out of a carton, out of the tin. Today, from the smell of it, it was onions, fried almost to a crisp till the sweetness came and all but went; sausages, too, fat ones, speckled with herbs, Lincolnshire. Though Calvin had a friend worked nights in a factory in the city, swore they were made right there.

'Hungry?' his father asked.

'Not very.'

His father spooned chick-peas on to one side of a plate, two sausages, then thinking about it for a moment before adding a third.

'Dad.'

'Yes?'

'I said I wasn't hungry, right.'

'That doesn't usually stop you,' his father said, although all that home cooking barely showed and Calvin, in his T-shirt and jeans, was still lean as cured bacon.

His father lifted the frying pan over the plate and tipped out half the onions, giving the pan a helpful shake. Finally, a thick tomato sauce distilled from several pounds of ripe tomatoes and molasses.

'Here,' his father said, passing the plate across to the breakfast bar where they usually sat to eat. 'You might need this.' He took the small, straight-sided bottle of Tabasco sauce from the shelf and set it close to Calvin's plate. 'Give it a little spice.'

Then he went back to serving himself.

A perfectly good dining-table in the living room, a picture window that looked right down across the park, and nine times out of ten they had their meals in the kitchen. Sixteen years they hadn't been able to get his father in there, now it was the devil's own job to get him out.

'Good?' Calvin's father asked.

'Mm,' Calvin responded through a mouthful of sausage. 'Umnh.'

His father had taken up cooking, but he hadn't any time for recipes. Making social security and his small disability pension stretch to feed the two of them took a special kind of enterprise and effort. He would spend up to half of each day wandering around the local shops, take the bus down into the city or up to Arnold, picking up stuff and feeling it, never seeming to notice when shopkeepers or stallholders told him to keep his fingers to himself. Once or twice a week he would get up at five and go down to the wholesale market at Sneinton, there and back on that old bike of his, pedalling home in laborious low gear, towing a little wooden trailer behind him – little more than a vegetable crate with wheels – loaded full of potatoes, cabbages, whatever was cheap and in season.

'You know all the colleges have started back now?'

Calvin grunted.

'I thought you were going to get yourself enrolled again?'

'I am.'

'When?'

'When I know what course it is I want to do.'

'And when's that going to be?'

'I'm still going through the booklets, in't I, prospectuses?'

'A little late, ain't it?'

'Takes time, I don't want to make another mistake.'

'No danger of that.'

Calvin set down his knife and fork. 'What's that supposed to mean?'

'Never enrol, no chance you've got of dropping out.'

It wasn't worth arguing. Every so often his father would nag him about it, he would stall and before long the matter would be forgotten. They would get back to what now seemed to have become their lives. Meals together, a couple of beers of an evening watching old films his father would rent on video. *Operation Petticoat. That Touch of*

Mink. He could never understand how his father could watch such garbage, laugh at it. Still, it didn't matter. Around ten he would go down to his room and lie back on the bed, headphones on his head. David Lee Roth, Eddie Van Halen. Calvin knew what he was supposed to play was Soul II Soul, New Kids on the Block, Niggers with Attitude. Crap like that.

Mouth still full, he pushed his plate aside.

'You haven't finished.'

'I've had enough.'

The local paper came through the front door and the flap of the letter box snapped back with a crack. Calvin fetched it through into the kitchen, unfolding it to show the front page.

'Seen this,' he said, pointing at the headlines: NURSE'S GRIM FIGHT FOR LIFE.

His father nodded gently and slid the paper away. 'What you left, I'll put in the refrigerator. You might fancy it later.'

Fifteen minutes later, Calvin was ready. He'd pulled a sweater over his T-shirt, black running shoes on his feet. A canvas bag hung from his shoulder, rested snug against his hip.

His father was at the sink, finishing the washing up.

'Right,' Calvin said, opening the front door.

'Where're you off to?' his father asked.

'Out.'

Twenty-three

'Dicey business, Charlie. Can't say that I like it.'

Skelton was on the prowl. Desk to window, window to filing cabinet, filing cabinet to coffee-maker, though it didn't seem to occur to him to offer Resnick a cup. The superintendent was so wired up himself, Resnick wondered if he'd been taking his caffeine straight, mainlining it into a vein. Truth was, likely he hadn't done any serious exercise for a few hours, needed a five-mile run to steady his nerves.

He'd been like this after the trouble had flared up with Kate, either hyped up or flatter than a slow Sunday out in the suburbs of Bramcote, Burton Joyce. Resnick wondered again how things were with Skelton's daughter, A-levels pretty soon – was that what they still called them? – off to be a student somewhere probably. Then let Skelton try and keep tabs on her. Or maybe with the new morality they didn't waste their energies on sex and drugs and rock 'n' roll? Straight into pension schemes and overdrafts to afford Paul Smith suits; long evenings lusting after fax machines while they listened to Nigel Kennedy or the Eric Clapton back-catalogue re-released on CD. He'd been a fair guitarist once; Clapton not Kennedy.

'What are you thinking, Charlie?'

' "Crossroads", sir.'

'Not bringing that back, are they? Thought it was all this Australian stuff, *Neighbours* and the like.'

'No, sir. "Crossroads". It's a blues. Robert Johnson. Skip James. It's . . .'

'Relevant, Charlie?'

'No, sir. Not really.'

Skelton gave him a short, hard stare and resumed pacing his office carpet. As a superintendent you get thicker pile and a choice of colours, replacement every five years if you had the right connections. The way Skelton was going, that might be something else to talk to Paul Groves about.

'It's distracting,' Skelton said, behind Resnick now and making him turn in his chair. 'That's what worries me. Leading us away from what I think should be our main focus.'

'But if it's there . . .'

'What, Charlie? What exactly?'

'If Groves and Dougherty were involved . . .'

'Come on, Charlie. We don't know that.'

'Seems pretty incontrovertible Groves is gay, bisexual at least.'

'Where's your evidence about Dougherty?'

'Close to thirty interviews, people who've worked with him, some of them for quite a while. Had a drink with him, socialized. Not a great deal, but a little. Never once, any talk of a girlfriend. Woman. Not once.'

'That means he's gay?'

Resnick shrugged. What was Skelton getting so worked up about? 'It's an indication.'

'Of what? That he doesn't like women? That he doesn't like sex? Maybe he's a very private person. Maybe it's his hormones. If we all had our sexuality determined by our rate of intimacy, where would that leave us?' Skelton was back behind his desk, constructing cages with his fingers. 'Come to think of it, Charlie, last couple of police functions, you haven't brought anybody with you, the opposite sex. Not significant, is it?'

Resnick found himself wriggling a little more than was comfortable. Either Skelton was accusing him of being a long time in the closet or being innately prejudiced, he wasn't sure which. Perhaps it was both. Or simply a game? No. The only games he could imagine Skelton being interested in had strict rules, required the utmost concentration and alertness, were important to win and absolutely no fun at all. Fun, Resnick thought, wasn't a concept the superintendent believed in.

Poor Kate!

'I'm sure there was something going on between them,' Resnick said. 'Something to make Dougherty leave early, more than this shift business. I saw Groves's face when I suggested they might have been having a row.'

'Lovers' quarrel, Charlie?' said Skelton dismissively.

'Could have followed him out of the bar, across the street. One thing, if Dougherty knew who his attacker was, that would explain why he was able to get close, get in the first blow.'

'From behind, Charlie?'

The thought set up possibilities neither man was prepared fully to consider. Skelton slid back one of his desk drawers and took out a blue folder, some papers clipped neatly together.

'Home Office statistics. Rise in recorded sexual offences, five per cent to twenty-eight thousand in '89, since then more or less holding.' Skelton flipped over two pages. 'Research into that extra five per cent, thirteen hundred cases, between half and a third indecency charges against men. One town's public toilets. You can imagine what the gays had to say about that. You know.' Skelton turned to another sheet, a photo copy of a magazine article. ' "The prosecution and persecution of gay men," ' Skelton read.

'With respect, sir . . .'

'Let the media get wind of this,' Skelton said, 'they'll have a field day. Gays carving themselves up in lavatories. The so-called silent majority will want officers on observation, armed with everything from mirrors to video cameras and everyone to the left of the Co-op Labour Party will be organizing demos and picketing police stations on behalf of their oppressed brothers.'

Resnick allowed a small silence to collect around them. Beyond it a car went by, all of its windows presumably down, loudspeakers blaring. From further along the corridor, not quite decipherable, the familiar cadence of swearing. Telephones, their urgencies overlapping.

'If he had motivation, sir. Groves. Opportunity.'

'Yes,' said Skelton, subdued now. 'I agree. We have to check it out. But, Charlie, low profile, low key, be careful who you use. And remember, if there is anything in it, where does that leave us with the attack on Fletcher? The hospital, Charlie, I still think that's where we'll find our answers.'

'Yes, sir,' Resnick said, getting to his feet.

'The wrong kind of publicity, Charlie,' Skelton said as Resnick reached the door, 'it can only get in the way.'

Patel was worrying over the information that had come back from the hospital, fussing with the computer, opening files, finding facts to cross-reference and concluding there were too few. If there was a clear link between Fletcher and Karl Dougherty he couldn't pin it down. Aside from the obvious; apart from the fact that they had survived. In Dougherty's case, just. His condition was still giving cause for concern.

Naylor and Lynn Kellogg were talking into telephones, opposite ends of the office.

'Nobody tramps the streets with a pram for eight hours,' Naylor was saying. 'Nobody in their right mind.'

'And when she made this application,' said Lynn Kellogg, 'did she say what she was going to do? . . . Mm, hm. Mm, hm . . . And did she say where?'

Resnick stood for a while behind Patel's desk, looking at the characters springing up on the green screen. Names, dates, times. It should all be checked against a list of patients Fletcher would have had dealings with, patients from Bernard Salt's list, but that list was slow in coming. The consultant's secretary had greeted Patel's request like an invitation to perform a particularly unsavoury sexual act.

If Skelton was right and the hospital was where they were going to get their answers, they would have to do better than this.

'I would go back there, sir,' Patel said. 'But with the best will in the world, I don't think it would make a lot of difference. She is a very determined lady.'

Resnick nodded. The sort that, generations back, would have travelled across the Sahara by camel without ever breaking sweat or needing to urinate behind the nearest pyramid; who held the Raj together in the face of disease, the caste system and the occasional difficulty in getting a fourth for bridge.

'If you might call her yourself, sir,' Patel suggested.

'I'll get the super to do it.'

'I don't know,' Naylor was saying. 'As soon as I can. What does it matter anyway, if you're not going to be there?'

'Thank you,' said Lynn. 'If she does get in touch, you'll let me know?'

Resnick watched as Naylor slammed down the phone and left the office with a speed that nearly left a startled DC, who happened to be coming through the door, minus an arm. Resnick looked questioningly towards Lynn Kellogg and slowly she shook her head. The number of times Resnick had seen it happen: young officers who think a kiddie is all they need to bring them and their young wives back together.

He headed for his office and Lynn followed him.

'Karen Archer, sir. I've checked with the university. Seems she saw the student counsellor and was advised to take some time off. Compassionate leave, sort of thing.

The department secretary assumed she'd gone home to her parents, but didn't know for sure. I've tried to contact them and can't get any response.'

'You're worried?'

'Just a feeling, sir.'

'She had obviously moved out, though. Signalled her intentions.'

'Yes.'

'It's not as if Carew's gone after her again, no suggestion of that?'

Lynn shook her head.

'The concern is, then, what? She might have harmed herself?'

'Something like that, sir. Rape. The way Maureen Madden explained it, at least if she'd agreed to press charges, that would have been acknowledging what happened and saying that it wasn't her fault. Not leaving her trying to suppress it or feeling guilty.'

'Her parents. Where do they live?'

'Devon, sir. Close to Lynmouth.'

'Put through a call to the local station. Ask them to contact the parents if they can.' He looked across at her, a stocky, earnest woman with worried, sympathetic eyes. 'Take it from there.'

'Yes, sir.'

Before Lynn had left his office, Resnick was getting himself put through to Skelton. The superintendent brought his rank and authority to bear on Bernard Salt's secretary, who promised she would have the necessary information available by the end of the day. Resnick thanked him and checked that he could pick it up himself. He had another call to make that would take him close.

A little after five, Resnick was standing in the back garden of the Doughertys' house in Wollaton, balancing a cup and saucer in his left hand. The sky was losing light and across a succession of privet hedges bungalows were falling into silhouette. Inside, in the kitchen, Pauline Dougherty was washing their best dinner service, the one that had been a wedding gift, for the second time.

'I'm sorry,' Resnick said to William Dougherty, who was standing to his left, staring at some non-existent blemish on the lawn, 'but there's something I have to ask you about Karl. Something personal.'

Twenty-four

'Helen, this is simply not the best time.'

'No?'

'No.'

'But then, Bernard, it never is.'

Bernard Salt put both hands briefly to his face, covering his mouth, tiredness; his eyes alone had any brightness left in them and even they were showing signs of strain. All the damned day in theatre and now this.

'Look,' he extended his hands towards her, palms up, fingers loosely spread; the way he approached relatives, persuasive, calming; the way he approached them when the prognosis was poor. Helen Minton knew: she had seen it in operation many times before. 'Look, Helen, here's what we'll do. Your diary, mine, we'll make a definite date for later in the week . . .'

Already she was shaking her head.

'Go somewhere pleasant, that restaurant out at Plumtree . . .'

'No, Bernard.'

'Give us a chance to talk properly . . .'

'Bernard, no.'

'Relax. Surely that's better than this?'

Helen Minton lifted her head and began to laugh.

'Look at us. You're tired, I'm tired. It's the end of the day.'

'Yes,' Helen said, still laughing. 'It's always the end of the day.'

He came close to taking her by the arm but thought better of it. 'Helen, please . . .'

The laughter continued, grew louder. Salt glanced anxiously towards the connecting door, the faint shadow of his secretary at her desk, the soft purr and click of the electric typewriter maintaining the same even tempo. The laughter rose and broke and was gone.

'Don't worry about her, Bernard. She'll think I'm just another hysterical, middle-aged woman for you to deal with. I'm sure she's used to them, trooping in and out of your office. The fact that this one's in uniform probably doesn't make a lot of difference. She'll never betray your confidence, expose you to anything as unsavoury as gossip.' Helen smiled without humour. 'She's probably in love with you herself.'

Salt shook his head. 'Now you are being stupid.'

'Of course,' she said, 'I always am, sooner or later. If I weren't, how could you dismiss me so easily. Ignore me as a fool.'

The consultant shook his head and sat down. 'I don't know what to do.'

'Yes, you do. It's simple. Give me an answer.'

He looked up at her and back at his desk. Slightly muffled, there was a knock at the outer office door. 'I can't,' he said.

They stayed as they were, Helen staring at Salt, at the fleshiness around his jaw, hating it, sickened by it, the sight of him; if he turned his head towards her now and said the right words, she would weep with gratitude and fall into his arms.

'Excuse me,' said the secretary apologetically, opening the door, 'but the inspector is here. To collect the patients' details. He wondered if you had a minute to spare.'

Without another word, Helen Minton hurried out, past the secretary, past Resnick, into the corridor.

'Of course,' said Salt wearily. 'Ask him to come in.'

The book shop was on the ground floor, close to the medical school entrance. Situated in the broad corridor outside was the telephone from which Tim Fletcher had tried to call Karen Archer the night he was attacked; around the corner and through the doors was the bridge where it had happened.

Ian Carew was wearing a sports jacket and underneath it a T-shirt with the slogan, *Medics have bigger balls.* Navy blue sweatpants and running shoes. In his hand, held against his side, were an A4 file and a textbook on anatomy and physiology. He watched Sarah Leonard walk into the corridor from the hospital and cross towards the bookshop and go inside. He gave her half a minute and went after her.

In amongst all of the professional sections there were a few general paperbacks, Booker runners-up and beach reading. Carew pretended to browse through these, watching Sarah all the while, the way the muscles of her calves tightened as she reached for something from an upper shelf.

Suddenly, she turned to face him, as if aware that he had been watching her and Carew had only two choices. He walked straight to her, finding his smile easily, glancing at the books in her hands.

'Teasdale *and* Rubinstein. Heavy duty, even for a staff nurse with ambitions.'

Sarah looked at him as if expecting him to move aside, allow her to get to the cash desk.

Carew didn't move. 'I recognized you,' he said. 'From the other night.' Pointedly looking at the engraved badge pinned above her breast. 'Sarah.'

'Yes,' she said. 'You were kerb crawling.'

Carew tut-tutted. 'I offered you a lift.'

'You tried to pick me up.'

'Yes,' he said. 'Yes, I did.'

'Why?' she asked, sensing immediately it was the wrong thing to say.

Because of your hair, Carew thought, the way you were walking, striding out. He didn't say those things; not yet. He wasn't so stupid or inept.

'Are you really getting both of those?' he asked, tapping the uppermost of the books.

'They're not for me. One of the doctors . . .'

'Don't tell me he's got you running errands.'

'He couldn't get here himself.'

'Too busy.' Just an edge of sarcasm.

'He was badly injured. A few nights ago.'

'Not Fletcher? Tim Fletcher?'

'Do you know him?'

Carew shook his head. 'I read about him. Poor guy.'

'Yes.'

'How's he coming along?' Carew asked. 'On the mend?'

Sarah nodded. 'Slowly, yes.'

Carew angled his head back a little and seemed to refocus on her face. Sarah knew that he was going to change tack, ask her to meet him after work, something of the sort. She was conscious of the roof of her mouth turning dry.

'Well,' Carew said, 'nice to bump into you.' Stepping away. 'Maybe I'll see you again some time.'

And he was on his way out of the shop, a thick head of hair, good, muscular body, something of a bounce to his walk. Perhaps, Sarah thought, I was being a bit harsh on him, maybe he isn't so bad after all.

There were days and far too many of them when the only time Bernard Salt felt free of pressure was when he was in theatre. Anaesthetized in front of him, a problem to be solved and he knew the surest, the safest way to solve it. Of course, there were surprises, emergencies even. But they were what kept it alive: and they were surmountable. Within the span of his knowledge, of his hands. He stood there and at his bidding instruments were put into his hands, sterile, sharp. If something was rotten you cut it out.

As to the rest of it . . .

Twenty-four years of a marriage that had decently laid itself to rest. A mixture of rapaciousness and boredom that had driven him to find a solace for which he no longer had the inclination or the need. Why couldn't she accept that? Let go. That eternal whining, you promised, you promised. Of course he had promised. Wasn't that what he was supposed to do? A married man. Senior consultant. Seven, eight years ago when it had started, he would have promised her anything. Had. Now he would promise her anything to leave him alone, only she no longer believed him. Not without words on paper, evidence, commitment. All the times you said what we might do if only you were free.

Well, now he was free and fully intending to stay that way.

She was waiting by his car again and he considered abandoning it, heading back to the hospital and calling a taxi, but she had seen him.

'Helen,' Salt said, resting his briefcase on the roof of his car, fingers in his jacket pocket circling around the keys, 'how long do you think you're going to keep this up?'

She had changed out of her uniform into a white blouse and navy cardigan, a calf-length pleated skirt and, unbelted at the waist, a camel coat. Her hands were small, tight fists. 'For as long as it takes,' she said.

'And if I say no,' Salt asked.

'That's easy,' Helen said. 'You know what I'll do then.'

He drew his breath. In the masked fluorescence of the car park, her skin looked sallow and old. 'All right,' he said, 'no. The answer's no. Once and for all, no.'

Helen Minton slid a half-step sideways and steadied herself against the side of the car. Her mouth opened and there was a sound, harsh and hissing, like stale air making its escape. She almost slipped as she turned away, recovered, and walked quickly between the avenues of other cars. Salt hesitated, started after her without conviction, and when she was lost to sight behind the door leading to the lifts, he stopped.

He had done it: said it.

Only then, quite still, did he realize the extent to which his own breathing had accelerated. He made himself stand for a full minute before heading back towards his own car.

Fitting the keys in the lock, fumbling a little, his head suddenly came up, alert. A movement off to his right, behind him. Moving then stopping. Salt looked off along the line of roofs, shadows. His first thought had been that it was Helen, calmed down, back to make her peace, apologize. He could see nobody: no doors opened, engines fired.

'Hello?' Salt's voice was oddly uncertain, hollow.

Then there was somebody, someone he knew, a fellow consultant making his way with crisp steps towards his Rover, waving: 'Hello, Bernard. Communing with the old carbon monoxide?'

Salt let himself into the car and waited until the Rover had slid from its space, reversing out and following it towards the exit.

By the time Calvin Ridgemount got home it was late. He let himself in, dropping his sports bag at the top of the stairs before going into the kitchen. There were two cartons of milk in the fridge, one already opened, so he opened the other and drank the contents down in four long swallows. From the living room he could hear the sound of recorded voices and soundtrack music, his father's laughter.

Calvin smeared plum jam on two digestive biscuits and put them together, taking a bite as he went towards the back of the house.

His father was sitting back on the settee, one leg hooked

over the side, can of Red Stripe in his hand, laughing at something Barbra Streisand had just said to what's-his-name? The one whose daughter married the tennis player Calvin couldn't stand. It didn't matter. He had seen it before, the film, something really stupid about boxing. His father had fetched it from the corner shop, two videos for a pound if you brought them back next morning, but this was being shown live, on TV, now.

'Where've you been?' his father asked, still smiling at what he'd seen.

'I told you,' Calvin said. 'Out.'

'Where you going now?'

'To bed.'

In his room, Calvin tossed the bag towards the far wall, below the window. Without bothering to switch on the light, he slipped *Fair Warning* from its case and switched the cassette player on. Lying back on his bed, he stared up at the ceiling, eyes growing accustomed to the blackness, watching the stars come out, one by one.

Twenty-five

Time was, Resnick thought, you would have walked into Manhattan's in the happy hour, and said the joint was jumping. Of course, he didn't know that for a fact. Just another bit of America that had found its way into his life via a record label. Thirty-seven or -eight. Herman Autrey on trumpet, Gene Sedric on tenor. Fats Waller and his Rhythm. Resnick had an uncle, a tailor with thumbs like sheet metal and fingers like silk; instead of coming to England in the months before the outbreak of the war, he had shipped out with his family to the States. Half a dozen of them sleeping toe to tail in a tenement off Hester Street. After VJ Day, the uncle had uprooted himself again, more opportunities in a smaller pond. Time had proved him wrong.

But Resnick could remember, as a boy, climbing to the upper floor of the house in St Anne's and poring over the enormous pile of 78s, black and brittle in brown covers of paper or card printed over with slogans for Vocalion, HMV. Sitting there, cross-legged, on his own, he had read the labels with fascination, inventing stories about the owners of those names before ever hearing their music: Count, Duke, Fats, Willie the Lion, Kid and King.

When first he heard them played, his friends were beginning to listen to – what? – Tommy Steele, Bill Haley and the Comets. Resnick had sat in hushed silence with black tea and dry cake while his uncle handsewed buttonholes and hems and his cousin swayed her legs softly to the Ink Spots, the Mills Brothers, four voices and a guitar. After a while, his uncle would tap his thimble on the table and wink at Resnick and then they would listen to Mildred Bailey, Billie Holiday, Luis Russell's 'Call of the Freaks', Fats Waller and his Rhythm, 'The Joint is Jumpin' '.

'You came back,' Maura said, as Resnick tried to edge into a space at the bar.

Her hair seemed to be suspended around her head, a mixture of fine gauze and candy floss. Since Resnick had last seen her, its colour had shaded from auburn towards orange. She was wearing a halter top, bright flowers on a black background. Rings on her fingers, earrings that brushed against her shoulders as she turned.

She set a bottle and a glass down in front of him and inclined her head towards the far side of the room, past the console where a hip black DJ was playing something Resnick was relieved not to recognize.

'I know,' Resnick said. He had spotted Groves as he walked in, sitting at a table against the wall with a couple of friends, back towards the door.

'You're not going to arrest him? In here?'

'What for?'

When Maura shrugged, her engraved metal earrings jingled. 'I've never seen anyone arrested, only on television.'

'That's where it happens most.'

She went back to serving customers and Resnick poured his beer, drank enough to get the remainder of the bottle into the glass and stood away from the bar, between there and the steps, occasionally glimpsing Paul Groves's prematurely balding head through the mass of drinkers. When he had finished his drink and Groves had shown no sign of leaving, Resnick moved to him around the edge of the dance floor and tapped him on the shoulder.

'Sup up,' Resnick said.

Beneath the volume of the music, Groves might not have

heard the actual words, but he caught their meaning. One of the young men with him, a white shirt with rolled-back sleeves and a wide paisley tie, looked as if he might be about to tell Resnick to mind his own business, but Groves shook his head and said it was all right and then stood up, leaving his lager unfinished.

'I've been reading your file,' Resnick said. They were crossing on to the pedestrian street that would take them to the rear of the Council House, the old Boots building. Usual for the time of year, it couldn't make up its mind whether or not to rain.

'I thought you might,' said Groves. His hands were in his trouser pockets, flaps of his jacket bunching back along his arms.

They were passing McDonald's, across squares of pavement on which a street artist had lovingly copied a madonna and child.

'What you are,' Resnick said. 'It doesn't matter, not to me. It doesn't make any difference.'

'Then why . . . ?'

'Except in so far as it's relevant.'

'Is it?'

'That's what I want to know.'

'You want to know if Karl and I were involved.'

'Were you?'

'What difference would it make?'

'I'm not sure. But your relationship with him, it would be different.'

'If we were both queer.'

They went right towards the square, past the girls with skimpy dresses and anxious eyes waiting between the lions, the Goths and Skins and would-be bikers gathered around the wall above the fountains, and sat on a wet bench in front of half-a-dozen damp and hopeful pigeons.

'How long have you known him?' Resnick asked.

'A year. More or less a year.'

Having learned when to question, when to listen, Resnick waited.

'I met him at the cinema. Late afternoon. It was my day off and Karl, well I suppose Karl's, too, or he'd worked an early. It doesn't matter. There we were in the smallest screen, the two of us and an old woman who ate her sandwiches and then fell asleep.' He gave Resnick a quick glance. 'We weren't sitting together, not anything like that. About as far apart as you could get. Karl spoke to me on the way out, something about the film, I don't remember what. We got outside and we were walking in the same direction. "I'm going for a pizza," he said, and laughed. "It's a wonder you didn't hear my stomach grumbling all through the film. I had half a mind to go and ask that old dear for one of her sandwiches." I laughed and there we were, sitting in the Pizza Hut, drinking large Cokes and arguing over which of us could build the biggest salad.'

A line of young women wearing fancy dress was congaing their way across the opposite end of the square, shrieking and singing. Paul Groves slipped both hands beneath the lapels of his coat.

'After that we'd meet up, usually once a week, go to a film, have a pizza, or if Karl couldn't get off in time we'd just go for a drink. Once in a while, after one of us had got paid, we'd go out for a meal. Karl wanted to go to that Japanese place, down in Lenton. Raw fish and it cost an arm and a leg.'

Resnick was aware of cramp spreading down his right leg, but didn't budge, didn't want to distract Groves from what he was saying.

'I nearly got him to come on holiday once. Greece, one of the small islands. Keen as anything until it came to paying the deposit and signing the forms.' Groves's voice was little more than a whisper; the conga line had moved off towards the Dog and Bear, to be replaced by a gang of jostling youths in Forest shirts, chanting and clapping their hands. The first of the police dog vans was parked at the north-east corner of the square. 'I went round to his place a couple of times. He had all these photos on the walls from when he was in the States, posters, more books than any normal person would read in a lifetime. Made a great thing out of grilling these hamburgers and having California wine. He'd never come back to my place, not once. Made excuses till I stopped asking.'

Groves moved his hands until they were gripping his knees.

'I touched him one time and you'd have thought I'd stuck a knife right in his back.'

'For Christ's sake,' Mark Divine said. 'What's your hurry?'

Naylor hesitated long enough for Divine to order two more pints.

'Fucking Friday night,' Divine said, elbowing his way towards a space by the doorway to the Gents, calling back over his shoulder. 'That's what it is.'

He glowered at a couple of underage lads and they slunk off.

'Ring her, tell her you're on obs. What's she going to know?'

'I already did.'

'You told her that?'

'Told her I was in for a half.'

Divine shook his head in disgust. 'Fucking women. Think they own you.'

'It isn't like that,' Naylor said.

'No? Tell us what it is like then?'

Naylor swallowed some more beer. He could no more begin to explain to Divine what it was like than he could get Debbie to talk about what it was that was wrong.

'Get these down,' Divine said, 'and we'll move on.' He

pushed at Naylor's shoulder with his fist. 'Strike lucky before the night's out, eh?'

Naylor drank his best bitter and didn't say a thing.

Resnick remained where he was, despite the dampness seeping up into his thighs and back, long after he had watched Paul Groves cross the square and climb into one of the cabs at the rank, heading home to Mapperley Top. If Karl Dougherty had only wanted companionship, a friend outside his work, Groves had wanted more. Sex. Love. It was difficult to believe that Karl had been ignorant of Groves's inclinations, that the younger man – he couldn't think of any other way to put it – fancied him. So what had he been doing? Pat phrases fell, fully formed, into his mind: stringing him along, playing with fire, dicing with death.

How frustrated would Groves have to be before striking out? How provoked? Two interviews in, Resnick did not consider Paul Groves to be a naturally violent man.

He remembered a pensioner who, after years of caring for his bedridden wife, waiting on her hand and foot, had blinded her suddenly with boiling tea; a fifteen-year-old youth who had stabbed his stepfather forty-two times with a bread knife and then tried to sever his neck with the end of a spade. Neither of them naturally violent, just driven till, like piano wire drawn tight inside them, their anger and frustration had sprung and snapped.

He passed the lavatory where Karl Dougherty had been attacked and thought about Reg Cossall. Likely he had seen which way the wind was blowing and been pleased to have the lot dumped into Resnick's lap, glad to be shot of it.

He could remember Cossall, a young sergeant then, still in uniform, fulminating against the openness in which a urinal close to the station was used for homosexual assignations. Men would gather there, two or three at a time, quick glances over their shoulders as they approached along the pavement that bordered the cemetery. Sometimes their cars were parked below on Talbot Street, ready for a quick retreat or later meeting. Sometimes a passing PC would whistle his approach, lean in and flash a torch. Occasionally, on the request of an indignant customer, caught short on his way home and unsuspecting, policing would become more positive. Word on the grapevine would pass along and the practice would fall away until things had calmed down and it was safe to return.

From time to dangerous time, the citizens of outrage, primed by beer and armed with sticks and worse, would take the law into their own hands. Resnick had watched as Cossall hauled out one who had been wading through the toilet's dim interior with the blunted bayonet his father had brought back from Cyprus.

'Go on, youth,' Cossall had said, retaining the weapon. 'Off with you, sharpish.'

One of the men they had helped out had been bleeding profusely from superficial wounds; another had to be stretchered to the ambulance, a gash opened up down his side, three layers of clothing exposed through to his ribs.

'Serves the bastards right,' Cossall had said, spitting towards the gutter. 'Bugger legislation, castrate the lot of 'em!'

There had been a high anger in his eyes and, seeing it again, in memory, Resnick thought of Karl Dougherty in the steady hum of intensive care, the blows that had been inflicted, Cossall's face as he had stepped down from the urinal, zipping himself into place. Was that what he had been thinking then? Serve him right. Just another bumboy getting more than he'd bargained for. Teach him a lesson.

Resnick wondered what the lessons were, exactly who was teaching whom? Queer-bashing. Paki-bashing. They broke out in phases, ugly and suppurating, cocky kids in short hair with right on their side. Something to do of a Friday night: someone to hit. Midway up that first stretch of Mansfield Road, Resnick turned and looked back at the city: nobody was learning anything.

Twenty-six

The only sign of Ed Silver was the broken glass shining dully in the light from the top of the front door. Bottle glass. The cats, anxious and eager and, as usual, late being fed, brushed around him and he shooed them away. When he went inside they scurried to the kitchen, where Resnick forked food into their bowls before going back out with an old newspaper. He wrapped the larger pieces of glass thickly inside its pages and dropped them in the green council dustbin. Then he used a dustpan and brush to sweep up as much of the rest as he could, finally down on his hands and knees to find any fragments that might end up in the cats' paws.

The envelopes he carried in from the hall floor were dull and brown and he left them beside the kettle while he ground coffee and gave the cats their milk. Pepper was losing hair in clumps along his back again and he would have to make time to take him to the vet: forty-five minutes of staring out the owners of schnauzers and Alsatians, pretending not to be embarrassed by his cat's whimpering.

One of the letters was from the Polish Club, reminding him that his subscription was overdue and inviting him to the eightieth birthday celebrations of one of its stalwart members. Second-class mail, it had taken five days to reach him, as the crow flies no more than a mile. A note had been penned at angles to the page: *Please come, Charles. We would all love to see you. Marian.* Marian Witczak, who kept the Polish flag in her window and an atlas open at Eastern Europe as if it were the A–Z. Step outside on to the street and the taxi that draws up will take you to the heart of Warsaw, fifteen minutes.

Resnick poured coffee, wondering about people who so strenuously denied the present, constructed a fantasy from the past. How many nights did Marian fall asleep dreaming of mazurkas and ball gowns? How much alcohol did it take before Ed Silver saw himself stepping up again on to the stand at Ronnie Scott's, slipping the shield from the mouthpiece, hooking his sax on to its sling, beating in time with his heel and launching into 'Dexterity' without even a glance back at the band?

He sliced the sausage he found in the back of the fridge and planned to fry it with pieces of cooked potato, a bulb of garlic, dust in a little dill and thyme. Before that he wanted something with his coffee and mourned for his lost cherry cheesecake. What he did have was honey, black bread it wouldn't take more than a minute to toast. Take it through and get the weight off his feet, a little rest and then the cooking. He was listening to Miles Davis, the trumpeter's namesake stretched purring between crotch and knee, a mouthful of coffee still in the cup, feeling better than at any time that day. He knew the phone would ring before the tune finished and it did.

There was one youth, hair cut like a mistake, boogying around the middle of the floor, doing a haphazard strip to Madonna, almost down to his boxers already and the bouncers anxious at the edge of the six-deep circle cheering him on.

'Any minute now,' said Naylor.

'What?'

'Trouble.'

Divine laughed. 'Fucking Friday night! What d'you expect?'

The girls he'd been eyeing up were back again, three of

them, standing close to the spiral staircase, pretending not to notice.

'Right,' Divine said. 'We're on.'

'What?'

'There.'

'Where?'

'Over there. Hanging out for it.'

All that Naylor could see was a trio of young women, nothing to differentiate them from the others packing the club. Hundreds of them. Lots of make-up, sun tan, streaked and permed hair, short skirts or low tops or both.

'Look at the state of that!' Divine nudged him urgently. 'Not wearing much more than a sodding belt.'

At least the woman who'd wriggled by might take his mind off the ones he'd been endlessly on about, but no, there he was again, looking interested, looking cool, wait for it, wait for it, now the grin. One of the three said something to the others and all three of them laughed.

'There you are,' Divine said. 'Let's get over.'

Out on the floor the impromptu stripper was shimmying a pair of boxer shorts with a design like psychedelic crazy-paving lower and lower on his hips. Half the crowd were clapping their hands and bellowing the chorus from 'World in Motion', the rest chanting, 'Off! Off! Off!' and the bouncers were flexing their muscles like substitutes about to be thrown into the action.

'We ought to do something about that,' said Naylor.

'Did we, fuck!'

'See what I mean,' Naylor said, as the first of the bouncers tried to barge through the crowd and took an elbow to the face for his pains.

'That's what we ought to do something about.' Divine turned Naylor round physically, the three girls looking at them openly now, the tallest giving them a touch of open mouth, letting the lip gloss do the work.

Two of the bouncers had broken through the cheering

cordon and made a grab for the stripper, managing between them to pull his shorts the rest of the way to the floor. 'Leave it,' Divine hissed. 'Just leave it alone.' A counter-section of the crowd had deserted the World Cup anthem for a few desultory lines of 'Why Was He Born So Beautiful?', dragged by the occasion from ancestral memory. Naylor found himself in front of the girls, only the tall one bolding it out, her friends turned away in embarrassment, real or feigned. 'Right,' said Divine. 'What are you lot drinking?' One of the bouncers grabbed up the stripper's clothes and tossed them in the direction of the nearest exit, while another held him by the shoulders and nonchalantly kneed him in the naked groin.

'What's he threatening to chop off this time?' Resnick asked.

'So far,' said Jane Wesley, 'nothing. He got into an argument with one of the regulars about football and there was a fight. Your friend came out of it rather the worse.'

'Far as I know,' said Resnick, 'Ed doesn't know a thing about football.'

'Exactly.'

Resnick sighed. All around them there was the smell of damp clothing and Old Holborn; urine, yesterday's and today's. 'Where is he?' he asked.

'In the office. I wanted to send for an ambulance, but he wouldn't let me.'

'Does he know you called me?'

'No.'

Resnick looked at her sharply.

'I thought, if he's going to have a go at somebody, rather you than some unsuspecting ambulance driver.'

'Right,' said Resnick. 'Thanks.'

Ed Silver was sitting, not on the chair but on the floor behind it, both arms wrapped around his head, which was resting on his knees.

'Will you be okay?' Jane asked.

Resnick nodded and she closed the office door behind them.

'Bastard, Charlie.'

'Who?'

'It's a bastard.' Silver's voice was muffled and even when he slid his hands clear of his face still sounded as if it were being filtered through cotton wool. 'Broken my bloody nose.'

In amongst the dried and drying blood and the swelling, it was difficult to see exactly what the damage might be. 'Looks like a trip to casualty,' Resnick said, already dreading it, far and away enough of hospitals recently.

Silver was shaking his head, even though it hurt to do so, mumbling no.

'You can't stay here with a broken nose.'

'Why the sodding hell not?'

'It needs attention.'

'I'll give it attention.' Silver placed his fingers to either side of the nose and began to push.

'Jesus, no!'

'What?'

'Don't do that.'

'Go back outside, Charlie. If you're squeamish.'

Instead, Resnick closed his eyes; it wasn't the blood, more the self-inflicted pain. There was a lot of squeezing, a quick click like balsa wood splintering and a lot more blood.

'There,' announced Silver, 'that's done it.'

'What exactly?'

'If the bastard wasn't broken, it is now.'

Naylor might not have believed it if he hadn't seen it with his own eyes, but there was Divine, leaning over these four lads and talking low and purposeful, smiling all the while.

A couple of minutes and the lads got up and vacated their table, great view down over the dance floor.

'What did you say to them?' Naylor asked as they sat down.

Divine winked. 'You don't want to know.'

The girls were all chatty enough now, not that it mattered what they were saying, most of it lost beneath the music and the low roar that rose from the floor and hung beneath the ceiling like hot air.

Divine put his arm around the tall girl's shoulders and she made a show of shrugging it off; Divine winking then, across the table at Naylor, giving him the thumbs-up when he thought the girl wasn't looking, though, of course, she was, pursing her lips at him, just a touch of tongue between the lip gloss.

'Fancy your chances, don't you?'

'I fancy yours.'

The other girls, sisters it turned out, in on the bus from Kirkby-in-Ashfield, Lord knows how they were expecting to get back, did some more nudging and giggling and Naylor thought, not for the first time, Christ, they can't be more than sixteen, seventeen.

'Mandy's a beauty queen,' said one of them, looking at the tall girl, who adjusted her profile into what she assumed to be a regal manner.

'Kevin over there's middleweight champion of the world, aren't you, Kev? Stings like a butterfly and sucks like a bee.'

Naylor blushed, the girls snorted into their banana daiquiris.

'I am, actually,' Mandy said.

'Yeh?'

'Yes. Miss Amber Valley. Two years running, as a matter of fact.'

'And she was runner-up the year before that,' added one friend.

'And she got into the heats for Miss East Midlands at Skeggy.'

'I can't cope with all this,' Divine said, getting to his feet, adjusting the crotch of his trousers as he did so. 'I'm off for a slash.'

'Coarse, your friend, isn't he?' the nearest sister confided in Naylor.

'Hey, Kev,' called Divine, turning back towards the table. 'What d'you reckon? Shall I get the coloured, the ribbed, or just the plain?'

The car hadn't been outside Aloysius House much more than twenty minutes, long enough for someone to throw up over the nearside of the boot.

'I hope you're not going to blame us for that,' said Jane Wesley, walking with Ed Silver and Resnick from the door.

'Wouldn't think of it,' Resnick said.

When they had manoeuvred Silver into the front seat, she said, angling her head away from the road, 'If this happens again, are you sure you want me to call you?'

'No,' Resnick shrugged.

'Does that mean you don't want me to?'

'No.'

'That's what I like,' she smiled, 'clear, decisive decision-making.'

Resnick raised one hand, open, towards her and went around to the other side of the car. A few more nights like this and he'd give up the idea of sleep altogether.

'Lovely woman,' Ed Silver said. 'Lovely.'

'So you said.'

'I did?'

'Last time.'

Silver picked at a scab on his upper lip and a thin line of blood began to run towards his unshaven chin. 'Have I seen her before? That woman?'

'Not clearly,' Resnick said.

'Hey!' Silver exclaimed some moments later, the car turning right to pass the central Probation Office and the old Guildhall courts. 'Was that a joke? Not clearly. Was that a joke?'

'No,' said Resnick. 'I don't make jokes.'

'Take 'em, eh Charlie. Take 'em. Not like that feller tonight, the one as did this. All that happened was, let me tell you this, he was blathering on about football or something, England, you know. That Parker, he said, not so bad but he'd play a damn sight better if he weren't black. You see, d'you see? So I goes, being black, that's part of it, makes him as fucking good as he is. Charlie fucking Parker. And he hit me, not with his fist neither, with his knee. Don't know how he managed it, but that's what it was, his knee. Ignorant drunken bastard, he calls me, don't even know his right bloody name.'

Resnick glanced sideways as they stopped at the lights below the Broad Marsh. The swelling round Silver's nose was certainly not going down; instead it was spreading across his cheeks, up towards his eyes. 'I knew he didn't mean Charlie Parker, somebody else . . .'

'Paul,' Resnick said. 'Paul Parker.'

'It was a joke.'

'Yes.'

'Fucking joke.'

'Yes.'

Silver rested a hand forward against the windscreen, blinking as he tried to focus. 'Where we going?'

'Casualty.'

'I'm not . . .'

'Ed?'

'Eh?'

'Shut up.'

One of those old Motown songs and Divine was pressing

himself up against the former Miss Amber Valley, grateful that she was tall enough for him to wriggle his tongue in her ear without having to bend too low.

'How about it, then? Shall we go?'

'What d'you mean?'

'Come on. Ready?'

'No.'

'Come on.' A tug at her wrist.

'No.'

No attempt at dancing now. 'Why not?'

'I can't.'

'Don't worry about your mates, Kev'll look after them all right.'

'It's not that.'

'What is it, then?'

'My boyfriend . . .'

'Your sodding what?'

'Boyfriend. He's meeting me here, picking me up.'

Divine shook his head in disbelief.

'One of his pals was having his stag night.'

'Well, that's it, then, isn't it?' He moved in again, hands low at her back, fingers against the top of her buttocks pulling her back towards him, edge of her little panties clear to the touch. 'You'll not see him till morning.'

'What d'you mean?'

'If he's been out on the piss with his mates, he's not going to turn up here, is he, ready to drive you home.'

'He will.'

'Be too drunk to stand up, most likely, never mind drive.'

She pulled herself away from him and stood there pouting, lip gloss all but gone. Divine had a sudden vision of the evening ending in nothing and he hated it.

'All right, then,' he said, grabbing her arm at the elbow, 'if he's out there waiting for you, let's go find him.'

Protesting, Mandy was pushed and pulled towards the

exit, until finally, grudgingly she walked with him out through the entrance, past the dinner-jacketed bouncers and round into the car park.

'Where is he, then?'

'I don't know . . .'

'Exactly.'

Divine ran his hand up her back and fondled her neck beneath the permed hair. He kissed her shoulder, slid his other hand over her breast as he turned her towards him.

'If you didn't want this,' he said, 'you should have said so before. But then you might not have scored so many free drinks.'

'You offered,' she said. 'What was I supposed to do?'

'This,' Divine said.

He was kissing her, pushing his tongue into her mouth, doing his best to stop her wriggling and get a hand inside her dress at the same time, when someone tapped him hard on the shoulder.

The second time it happened Divine turned to give whoever it was a mouthful and got hit by Mandy's boyfriend, a fourteen-stone West Indian, who brought an eight-inch spanner smack down on to Divine's left eye.

Resnick wanted to drop Ed Silver off at the doors to casualty and leave him there, but he couldn't bring himself to do it. Almost the first things he saw, after steering Silver towards reception, were two familiar faces amongst those waiting for attention. 'Naylor,' Resnick said. 'Divine. What are you doing here?'

Twenty-seven

'Course, I'd heard the records, a few of them anyway, but I'll tell you, Charlie, first time I ever saw Bird and Dizzy live, I almost pissed myself.'

One of the other problems with drunks, Resnick was thinking, they never knew when it was time to go to sleep. The visit to casualty had been shorter than some, less painful than many; Ed Silver had emerged with a well-washed face, a slightly remodelled nose and good intentions. 'One thing, Charlie,' he had claimed, getting into Resnick's car, 'this has done it for me, I mean it. My drinking, from now on it's going to be seriously under control. So help me. And you can bear witness to that.' They hadn't been back at the house half an hour, before Silver was going through cupboards, searching at the back of shelves. 'Just a tot, Charlie. Nobody can be expected to give up totally, just like that. The body wouldn't stand for it.'

Resnick had found tins of frankfurters and Czechoslovakian sauerkraut, the nub ends of a loaf of black rye, pickled gherkins; he had opened the only bottle of wine he possessed, the cheapest dry white he had found in the Co-op, bought months ago to make a recipe he had since forgotten.

Nervous of all this unwonted night-time activity, Bud chased his tail from room to room, occasionally stopping to look perplexed, the White Rabbit in *Alice*, terrified that he was late but with no idea what for.

'The first of the Dial sessions, Charlie, the ones with Miles and Max Roach, you must have those, eh?'

So they sat through the night, listening to the Charlie Parker Quintet – 'The Hymn', 'Bird of Paradise', 'Dexterity' – while, around them, Resnick's neighbours slept on, dreaming straight dreams unthreatened by flattened fifths.

Ed Silver's first attempts to play jazz had been as a clarinettist with a revivalist band in Glasgow, doing his best to sound like Johnny Dodds in the twenties. The first thing that changed that was, down south for a rare date at the Hot Club of London, this skinny guy had come up to him and started talking, an accent that stretched across the Atlantic and back to Aldgate. A musician himself, he'd played with a number of USAF band personnel stationed here during the war, taken a job immediately afterwards, polite music for dancers on one of the liners travelling from Southampton to New York. It was in his East End flat that Silver heard his first bursts of Charlie Parker, records he'd made with Jay McShann's band; each time Parker soloed, the everyday was suddenly pierced by the sublime.

Next day, Silver had pawned his clarinet in exchange for an alto and talked his way into a band working the boats. Anything to get to the Apple, 52nd Street, the Three Deuces and the Royal Roost.

'This is the group,' Silver said now, listening, catching a piece of cucumber at the third attempt and slipping it into his mouth, 'I saw at the Deuces. Amazing. Every last dollar I had on me I spent seeing them, three nights in a row, each time it was hotter and better.

'Anyway . . .' A gulp at the wine now, wincing a little as he moved his mouth. '. . . there I am the next day, pretty late on, due on board ship at half-seven, taking my last look down Broadway and there's Bird, crossing the street ahead of me, sax case in his hand. First reaction, Charlie, I'll tell you, no, it's not him, can't be. Then it is and I'm hurrying after him, slapping him on the back, shaking his hand, telling him I've come all the way from England just to hear him, every solo he's played the last three nights has been a fucking inspiration.

'Bird looks at me a shade off and then he smiles. "Hey, man. Lend me fifty bucks." I would have given that man every stitch of clothing on my back if he'd asked for it, but right then I didn't have five bucks, never mind fifty. I can't think of another damn thing to say and all I can do, Charlie, I think of it to this day, is watch him walk away.

'By the time he got to the studio, just a couple of blocks down, he'd copped from somebody else. Story goes he shot up in the studio bogs before going right in and cutting this stuff.'

Ed Silver leaned back and closed his eyes as, unison theme over, Parker's alto sailed out, clean and clear, over the swish of Max Roach's cymbals.

' "Dexterity",' Ed Silver said.

'Story also goes,' said Resnick, 'he'd killed himself before he was forty. Heart, stomach, cirrhosis of the liver.'

Ed Silver didn't say a thing; continued to sit there, eyes closed, sipping now and then at the last of the white wine.

Saturday: Debbie Naylor sat in the living room, curtains still drawn, trying to get the baby to feed. Up on the first floor, she could hear Kevin retching, head over the lavatory bowl. Serve him right, she thought, though with little satisfaction, let him find out what that's like, at least.

'What d'you call this?' Graham Millington asked, staring down at his plate. His wife was eating wholemeal toast, drinking camomile tea, reading the women's page of the *Mail*. If she could persuade Graham to drop her off at Asda and collect her, there would be time to get her evening-class homework finished before the boys needed ferrying to that party in West Bridgford. 'This isn't what we normally have, is it?' Millington persisted.

'Extra bran,' she said, 'fifteen per cent more fruit and nuts. No added sugar or salt. Thought it would make a nice change.'

Graham Millington mumbled to himself and carried on chewing.

Lynn Kellogg sat in the parked car and poured coffee into the flask's white plastic cup. When she'd been little, six and seven and eight, Sunday afternoon drives with her parents, east to the sea, south to watch the horses canter on Newmarket common, there had been milk in Tupperware containers, sugar – lumps for the horses, granulated for themselves, spooned from a paper bag – a packet of ginger nuts and another – treat of treats! – of jaffa cakes. Sitting there, watching the still deserted street, she could remember the first taste of jam, the quick sweetness of it the moment the chocolate coating broke through.

'What time did she get in last night?' Skelton's wife asked, tightening the belt of her dressing-gown, turn and turn and pull, a double bow.

'I don't know.'

'Of course you know.'

Skelton shook his head. Take the kettle to the pot, not the pot to the kettle: amazing how our parents' precepts stuck with us, governed the trivia of our lives, amazing and terrible. 'It doesn't matter,' he said.

His wife opened the glass-fronted cupboard, took out saucers, bone-china cups, white with a tasteful floral design. 'If it doesn't matter, why spend half the night sitting up, the rest of it lying in bed not sleeping?'

Divine blinked into the bathroom mirror with his one good eye. The other was swollen, yellow, stitches like Biro marks, blue-black, across it. 'Shit!' He leaned over the toilet bowl to urinate, one arm resting against the wall;

when he cleared his throat and spat it was like dredging Trent Lock. He didn't know what had been worse, the initial blow, the embarrassment or Resnick's face. Well. The swelling would subside, the stitches would come out and there was the inspector still to face. 'Slag!' wincing as the sound reverberated around his head. 'Slag!' slamming the wall with the flat of his hand. 'Fucking see her again, I'll teach her a fucking lesson!'

Calvin Ridgemount woke to the smell of bacon frying and knew instantly which day it was. He cleaned his teeth and splashed cold water up into his face. Same black jeans but a new T-shirt, Stone Roses, he liked the shirt design better than he liked the band. Smack on time, as Calvin entered the kitchen, his father was breaking the first of the eggs against the edge of the pan.

'You goin' to see your mother today?'

'You know I am.'

'That's fine. Just a couple of things I'd like you to do for me first.'

'Sure,' said Calvin, picking up one of the slices of bread his father had already buttered, folding it in half and starting to eat. 'No problem.'

'I've got a note somewhere for your mother, too. You give it to her, see that she reads it.'

'Sure.'

The same thing every fortnight, the same note, more or less, same words on blue-lined paper bought in a pad from the shop down on the corner and written painstakingly with a pencil. Knowing what would happen to them at his mother's hands, Calvin no longer bothered to deliver them, tore them into tiny pieces and pushed them out of sight behind the seat on the bus instead.

Helen Minton had thought she might write the letters by hand, but had decided instead that typing them would be better. She had a small Silver Reed, a portable she'd bought at Smith's, oh, so many years ago she couldn't remember. Typing was far from natural to her, far from fast. Not often did she get through a sentence without having to wind the paper up, dab on the Tippex, wind it back down. She had been up since well before light, curtains open just a crack, lamp by her elbow, the typewriter on the living-room table. Four envelopes were fanned across one another like cards, addressed and ready, stamped. The tea had long gone cold in its mug and formed a viscous, orange rim. *Dear Mrs Salt,* she wrote, and *now that you and Bernard are divorced you may not think this concerns you directly*, and *during the last eight years of your marriage . . .*

Dear Father, wrote Patel, another letter of appeasement and promises, what he was doing, how close he was to sitting his sergeant's exam.

Dear Mum, wrote Paul Groves, *I don't want you to be too upset, but I might not be able to get home next week, something's cropped up . . .*

Dear Helen, wrote Bernard Salt and immediately tore it up.

In the intensive care ward, Karl Dougherty opened his eyes when the nurse spoke to him and, for the first time since he had been admitted, knew exactly who and where he was.

Amanda Hooson, a second-year social sciences student at the university, sweated on the floor of her small room, no way of knowing that she was pushing herself through her morning exercises for the very last time.

Twenty-eight

'Are you following me?'

'Not at all.'

'So what are you doing here then?'

'Not following anyone, just sitting.'

'You just happen to be sitting.'

'Yes.'

'In a parked car.'

'Yes.'

'At the end of my street.'

'Your street?'

'You know what I mean.'

'The street where you live.' Lynn had a sudden flash of memory, one of her mother's few records, its cover torn and bent at the edges, stained with greasy fingerprints and ring-marked by mugs of tea, Rex Harrison and Julie Andrews, *My Fair Lady*.

'What's so funny?' Carew said, a vein above his right eye standing out through the sweat.

'Nothing.'

'Then what's that smirk doing on your face?'

The smirk disappeared.

'I suppose you're here for the view?' Carew said.

'How was your run?' Lynn asked.

'Fine.'

'A little over twenty minutes. What's that, two miles, three?'

'Four.'

'Really? That's pretty good.'

'What? You want to be my coach or something?'

'Depends what you need coaching in.'

He leaned low towards the car window, a few drops of sweat falling from his nose down on to the sill. 'What would you suggest?'

'Oh,' Lynn said. 'I don't know. I should imagine it's difficult teaching much to a man like you.'

He gave her a glare and turned his back, started to walk away. He was wearing shorts this morning, despite the fall in the temperature, brief and tight across his buttocks. The muscles at the backs of his legs were thick and taut and shone with the dull glow of sweat. The hair along his legs and arms was thick and dark.

'When did you last see Karen Archer?' Lynn called after him.

Carew stopped instantly and Lynn repeated her question.

He faced her slowly, began to walk back. Lynn read the expression on his face and thought for a minute he was going to reach in and try to drag her from the car. The moment passed. 'You know I'm not allowed to see her,' Carew said.

'Does that mean you haven't seen her?' Lynn said.

'Remember? I'm warned off.'

'Not everyone pays attention to warnings.'

'Perhaps I do.'

I doubt that, Lynn thought. 'So you haven't spoken to Karen since you were at the station? You haven't seen her, there's been no contact?'

'That's right.'

'Because she's missing.'

'Oh, well!' Carew threw out both arms like a bad stage tenor. 'That's it then. It's obviously me. That's what you're thinking, isn't it? Karen's hidden in a cupboard somewhere. Ian Carew. No other explanation.'

'Is there?'

'What?'

'Another explanation?'

'I should think so, hundreds of them. You just like this one.'

'Why should I do that?'

'Because it's easy. You don't have to think further than the end of your nose.' He made a gesture, maybe automatic, perhaps not, a tug at the front of his shorts. 'Because you resent me.'

Lynn bit her tongue, best to let it ride. 'Why did you say a cupboard?' she said.

'Did I?'

'Hidden in a cupboard somewhere, that's what you said.'

'The sweat's drying on me,' he said. 'I need to take a shower. It's getting cold.'

'A cupboard,' Lynn persisted.

'That's right,' Carew smiling, 'that's where I've dumped her. Inside a sack after I hacked her to pieces.' He leaned close and leered. 'Why don't you come in and look?'

Lynn stared at him, stone-faced.

'Come on, search. You do have a search warrant, don't you?'

Lynn turned the key in the ignition. 'If Karen gets in touch with you, please let us know. Ask her to contact the station, ask for me.'

Carew sneered two soundless words, unmistakable. Lynn made herself let out the clutch slowly, check the mirror, indicate. When she reached the main road and swung up past the hospital towards the station, she was still shaking.

It was raining again: a fine, sweeping drizzle that seeped, finally, into the bones, chilling you as only English rain could. On a makeshift stage at the centre of the old market square, the Burton Youth Band were playing a selection from the shows to a scattering of casual listeners and a few sodden relatives who had made the journey over on the band coach. Off to one side of the stage, in a row of their own, a boy and a girl, eleven or twelve and not in uniform like the rest, sat behind a single music stand, mouths moving as they counted the bars. Resnick watched them – the lad with spectacles and cow-licked hair, the girl thin-faced and skimpily dressed, legs purple-patched from rain and wind – nervously fingering the valves of their cornets as they waited to come in.

It was close to where Resnick was standing that Paul Groves had sat, staring off, and talked about his friendship with Karl Dougherty. *I touched him one time and you'd have thought I'd stuck a knife right in his back.* Once, while he and Elaine were still sharing the same house, truths spilling like stains everywhere between them, they had passed close together near the foot of the stairs and Resnick, unthinking, had reached to touch the soft skin inside her arm. He could picture now the hostility that had fired her eyes; the already instinctive recoiling.

The band hit the last note of 'Some Enchanted Evening' more or less together and Resnick clapped, startling a few dazed pigeons. An elderly lady wheeled her shopping trolley across in front of the stage and dropped a coin into the bass-drum case that was collecting puddles and contributions towards the band's winter tour of Germany and the conductor announced the final number. Time to go, Resnick thought, but he stayed on as the two beginners lifted their instruments towards their lips. The conductor waved a hand encouragingly in their direction, the wind lifted their sheet music from its stand and their chance was lost. Without hesitation, the boy retrieved it and Resnick watched the girl's pinched serious face as, biting the inside of her mouth, she struggled to find her place in time for the next chorus. Only when they had played their sixteen bars and sat back, did Resnick turn away, tears, daft sod, pricking at his eyes.

Carew had taken his time over showering and now he sat in his room with the gas fire turned high, just blue-and-white striped boxers and a lambswool V-neck, eating a second apple and glancing through the review section of *The Times*. So many sections, it was getting difficult to tell Saturdays from Sundays. At hand but unopened, a book on neurosurgery that needed returning to the library, notes for an essay that should have been submitted the week before and for which he had every intention of applying for a further extension.

He refolded the paper and dropped it to the floor, walked on bare feet to the window. The car was back again, square to the end of the street, he could see the dark-haired silhouette clearly enough but not the face. Well, fuck her! He pulled on faded jeans, clean from the launderette, replaced his sweater with a white shirt. His black leather jacket was hanging behind the door. The door at the side of the kitchen led past an outside toilet, now disused, across a small flagged yard to a narrow entry. Half-way along, Carew let himself through someone's rear gate and slipped through the side passage into the adjacent road.

He wondered if she'd still be sitting there when he got back, or whether her patience would have run out. On the whole, Carew thought with a smile, he preferred the former. Maybe then he would make a show of walking past, returning when she didn't even know he'd left, give her something to think about. Or simply go back in the way he'd come out, leaving her none the wiser. Either had its advantages.

And which one Carew chose, what would that depend on? Whim, mood, or how he got on where he was going?

Lynn Kellogg shifted her position behind the wheel yet

again, stretching her legs as best she could before beginning another set of exercises to keep the circulation flowing, raising and lowering first her toes, then all of the foot, circling and lifting, pressing down. Ankling, her former cyclist boyfriend had called it, one of the few techniques he could be relied upon to demonstrate successfully, those times she caught him flat on his back on their bed. She told herself not to check her watch but, of course, she did. She tried to clear her mind and concentrate, not wanting to think about the state of her bladder, how many more Sundays she could go without driving home to Norfolk, exactly what Resnick would say if ever she had to explain what she was doing.

Twenty-nine

Cheryl Falmer looked at her watch for the second time in as many minutes and walked across to the desk to check that it was correct. She had arranged to meet Amanda on court at four and there she was, changed and ready, twenty past four and no Amanda. She was beginning to feel stupid, standing in the sports-centre foyer in that skirt, pretending not to notice the rugby players staring at her legs as they came in from training.

'It is four o'clock?' she asked the woman at reception. 'Badminton. Booked in the name of Hooson.'

'That's right. Not turned up?'

'No.'

'Maybe she's forgotten.'

Cheryl moved away, shaking her head. Amanda wasn't the kind to forget. Not anything. Every week they'd been playing, through the last two terms of the previous year and carrying on in this. She knew that Amanda marked it down in the little diary she always carried. Green dot with a four alongside it: badminton. Blue dots for essays in. Yellow for tutorials, red for you know what. Unlike a lot of her group, Amanda was serious, organized; not a stick-in-the-mud, not po-faced like the few feminist-Leninists or whatever they were, always scowling from behind their hand-knitted sweaters and hand-rolled cigarettes; a little older, more mature, she had chosen social sciences with a purpose, not fallen into it as an easy option or an academic back door.

Even so: nearly twenty-five past and no sign.

If it had been squash, it would have been worth going on to the court by herself and thwacking the ball against the wall for half an hour. But the prospect of lofting shuttles high above the net, practising her serve, didn't appeal. She would go back into the changing room and get into her Simple Minds sweatshirt, her denim jacket and jeans. If she cut across between the practice pitches, it was easy enough to call by Amanda's hall of residence and find out what had happened, what had gone wrong.

Jazz Record Requests was just finishing as Resnick entered the house. Hearing the signature tune, he assumed that Ed Silver had switched the radio on and left it playing, hardly expected him still to be there. But he was at the kitchen table, so intent upon Resnick's battered copy of *The Horn* that he scarcely looked up. Miles, who had been spread the width of Silver's bony knees, leapt off at Resnick's approach and ran towards his bowl.

'Thought you couldn't stand cats,' Resnick said.

'I can't,' not looking round.

Resnick shrugged off his damp coat and leaned his plastic bag of shopping against the fridge. The other cats were there now, all save Dizzy, and Resnick ministered to them before grinding coffee for himself.

'Cup?' he asked Silver.

Silver didn't answer.

The legs of Resnick's trousers were wet through from the knees down, his brown leather shoes stained nearly black and he knew that when he took them off his socks would be ringed with dye and all but soaked through.

'This book,' Silver said, eyes not leaving the page, 'bloke who wrote it, wouldn't know a real musician if one jumped up and bit him in the arse.'

A novel about drugs and jazz in New York, Resnick remembered it as being romanticized but readable; at least it wasn't *Young Man with a Horn*.

'This, f'r'instance. Listen to this.'

But Resnick wasn't in the mood to be read to. He left Ed Silver competing with Radio Three and went into the bathroom. Clothes off and dumped in a corner he considered playing truth with the scales, but decided he wasn't up to that either. In his experience, grey days such as this only got greyer. One hand holding in his paunch, he stepped under the shower. Having failed to sell the house he would have to get the bathroom retiled, cream wallpaper beginning to darken and buckle where it was exposed to the water.

'Persistent, isn't she?'

Opening his eyes, Resnick realized that Silver was standing just beyond the open doorway, book by his side.

'Who?'

'I don't know, do I? Same one as called before, I s'pose.'

'You suppose?'

'Sounded the same to me.'

'What did you tell her?'

'Asked her if she wanted to meet me later, buy me a drink.'

Silver's silhouette was fading behind a shimmer of plastic and steam. 'What did she say?' Resnick asked.

'Unprintable.' He flapped the paperback against his leg. 'Even in crap like this.'

'Did she leave a name?'

'No.'

'Number?'

'Too busy hanging up.'

Resnick tilted his face towards the stream of water and soaped his belly, buttocks, beneath his arms. He thought Silver had walked away, but when Silver spoke again, the voice was as close.

'The other call, some bloke, he said for you to ring back. Soon as you could.'

'Great.'

'What?'

'Telling me when I got in.'

'Forgot.'

'Yes. Too engrossed in that appalling book.'

'No,' Silver said. ' 'S'not that bad.'

'This bloke,' Resnick said, 'any chance he left a name?'

'Skelton,' Silver said. 'Wrote the number down somewhere. Lessee.' He fumbled through his pockets. 'Know I got it here somewhere.'

But Resnick had already switched off the water and was stepping out of the shower, reaching for the towel; the number he knew by heart.

The hall of residence was built around a central courtyard, dark pointed brick and uniform windows, a path that wound down towards it through a meadow of grass from the university itself. Only the police vehicles parked off the inner ring road suggested anything less than ideal. Resnick nodded at one of the forensic officers who was leaving, followed the directions of the constable standing inside to keep any of the curious at bay.

'DI in shot,' grinned the scene-of-crime officer with the video camera. Resnick held his ground while the man zoomed in hard on the bed and then out. Stick a camcorder in their hands and suddenly they're Alfred Hitchcock.

'Sorry, sir,' said Resnick. 'Came as soon as I could.'

'Not to worry, Charlie.' Skelton dropped the pair of white cotton pants he was holding into a plastic envelope and left it to be labelled and sealed. 'Just about through.'

The room looked as if it had been in the eye of a storm. Bookshelves had been torn from the walls, books strewn over the ground. Bedclothes were almost anywhere but on the bed. Shoes, a sports bag, articles of clothing; a tube of toothpaste caught inside a trainer. A4 file paper bearing orderly writing in purple or green ink, diagrams designed to give comparative readings in levels of employment, take-up of housing benefit.

'Lucky the girl found her when she did,' Skelton said, crossing towards him. 'Even so, she lost one hell of a lot of blood.'

Resnick hadn't needed telling, evidence of it enough on the striped duvet, sheets of paper, a pillow; a splash of it like paint someone had flicked against the porcelain of the sink.

'This done after or before?' Resnick asked, still surveying the mess.

'During. She put up quite a fight.'

'Is she going to be okay?'

Skelton shook his head. 'Let's go outside.'

They stood in the courtyard, two middle-aged men in raincoats, Skelton still wearing his gloves, heads together, talking. From different parts of the building, a handful of students stared down at them through glass. Not long from now, Skelton was thinking, my Kate could be one of these. He did not allow himself to think she could have been the one they were discussing.

'How long,' Resnick was asking, 'between when it happened and she was found?'

'Not less than two hours, likely not more than three. She was due to play badminton, four o'clock. When she didn't show, her friend came looking for her.' Skelton glanced at Resnick and then off towards the middle distance, trees glimpsed against the horizon, dark against darkening clouds. 'She was found around half four. Last anyone had seen her before that, as far as we can tell, far as we've been able to check, about half twelve she walked up that path to the university.'

'No one saw her come back?'

'Apparently not.'

Resnick turned in the direction of the room. 'No matter how quick that all happened, somebody must have heard.'

Skelton shook his head.

'There must be – what? – sixty students living here. More.'

'Most of them home for the weekend. Those that weren't, out somewhere. Shopping in the city. Working in the library. Just out.'

'Any sign of the weapon?'

'Not so far.' Skelton stood looking out across the slope of meadow. 'If it's out there somewhere, we'll find it but it'll take time.'

'The wounds,' Resnick said, 'were they . . . ?'

'Not too similar to the hospital incidents, if that's what you're thinking. More random. Frenzied. Whatever she was cut with, my guess is that it was a heavier instrument altogether, a thicker blade.'

Or whoever attacked her was angrier, more frightened. *Frenzied* – the superintendent didn't throw words like that around carelessly. Resnick looked directly at Skelton and Skelton read the question in his eyes.

'I don't know, Charlie. From the visual evidence alone, it was impossible to tell. But only the upper half of her body was clothed.'

'She could have been dressing when whoever it was broke in.'

'Or while he was there.'

Both men knew the other alternative. Until she was well enough to give an account of what had happened, or there had been time to examine all the evidence more closely, reconstruct as best they could what had taken place, they would not know.

'God help me, Charlie,' Skelton said, 'I know nothing good can hope to come of this, but something's been nagging away at the back of my brain denying any connection with all that other business; this isn't another Tim Fletcher, another Karl Dougherty. Poor woman, at least she was a student and not a nurse.'

'Was, sir?'

Skelton lowered his head. 'Figure of speech, Charlie, slip of the tongue. Let's pray it's nothing more than that.'

Resnick nodded. Amen to that.

Patel was sitting in the common room opposite Cheryl Falmer, notebook on his lap. The curtains had been drawn part way across and no one had thought to switch on the lights. It had been made clear to her that she could make her statement later, when she was feeling stronger, after she had recovered from the shock. But if you waited for that, you might be waiting forever.

Patel had been patient, letting the words fall out in broken clusters, content to piece them into sentences, a picture, a sequence of events. First she had knocked on the door, knocked again and turned to go away and for no reason she could think of now she had gone back and tried the handle. She did this and then she did that. Yes, Amanda had been inside.

'Would you like me to get someone to take you home?' Patel asked, when the story was finally told.

Cheryl shook her head. 'I think I'd like to sit here for a little longer.'

'All right.' Patel nodded understanding and sat with her, waiting as the shadows claimed the room.

The faces had disappeared from the windows. Lights burned behind several, illuminating photographs of families and boyfriends, posters for Greenpeace. A few TV sets or radios had been switched on. Those students who were in residence either sat on their beds stunned or got ready to go out for the evening. Saturday night. The search for a weapon had been abandoned and would be resumed at first light. Resnick had no excuse for not returning to his car and as he did so he was intercepted by a constable who had just taken a message on his personal radio: Resnick knew from the officer's expression that Amanda Hooson was dead.

Thirty

He wanted Ed Silver still to be there, reading his borrowed book with rapt attention and complaining about every paragraph, every other word. It was a night for company, conversation, a little controlled drinking: it was not an evening Resnick wished to spend alone. There were cups and glasses, unwashed, in the sink; upstairs Resnick's wardrobe door stood open and he wondered which of his clothes would come home next morning stiff with puke and cold. He thought of all the people he might call on the off chance and the list did not amount to much. Graham Millington had said to him, a month or so back, you must come round again and have a meal, the wife was asking. But Millington was parked in some motorway service area, a lorry park off the A1, cold and getting colder, asking himself over and over if all he'd joined the Force for had been this.

By the morning a murder incident room would have been set up, more uniformed officers drafted in, civilians to access all information, checking it via the Holmes computer. The investigation into the hospital attacks would continue side by side; CID resources would be stretched and stretched again. The DCI would be breathing down Skelton's neck, wanting a result. All of that was tomorrow: tonight Resnick didn't trust his own company.

Never having removed his coat, he let himself out again and hesitated between his front door and the gate. He sat in his car for fifteen, twenty minutes, letting the blackness thicken around him. Once, he thought he heard the telephone, muted, from inside the house. When it was quiet he got back out of the car and Dizzy ran along the top of the wall towards his hand. Against the black sheen of his coat, Dizzy's eyes were alive and dangerous. This was his time. Where Resnick wanted to be was somewhere dull and safe. Known. Hands in his pockets, he set off towards the main road, past homes where the plates were being dried and stacked away, something good on the box at half-past eight, be quick, don't be late.

Please come, Charles, we would all love to see you.

Only a dull light seemed to be burning deep in the hallway, faded orange through the triptych of stained glass beside the heavy wooden door. Resnick tried the bell again and heard another door, within the house, being firmly closed. Footsteps, brighter light, turning of the lock: when Marian Witczak appeared, the first of several clocks began to chime from different rooms, none pitched or set the same.

'Charles.' Surprise and pleasure mixed in her voice.

'The invitation, I know I should have replied . . .'

'Charles! Really, you are going to come? How nice.' She reached forward and took his hands, leading him into the tiled hall. 'I hoped, of course, but never really expected . . .'

'I know. I've not been a good friend.'

'Always, you are so busy.'

Resnick nodded and offered up something of a smile. He was already beginning to wonder if he should have come. Marian had obviously spent time getting ready. She was wearing a tightly-waisted orange dress that fell away in loose pleats almost to her ankles; her collar bones stood gaunt below thin straps, a silver brooch like a spider above her breast. Lifted off her face and tightly coiled behind, her hair accentuated the hollowness beneath her cheekbones. Her flat, black shoes had silver buckles, large and square.

'I shall not be the only one pleased to see you,' Marian said. 'There is a feeling, perhaps you have deserted us.'

Resnick shook his head. 'Don't make me feel guilty, Marian. Besides, it's you I've come to see, not the whole damned community.' He saw her disapproving face and found a more convincing smile. 'You did say it was a party. I remember how you like to dance.'

Marian reached out again and patted his hand. 'Please come and wait for me. I shall not be long.'

Holding his arm, she led him along the wide, tiled hall into a room of oak and dried flowers that had scarcely changed since Resnick had first seen it, more than thirty years before. Marian left him for a moment then returned, pressing a small cut glass into his hand. It was sweet plum brandy and he sipped at it as he stood by the French windows, looking out. It wasn't simply that Marian, more or less his contemporary, made him unusually conscious of his age – stepping across this threshold was like stepping into another country. One which had little place in reality, least of all, perhaps, in Poland itself.

During the strikes, the demonstrations, the celebrations of democracy, Marian and her friends had watched in fascination every television picture, scanned newspaper after newspaper, each of them searching for a face they recognized, a street corner, a café. Resnick had never been there, where Marian Witczak still called home. Whenever he said the word, Resnick saw different pictures in his head, heard different voices, St Anne's rather than the Stare Miasto, not the Vistula but the Trent.

'See, Charles, I am ready.'

She stood in the doorway, a shawl of rich, black lace around her shoulders; small, white flowers pinned above her waist. She smelt of lilies of the valley. 'Of course, Charles,' she said, 'I am grateful that you are here. But let us face the truth: I have written you such notes before.

What brings you here is less to see me, more whatever it may be you wish to turn your back upon.'

She put Resnick's glass aside and offered him her gloved hand. 'Tonight,' she said, 'we will have a fine time. You see,' glancing down at the gleaming buckles, 'I have on my dancing shoes.'

At first Resnick sat near the back of the main room, nursing his beer while Marian moved from table to table, table to bar, greeting those she had not seen since last year or last week with grave enthusiasm. The younger men stared at Resnick sullenly, knowing who he was and what he did.

At the head of the main table, the guest of honour drank peppermint vodka on the quarter hour and chainsmoked small dark cigars pressed upon him by his eager sons-in-law, mindful of what might one day soon be theirs. His daughters brought out a cake, festooned with chocolate flakes and candles and icing in red-and-white horizontal stripes: the committee made him a presentation and in the middle of his speech of thanks, the old man lost interest and sat back down to light a fresh cigar.

Resnick and Marian waltzed and polkaed and once essayed a nifty quickstep, until Resnick's subliminally remembered fishtail came to grief amongst the swirl of small children that jigged about his legs.

After that they ate *pieroqi*, and when the treasurer tapped Resnick on the shoulder, he reached for his cheque-book without delay.

'You see, Charles, you should join us more often. Then you would not look, always, so sad.' She touched the backs of her fingers lightly to his face. 'Here it is a haven; here you may forget.'

The accordion player did a passable job on Chuck Berry's 'Johnny B Goode' and then led the band into an old Polish dance that had the men dropping alternately to right knee and left, lifting their partners off the ground and whirling them round.

Marian clapped along until her hands glowed.

Someone came and whispered in her ear and she blushed and agreed, excusing herself from Resnick to climb on to the stage and stand well behind the microphone. In a small, strong voice, to a lilting tune, she sang about a young girl who has been abandoned by her lover and still waits for him at the field edge, before a bank of trees.

When my hair turns white
Will you remember
that I was once young here?
I'll keep faith forever
till only death overtake me.

There was a pause and then applause, those at the rear slapping the tables, stamping their feet. The band began a waltz and she stepped off the stage towards Resnick, hands outstretched. What else could he do? They made two circuits of the small floor to more applause, before others joined them and when the dance at last ended there was scarcely room to move.

'I sang that once when I was twelve,' Marian said. 'We were all here, my family, your family. My father lifted me up on to a chair to sing and when it was over, your mother pushed you forwards to give thanks. Do you remember?'

'Yes,' Resnick said, remembering nothing. Surely it had been another boy, not him at all?

As they walked back towards their table, Resnick was aware of people looking at them, weighing their futures in the balance.

'At least,' Marian smiled, seeing his embarrassment, 'they're not saying what a lovely couple we make.'

'Oh, but you do!'

The exclamation came from close behind and as both

Resnick and Marian turned, a woman lurched towards them, dark hair and wild eyes.

'You do, you really do.'

Startled moments before Resnick recognized his former wife, before he recognized Elaine: sunken cheeks and patched skin, fiercely hacked hair, eyes that glowed back at him as if from the centre of another face.

'Well,' Elaine said. 'Old times. Me and you and Marian. This place.' She was standing unsteadily, never quite still. If she stops waving her arms, Resnick thought, she might fall down. 'Pretty wonderful out there, the two of you, prancing about. The light fantastic. Ginger Rogers and Fred Astaire.'

She smiled lopsidedly, slipped and when Resnick reached out a hand to steady her, she flapped him away.

'Got to hand it to you, Marian,' she said. 'The way you've prised him out of his shell. More than I could usually manage.'

Marian's eyes focused on Resnick, distressed, appealing. Around them people were ceasing to drink or talk, no longer pretending not to be watching.

'One quick turn round the floor at the end of the evening,' Elaine was saying. 'If I was lucky.' She smiled conspiratorially at Marian. 'It gets like that towards the end. They lose interest. All of them. You'll see.'

Marian looked away but it didn't matter: the words weren't really for her, and Resnick and Elaine both knew it.

'Elaine,' Resnick said. 'Please.'

'*Please*, Charlie? Is that pretty-please, or is it the other kind?'

Resnick sighed and looked towards the floor.

'Don't look so hangdog, Charlie. It's just girl talk. Marian and I having a nice little chat . . .'

'Elaine,' Resnick said.

'Yes?'

'This isn't the place.'

'Oh, but it is. You're here. She's here . . .'

'No.'

'Charlie, you're not embarrassed? Don't tell me you're embarrassed? Not after watching Marian singing about a late lamented lover. Some people might have thought that was a bit of a spectacle, Marian pretending to be a sweet little virgin, but there you were, Charlie, clapping along with the rest of them.'

Tears of shame in her eyes, Marian pushed her way towards the exit. Resnick started after her, stopped, turned back.

'Difficult, isn't it?' Elaine said. 'Which way for that famous bleeding heart to jump? Your lover or your wife?'

'She's not . . .'

'Your lover? I daresay. And I'm not your wife.'

The band had stopped playing. There were hardly any other voices to be heard.

'But you know all about that,' Elaine said, backing towards the dance floor, looking all around. 'Charlie's tragic divorce. You were at the wedding, some of you. Remember? Whom no man shall put asunder. Except you, Charlie. Not so much put asunder as shut out. And you know the reason? I expect you all know the reason, but just in case . . .'

'Elaine . . .'

'Just in case you don't . . .'

'Elaine . . .'

'The reason was I didn't want to have babies . . .'

'Elaine, for God's sake!'

'Pretty little babies to make him tall and proud . . .'

Resnick slid his face slowly down into his hands.

'. . . and call him Da-da.'

Resnick didn't move. Blood was pumping fiercely inside his head, against his ears and he didn't move.

'What's the matter, Charlie?' Elaine said. 'Too near the truth?'

He lowered his hands, opened his eyes and looked at her, anger thick in his face.

'You'd rather everyone thought you chucked me out because you caught me on the mattress of someone else's bed, fucking another man. They'd understand that, not, but not . . . No, Charlie, let me finish. Don't pull me! Don't touch me! Let me finish telling them what kind of a caring, compassionate man you really are. Let me tell them about the letters, Charlie. All the letters I sent you, the ones you never answered. All the times I rang up in pain and you hung up without a word.'

He wanted to strike her, hit her, wanted to smother her mouth, shelter from the taunt of her words and eyes. Her words broke over him as he turned and walked away.

'Stay and tell them about all that, Charlie. How you helped me with everything I've been going through. How you fucking helped . . .'

The sudden rush of cold air rocked him on his feet; a lorry climbing the hill missed a gear and he jumped. A black and white cab turned up from the city with its roof light shining and Resnick flagged it down, bundling himself into the warm upholstery of the back.

'Where to?' the driver asked.

'Anywhere,' Resnick said. 'Just drive.'

Thirty-one

'Shit!' Calvin exclaimed, stepping barefooted into the splashes that his father had left around the toilet bowl. 'Grown man, might have thought he'd've learned to piss straight!' He finished his own business, dabbed at the soles of his feet with a towel, tore off some sheets of paper and wiped up the floor. Might as well do the rest while I'm at it. Calvin used more paper around the rim and just a little way down into the bowl, dumped it inside and flushed. Now rinse your hands under the tap. Last thing he wanted to do, catch some kind of disease, end up in hospital: last place he wanted to be. Let those doctors get their hands on you and you never knew where it was going to end.

His father was in the kitchen, drinking black tea with lemon – his Sunday favourite – and reading his way through the *News of the World*. What was the matter with *Sunday Sport*, that's what Calvin wanted to know? Women with 62-inch chests and three-headed babies, something truly gross to get the day on its way.

'You ready to eat?' his father asked, scarcely looking up.

'Just about.'

'Pancakes?'

'Why not?'

Every week the same little ritual. The batter was already mixed, buckwheat flour and plain, a nub of lard that his father would wipe round the inside of the pan, barely greasing it over before cooking each one. Sugar. Lemons. Strawberry jam. Calvin checked to see if there was any juice in the fridge, but was out of luck. He flicked on the kettle and reached for the huge caterer's tin of Nescafé his father had found on one of his foraging trips. Special offers, past-the-sale-date bargains, he would cycle half-way across the city to save fifty pence.

'You got in late last night,' his father said, refolding the paper.

'So?'

'Nothing. Simply a remark.'

'Yeh, well,' Calvin said, stirring hard to prevent the powder from collecting on the top of his mug, 'keep them to yourself, right?'

His father hummed a few bars of some old song Calvin vaguely recognized and lit the gas beneath the pan. 'How was your mother?'

Calvin shrugged, hunched over his drink, thin-backed in black. 'Same.'

'Sister?'

'Same.'

'Damn it, boy!'

'What?'

A rare anger flared briefly in Ridgemount's eyes and then it was gone. Shaking his head, he turned back to the stove, tilting the pan this way and that before pouring in the first of the batter. Calvin read the soccer reports. His father shook the pan to make sure the pancake wasn't sticking, tossed it through a lazy somersault and set it back down on the gas for a final minute.

'Your mother and me, we were together a long time. I just want to know how she is.' He slid the pancake, speckled brown, on to Calvin's plate. 'That so difficult to understand?'

'Yes.'

His father shook his head slowly and looked away.

'She left you. Walked out. Now she's living with some other bloke, won't hear your name mentioned in the house. Minute I walk into it, he sods off down the garden into his shed or takes their pathetic dog for a walk. No, I don't understand.'

'She had her reasons.'

'Yeh, didn't she just!'

'Calvin . . .'

'Yeh?'

But his father was back at the stove, the next pancake soon on its way. 'Marjorie,' he said, eyes on what he was doing, 'she asked about me, didn't she? Asked about her daddy?'

'Yes,' Calvin said, through a mouthful of breakfast, 'course she did. I told her you were fine.'

'You say I was missing her?'

'That, too.'

'Good, good. Now here,' lifting the pan, 'you get ready for this one. I'll make mine next.'

Marjorie had asked about him, Calvin was thinking, just found time to stick her head round the door and squeeze the words out. Looking like she'd just spent more getting her hair done than Calvin had to spend in a week. Two weeks. 'How's school?' Calvin had said, but she was already lost to sight. 'She has such a lot of friends now,' his mother had said. 'Nice young people.' Calvin had watched a film with his father once, about a girl whose skin had been light enough for her to pass as white. Nice young black people, he wanted to ask his mother, or now you're stuck out here in Burton Joyce isn't there any such thing?

He squeezed some lemon juice, sprinkled sugar. 'How is your dad?' she had asked. 'Still having his attacks?'

'What attacks?'

'Oh, you know, nightmares. Whatever you want to call them?'

'No,' Calvin had said. 'No, he doesn't have them any more. He's fine.'

'Ready for another?' his father asked.

'In a minute. Do your own.'

How would he know the frequency of his father's screams, used as he was to falling asleep with the sounds of Aerosmith or Led Zeppelin throbbing in his ears, leaving the headphones in place all night long.

Certain that after his confrontation with Elaine he would never be able to sleep, Resnick had been fast off the moment his head had eventually hit the pillow. When he awoke it was to the rhythmic clawing of the cats and the rasp of an eager neighbour's hedge trimmer. His hair had been matted to his scalp by sweat and his sheets were a damp, cold tangle from which it was difficult to move.

He got ready as soon as possible, listening all the while for evidence that the previous night had not been a guilty dream. Now, more than before, when the telephone rang his first fear would be that it was Elaine. A taxi drawing up outside, ringing at the door – he didn't know when she would come, yet suspected that she would. Where had she gone at the end of that ghastly evening? Where in the city might she be staying? Questions that Resnick needed answering; answers he didn't want to know. He held his breath as he opened the front door, glanced along the street in both directions before letting himself into the car. Relax, Charlie, she won't skulk in shadows. Not now. She's spat all that out of her system, hawked the worst of the anger off her chest. Resnick slipped the engine into gear, indicated and pulled away. Now, he smiled ruefully, that she's broken the ice. Reaching the main road he turned right. We all know what waits beneath the ice, black, cold and seemingly unending.

He parked outside Marian's house and rang the bell.

Upstairs the curtains were forbiddingly drawn across; otherwise there was no sign of life. He could understand if today Marian had no inclination to speak to anyone, himself least of all. Still he tried again and waited. If she weren't inside, waiting for him to leave, she would be at

Mass. Resnick considered, but only for moments, waiting outside the Polish church for her to leave. All too easy to picture the scorn and curiosity on the faces of the congregation when they walked out of the incense and into the daylight, staring at him from their state of grace.

He got back into his car and set off towards the hospital. While there he would be able to buy some flowers, leave them on her doorstep with a note, *Dear Marian . . .* Perhaps in another six months he would pick up the phone and she would answer, perhaps not. Now, thank God, there was police business to attend to.

Karl Dougherty was no longer in intensive care, back down on the same ward as Fletcher, though not the same bay. A nurse approached, smiling warily, about to shoo Resnick away until the start of proper visiting, but his warrant card and a returning smile won him access to the bedside and the expected warning. 'Don't stay too long now. He's still quite weak. Don't want to tire him out.'

Dougherty looked pale but pleased to have a visitor, sucking up pineapple juice through a bendy straw. 'I've been talking to a friend of yours,' Resnick said, the conventional queries and formalities over.

'Paul.'

Resnick nodded.

'Yes, he told me. Apparently he's your prime suspect.'

'I wouldn't call him that, exactly.'

Dougherty managed a grin. 'I'm sure you could do better. At least, I hope so. Wouldn't want to think that whoever did this was about to do it again.'

'I suggested to Paul you'd been having a row before you left Manhattan's. He didn't deny it.'

Dougherty was quiet. A domestic walked past, pushing a heavy, insulated trolley. Late breakfast, Resnick thought, before reasoning that it was early lunch.

'What were you arguing about?'

'The usual.'

'Which is?'

'Oh, you know, inspector. Who's the greatest psychologist, Jung or Freud? If you had three people in an air balloon, Mother Teresa, Bob Geldof and Princess Di, who would you throw out first and why?'

'Seriously,' Resnick said.

'Geldof,' said Dougherty. 'He's the worst singer.'

'No, I mean seriously.'

'Sex,' Dougherty said.

'When, where or how?'

Dougherty smiled and shook his head. 'If.'

'Paul was interested and you weren't, is that it?'

Dougherty nodded. 'Just about.'

'Why carry on seeing him?'

'Because I liked him, because ordinarily he's good company. Because he isn't a nurse. I was prepared to overlook the final five minutes of why won't you come back to my place, why can't I come to yours?'

'And that's what you were arguing about? That evening?'

'It was a routine Paul went through. We both expected it.'

'Then why leave early?'

'What?'

'Why leave early? You left early, left Paul there to finish his drink. If it was no different to the end of any other evening, why did you do that?'

'Paul,' Dougherty said after a moment, 'he was getting more and more insistent. Said that it was as if I was ashamed of him, he said I was using him, he said a lot of things. I didn't want to listen to it any more.'

'You walked out on him?'

'I suppose so. I suppose you could say that, yes.'

'That's the way he would have seen it?'

'He might.'

'He was angry with you already. Frustrated.'

'He didn't do this.' Dougherty glanced down and Resnick imagined the wounds beneath the blanket. 'He couldn't.'

'He could have followed you from the club, seen where you were going.'

'I didn't mean that. I mean, psychologically, he couldn't have done it.'

'Is that according to Freud or Jung?' Resnick asked.

Dougherty almost smiled. 'Both of them, probably.'

'Physically,' Resnick said, 'could Paul Groves have attacked you?'

'If he was worked up enough, I daresay he could have found the strength, but he could never have got that close to me without my hearing him, I'm certain of that.'

'You want to be certain. The last person in the world you want it to be is him.'

'Of course. But whoever it was, they came from directly behind me. From one of the lavatories, the stalls.'

'You heard them?'

Dougherty didn't answer straight off. 'I don't think so. Though sometimes when I'm running it all through, only sometimes, there's this faint half-remembered click, like the bolt of the door being pulled back.'

'And you saw?'

'As I said before, very little. A boot or maybe a shoe, black. Everything was black. Trousers . . .'

'Trousers, not jeans?'

'I think so, yes.'

'And size? Did you get some idea of that? How big? How tall?'

'Around my height. Strong, obviously. But I don't think he was, you know, I don't think he was a body builder or anything like that.'

Already the nurse was hovering at the end of the bed and Resnick could see that he was coming close to outstaying his welcome. 'Karl,' he said, getting to his feet, 'you rest now. Someone will be in to talk to you again.' He lowered his hand as if to pat the foot of the bed and Dougherty winced. 'Take care,' Resnick said. 'Get better.' He would walk along and have a word with Tim Fletcher while he was there, find out if any little memories had clicked into place in his brain.

The Yorkshire puddings had sat there in the gravy, staring back up at him like little brown diaphragms, but otherwise Sunday lunch hadn't been too bad. Now Naylor was sitting in the living room with his feet up, listening to James Hunt and Murray Walker disagreeing about who was in pole position for the World Championship. With a murder investigation about to get underway, he was going to need what little rest he could snatch. Not so often the baby slept through an hour without waking to tears and you didn't waste it.

Debbie came into the room but Naylor didn't look up.

'We ought to be going soon,' she said.

No response. Mansell made as if to overtake on the inside, but at the last moment chickened out.

'Kevin.'

God! The whine in that voice!

'Kevin!'

'Yes.'

'I said . . .'

'I heard you.'

'But you haven't moved.'

'That's because I'm not coming.'

'You're what?'

'You heard.'

'Mum's expecting us.'

I'll bet, thought Naylor. I can just see the corned beef sandwiches, turning up their edges in delight. He leaned further towards the screen and didn't say anything.

'You can't stay in all day, watching that.'

'Why not? Anyway, I shan't be staying in. I'm going out.'

'Where? Where if it's not . . . ?'

'If you must know, I'm going to see how Mark is.'

'That's right. You do.'

'I will. Don't you worry.'

'Sooner spend time with the likes of him than with your own family.'

'It's not my family, Debbie,' turning to face her now, splutter of engines from the set behind him, 'it's yours. She's your mother, you go and have tea with her. Get yourself bored stupid listening to her prattle on.'

The tears were there, but she was fighting them back. Naylor was looking at her and then he was looking at the flat, painted wood of the door. When he swung back to the screen, Mansell had accelerated into the straight and was going into the final lap in second place.

Thirty-two

Lynn Kellogg had drawn the early shift and the logs were on Resnick's desk and ready for his inspection a full fifteen minutes before he set foot in the station. Amongst the usual spate of break-ins that would require Lynn's attention was one in which some enterprising soul had squirted WD 40 through the letter-box to stun a pair of angry Rottweilers, picked the lock and walked away with several thousand pounds' worth of jewellery and furs and the dogs' studded collars as souvenirs. The distraught owner had woken to find the front door wide open and the animals wandering around the garden in a dazed state, unusually beatific expressions on their faces. The first phone call had been to the PDSA, the second to the police.

Graham Millington was in next, limping as a result of half the night cramped up in the rear of a hastily converted transit van, watching the lorry park off exit 29 through a hole the size of a new five-pence piece. He was experimentally jumping up and down in an attempt to get the circulation going when Resnick entered with a headache and a Brie and apricot sandwich he'd picked up at the deli across the road.

'Going into training, Graham?'

'Not exactly, sir,' said Millington, embarrassed, casting a sideways glance at Resnick's feet to see if he was wearing odd socks again.

Resnick went through to his office and nodded for Millington to follow. 'Good weekend?' he asked, making a space on the desk for his sandwich.

'Not bad, sir. Pretty good, really. The wife and I . . .'

Resnick skimmed through the night's reports, half an ear on his sergeant's domestic ramblings. What was it that made for a happy and lasting marriage, he caught himself asking? Perhaps it was a lack of imagination.

Lynn Kellogg brought in mugs of tea and cut the catalogue of grouting and trips to the garden centre mercifully short. After that lot, Resnick was thinking, it might come as a relief to be shut up in a van for six hours.

'These obs, Graham,' Resnick asked. 'Any luck?'

Millington shook his head. 'We were wasting our time up round Chesterfield, while they were in business outside Ashby-de-la-Zouche.'

Resnick spotted Naylor through the glass of the door and got to his feet, waving to get the DC's attention and losing a bright sliver of apricot jam to his shirt front in the process.

'Any sign of Divine?'

'Saw him yesterday, sir,' said Naylor. Sitting in Mark Divine's new studio apartment near the marina, watching a worn video of *9½ Weeks* while they worked their way through a six-pack of Carling Black Label.

'Coming in today?'

'No, sir. I don't think so. He's . . .'

'Wrong,' said Resnick. 'Wrong answer. Injured in the line of duty, one thing. Getting smacked for behaving like a yob with libido problems, that's another. Ring him now, tell him I expect to see him in thirty minutes. Here. Right?'

'Yes, sir.' Naylor went back into the main office, doing his best to figure out what a libido was; he thought that Divine had only had stitches above the eye.

Millington was midway through making a tortuous request to be relieved of working with the West Midlands Force, at least while there was so much heavy activity on his own patch, when Lynn Kellogg came back to the door. 'It's Ms Olds, sir. Wants to see you now.'

Wonderful! thought Resnick. 'Stall her,' he said. 'Try and interest her in the delights of the canteen.'

'I did, sir.'

'And?'

'She laughed in my face.'

Resnick sighed. 'All right. Five, no, ten minutes. Tell her it's the best I can do.'

Lynn nodded and withdrew.

Suzanne Olds tilted back her head and released a film of smoke from between perfectly made-up lips. When Resnick was using the perfumery floor of Jessops as a cut-through, making for the market, that was when he saw women the like of Ms Olds, perfectly groomed and hard as teak. He guessed one difference might be Suzanne Olds had the brains, too.

'Are you saying this is an official complaint?' Resnick asked.

Unnervingly, the solicitor smiled. 'Not yet.'

'Maybe we should wait till it is?'

She swivelled towards him in her seat. 'Police Complaints Authority, officers from an outside force, one of your own suspended. To say nothing of the possible accusations: victimization by a ranking officer, harassment, bias.'

'If, if Ian Carew was under surveillance, it was with no knowledge of mine.'

Suzanne Olds was enjoying this. 'In that case,' she preened, 'perhaps we should add incompetence to the list.'

'Jesus!' sighed Resnick.

'Yes?'

'It's a game to you, isn't it? Somewhere between Monopoly and Scruples.'

'There's nothing funny about a citizen having his civil rights . . .'

'Oh, come on!' Resnick on his feet now, turning away,

turning back. 'Don't give me Carew and civil rights in the same breath. It doesn't wash.'

'Somehow he's forfeited them? If that's what you're saying, I'd say it was a difficult argument to sustain.'

'Yes? Well, there's a girl out there who had her civil rights severely curtailed when your client beat her up and raped her.'

'Wait.'

'No.'

'Wait a minute.'

'Why?'

'My client, these alleged offences, has he been charged? Never mind brought to trial, found guilty, sentenced.'

'The only reason he hasn't, the girl withdrew the charges.'

'Maybe she changed her mind. In the light of day, decided she'd been rash, making accusations in anger. Who knows?'

'How about this? What happened to her was so appalling she couldn't face being dragged through it again, in front of witnesses, knowing that he would be there watching her.'

'Melodramatic, inspector.'

'Better than being smug.'

'And rude.'

Resnick made himself stand straight and still and with an effort brought his breathing back under control. 'I'm sorry,' he said.

'Apology accepted.'

'He was given an official warning,' Resnick said, 'as to his future behaviour.'

'Towards the girl?'

Resnick nodded.

'As far as your knowledge goes, has he seen her again?'

'No.'

'Has he made any attempt to?'

'I don't think so.'

'Then how is planting a police car at the end of his street to be construed? Exactly.'

'I've explained . . .'

'You know nothing about it.'

'Exactly.'

Suzanne Olds was smoothly to her feet. 'If I were in your shoes, inspector, I'd be at pains to find out. On this occasion I was able to persuade Mr Carew an informal approach might be best; if he's given any further cause for complaint, I suspect he won't be as charitable. Oh . . .' pausing at the door, a trace of warmth around the edges of her smile, '. . . and there's a smudge of jam, just there . . .' With one long, painted fingernail she traced a line down the silk of her blouse. '. . . the corner of your handkerchief and cold water, that should do the trick. Good day, inspector. I know my way out.'

'Where's Lynn Kellogg?' Resnick demanded, pushing angrily into the CID room.

'RSPCA,' said Naylor. 'PDSA. One of those.'

Divine sat at the furthest end of the room, one-half of his face like a battered pumpkin several days after Halloween.

'You!' Resnick said, jabbing his finger. 'My office. Now.'

Information about Amanda Hooson was being laboriously obtained, systematically annotated, organized. As an exercise it was less than cost-efficient, heavy on personnel, essential:

'Mandy,' said a student from her social-sciences group. 'God! She used to hate it when I called her that. Anyway, yeh, she was just, you know, pretty straight, together. All she wanted to do was get her 2.1 and get back out into the real world. Wasted too much of her life already, that's what she said. Mandy. God, I still can't take it in. Amanda.'

The lecturer tapped the bowl of his pipe and began scraping away at the interior with the blunt end of a penknife. 'She was rather more serious than a number of our students, that would have to be said. Older, you see, not old, but older. Here from choice, real choice, not like so many of them, arriving on the doorstep straight from school simply because they forgot to get off the bus.' After the dredging came the replenishing, the tamping down. 'Great shame, picked up a bit in her final year, might even have got a first.'

'Hot weather, oh yes, sit out on the grass across from PB, hoick her skirt up and sunbathe for hours, ginger-beer shandy and some book about the extended family in Mozambique, homelessness in the inner cities. Not like some of them, stagger about between the Beano and Viz and still end up with a headache. No, she was a serious girl, woman, I suppose you'd have to say. I liked her. Liked her a lot.'

'Amanda! You're kidding! I mean, I don't want to put her down, especially after what's happened, that's dreadful, it really is. But, I don't know, the idea of Amanda going out with any bloke, especially a student, well, if you'd have known her . . . I can't think of another way of putting it: stuck-up, that's what she was. No social life. Anything that wasn't on the syllabus, forget it!'

'Yes, I don't know who he was, don't know his name or anything, but yes, she was seeing somebody. I'm sure of it.'

'Amanda came to my seminars, sat there writing it all down, sometimes if I coughed I think she made a little notation in brackets. Good essays, of course. Solid. But discussion – never contributed a word. Not my idea of a good student, I'm afraid, but there you are. I could show you her grades, if you think that might be of any use.'

'Terrible, terrible, terrible. A tragedy. A tragic waste of a young life. Truly, truly terrible. Tragic. Um?'

'We went through this period, last year. Badminton, right? I was beating her time after time, 15–6, 15–7, 15–5. Found out that if I kept it high to her backhand, she just couldn't cope. Amanda came back after the holiday and wiped the floor with me. She'd found this guy, county player, talked him into teaching her, two hours a day for three weeks. Backhand smash, drive, backhand lob, she could do the lot. Not brilliantly. She was never what you'd call a natural. But she was like that with anything, anything she wanted, *really* wanted to do. Got down and worked at it, hard as she could. Little things, important things, it didn't matter. Amanda had these lists in the back of her diary and she'd tick them off one at a time until they were done. After that she'd start a new list. Goal-oriented, I think that's the term for it. Amanda would have known; if she didn't she'd have been off to the library to look it up.'

'This diary,' asked Patel, 'can you describe it?'

Cheryl pursed her lips and nodded. The shadows beneath her eyes were deep and dark from crying. 'Nothing special, not one of those – what-d'you-call-'em – Filofaxes, nothing like that. Sort of slim and black, leather, you know the kind? Student year, I think it was, September to September. Carried it with her all the time.'

'I see.'

'You haven't found it?'

'I don't think so. Not yet.' Patel smiled and when he did so, Cheryl thought, not for the first time, what a nice man he probably was; what a shame he was a policeman. 'I don't really know,' Patel said. 'I'll certainly check. Now . . .' turning a page of his note book, '. . . perhaps you can tell me something about her friends . . .'

It was Millington who, having temporarily talked himself

out of the hijack detail and finding himself with half an hour in the enquiry room, chanced to glance at a report form waiting to be accessed on to the computer. Amanda Hooson, twenty-six, previous education, West Notts College, previously employed for two years as an ODA at the Derbyshire Royal Infirmary and then back to the main hospital in the city.

'ODA?' Millington asked. 'What's one of them?'

'Search me.'

'Lord knows.'

'Wait up,' called one of the civilian operators, looking away from his screen, 'I don't know what the initials stand for exactly, but what it is, what they do, assist the anaesthetist, make sure the gear's all in working order, operations and the like. That's what it is. ODA. Yes. Saw one on television once . . .*What's My Line?*'

Thirty-three

Lynn hadn't been able to work out if the woman was more worried about her floor-length musquash and her sable stole or the stupid dogs. She didn't know which might raise the woman up higher in her opinion and finally decided it was neither. How could you have respect for someone who drank Perrier out of cut glass and allowed her Rottweilers to crap on the kitchen floor rather than take them for a walk after dark? Nervous of getting mugged, she got burgled instead. 'It was stripped down to the original boards in here,' she'd said, pointing at the kitchen floor, 'but we had that taken up and new quarry tiles put down. So much easier. Scoop up and swab down, a matter of minutes.' Right, Lynn had thought, that and the money to pay someone to come in every morning, do it for you.

Five hundred yards away, Lynn knew there were families living in flats with rising damp, cockroaches, hot-water systems that broke down again before the repair van had reached the end of the street. 'It doesn't matter, Lynnie,' her mother had used to say, 'not where you live, it's how you live. My great-aunt brought up a family of five in two rooms with a tin bath you set down before the fire and an outside lavvie where the water froze across the bowl November to March. And you could walk into that place anytime, no warning, and not find a cup that wasn't washed up or a half-inch of dirt on or under anything.' Well, good for Great-aunt Queenie. Knew her place and kept it spotless. Huge bosoms and facial hair; a backside that made horses tremble. Lynn would have loved to see her weighing into the hardship officer at the DSS.

She swung left off the main road and turned quickly left again opposite the disused lido, bringing the car to a halt facing the university lake. Without thinking, she had been heading, not towards her own place, not back to the station, but to Ian Carew's. God's gift, that's what he thought he was. God's sodding gift! The way he'd come prancing past her while she was sitting behind the wheel, hours watching the short length of street, front of his house. Clever bastard, just to prove he could do it, show he didn't care. Sneaked out the back and gone off who knows where. A lot of people would have gone back in the same way, left her thinking he was inside all the while, a good boy, doing whatever good boys did. But, no, not in his nature. Cocky! Couldn't resist letting her see him, supercilious grin on his face and knowing she'd be looking at the way the material stretched tight across his behind. Much as Lynn hated to admit it, he had a great arse!

That wasn't what she was doing, was it? Fancying the man? Fantasizing about him? If she were, one picture of Karen Archer should do the trick.

Did you want him to have sex, make love to you?

The marks on Karen Archer's face, the eyes that could never once return your gaze.

He said he didn't believe me. Said I was dying for it.

The police in Devon had reported no sign of her; she still had not contacted her parents. What happened next? Posters in shopping centres and outside police stations up and down the country? An urgent message on Radio Four, between the weather forecast and the news? Or wait until a body turned up somewhere months from now? The wasteland south of Sneinton, along by the railway line. Wedged between the lock gates on the Trent Canal. Under a mulch of leaves and earth in the middle of Colwick Woods.

And now . . . ?

Amanda Hooson had been murdered in the early hours of Saturday afternoon, exactly when Carew had apparently been out of the house she had been so uselessly watching. Common sense told Lynn that if he had had anything to do with that, the last thing he would have done was strut past and throw suspicion on himself. Not with Lynn sitting there, unwittingly providing him with an alibi.

Or would he? It depended just how clever, how cool he really was.

Lynn locked the car and walked towards the lake, not the crowds today of youngsters waiting to hire rowboat or canoe and get out on the lake; lads who splashed each other with oars, occasionally overturning their boats and falling in; couples who moored alongside the small island and made love in the undergrowth, feeding the condoms afterwards to unsuspecting ducks. A stroll around might clear her mind of this, at least, encourage her to think of other things: whatever was going on with Kevin and Debbie Naylor, whether they'd get through the year without divorce; if her mother could persuade her dad to talk to the doctor about his depression, and if ever he did what the doctor might say. There were days, Lynn thought, buying herself one of the last ice-creams of the year, when she wished she had more problems in her own life, save her worrying so much about those of others.

'I was wondering,' Resnick said, 'if you had five minutes? Couple of things you could help me with. Perhaps.'

'Five pairs of hands might be more useful.' Sarah Leonard brushed an arm across her forehead; a curl of dark hair had escaped beneath the front of her blue and white cap. Something about a woman, Resnick thought, almost as tall as yourself; the closeness of the mouth. If last time she had reminded him of Rachel, now there was no such misrecognition: he knew who she was and she was herself

'Let me change this catheter and I'll be with you,' Sarah said.

'Fine,' Resnick nodded, wincing a little at the thought.

'Don't worry, I'll wash my hands first.'

They went out into the corridor and stood at a window, looking down on to Derby Road. 'I don't know how you do it,' Resnick said.

'What? Catheters, colostomy bags, enemas, that sort of thing?'

'I suppose so. Partly, anyway.'

Sarah grinned. 'It isn't all piss and shit, you know. James Herriot without the friendly collie dog yapping encouragement round your feet. A lot of the time it's a good laugh.'

Resnick looked back at her, disbelieving.

'The other day,' Sarah said, 'this young lad on the ward. Asked one of the student nurses to fetch me over, something seriously troubling him. "Staff," he says, "I don't know what to do, I've got this erection and it won't go away. Can you help me do something about it?" ' Sarah laughed again, remembering.

'Dare I ask?' said Resnick.

'Took him along a bucket and told him to get on with it.'

'What I wanted to know . . .' Resnick began.

'Not you as well?' A knowing grin, sending him up just a little.

Resnick could see his own reflection in the glass, a mixture of embarrassment and pleasure. One day, he thought, if I should ever get to know you better . . . 'What I need,' Resnick said.

'Yes?'

'More in the nature of information.'

'Go ahead.'

'An ODA.'

'What about them?

'What do they do? That would be a start.'

'Operating Department Assistant. Attendant. Some hospitals, they call them Anaesthetist Technicians.'

'And that's their function, assisting the anaesthetist during an operation?'

'The main one, yes. Supervising the machines, making sure they're connected correctly so that the right mixture of oxygen and gases gets through to the patient. But they can do more than that, act as scrub nurse . . .'

'Scrub nurse?'

'Handles the instruments during the operation, passes them to the surgeon . . .'

'Scalpel.'

'Scalpel. Exactly. Whatever he's using. Hands them over, takes them back.'

'Responsible job.'

'And she doesn't spend the day dealing with faecal matter.'

'Amanda Hooson,' Resnick said. 'Don't suppose you knew her?'

Sarah shook her head. 'Should I?'

'Apparently she used to work here.'

'As an ODA?'

Resnick nodded.

'We've twelve theatres, fifteen to twenty ODAs. When was she here?'

'Left around two years ago.'

Sarah gave it a little thought. Below, traffic was driving into the hospital in a constipated stream. 'No, I'm sorry. Though there is something about the name.'

'How recently have you listened to the news?'

Sarah's shoulders slumped. 'Oh, God, it's her.'

'Afraid so.'

'At the university, the student who was murdered.'

'Yes.'

For a moment, she rested a hand on his upper arm, a grip strong enough for Resnick to be aware of each finger separately through his sleeve. 'I thought,' Sarah said, 'when I heard it, a woman attacked with a knife, whatever, stabbed, I thought it isn't, it can't be anything to do with us here, at the hospital. She's not a doctor, a nurse, she's a student.'

'I know,' Resnick said. 'That was what I thought, too.'

He knew he didn't want her to move away, not yet, but, of course, she did, the bounce and the snap that was there before quickly returned.

'We'll be talking to staff about security,' Resnick said. 'Officially, I mean. Leaflets, possibly, I don't know. In the meantime . . .'

Sarah grinned, broader than before. 'Be careful out there?'

'Sorry?'

'*Hill Street Blues*. The sergeant, at the end of roll call . . . you never saw that?'

Resnick shook his head.

'Shame. I think you'd have liked it.'

Resnick didn't think so. Police series, films, he liked his fantasies a little less close to home.

'Sarah . . .'

'Um?' She was at the end of the corridor, making a fool out of whoever thought the wearing of a uniform put her on a par with all the others. Eyes, Resnick thought: why is it always the eyes?

'Inspector?'

'Thanks,' Resnick said. 'Thanks for your help.'

Sarah pulled open the door. 'Whoever's doing this, catch them before they do it again.'

The way to prevent your take-away tipping over or getting thrown around the floor of the car, Lynn had discovered, was to slip the handles of the plastic bag they packed it in over the gear stick, then turn them twice, three times. One king prawn danshak with pilau rice home intact. She was so concerned about getting it across the courtyard and into the flat before it got cold that she failed to notice the figure moving forward from the shadow until it was almost at her shoulder.

Lynn gasped and whirled around, bag ready as a weapon, poised to swing into her assailant's face.

'Whoa! Steady. I didn't mean to startle you.'

Lynn recognized the voice the same moment that she saw the face. 'God, sir! Don't do that.'

'I'm sorry,' Resnick said. 'I thought you'd have spotted the car.'

Lynn's breathing was less than steady. 'Other things on my mind.'

Resnick pointed to the white bag. 'Whatever you've got, think you could slip it into the oven on a low light, keep warm? By my reckoning, it's about time you and I went for a drink.'

Some pubs you ruined by making them over, rendering them new; others cried out for ruining before a dividing wall was pulled down or four generations of tobacco smoke was sandblasted from the walls. Sometimes the result was a freshened-up local with taramasalata or devilled prawns on the snack menu alongside cheese and onion cobs and pickled eggs. If you were lucky.

Resnick stood with one elbow on a convenient shelf and sipped at his Guinness, watching Lynn get down half a lager like it was water, which likely wasn't so far from the truth.

'I'm sorry,' she said, not quite bringing herself to look at him, unusual for her. 'I knew all the time I was sitting there it was stupid. Somehow, once it had started, especially after he'd come up to me, Carew, and done his macho bit . . . if I leave now, I thought, it's because he's intimidated me into doing so. And he'll know it.' She drained her glass. 'I wasn't going to let him do that, sir.'

Resnick didn't say anything until he'd fetched her another drink.

'You really think he's done something to Karen Archer? Something more?'

'I don't know, sir. I do think he's capable of it.'

Resnick glanced around. 'So are half the people in this bar, given the right circumstances. We don't stick officers outside their front doors at weekends, twelve-hour watch.'

Lynn looked towards the floor: black tights, sensible shoes.

'You've got good instincts,' Resnick said. 'A good copper. You've got a nose for it.'

Blood darkening the length of the landing until it stopped at the door to the small bedroom at the back of the house. The first time Lynn had interviewed William Doria in his office, something about him had prickled uneasily beneath the skin. At that time, there had been little enough reason for suspicion, a successful university academic, an expansive and loquacious man. Now, when there was more reason to regard a suspect with caution, why was Resnick holding her feelings up to question?

'Karen Archer,' he said. 'I wonder if that is where we should be looking?'

'You mean the new one, Hooson?'

'The timing could be right. We know he slipped out of the house, plenty of time for him to cut across the campus, meet Amanda, go back to her room.'

'Is there any reason for supposing he knew her?'

Resnick shook his head. 'She was seeing somebody, a man, we don't know who he was.'

'But Carew, isn't that too much of a coincidence?'

'Probably.'

'And besides, if I'm fool enough to be sitting there providing him with an alibi, why would he break it himself when he doesn't have to?'

Resnick gave her a quick grin. 'I don't know.'

'To say nothing of talking to a lawyer, making a complaint.'

A woman in Salvation Army uniform had come into the bar selling copies of the *War Cry* and Resnick reached towards his pocket. 'Maybe he likes drawing attention to himself, being at the centre of things, simple as that.' He gave the woman fifty pence and gestured that she should keep the paper. 'Unless he's being more devious, reckoning if he acts this way, it's going to take him out of the running.'

'Has it, sir?'

Resnick set down his half-finished glass. 'I don't want you getting into trouble on this, giving him cause to make his complaint official. And I don't want to be left feeling foolish again, not knowing what one of my team's up to.'

Lynn flushed, 'Sorry, sir.'

'On the other hand, I m not saying you're wrong. Let's keep him well in mind, see if something turns up that gives us reason for talking to him again.'

'Yes, sir.'

'Now, best get back to that curry before it's all dried out.'

Lynn smiled, close-mouthed. Resnick had one more swallow at his Guinness and followed her out of the pub.

He half-expected a letter from Elaine, a note; even his ex-wife herself, in the front garden of the house, waiting for what? Apologies? Reconciliation? Another burst of recrimination? Outside there was nothing, not even Dizzy, patrolling the night watch. On the living-room sofa, Ed Silver slept like a baby, wrapped in a blanket and still wearing a pair of Resnick's shoes that were several sizes too large.

Thirty-four

MURDER HUNT WIDENS

Police are stepping up their hunt for the sadistic killer who viciously attacked pretty 26-year-old student, Amanda Hooson, and left her for dead.

They have refused to confirm or deny that Amanda, who was half-naked when her body was discovered, had been sexually assaulted.

Police Superintendent Jack Skelton admitted yesterday that he fears a connection between this cruel and senseless murder and recent attacks on hospital personnel in the city.

Amanda, who had been studying for a Social Sciences degree, had previously worked as an Anaesthetist Technician.

Superintendent Skelton is anxious to contact a man whom they believe met Amanda for a drink at the University bar only an hour before the slaying. They are also urgently tracing her boyfriend, so far unidentified, so that he can be eliminated from the enquiry.

Amanda's mother, 52-year-old Deirdre Hooson of Amber Crescent, Belper, Derbyshire, said to our reporter yesterday, 'Amanda was a quiet, thoughtful girl. All she ever wanted was to help other people. I still can't believe this has happened to her.' Mrs Hooson continued tearfully, 'I keep expecting her to come walking through the door.'

'Let's be clear on one thing,' Tom Parker said, 'no matter what you may have heard or read with suggestions to the contrary, none of the medical evidence points to a sexual attack of any kind. That's not to say there might not have been some kind of sexual motivation; you've all seen the photographs.'

They were still pinned high along one wall of the room, curling already at the bottom corners. One glance was enough to remind the men sitting there of what they were engaged in and why. Aside from Resnick, the other DIs were Reg Cossall and Andy Hunt; the officer in charge of uniforms was Paddy Fitzgerald. Once this briefing was over, they would report back to their respective teams and set them on their way.

'We need something to break this open and quick,' the DCI continued. 'There's already panic talk out at the hospital, staff phoning in and crying off late shifts if they haven't got their own transport: the whole business will get worse before it gets better.'

'Surely, sir,' said Andy Hunt, 'the dead girl's connection with the hospital, tenuous at best?'

'That's what we're working to find out. Hopefully, by the end of today, we might have some answers. Meanwhile, we carry on exploring all the avenues we can.' The DCI stepped back, automatically buttoning his sports coat, unfastening it again as he sat down.

Jack Skelton got up and moved towards the Al flip chart suspended from an easel alongside the desk. 'Should've been bloody Rommel,' Reg Cossall murmured.

'Wrong side, Reg,' whispered Paddy Fitzgerald.

'Huh,' Cossall snorted, 'bugger wouldn't have given a toss which side, long as he was running the show.'

Bernard Salt misjudged his turn, colliding with the end of the bed and banging his leg; he cursed beneath his breath and shot a fierce look at one of the nurses who was fighting hard to stifle a snigger. He'd been aware of them that morning, the way they were all looking at him, staring when they thought he wasn't noticing, openly some of them, curious, dismissive. Salt wondered what Helen had done. Pinned up a notice in the staff cafeteria? Called a meeting? All around him he could hear the tainted wriggle of tongues. The letter Helen had sent to his former wife, crammed with accusations and half-truths. The copy which had been delivered to the hospital by hand, together with a note: so reassuring after all these years to have my worst fears confirmed. I only hope the poor woman realizes how fortunate she is that you are letting her go too.

He looked at her now, Helen, fussing down the ward in her sister's uniform and it was beside belief that he had ever seen anything in her. A small-minded woman with a look of permanent disappointment in her eyes. Even then, when their affair had been at its height. Weekends in Harrogate and nights at the Post House near the Ml. Escorting Helen down to dinner when she was wearing that awful red dress, velvet, that looked as if she'd taken it down from the curtain rail and put it through the machine. Now he despised her. One look enough to turn his stomach, the sight of her thick calves sufficient to make him feel sick. There was a way of quenching her anger, but he knew that he could never take it. Not now.

He swept off the ward and stalked back to his office; damned secretary had been the worst, the look she'd given him, anyone would think it was her he'd been unfaithful to. A typed note waiting for him at the centre of his desk, cow asking for a transfer to another consultant, to be expedited as soon as possible.

Bitches the lot of them!

And there was that bloody inspector, loitering in the corridor like a shop steward from the TGWU. Man in his position ought at least to shine his shoes in the morning, see to it that, if he was going to wear a white shirt, it was decently ironed.

'All that guff you wanted,' Salt asked, showing Resnick through to his office, 'lead you anywhere?'

'Not yet,' Resnick said, relieving the consultant of the chance to keep him standing by sitting down.

'Some crackpot,' Salt said, settling behind his desk.

'Possibly.'

'Damned certainty. Lunatic with a bee in his bonnet. Been put out on the streets, most likely, instead of being kept locked up, safe where he belongs. Don't mind telling you, I think this government's come in for far too much stick, but health policy, mental care in the community . . . Saving pennies by wasting lives.'

'Amanda Hooson,' Resnick said.

'Worked here, ODA.'

'You knew her, then?'

'Yes, but not well. Consultant anaesthetists, registrar, that's who you should be asking.'

'Oh, we will,' Resnick said. 'We are.'

'Well, inspector, of course I'm anxious to help. But this is an especially busy day for me . . .'

Resnick was already on his feet. 'There's nothing out of the ordinary strikes a chord, nothing that would have involved Amanda Hooson with either Dougherty or Fletcher?'

'Not that I can think of. She could have had contact with Dougherty, of course, dealt with patients from the ward on which he worked. But only in the natural process of things.' He signalled with opened palms that Resnick's time was up.

'If anything does come to mind . . .'

'Of course.'

Resnick let himself out, past the secretary pecking away at her keyboard like a demented hen. One of the anaesthetists who'd worked with Amanda Hooson quite frequently had since retired, but Resnick had spoken to two of the others and their responses had been largely identical. Neither of them could think of anything about Amanda's work at the hospital that would have drawn attention to herself in any way; certainly there had been nothing about what she did or the way she did it which would have invited such violent wrath and anger.

Dougherty was still in bed, the number of tubes running into and out of him down to two. He smiled as Resnick sat down, then grimaced.

'What can you tell me,' Resnick said, 'about anaesthetic failure?'

'Simply as I can, it's this. Patient going into theatre, okay? They have an intravenous anaesthetic to start them off, but that's not going to last for more than the first few minutes. After that they're breathing in a mixture of oxygen and anaesthetic gases. What these do, they send the patient to sleep, numb all sense of pain, absolutely relax the muscles. Now occasionally, thank God not too often, but it happens, only the muscle relaxant works.'

Dougherty paused for a while, regaining his breath, allowing Resnick time for the implications to sink in.

'So,' Resnick said, something akin to nausea starting up at the pit of his stomach, 'the patient's lying there, unable to move, and all the while . . .'

'Exactly.'

'Jesus!'

'Uh-huh.'

'When this happens, they can feel everything?'

'Not necessarily, not always. Most times, probably not.'

'But sometimes?'

Dougherty nodded.

'During the actual operation?'

He nodded again. 'Right through it.'

'Not able to move.'

'Or scream.'

Resnick was thinking about what had happened to Amanda Hooson, to Fletcher, to Karl Dougherty himself.

'At least I could do that,' Dougherty said. He was smiling, but it wasn't at the memory.

'Not the sort of thing that gets broadcast about, is it?' Resnick said.

Dougherty winced and eased himself forward, encouraging Resnick to lean past him and push his pillows into shape. 'When I was in the States, just a twinge coming out of the anaesthetic was enough to bring down lawsuits like they were going out of style. Everyone from the head of the hospital to the relief cleaner. It's not like that over here, not yet, but with the spread of private medicine we'll be getting there.'

'You saying that's a bad thing?' Resnick asked. 'Compensation in cases like this.'

'Absolutely not. But it does make a naturally secretive profession even more so. You know what it's like trying to get a straight answer out of a consultant at the best of times.'

Resnick nodded and poured him some Ribena, pinched a handful of grapes and thanked him for his help. 'How about your parents?' he asked. 'How are they coping?'

For a moment Dougherty closed his eyes. 'My mother came in a couple of days ago. I was in a worse state than this, I don't know if she knew what was happening. I'm not even positive she knew who I was. I mean, she said my name, stuff like that, but twenty minutes after she'd arrived she was on her way again.' He smiled gently. 'My guess is, she thought it was all a big mistake.'

'And your father?'

'Doing pretty well considering. Comes in every day, sits for an hour, eats my grapes . . .' Resnick swallowed the last one guiltily, pips and all. '. . . doesn't say much, but then I suppose he never did.'

Resnick backed away from the end of the bed, raised a hand in farewell.

'How about Paul?' Dougherty asked. 'Is he still a suspect?'

'I don't think so.'

'If he doesn't know that already, it might help him a lot to be told. He's not finding any of this easy, either.'

'Okay,' said Resnick, 'you're right. I'll see that it gets done.' As he left the bay, sidestepping the tea trolley, his stomach gave a definite grumble. He wondered what the chances were of trying the new sandwich bar on Bridlesmith Gate before reporting back to Skelton.

Going into the hospital with a group of other medical students for one of their ward visits, a tasty little episiotomy to be viewed and mulled over, Ian Carew had spotted Resnick, recognized him from the rear and slowed his own pace, no wish to remind the inspector of his presence. That gormless little policewoman was one thing; Resnick, he guessed, was quite another.

Coincidence wasn't going to bring him so close to Sarah Leonard and, visit officially over and the students beginning to disperse, Carew took the lift up to the ward where he knew she worked. Through the end doors, he saw her, leaning across some old codger's bed and laughing; Carew only able to see the light in her eyes, dark opening of her mouth, not hear the sound. So simple to walk through, fall into step alongside her as she went back down the ward, pretty words in her ear. No. Not now, he told himself. Not now: wait for the time to be right.

Thirty-five

The senior Consultant Anaesthetist was a trim-looking man of medium build, a livid mark high on his left cheek, birthmark or burn. He greeted Jack Skelton as though he and the superintendent might long ago have been at school together, even shared the same dorm, eaten at the same refectory table, though, of course, they had not. The two men hadn't even leaned elbows against the same golf club bar, though, true to say, the consultant had done so with the Chief Constable. Yes, and the Chief Constable before that. Skelton was a runner not a golfer, a few rounds of pitch and putt on long-past family holidays the nearest he had ever come to a tight-fought eighteen holes then large gins and business at the nineteenth. His education had been grammar school, a good one at that, bringing the industrious middle classes the trappings of a public school – houses, prefects, an emphasis on keeping a straight bat while all around you are flashing across the line – without the expense. Or the kudos, automatic entry into the élite.

It would have been easy for the consultant to have patronized Skelton, so easy as to be automatic. Better, though, to rein that back, keep it under control; treat the man as a fellow professional, one who's risen to the top, an equal.

They shook hands and sat in comfortable chairs inclined towards the window; with only a slight effort it was possible to see the trees along the avenues of the university park, those around Wollaton Lake and the ornate turrets and chimneys of Wollaton House itself.

Skelton declined sherry, accepted the offer of coffee, which came in white china and with biscuits on the side. There was a preliminary feeling-out, during which the consultant let Skelton know how many of ficers he knew in the Force who were senior to the rank of superintendent. In total it didn't number many and the consultant knew nearly all of them.

Skelton had his best suit on and he felt scruffy; the fact that the man was so clearly making an effort to be pleasant and polite made it all the worse. He set down his cup and saucer and explained in terms as sharp and defined as the crease of the consultant's trousers what he needed to know and why.

'Anaesthetic failure,' the consultant said.

'Exactly.'

'You really believe, as a line of enquiry, this is . . . er . . . germane?'

'Amongst others, yes. Otherwise, I wouldn't dream of wasting your time.'

Don't patronize me, the consultant thought, taking his china cup towards the window and gazing out. To the left, just out of sight, was the bridge across the ring road where this wretched business had all started.

'What do you want to know?' he asked.

'Everything,' Skelton said. 'Everything that's relevant.'

The consultant drew a breath. 'What you must realize. First. The phenomenon we're talking about here is precisely that. Its occurrence is restricted to a tiny number of cases.'

Skelton waited.

'I wonder if you know how many operations are carried out each year in this country?'

The superintendent shook his head.

'Somewhere in excess of three million. So whatever incidents we're discussing, they have to be seen against that context.'

Skelton crossed his legs and waited some more.

'Recent research suggests – and like all research of this nature these results should not be considered conclusive – there may be some degree of anaesthetic failure in as few as one in every five hundred cases.'

It was very quiet in the room.

'As few?' Skelton said.

'Exactly.'

'But not exactly.'

'I'm sorry . . .'

'The figures, one in five hundred, you said they shouldn't be thought of as conclusive.'

The consultant nodded. 'They could be less.'

'They could be more.'

'In theory, yes, but . . .'

'But that's not a theory you would necessarily go along with.'

'That's correct.'

Time for Skelton to nibble a biscuit, recross his legs; for the consultant to check through his window that the trees were still there.

'As far as the patient is concerned,' Skelton said, 'some degree of anaesthetic failure means . . .'

'It means,' interrupting sharply, 'there is likely to be some small form of awareness . . .'

'Small form?'

'Some awareness of what is happening.'

'To the patient?'

'Yes, yes, of course. That's what we're talking about. For some reason, some mechanical failure, or mismanagement, or something unique to that particular patient, the nitrous oxide, the anaesthetic gases fail to function correctly.'

'The patient feels pain.'

'Yes, of course. The patient is being operated upon. The . . .'

'Cut open.'

'Generally, yes. The whole technique, the reason . . .'

'Then why doesn't he scream? He or she, whoever it is, as soon as the surgeon makes the first incision, why don't they scream?'

The consultant shook his head. 'They can't.'

'Why ever not?'

'Because, usually, although the anaesthetic is failing to have the desired effect, the other substance that is being breathed in, the muscle relaxant, is effective.'

'Effective?'

'Yes.'

'Please explain.'

'The patient's muscles are totally relaxed, any movement is impossible; there is no effect on either consciousness or the control of pain.'

There was a fly now, in the still room, somehow a fly, impossibly loud.

'All the patient can do, while the surgeon does his work, is lie there and give no sign.'

'Not actively, that is correct.'

'But there are signs?'

'Oh, yes. Generally. Arhythmia of the heart, a rise in blood pressure – the difficulty is that these same signs more commonly occur in association with other causes.'

'So there is nothing specific? Nothing that somebody around the patient might recognize as a sign of pain, a cry for help?'

'Sometimes,' the consultant said carefully, 'the patient may sweat and sometimes . . .'

'Yes?'

'Sometimes, although the eyes are taped shut, there may be tears.'

Thirty-six

Otis Redding, that's who the DJ was playing when Resnick went down the curved steps into Manhattan's. 'I've Been Loving You Too Long (To Stop Now)'. It hadn't been altogether true, what Elaine had accused him of that evening at the Polish Club. About having to drag him on to the floor, one dance before fumbling for the cloakroom ticket, fetching the coats. When they'd first been going out, going steady – only Elaine's grandmother had used the term 'courting' and then with the slyest of grins – there was a spell they'd be dancing – what? – every Friday night without fail. Once, at the second-string Palais that was now the MGM, the corner of Collin Street and Greyfriar, they'd walked in on some kind of Otis Redding tribute, some anniversary, and just about every number that was played or sung had some association with him. 'Sitting on the Dock of the Bay'. 'Mr Pitiful'. 'Fa-Fa-Fa-Fa-Fa-Fa-Fa (Sad Song)'. If they heard 'My Girl' once that night, they must have heard it a dozen times. Resnick scarcely moving, pushed up against Elaine and her arms round his neck, saying, 'See, just because it isn't jazz, doesn't mean it isn't any good.' Right there and then, Resnick would have listened to Alma Cogan, Clodagh Rogers, Des O'Connor, thought they were wonderful.

Maura was collecting glasses from the tables, her hair like orange whip. 'Hey!' she exclaimed. 'What're you doing here?'

'It's okay,' Resnick said, 'I'm not wearing a cap.'

'How about cheesecake?'

'I'm not wearing that either.'

Maura picked up another couple of glasses with her left hand and transferred them to the column she was balancing from the palm of her other hand all the way up to her shoulder. 'That bloke,' she said, nodding behind where Resnick was standing, 'he's over there.'

'Good,' said Resnick. 'Thanks.'

Paul Groves was sitting with a young Asian who was wearing a light-green polo shirt, bottle-green trousers and ankle-high trainers with the tongue out and the laces mostly undone. Groves was wearing the same suit, tie slacked down to half-mast.

Resnick pulled over a stool and sat opposite them and Groves introduced him to his friend, who had an accent that was Handsworth via Hyson Green.

'I was in to see Karl,' Resnick said.

Maura leaned between them and placed a bottle of Czech Budweiser and a frosted glass on the table.

'Thanks,' Resnick said.

'I'll put it on the manager's tab.' Winking, moving away.

'How was he?' Groves asked. 'Karl?'

'Seemed a lot better. Amazing, when you consider.'

Groves glanced at his friend, flicked ash towards the ashtray and missed. 'Did you see him?' he asked. 'When he was in there, after it had happened? Before they took him off in the ambulance.'

'No.'

Groves blinked away the smoke that was drifting up past his eyes. Two girls, couldn't have been more than sixteen, pushed past the back of his stool on their way to the ladies. 'Bleedin' cheek!' one said. 'All right, though, isn't he?' said the other. 'Well, wouldn't kick him out.' Giggling, they pushed into the crowd standing around in front of the DJ.

'I keep thinking about it,' Groves said. 'Trying to picture it. What he must have looked like.'

'Don't.'

'Lying there in all that . . .'

'Don't.'

'No. No, suppose it's stupid. Daft.'

'Want another?' his friend said, making the nail of his index finger ring against the rim of Groves's glass.

'Yeh, thanks.'

'You?' he asked, standing, looking over at Resnick.

Resnick laid a hand flat across the top of his glass. 'I'm fine. Thanks.'

There was an instrumental coming through the speakers, organ and sax, a churning, rolling blues and a few couples had started moving around the small dance floor.

'Firm I work for,' Groves said, looking not at Resnick but at his almost empty glass, 'got a vacancy. Northampton. I was thinking, you know, time I had a bit of a change. Might, like, take it.'

Resnick nodded.

'What d'you think? I mean . . .' Groves shrugged.

'New place,' Resnick said. 'Fresh start. Sometimes it's a good idea.'

'But as far as you're concerned?'

'Personally?'

'The police.'

'Oh. No. Let us know where you are if you like, but no, far as we're concerned, feel free.'

Groves relaxed on his stool, unfastened another button of his shirt. His friend was on his way back from the bar, carrying the drinks. 'Pursuing a new line of inquiries, then?' Groves half-smiled.

Resnick said he supposed that was true.

'I know.' Groves pulled out the newspaper from beneath his stool and folded it back at the front page. 'I was reading it in here.'

UNDER THE KNIFE

Hospital staff in the city are now working in fear of their lives after police confirmed today they are investigating a connection between the murder of attractive student Amanda Hooson and the earlier violent attacks on two young men employed at the hospital. Security precautions have been stepped up and there is a strong possibility that visitors will be routinely questioned and searched.

Detective Chief Inspector Tom Parker said that connections between the three victims were being pursued as a matter of urgency. 'The one thing we don't want the general public to do,' the Chief Inspector told our reporter, 'is panic.' He would neither confirm nor deny that until the present danger has passed, both plain-clothes and uniformed officers would be on duty in and around the hospital buildings and grounds.

Resnick passed back the paper and stood up to go. 'What if he wants to go to Madisons?' asked one of the girls, coming back. 'Yeh, well,' said her friend, 'what if he doesn't?'

Resnick offered Groves his hand. 'If you go through with it, the move, I hope it works out for you.'

'Thanks.'

Resnick looked for Maura on his way out, wanting to wave goodbye, but she was intently talking at the bar, uncorking a bottle of Bulgarian red without taking her eyes off a man in a blue mohair blazer, short fair hair and a stud in one ear, more muscle across his shoulders than Resnick had in the whole of his body and roughly half Resnick's age.

There was nothing for it but to head home.

The smell of charred meat was strong, as though someone had decided to hold a barbecue there in the middle of the house. Smoke lingered close to the coving in the hallway and Ed Silver stood in front of Resnick's stove like the man who's discovered the wheel but can't immediately think what to do with it. 'Bastard thing!' Silver said, grudging admiration in his voice. He was wearing one of Resnick's light-blue shirts as an apron, sleeves knotted behind his back. Small darts of flame were sparking out from beneath the grill. 'Not be long, Charlie. Have it on the table in two shakes of a monkey's tit.' If the kitchen didn't burn down first.

Pepper's head lolled from the tin hat of the colander, half-asphyxiated, a cat in need of a gas mask.

Resnick went to take hold of the grill pan, but Silver stuck a bony elbow into his side. 'Relax, Charlie. S'under control.' Catching Resnick's breath, he turned to him disapprovingly. 'Bit early in the day to have been at the bottle?'

Whatever was simmering away in the various pans Silver had going on top of the stove was going to give new meaning to the words, well done. 'Right,' Resnick said through gritted teeth, 'I'll leave you to it. Everything you want's over there – salt, tomato sauce, fire extinguisher.'

He went upstairs to sluice his face, change his socks, work whatever had got lodged there out from his upper back teeth.

'What you've been missing, Charlie, someone to do this sort of thing for you. Make sure you've got a proper meal waiting for you when you get home. Never mind this sandwich, sandwich, sandwich. You must have a digestion like the M26 at rush hour.' It was always rush hour on the M26. Perhaps that was his point. 'Grazing, that's what it's called. Eating like that. Heard it on the wireless.' He gave Resnick a sharp, pecking look over his forkful of mashed potato. 'When I was with Jane.'

Let that one sink in.

'Jane?'

'You know. Wesley.'

'Wesley.'

'Yeh, that's her. I was helping her out.'

'At Aloysius House?'

'Yeh. Nothing, like – how would you say? – too specialized. Bit of cleaning, few things she wanted humping out the way . . .'

'No cooking?' Resnick had given up trying to cut what, in a former life, had been a lamb chop and was holding it between his fingers.

'Not yet, eh?' Silver winked. 'Got to ease into these things. Never does to go at it too hard. Full frontal, know how I mean?'

Resnick thought it was probably better that he didn't. He wondered if mushy peas had been Silver's original intention, or whether they'd simply happened along the way.

'Good, eh?' Silver said, pointing towards Resnick's plate with his knife.

'Distinctive.'

Silver beamed. 'S'what I said, Charlie. How it should be all the time. Job like you've got, can't be expected to cook for yourself. You need someone to do it for you.'

Was this how Ed Silver saw his future? Mornings doing good works for homeless alcoholics like himself; afternoons as Resnick's resident cook and butler.

No.

'She was here, Charlie. You know that?'

'Jane Wesley?'

'Elaine.'

Air clogged at the back of Resnick's throat.

'Earlier. Came to the door, didn't see as I could turn her away.'

'She came into the house?'

'Well, it did used to be half hers, Charlie. 'Sides, she looked terrible.'

'Ill?'

'Face like a bleached nappy. I had her sit down and made a pot of tea; slipped a drop of gin into it.' Whose had been the gin, Resnick wondered, Ed Silver's or Elaine's? 'We had quite a little chat.'

I'll bet you did!

'She's had a hell of a life, Charlie. Since she left you. One hell of a life.'

Resnick set down his knife and fork and pushed the plate aside.

'You've never finished! There's another chop waiting to be eaten. Apple pie in the oven, Mr Kipling, can't beat them. Winner every time. Charlie . . .'

'Let's be straight on this,' Resnick on his feet, back of his chair, staring down, 'it's fine for you to stay here, for a while, till either you get a room somewhere or decide to move on. But I don't want a nanny, I don't want a housekeeper, I don't want a cook and if I did, with the best will in the world, I don't think you'd get the job.' Silver sat there absolutely still, looking up at him. 'And I don't want a wife: especially the same one I had before.'

'Some people,' Ed Silver said a few minutes later, trying to coax Bud on to his lap with a piece of fat, 'don't know the meaning of the word gratitude.'

When the cat only sniffed the meat but wouldn't come any closer, Silver popped it into his own mouth, got up, and carried the plates towards the sink to do the washing up.

Ben Franks had been in the Buttery, taking his mind off an overdue essay with several bottles of Newcastle Brown, a couple of games of pool and the last half hour bopping around to a retro post-punk band with reggae leanings called Scrape the Barrel. He saw a bunch of students he knew ahead of him and called after them, running in a shambling sort of fashion past the library to catch up.

Four of them, three lads and a girl, they'd been across to the Showcase to see a film about a legless Vietnam vet who dies in a traffic accident and is reincarnated as a kung-fu Buddhist priest who's vowed to eliminate the Colombian drug lords. Chuck Norris, the girl said, was better than you'd have given him credit for. Especially playing the entire ninety-four minutes on his knees.

Somehow, heading down the grassed slope towards the hall of residence, all five became involved in a re-enactment of the plot, with the result that Franks finished up twisting his ankle and having to be supported the rest of the way home. Down on the level, they decided he could manage to hobble by himself and after a few steps his ankle went again under him, he pantomimed a dying fall and came down with a clatter amongst the dustbins. Groaning theatrically and allowing himself to be hauled to his feet, Ben Franks's hand brushed against something and he called for them to stop.

He picked it up and turned in the direction of the overhead light; he blew on it a couple of times, brushed away a persistent beetle and opened it up. There in his hand, Amanda Hooson's diary.

Thirty-seven

The slimline diary with the black imitation-leather binding and trim, metal corners at its four edges, lay on Skelton's desk, the sunlight shafting in from a cloudless sky, Indian summer. In a neat hand on the prelim pages, Amanda Hooson had written her name and both addresses, university and home, together with their respective phone numbers. Beneath she had put her passport number, current account number, national insurance number; the telephone numbers of her bank, doctor, dentist; the internal numbers for the Social Sciences Department and the Health Centre. Columns requesting dress size, hat size, shoe size had been left blank. At the foot of the right-hand page, she had filled in the name and address of her next of kin, to be informed in case of accident or emergency. There was an organ donor card sellotaped inside the back cover, but the necessity for a police post-mortem would have prevented it being used.

'Well?' Skelton said, early in the day but down to shirt sleeves already; things were going to get hotter as this day wore on.

Resnick and Paddy Fitzgerald were side by side, close against Skelton's desk. Resnick was wearing a green-hued tweed jacket with sagging pockets and frayed cotton at the cuff of its left arm. Fitzgerald was sweating through the dark blue of his uniform, little to do with the temperature or the unlooked-for sunlight.

'Well?'

Paddy Fitzgerald glanced, stiff-necked, at Resnick and Resnick looked away.

'I've had them in, sir, every man jack of 'em. Gave them a right bollocking.'

'If you'd done that sooner,' Skelton said, 'might have had some effect.'

'Yes, sir.'

'How many days searching that area?'

Fitzgerald blinked.

'Days?'

'Three, sir.'

'Officers?'

'Sir?'

'How many officers?'

'Twelve. All told, sir. Not, I mean, obviously not all at the same time, same shift . . .' Words withered away under Skelton's unflinching glare.

'I'm sorry, sir,' Fitzgerald said.

'You're . . . ?'

'Sorry, sir. I don't know how they . . . I don't understand how it wasn't spotted.'

'Maybe it was only put there last night,' Resnick suggested. 'Maybe whoever took it, kept it until yesterday, decided to get rid of it.' He shrugged. 'Always possible.' Even to himself, he didn't sound very convincing.

'Seen the state of it, Charlie?'

'Yes, sir.'

'Read it? The relevant pages?'

'Yes, sir.'

'You, Paddy?'

Fitzgerald nodded. The ripe scent of sweat was permeating the room and if things continued this way there was liable to be a puddle in front of Skelton's desk, not necessarily perspiration.

'What if,' the superintendent said, measuring every word, 'what if our laddie had sharpened up his blade, found another victim, some young nurse say, walking home alone, what if there was another body on our hands? What would you think then?'

Fitzgerald stuttered. 'I don't know, sir.'

'It only takes five minutes,' Skelton said. 'Ten at most. You gave him seventy-two hours.'

The sun was strong on the right side of the superintendent's face, highlighting the fine strands of hair above his ear, making the skin at the curve of the ear gleam.

'It would be nice to think,' Skelton said, that when your men go back over the ground this morning, any weapon that might be lying around underneath the odd dustbin might be found before it takes another half-cut student to do their job for them.'

'Yes, sir.'

Skelton nodded and looked down towards the desk, allowing Fitzgerald the grace to leave the room. After another moment, Skelton picked up the diary and leafed through it, all the colour-coded dots beneath or alongside dates, the times of tutorials and seminars, notes of books to return to the library or pulses to buy from Hizicki or Oroborus, her father's birthday. When he found the right week, he angled the page across the desk so that they could both read what was written in the column for Saturday: *Buttery. 1pm. Ian.*

Resnick pushed the door to the CID room open wide enough to call round it. 'Mark, Kevin. Job for you.'

Carew had found a light cotton sweater, pearl grey, and he wore it now, draped across his shoulders, a deep purple singlet underneath, white running shorts with stripes in two shades of green and a high vent at the sides. Reactolite Polaroids with silvered frames. On each wrist a purple and green sweatband. He didn't want her to think he wasn't taking this seriously.

He rocked forward, legs straight out, and flicked an ant from the toe of his left shoe. Brand new LA Gear, he'd made a trip specially into the city to buy them that morning. What was the point of having parents who were prepared to supplement your grant if you didn't take full advantage?

'You didn't just happen to be here?' Sarah Leonard said.

'Uh-uh,' grinning that cocky grin of his, 'I was waiting for you.'

'How did you know I'd be here.'

'Easy. I checked your ward rota.'

'You checked . . .'

'Lying around on the sister's desk.' Carew touched the side of his sunglasses, but didn't take them off. 'It's hardly confidential. Surely?'

'I'm early.'

'I know.' All right for some, Sarah thought, bit of sun and they're lazing around, taking it easy; here he was, didn't care if he had to wait over an hour, just as long as he got a little more tanned. But instead Carew said, 'You're often early.'

'Am I?'

'More often than not.'

'You'd know, would you?'

He did take off his glasses then and smiled. Conceited bastard! Flashing those blue eyes, Sarah thought. Why are the good-looking ones always so conceited? Or gay?

'You sound as though you've been watching me.'

'I have.'

Something prickled at the root of her scalp, along the backs of the arms and legs: not the attraction, not the heat. Though they were part of it.

'Why?'

'Oh, come on!'

'No, why are you watching me?'

'Now? Take a look at yourself.'

Sarah was wearing a loose dress which buttoned up the

back, deck shoes, no tights. Sometimes she wore a slip with the dress and today, seeing the weather, she hadn't, so there she was now, wishing that she had. Her hair wanted cutting, she had no makeup save for a touch above her eyes, a smudge of blue; she knew exactly what she looked like.

'I don't mean why are you watching me now, I mean why before? Why the interest in my hours, when I come in and out? What?'

'You know,' Carew said, treating her to a lazy smile.

'So tell me.'

'Why?'

'If I already know, tell me again.'

'What's the point?'

'Maybe I'm wrong. I want to know if I'm right.'

'It's simple. I've already told you. I think you're attractive. I want to go out with you. I fancy you, all right?'

Sarah turned to walk away.

'Wait!' He was on his feet in a second, rolling back on his buttocks then springing up, jumping in front of her just as the unmarked car swung round from the main entrance and Resnick, seated in the back, leaned forward between Naylor and Divine, pointing, and said, 'There he is.'

'What?' Sarah said, Carew not looking at her now, somewhere else beyond her shoulder, something that changed his expression to one of concern, almost alarm.

When Sarah turned her head, the car had slewed up on to the grass, two of its doors already open, front and back, two men in the process of getting out. She didn't recognize the first, a tall man with a large plaster on one side of his face, but there was no mistaking the second.

'What's happening?' she asked.

Carew didn't reply. For a moment, she thought he was going to turn and run, saw his body tense and then relax, the moment passed now. By the time the officers were in front of him, each a little to one side, he was almost relaxed.

'Detective Inspector Resnick, this is Detective Constable Divine.' Sarah watched the faces, impassive, saw the warrant cards in their hands. Resnick reached out a hand, not quickly, and placed it firmly on Carew's right arm, midway above the elbow. 'We are arresting you in connection with the murder of Amanda Hooson. You do not have to say anything unless you wish to do so, but what you say may be given in evidence.'

Carew glanced at Sarah, much of the colour gone from her face; he looked at Resnick's fingers, quite tight around his arm. 'Made up your mind, hadn't you?' Carew said. 'Couldn't get me for one thing, you were going to get me for something else.'

Resnick withdrew his arm and the three men walked in close formation towards the waiting car. The last image Sarah had of Ian Carew was his face swivelled round toward the rear window, searching for her, smiling.

Thirty-eight

'Don't suppose either of you saw the match last night?' Carew said from the back. They were turning left into Gregory Street, passing the houses the health authority had built for doctors, but the doctors hadn't wanted to live in them. 'Highlights,' Carew said.

Nobody answered.

Carew was looking at the side of Divine's face; someone had fetched him one hell of a whack.

'What happened?' Carew asked. 'Your eye.'

Divine stared out through the opposite window.

'I suppose,' Carew said, 'they don't all come as quietly as me.'

'You call this quiet?' Divine said. 'Haven't shut your mouth since you got in the car.'

'It's called being sociable,' Carew said.

'It's called being a pain in the neck, that's what it's called.'

'It's . . .'

Resnick laid his arm along the top of the front seat. 'Sociable is what you do on day trips to Skegness,' he said. 'You'll get all the time you want to talk later.'

'I . . .'

'Save your breath.'

'We wouldn't make a detour via my place?' Carew said to the back of Resnick's head. 'Pick up some other clothes?' He was beginning to think that running shorts weren't going to be the most serviceable form of clothing.

'You have the right,' the custody sergeant said, 'to inform a relative or close friend that you are being detained.' Carew wasn't looking at him directly, but off to one side. Resnick and Divine were behind him, ten feet apart. All four men were standing. 'You have the right,' the custody sergeant said, 'to consult a solicitor.' He handed Carew a typewritten notice conveying the same information. 'Is that understood?' the custody sergeant asked.

Carew nodded and set the notice back upon the desk.

'You also have the right to examine the Code of Practice for the Detention, Treatment and Questioning of Persons by Police Officers, should you wish.'

'I want a solicitor,' Carew said.

'You wish to inform anyone else that you are here?'

'I want to inform my solicitor.'

'Nobody else?'

'How many times,' Carew said, 'do I have to tell you?'

The sergeant's eyes met Resnick's for just a moment then flicked back to Ian Carew's face. 'Twice, I think, will be enough.'

The first thing Suzanne Olds did when she walked into the police cell was to turn right around again and walk out. 'What the hell's going on in there?' she asked. Resnick and the custody sergeant were waiting by the sergeant's desk; the constable who'd escorted the solicitor to the cell wavered uncertainly in her wake. 'Well?'

Resnick and the sergeant exchanged questioning glances. 'You tell us,' the sergeant said.

'I didn't know,' Suzanne Olds said, 'you went in for this kind of thing. I'm surprised you didn't order him to strip and have done with it.'

'I don't quite follow . . .'

'He's in there in shorts. A skimpy pair of shorts and whatever the temperature might be outside, it's pretty damned cold in there.'

'He has a blanket,' the sergeant observed.

'In Northern Ireland,' Suzanne Olds said, 'it gets called sensory deprivation.'

'Really? Here we just call it sitting around in shorts.'

'I presume you're intending to question him like that as well?'

'I hadn't thought about it,' Resnick said. 'Not as an issue.'

'You don't think it might put my client at a disadvantage?'

'As I recall,' said the sergeant, 'he's got a good, strong pair of legs.'

'Has he complained?' asked Resnick.

'He will.'

'I'm sure of it.' The beginnings of a smile around the corners of Resnick's mouth.

'Did he ask you for some other clothing?'

'No,' the sergeant said.

'Yes,' Resnick said. 'When we were bringing him in. I didn't think he was very serious about it.'

'Perhaps you should have thought differently?'

'If your client would like to provide us with a key and permission to enter his property, I'll send someone round straight away. Whatever clothes he wants.'

'And a chance for you to search from top to bottom.'

'Difficult sometimes, putting your hands on the right pair of trousers.'

Suzanne Olds turned to the sergeant. 'Why don't you find something suitable he can wear? Something other than a blanket. I'll wait with my client while you see what you can do.'

Outside, the sun seemed to have exhausted itself early and given up. An articulated lorry carrying an assortment of toilet-roll holders, towel rails, toothbrush racks and toilet seats had been in collision with a blue five-hundredweight van at the south-eastern corner of Canning Circus. The van had run the lights off Derby Road and gone smack into the side of the lorry, which had been crossing lanes on the opposite diagonal, the driver having taken a wrong turning in his search for Texas Homecare. A 67-year-old woman, listening to Postman Pat as she drove, anything to keep her grandson in the back from yelling on and on about his lost marble, had swerved to avoid the rear of the lorry, done so successfully, but then swivelled round in alarm as she heard her grandson fall forward from his seat. Not looking where she was going, she had driven into a brand-new caravan setting out on its first trip to enjoy the autumn in Mablethorpe. Now traffic was backed up as far as you could see on all six roads leading into the circus, and those officers who weren't involved with sorting out the chaos were standing at the first-floor windows getting a lot of laughs out of the efforts of those who were. They were making bets, back and forth: first traffic warden to be verbally abused, first driver to get arrested, first punch to get thrown.

'To be clear,' Resnick said, 'Saturday lunchtime. You went into the university, to the Buttery, the bar, to meet someone for a drink?'

'I told you.'

'Someone you didn't know?'

'Of course I knew them. If I didn't know them, how could I expect to meet them?'

Resnick opened his hands and examined them, palms up against the edge of the desk. 'Tell me.'

Carew breathed deeply. 'I didn't know her name.'

Resnick's gaze came up slowly from the palms of his hands to Ian Carew's face. There was some sign of sweat at the temples and he was finding it difficult to look anyone in the room in the eye for more than seconds at a time. He was beginning to be uncomfortable, but he wasn't uncomfortable enough. A shame the uniform trousers the custody sergeant had found for him hadn't been tighter still, biting into the crotch.

'I bumped into her a couple of days before, in the video shop. She said she was a student, well, most people living round here, they are, one sort or another . . .'

'Which sort was she?'

'Sorry?'

'Student. Which sort of . . . ?'

'English.'

'Was English or she was doing English?'

'Both. Except it's called reading English.'

Sitting beyond the end of the desk, Divine looked up sharply. How the fuck else would you do English if it wasn't by reading it? Stupid tosser!

'Have you remembered her name?' Resnick asked.

'I told you . . .'

'Oh, yes. You never knew her name.'

'It didn't matter. It was no big deal. All I said was, if you're not doing anything Saturday lunchtime, why don't you meet me at the Buttery? We'll have a drink. You can tell me what you thought of *Wall Street*.'

'Where?' Divine said.

'It's a film,' said Carew disparagingly. 'A video. We were in a video shop.' Pronouncing each word as if addressing someone who was hard of hearing or short of understanding.

Five minutes, Divine thought, that's all I want with you. Five minutes. Alone. Later.

Feisty, thought Resnick, senses he's getting pushed back on his heels and fighting back. All right, let's see if we can't get him to overstep it. 'Did you meet her?'

'She wasn't there.'

'Wasn't that surprising?'

'I don't see why.'

'Oh? Surely you expected her to come? You had asked her, wasn't that enough?'

Carew bit back the word, *Usually*, looked across at Suzanne Olds instead. Sitting there with her notepad on her knee, spiky notes made with a gold-tipped fountain pen, skirt slipping back along her thigh, good legs. Maybe later, when this was over . . .

'Are you saying,' Resnick persisted, 'you went to the bar specially to meet someone whose name you didn't know, who you'd only seen once before for five minutes and who you didn't think anyway was necessarily going to turn up?'

'Yes.'

'You must have wanted to see her badly, then? Wanted to see her a lot.'

'I didn't give a toss.'

'You didn't . . . ?'

'One way or the other, I didn't care. I was going anyway.'

'For a drink?'

'That's right.'

'Pretty much a habit, was it? Saturday lunchtimes? To the bar for a drink?'

'No, not really. Not often. Better things to do.'

'Not this Saturday? The one in question?'

'That's right.'

'Besides, there was this girl to meet.'

'Yes.'

'The one without a name.'

'She wasn't without, I just . . .'

'The one you didn't really care if she turned up or not.'

'Yes!'

'So, to meet this person you scarcely knew and weren't even bothered about seeing, to do this, you went to the trouble of climbing out through the rear of the house where you were living and trespassed across someone else's property? Is that correct?'

'I've told you . . .'

'What have you told us?'

'Play it back, for God's sake! I've told you I went out that way because there was one of your lot out the front keeping watch.'

'Detective Constable Kellogg. And you didn't want her to see you leave the house.'

'Right.'

'Why?'

'What?'

'If what you had in mind was as innocent, as casual as you've said, why didn't you simply come out of your front door like anyone else?'

'Anyone else doesn't have a bloody policewoman parked outside the door!'

'Did that annoy you?'

'You know damned well it annoyed me. You know damned well I complained.'

'It made you angry?'

'You bet it made me angry.'

'So when you went out the back, letting DC Kellogg believe you were still inside the house, that was in the way of putting one over on her?'

'Yes, if you like.'

'Teaching her a lesson.'

'Yes.'

'Bit of a habit with you, isn't it? Teaching women a lesson.'

Suzanne Olds was fast to her feet. 'Inspector,' she said, 'I want to talk to my client, please. Privately. Now.'

Out on the circus, the lorry driver and the owner of the blue van had got into an altercation about lane and blame. One of the more maternal of the traffic wardens had offered to look after the little boy while his grandmother made her statement and the boy had taken a bite out of her calf. When the AA man with a tow truck tried to attach the crane to the rear of the van, its owner backed off from his argument with the driver of the lorry to ask him politely what in fuck's name he thought he was doing. The AA man said if he needed to ask that there must be a six-inch square vacuum in the centre of his head where his brain was supposed to be. The van owner punched him in the face, whereupon he was promptly arrested by Ginger Houghton, who had been standing less than six feet away, watching. The crane was set in place, the back of the van swung round a shade too quickly so that the doors swung open and cartons of cigarettes began to tumble out.

'Any idea where your DS is?' Houghton asked from the door of the CID room.

'Sorry,' answered Patel from the midst of a half-ream of computer print-out.

'Only when you see him, tell him we've got a vanload of fags he might be interested in, bloke in the cells he might want to talk to.'

The sun might have packed it in for the day, that didn't mean it was getting any cooler. It was muggy instead. Suzanne Olds had removed her suit jacket and the cotton of her blouse was sticking to her; anywhere else, any other time she might have slipped into the ladies and removed her tights, but not now, not today.

'The name wasn't Amanda?' Resnick asked.

'No.'

'You're sure?'

'How can I be? I don't know what it was. That's the point.'

'Then it could have been?'

'Yes. I suppose so. It could have been anything.'

'Amanda Hooson.'

Carew scraped his chair until it was at right angles to the desk.

'Do I have to answer that?' he said, looking at Suzanne Olds.

'You already have.'

'Right.' Carew looked back towards Resnick. 'Right?'

Resnick nodded at Divine and Divine slid a 10" × 8" from inside a paper wallet and set it centre table. 'No,' Carew said, barely looking. 'That's not her.'

'Not?'

'The girl I was meeting. That's not her.'

'One o'clock.'

'What about it?'

'Saturday. The Buttery. One o'clock.'

'What?'

'You were meeting her?'

Carew was half out of his seat, eyes fixed on Suzanne Olds who shook her head and slowly he sat back down.

'Amanda,' Resnick said again.

'Inspector,' said Suzanne Olds, closing her notebook, fastening her fountain pen. The watch on her wrist was gold and told the phases of the moon. 'My client has been questioned now for a little over two hours. He's entitled to refreshment, a break.'

'Amanda Hooson,' said Resnick flatly.

'No,' said Carew, 'I don't know her. No. No. No. No.'

Resnick glanced at Divine, who reached into the wallet and removed a slim black book inside a plastic wallet and handed it to Resnick, who unfastened the wallet and lifted out the diary and opened it at the page marked by a thin strip of light brown thread and, placing it on the desk in front of Carew and pointing, read: *Buttery. 1 pm. Ian.*'

'I insist,' Suzanne Olds said, still pointing at her watch, standing now alongside her client's chair. 'I really must insist.'

'You know how many men there must be at the university called Ian?' Carew asked. 'Never mind the medical school. Have you got any idea?'

'I wonder,' asked Resnick, feeling oddly relaxed now, 'how many of those Ians bothered to avoid police surveillance on Saturday lunchtime in order to go for a drink?'

'Inspector!'

'I wonder how many of them, within the last ten days, have been given an official police warning after attacking and in all probability sexually assaulting a young woman?'

Thirty-nine

In the bad old days before PACE, Carew might have been questioned through the night; kept awake by interchanging pairs of detectives until he was too tired to know what he was saying, so exhausted that he would say anything if it meant he could get some sleep. In some places Resnick was pretty sure such things still went on. On Jack Skelton's patch, especially with someone as sharp as Suzanne Olds looking over his shoulder, Carew was assured his hours of undisturbed rest, usually to be taken during the night.

But, Christ, he was a difficult bastard to shake, impossible so far to break down and maybe that was because, beneath it all, there wasn't anything to break. He'd quizzed men who were belligerent before, and clever, men for whom the interview was a challenge, a situation where you dug in your heels and won at all costs. He still hadn't been able to disentangle two thoughts in his mind: Carew was guilty of something; but try as they might they were not going to prove that he was guilty of this.

And if he were, what about the others? Fletcher? Dougherty? Motivation? Opportunity? Resnick crossed the street. Inside the entrance to Aloysius House, Jane Wesley was standing up to a stubbly young drunk with odd shoes on his feet and the behind falling out of his trousers.

'Look,' Jane was saying, 'I'm sorry, but I've already told you. You can't come in here in that condition.'

'What fucking condition's that?'

'You've been drinking. This is a dry house.'

'Of course I've been drinking. What the fuck else should I have been doing?'

'While you've got that much alcohol inside you . . .'

'Are you saying I'm drunk? Is that what you're fucking saying? 'Cause if it is . . .'

Resnick tapped him on the shoulder and the man turned faster than he should have been able and aimed a head butt into Resnick's face. Instinct swung his face away, enough for the man's forehead to clash with the protective corner of bone at the corner of Resnick's right eye. The man stumbled back against the doorway, blood beginning to run from a cut above his nose.

'Oh, God!' Jane Wesley said, quietly, a reflex sigh.

'Who in fuck's name d'you think you are, pal?'

Resnick told him.

Contempt seared the man's face. 'What's it now then? Assaulting a police officer? Eh? Resisting arrest?'

Resnick said nothing, didn't move.

'Resisting fucking arrest, eh? That what you fancy?' He turned and smacked his head against the inside of the door jamb, trying for a second time when Jane shouted out and tried to push herself between him and the door and Resnick caught hold of him by the arms and swung him round.

'Hey!' called the man. 'Hey!' A light in his eyes. 'Don't you fucking manhandle me! Enough fucking damage already, you! This . . .' He went unsteadily back across the wide pavement, pointing towards the blood that was now running freely down his face. 'Fucking this! You see that? You see that? Fucking police, bastards, they never change. Never change. But I'll see you done for this, I'll see you lose your fucking job over this. Bastard!'

'Okay, Charlie. Why don't you step inside, out the way while I get this sorted?' Ed Silver by Resnick's side, looking shaved and close to sober in a jacket Resnick was sure he recognized.

The two men looked at one another, a small crowd on the

pavement becoming less small every moment, the drunken accusations pouring on and on.

'Go on, Charlie.'

Resnick nodded and went through the small square entrance and into the main room, the same smell of damp clothing and urine and cheap tobacco, the same as it always was.

'Will he be all right?'

'Ed? Yes,' Jane smiled, relieved. 'You don't have to worry about him.'

'What will he do?'

'To calm him down? Oh, I don't know, give him a lecture, give him a hug, send him off down the road with a couple of quid to get another drink. I don't know.'

They stopped outside the door to Jane's office. 'You came to see how he was getting on, I suppose? Checking up on him. He said you would.'

'That makes it sound awful. I suppose I just . . .'

'Feel a sense of responsibility, I understand.'

'Maybe that's wrong.'

She shook her head, smiling with her eyes. 'It's not wrong. Not at all. If a few more people did . . .' The sentence remained unfinished, the smile disappeared from her eyes. 'It's not that type of world any more, is it?'

'No,' agreed Resnick. 'Though I'm not too sure it ever was.'

For a moment neither of them spoke.

Resnick nodded towards the door. 'Has he really stopped drinking?'

Jane shook her head. 'No. But he's cut down. He's getting it under control.'

'So what's going to happen here? I mean, is he going to work here, stay here? Are you actually employing him?'

'I think it's more Ed employing us,' Jane laughed. 'I think he's decided we're the therapy he needs. Situations such as the one you walked into, they're not infrequent. I like to think that I can talk to these men, I can, I have done, but Ed, well, let's say, those that won't listen to me, they listen to him.'

'I'm glad. I only hope it works out.'

'Oh, you learn not to be too optimistic, but I think there's a chance.' She smiled again. 'As long as he stops trying to get his hand up my skirt whenever I walk upstairs.'

'You could try going up backwards.'

'Not the best logistical advice, inspector, if you think about it. No, the thing to do, I'll have to go back to wearing jeans.'

The baby was crying. Jim Davidson was telling jokes about Arthur Scargill and AIDS and Asians, and the baby was crying. Kevin had gone up and picked her up, petted her, patted her, changed her, set her back down. There was a lasagne drying out in the oven, pieces of the foil it had come packed in still sticking to the tomato sauce. Debbie was still wearing the dressing-gown she had been wearing when he'd left for work that morning. The baby was crying.

Kevin Naylor slammed shut the oven door and reached for his coat.

'You're not going out again?'

'No,' Kevin said. 'I was never here.'

The echo of the front-door slam was still reverberating in his head as he unlocked the car.

What I'll do, Resnick was thinking, make something to eat, coffee; half of the evening still ahead of him, he could play Lester Young and Basie, with Billie Holiday, Lester with the Kansas City Seven, the Kansas City Six, maybe the Aladdin Sessions, Jazz at the Philharmonic, 'This Year's Kisses' in '56 with Teddy Wilson, so slow that to listen to it was to feel the loss, the pain.

'Charlie.'

He turned sharply, the sound of her voice shuttling him through twenty years and back again, before she stepped from the shadows of the house they had lived in together: Elaine.

'The other evening,' Elaine said. They were standing stranded in the hall, not knowing where to go or why. 'When I was here with that friend of yours . . .'

'Ed Silver.'

'Yes.' The light from the stairs was making her face more gaunt than ever. 'Strange. Somehow I never thought I'd stand in this house again.'

'Neither did I.'

'You kicked me out, Charlie.'

'You went. He had the bloody Volvo outside with the engine running and you went.'

'And if I'd changed my mind? Said I'm sorry, Charlie, please forgive me, let's start all over again, would that have made any difference?'

'Probably not.'

'Don't forgive easily, do you, Charlie?'

He was breathing through his mouth, seeing her and not seeing her, under water, through glass. 'I suppose not,' he said.

'All those things I wrote to you . . .'

'I didn't read them.'

She stared at him.

'I didn't read them, tore them up, burned them, whatever.' He was staring at the floor, carpet close to threadbare from use, he could remember the day she'd met him off shift, driven him to Hopewells to look, pay the deposit, arrange delivery.

'What it took,' Elaine said, 'writing to you like that, forcing it all on to paper.'

'I'm sorry.'

'I was in hospital, Charlie.'

He turned his head aside.

'The valium wasn't working, it never did, not really. I went back to the doctor and he made an appointment for me at the hospital and they admitted me the next day. Once a week we'd sit in this room, all of us, and talk, but mostly there wasn't anyone to talk to, not anyone who was sane enough to listen, and besides there were the drugs and there were, oh, Charlie, there were other kinds of treatment, and because I needed to talk to someone about it I wrote to you.'

Now he was having trouble breathing at all, even through his mouth, though his mouth was still open and he knew the crying wasn't going to help either of them, hadn't then and it wouldn't now.

'Charlie,' she said, 'go and put the kettle on, for God's sake make us something to drink.'

There was a box of PG Tips that Ed Silver must have brought into the house and Resnick dropped three bags into the large pot, poured on water and together they waited in silence. After a while, Elaine left the room and when he found her again she was in the living room, leafing through last night's paper.

'It's you, isn't it? This girl who was murdered. That's what you're working on.'

He pushed a clearing on the table and put down the tea. 'Yes. One of the things.'

Elaine nodded. 'I used to sit here, when we were first married, worried sick over what might be happening to you out there, frightened that something would happen, that you wouldn't come back.' The mug of tea was in her hand, less than steady. 'Then later, when it had all changed, I used to sit here hoping you wouldn't come back at all.' She looked up at him. 'Does that shock you?'

'No,' sitting down. 'No.'

'I wished you dead, Charlie.'

'Yes.'

'So I could escape out of here and live happily ever after.'

'Yes.'

'You know, he had offices all over the Midlands, a house in Sutton Coldfield, a place in Wales with tennis courts and a swimming pool and I don't think he waited more than a couple of months after I'd moved in with him before he started screwing one of his secretaries. At the wedding reception I caught him in the bathroom with one of the bridesmaids. Last little fling, he said, and winked.'

'You should have left him then.'

'I'd only just left you. And, I suppose, part of me thought, all right, two can play at that game.' She glanced about her. 'I'd been dying here, Charlie, this house. I wanted something else.' She sipped at the strong tea. 'We screwed around for years, foursomes a few times, hard to believe, eh, Charlie, all those years with you when I wanted the lights out?'

Resnick sat there mesmerized by her face, this woman whose features were only half-recognizable, talking about a life he could only imagine.

'I was careless and I got pregnant. He wasn't interested, called me a daft cow, a stupid bitch, anyway, he needn't have worried. I took on all this fluid, problems with my blood pressure. Finally they got me into hospital just in time. The baby died and they told me I was lucky to be alive.

'No more babies. That's what they said: no more babies.

'Suddenly, the one thing more important than all the rest, now he knew I couldn't have one, he wanted a child, a son, an heir. God, Charlie, he turned into you. Except that he hit me. He drank more than usual, more than before, and he started hitting me. Places where it wouldn't be seen, wouldn't easily be noticed. Here, the lower back, the kidneys. My breasts. I backed his Volvo into the pool and I left him, sued for divorce. One after another his friends, the friends we'd had together, more ways than one some of them, they went up into the witness box and lied to their hind teeth. His barrister tore me apart and I was lucky to leave the court with the clothes I stood up in.'

She looked at Resnick and smiled ruefully.

'That was when I should have come back to you, Charlie. If I was going to do it at all. Instead of waiting till I became like this.'

'Elaine . . .'

'No.'

'Elaine . . .'

She placed her finger firmly on his lips.

'Don't, Charlie. Whatever you say now, by the morning you'll regret it.'

He would have been able, at that moment, to have taken her in his arms and forgiven her what little there was to forgive, maybe even forgiven himself. He could have foraged amongst the albums he never played and found *Otis Blue* and set it on the turntable and stood with his arms around her and said, 'Let's dance.'

Elaine stood up. 'If the phone's still where it used to be, I'm going to call a taxi.'

Resnick shook his head. 'No need. I'll drop you.'

'Charlie, you don't want to know where I'm going.'

At the front door, he said, 'Take care.'

'I'll try,' she said. And, 'Maybe I'll drop you a line some time.'

'Do.'

Elaine smiled. 'You can always tear it up.'

Forty

'Helen!'

Bernard Salt was wearing his white coat over shirt sleeves and a pair of tan cavalry twills that he'd bought from Dunn's more than ten years back and were still going strong. His tie was the one with little pigs on it his elder daughter had given him one Father's Day as a joke. That morning he'd slid it from the rack and knotted it swiftly, left the house before he realized and now he was stuck with it, no intention of appearing on duty without a tie. Besides, look at it this way, with half the hospital privy to his private life, half of those despising him as a heartless chauvinist, the remainder thinking, himself and Helen Minton, there wasn't much to choose between them, well, it was a gesture. Let them think he didn't care. If they were brainless enough to take the word of a neurotic woman, superficial judgements, well and good. He'd pig it out.

And with this other business, checks in and out, escorts and taxis home, extra security cameras, the staff whose job it was actually watching the screens instead of playing Find the Ball and reading the *Sun* – there were other things to preoccupy the hospital mind.

'Helen!'

This time she half-cocked her head, the slightest acknowledgement, before disappearing into her of fice and closing the door.

Salt opened it again and left it open, standing just inside.

Witnesses, no more meeting in car parks, fumbling behind closed doors. Fine!

'What do you want, Bernard?' Somehow she'd found time to have her hair re-permed and it was more like wire wool than ever. She stood ramrod straight, staring at him, this woman who had once teased from him a tenderness he had been almost frightened to realize he possessed.

'Very little, except to say how much I welcome what you've done. You were right, I have a freedom from personal responsibilities such as I haven't experienced in thirty years. Now that you have acted as you have, there is no way in which you can threaten that again. I didn't want you, Helen, I haven't wanted you for a long time. I don't love you and if I ever did, the way you have behaved is guaranteed to make me forget it.'

There was a slight tightening of the muscles in Helen's face, nothing more.

'Thank you,' Bernard Salt said.

Helen said nothing. A nurse came towards the open door, hesitated, went away again.

'I was chatting with the Senior Nursing Officer over coffee; I shouldn't be surprised if the hospital doesn't offer you early retirement, obvious stress, neuroses, maybe you could carry on doing a little part-time work . . . at a more junior level.'

Helen willed herself not to move until he had gone, from her office, from the ward. She willed herself not to cry. Tears enough already and what good had they done her? From the side drawer of her desk, she took the photocopy of the theatre report book and folded it carefully in half and then in half again before placing it in an envelope and sealing the envelope down. Better than crying.

'How long, inspector, are you intending to detain my client?'

'For as long as it takes?'

Suzanne Olds gave a quick little shake of the head. 'You don't have that long.'

'I'm sure the superintendent will authorize an extension of custody. In the circumstances.'

'The circumstances being that, aside from the girl's diary, you haven't been able to come up with a single piece of evidence that places my client in any relationship with the victim.' She used a small gold lighter to light a cigarette. 'Getting on for eighteen hours of frantic searching for what? A fingerprint? A sudden reluctant witness?'

'We can apply to the magistrate . . .'

'An application we would have every chance of successfully contesting.'

Resnick shrugged and wearily smiled. 'You'll do what you have to do.'

'And so will you.' She shifted the balance of the bag slung over her arm. 'The trouble is, you want to find him guilty for all the wrong reasons. You don't like him, do you? Not one little bit.'

Resnick looked back at her. 'Do you?'

Calvin didn't know what had got into his father lately. Dinner last night had been those little beef patties from the butcher down on the High Street, the one he'd sworn never to use again on account of some racist jibe he thought he'd overheard. Patties and tomatoes out of a tin, swimming around in all that pale red juice. Calvin hated that.

Breakfast today had been toast, toast and toast. The jar of beyond-the-sell-by-date honey had had a fungus growing over it a quarter-inch thick. And just as Calvin had been on the point of sweetening his tea with a couple of spoonfuls of that sugar substitute his father had bought by the twenty-eight-pound bag, he happened to look across at the paper and there the people who made the stuff, NutraSweet, were being accused of falsifying their research and pushing a product that could cause headaches, nausea, dizziness, blurred vision, depression, loss of memory, mood swings and swelling of the bodily extremities. Calvin let go of the spoon and sipped the tea as it was. He knew there wasn't a granule of real sugar in the house and though he knew some people liked to use honey to sweeten what they were drinking, he wasn't about to take a risk with that gunk.

Jesus! The tea had tasted terrible.

And Calvin never quite believed what he read in the papers anyway. He spooned in the NutraSweet and started to flip through, looking to see when Guns and Roses were appearing in the city, one thing they couldn't lie about, announcements, and he noticed that one of the pages had been torn away. The front one. He'd found the ad he was looking for and there was *Cancelled* printed all the way across it. Refunds available on receipt of the original tickets. Even when they didn't lie, newspapers, what they were full of was bad news.

His father had come back in from doing something to his bike, the chain slipping, something like that, and Calvin had asked him when they were going to get some decent jam again, out-of-date Oxford marmalade there was never anything wrong with that, what was he going to do with twenty-eight pounds of poisonous artificial sweetener, where was the rest of the paper?

His dad had mumbled something and rinsed his hands under the tap, wiped them on a tea towel and gone back outside to get them all oily again.

Calvin had found the missing front page in the bin under the sink, tea leaves and what hadn't been eaten of the tinned tomatoes wrapped inside it. Stained with a sort of dark orange, he'd read the headline: NEW HOSPITAL ALERT, the first few lines about somebody being arrested in the grounds, helping the police with their enquiries.

One of Calvin's friends had helped the police with their enquiries. He'd been off work for six weeks and lost his job, bruises consistent with falling down a flight of steps his parents had been told. Bruises consistent with being called a black bastard and out on his own with a holdall at one in the morning, that was more like it.

Calvin had pushed the paper back down into the bin and headed off to his room. He was fast running out of dope and just a quick hit listening to some music, that would set him up for the day, get out on the streets and score some more.

Skelton and Resnick were in the corridor, trying to ignore the phones that were ringing everywhere, footsteps, the rise and fall of voices. Graham Millington passed between them with a murmured *excuse me*, a man in a sense of dazed elation: twelve dozen cartons of cigarettes traceable to two different robberies and at that moment the magistrate was issuing a warrant to search a lock-up in Bulwell.

'Forensic have checked every print in the girl's room,' Skelton was saying. 'Nothing that doesn't come from the girl herself.'

'Still hoping for something from the university, sir. Someone must have seen them together.'

'If they were.'

'Apart, then. Carew admits he was there; the girl's diary suggests she was. We've got two officers sitting there in the bar interviewing people and so far no definite sighting of either of them. Might have been her, might have been him, all of that.'

'Ms Olds has been wearing out the carpet to my door, Charlie.'

'Mine, too, sir.'

'We need a break on this and soon.'

'Yes, sir.'

It was Lynn Kellogg who remembered something the nurse, Sarah Leonard, had said while being interviewed. The first time he spoke to me, Sarah had said, meaning Carew, I was walking home and he pulled over in his car, asked if I wanted a lift. One of those sports jobs, I can't tell one from another. Lynn could see the car clearly in her mind's eye, parked higher up the street and on the opposite side of the road from the house where Carew lived. She had thought nothing of it.

She needed written authorization and with Resnick back in the interview room she went straight to Skelton and got it within minutes, neat and precise and with his blessing. Her heart seemed to be alternately pumping faster and hardly functioning at all when she drew up alongside Carew's car and got out. There were a couple of medical textbooks on the back seat, a towel and an empty Diet Lilt can on the floor; as far as she could see only maps and some old Mars Bar wrappings at the front. The boot was locked and it took her an age to find a key that would fit. Squash racquet, tennis racquet, a pair of sports shoes, a can of Duckhams Multigrade, a sweatband, a Ruccanor sports bag with a white sports shirt stuffed down through the top. Lynn gingerly removed the shirt and slid the zip back.

Beneath a jock strap and a single white sock with blue and red bands at the top, a slim metal rod, silvered, five to six inches long.

'Tea?'

Ian Carew nodded and reached up for the styrofoam cup that Divine was offering him. Instead of letting go immediately, Divine held on and their fingers briefly overlapped, their eyes locked.

'What's this?' Resnick slapped the implement against the table hard, not waiting for Divine to return to his seat.

Despite herself, Suzanne Olds jumped in her seat.

Hot tea splashed over Carew's fingers.

'What – oh, Jesus!'

'Hardly an answer.'

'Where did you find that?'

'You tell us.'

Carew shook his head, did his little trick of pretending to

get up, settling back down. Trick or nervous habit, Resnick couldn't be sure. 'I don't believe this,' Carew said to Suzanne Olds.

Suzanne Olds was the only person in the room who, at that moment, didn't know what the object lying on the table was.

'It's a scalpel holder,' Resnick said. 'If I'm correct.'

Carew shifted his weight on the chair and folded his arms. He'd been offered the chance to shave after several broken hours trying to sleep in the cell, while somebody through the wall alternated between throwing up and blaspheming. He pushed his fingers into the corners of his eyes, then pushed up on the skin around the eyebrows, he was buggered if they were going to get him to say something he didn't want to say. Couple of smart-arse policemen, think they're so bloody clever!

'Carew?'

'It's a scalpel holder, so what?'

'You recognize it? I mean, this one in particular?'

'No, inspector, I do not. A bit like the police, see one, you've seen the lot.'

'Ian,' said Suzanne Olds, warning tone, warning look.

Oh, please, Divine was thinking, please give me just one chance. 'And you've no idea where we found it?' Resnick persevered. 'This particular one.'

'Well,' Carew leaning forward now, a little adrenalin jolting through him, take the high ground, 'the only point of asking me is if one of your minions found it somewhere in the house. Maybe even in my clothes. So, yes, all right. It was in the house.'

Resnick shook his head. 'The car.'

For a moment, Carew seemed genuinely bemused. 'The car? My car? What on earth was it doing in the car?'

'You tell us,' Divine said, easy on the menace.

'Oh,' Carew said. 'Right. The car.'

Resnick and Divine exchanged glances. Suzanne Olds

uncrossed her legs, turned the page of her notebook; after holding out all this time, there wasn't a confession coming?

'I nicked it,' Carew said.

'Say again?'

'The scalpel holder. Saw it lying around. At the hospital. I thought, right, that might come in handy, slipped it in my pocket. I think then, yes, that's what it was, I was driving up to Cripps for a game of squash. Dumped it in the bottom of my sports bag.'

'When was this?'

Carew shrugged. 'Oh, whenever we were in theatres, couple of weeks back now, must have been.'

'It's been in your possession all that time?'

Again a shrug. 'I suppose so, yes.'

'Thieve stuff from the hospital often, do you?' Divine asked.

'No.'

'Just scalpels?'

'Scalpel holders.'

'Easy to get the blades though, is it?'

Carew actually smiled. 'Easy enough.'

'You haven't told us why you bothered to take this implement,' Resnick said, 'and then, according to your version, leave it at the bottom of your sports bag for two weeks. That is what you're claiming?'

'Look, I saw it lying around. No use to anyone else. I thought it might come in handy. Then forgot about it.' He looked over at Suzanne Olds for support. 'Nothing sinister about that, surely?'

'Come in handy for what?' Resnick asked.

Carew shook his head and made a sound of mock exasperation. 'Oh, come on! I wouldn't have thought that was too difficult to work out, even for you. What am I?'

A jumped-up little prick, Divine thought.

'A medical student,' Carew continued. 'One day I might

decide to specialize in surgery. In fact, I think I shall.' He held Resnick's gaze. 'I suppose I thought it would come in handy for practising.'

'On what?'

Carew laughed in his face. 'What's the matter, inspector? On whom, isn't that what you mean? Although it would probably be on who if you actually said it. No, I could fit some blades and try it out on all kinds of things. Rabbit from the lab. Frog. Carve the Sunday bloody chicken with it, if you like.'

'Carve a body,' said Resnick.

'What about the anatomical skeleton you must have found in my room?' Carew asked. 'Maybe that was the one. Carved her up, boiled down the flesh and tied it up in neat little parcels, swilled away the blood, painted the ribs and spine that funny sort of flesh colour when I'd finished scraping away any last fragments of tissue. I expect this was what I used for that, too. Slice them up one minute, clean them up the next. All in a studious medic's work.'

'Ian,' Suzanne Olds was standing close to the door, about to pull it open. 'A break. A break, inspector.'

'Fuck breaks,' said Carew. 'I've had it with this. Old bloody scalpels, it's pathetic. The same name as mine in some girl's book. If that's all there is, all the so-called evidence there is, I'm walking out and not coming back.'

'You can't do that,' Suzanne Olds told him. 'You're still under arrest.'

'How much longer for?' Carew asked her.

Suzanne Olds looked at her watch. 'Between four and five hours, unless the inspector approaches a magistrate and requests an extension.'

'He needs evidence for that, does he? The magistrate has to hear the evidence and be convinced by it?'

'Yes.'

'Well, then,' Carew said, 'in that case we're laughing.'

Forty-one

The page had been photocopied from an operating theatre record dated 17 April, three years earlier. Cholecystectomy. Time operation began: 11.42 a.m. Time operation finished: 13.17 p.m. Surgeon's name. Assistant surgeon's name. Anaesthetist. Scrub nurse. Circulating nurse. Nature of operation. There were others noted on the same page, but Patel was in little doubt this was the one he should be concerned with. Whatever the exact reason the sister had handed him the envelope containing the copy, he was certain it had to do with this particular operation.

Cholecystectomy: he'd have to look that up.

Bernard Salt's signature at the end of the page; dashed off in no time at all, pitched between a scrawl and a flourish.

'Who usually fills in the record book?' Patel had asked, polite and always eager to learn. 'Yes, after an operation.'

The answer was the circulating nurse and this particular one was still at the hospital, that day, that moment in the recovery ward, a broad-boned woman with skin like raw washing left too long in the wind.

'Oh yes,' she said, Midlands accent, uncertain. 'Yes, that was me. You see, my handwriting, I'm afraid it's not the best.'

'And this operation, a long time ago, I know, but I was wondering . . . perhaps there is something you remember?'

The look in her eyes told Patel that there was.

'I don't know,' she said, casting her eyes about her

already, concerned that she might be overheard. 'We were asked, you see, not to talk about it.'

'Of course,' said Patel reassuringly. 'I understand. But this is a police enquiry.'

'Into this?'

'No. Oh, no. Of course not. But we think, well there is a possibility, there might be some connection.'

The nurse sucked in her lower lip, distorting her face.

'If it might help to put a stop to what's going on, you'd want us to know, wouldn't you. I mean, you'd want to help put a stop to all this, these attacks?'

'But this was three years ago. More than that even. I can't see . . .'

'Trust me,' Patel said. 'If it isn't relevant, nobody need ever know we've ever talked about it. I can promise you that.'

She sighed and he could see that she had made up her mind. 'The patient . . . he was on his way out of the theatre, being wheeled, you know, here to recovery, and I could see that he was crying, really crying, and I stopped, you know, the trolley and went to touch him, just on the shoulder, to touch him and he screamed. Screamed and screamed and screamed. Ever such a fuss and palaver we had calming him down. And then he told us – well, you don't know, do you? – but what he said was, right through the operation, he knew everything that was going on. He'd been able to feel the whole thing.'

Once, back in Bradford, Patel's paternal grandfather had been taken suddenly ill and rushed to hospital. Even as the old man lay there in the middle of a ward of strangers, palpably dying, it had been all but impossible to extract information from the doctors. Don't worry. No need for anxiety. The best thing you can do is not get upset. Nothing more than an exploratory operation. Tests. Examination.

Before the results had come through, his grandfather had been dead.

Trying to get information here had been little better: men and women, but mostly men, so used to obscuring the truth that it was second nature. Any question either ignored as by rote or weighed in the balance against any possible slur or taint of redress. Such records as existed were incomplete for the police's purposes and jealously guarded. So they had gone off digging, never sure of what they were searching for, another member of staff with a professional or private grudge or family with grounds for retribution? One veil prised away only for another to fall into place.

Excited by Helen Minton's gesture, Patel drove far too fast to the enquiry room and bullied his way on to the computer. Less than half an hour later he was knocking on the superintendent's door.

Carew had shifted gears: the bursts of belligerence, the bravado were gone and now he was playing for time, a straight bat, content to sit there and give the same answers, short as possible, again and again and again. More than one eye on the clock.

'I was wondering, sir . . . ?' Lynn Kellogg on her way across the CID room the moment Resnick appeared.

Resnick looked at her forlornly and shook his head.

'But the scalpel . . .'

'No way we can tie it in, nothing that puts him with the girl that lunchtime, any other time, nothing at all.'

'We've got his name in her diary, surely . . . ?'

'Eighth most popular name, A and B group parents, kind of statistic Amanda Hooson would have loved. Medical school, university, probably full of them.'

'If it is somebody else, he must know who he is, why hasn't he come forward?'

Resnick shrugged. 'Who knows? But Naylor did come

up with a student, positive he saw Carew sitting in the corner of the Buttery, watching the pool. Says he was on his own.'

Lynn Kellogg closed her eyes.

'His solicitor said it, I don't like him. Neither do you. Sort that gets under your skin, blurs your judgement.'

'Karen Archer, sir, you have questioned him about her as well?'

'He swears not to have set eyes on her after he received his warning. Hasn't heard from her, no idea where she is.'

'I don't believe him.'

'Isn't it what I just said? You don't want to believe him.'

'I don't think, where women are concerned, he's the kind of man that ever gives up, lets go.'

'I hope you're wrong,' Resnick said. 'I hope to God you're wrong. Meantime . . .'

'We're releasing him.'

'Maybe soon,' Resnick said. 'Not yet.'

Salt had screamed at the scrub nurse in theatre, fumbling with a clamp instead of slapping it down into his hand and the poor bugger on the table into a bleed that had his kidneys bobbing around like a coxless pair catching a crab. Of course, he'd apologized to her afterwards, no excuse for snapping like that and she'd said, no, it had been her fault, her fault entirely, but it had been her eyes that had told the truth.

Interesting, the way they were polarizing, attitudes towards him inside the hospital. Well, not interesting at all, really, take that back, more what you'd expect. Most of the nurses, female ones, the secretarial staff, social workers, their sympathies were with Helen, the other woman, used and then abused. Whereas the men – some of them it was nudge, nudge, wink, wink, sly old goose keeping a bit going on the side and pretty much getting away with it; others who'd found themselves on the receiving end of

Helen's tongue, they thought he was well shot of her. All brimstone and spare the treacle.

There was a message on his desk – he'd swear his secretary's handwriting had become more crabbed since this had come out into the open – would he please get in touch with a Superintendent Skelton as soon as possible?

Soon as he felt up to it: later.

Right now what he needed was a brisk walk, fresh air. He knew some surgeons who kept a silver flask topped up with one form of spirits or another, a quick tipple between jobs to keep the hands steady. Or so they claimed. One of his former colleagues, now gone to meet the great consultant in the sky, hadn't been above grabbing the mask when no one was looking and having a furtive go at the ether. Nine operations a day, that man, matter of routine. Of course, it had killed him. Heart. Four years short of fifty. Wife had remarried within six months, junior surgeon. New blood. Probably something going on there beforehand as well. Truth were known, they were all at it. Most of them. Human nature. What was that play? Restoration. Damn. English teacher had them read it at school. One that got the sack. *Way of the World*, that was it. True enough.

Bernard Salt stopped at the slip road to the car park and for only the second or third time since it had happened, he was thinking about the incident that evening after talking to Helen. A sound like a footstep, a movement, definitely a movement, and close, close to him. But then someone he knew had come along and after that, nothing. Which was in all probability what it had been.

Except . . .

That houseman, Fletcher, then Dougherty, it hadn't seemed anything that concerned him, that might impinge on his life, touch him at all. And then that young girl, the one who'd been an ODA. He had never wanted to admit to himself that there might be a connection.

Then he turned back towards the hospital and saw the

two men standing close to the entrance, neither of them men that he recognized as such, but the way they stood and waited, you didn't need to know their name.

'Superintendent Skelton,' said the taller man, showing his card. 'This is Detective Constable Patel. We appreciate that you have a busy schedule, but we were wondering if you could find time to talk to us. It may not take very long.'

Salt made a brief nodding motion, almost imperceptible. 'I have a cholecystectomy scheduled, which I should imagine, barring complications, will take an hour to an hour and a half. After that . . .'

'Will be fine,' said Skelton. 'There are other matters we can be checking into while we're here.'

Salt didn't ask what these might be; some of them he thought he might guess.

'Cholecystectomy,' said Patel, 'an operation to remove the gall-bladder, is that right?'

'Yes,' said Salt, 'it is. Absolutely.'

'What did you get your degree in?' Skelton asked as they were walking into the hospital.

'Mechanical engineering, sir,' Patel said, holding the door to let the superintendent step through.

'Rightly or wrongly,' Bernard Salt was saying, 'the impulse is always to calm the patient down, give something to deal with the residue of the pain, basically ensure as little agitation as possible. Last thing you want them to do, dwell upon what happened. Difficult enough to forget, I should have thought, without willingly reliving it all the time. No, you can apologize, you can try to explain.'

'Smooth it over,' suggested Skelton.

'Absolutely.'

They were in the consultant's office, Skelton and Salt facing one another from the two comfortable chairs, Patel off to one side on a straight-backed chair with a leather seat. Among the questions he wanted to ask, why wait until someone else gave us this information, why not come forward with it yourself? The sister who did point them in this direction, what were her motives? Another of a different kind, what was Skelton's degree in? But he remembered somebody saying, the superintendent was not a graduate at all. When Skelton had entered the Force, relatively few recruits had been graduates; even fewer had been Asian, black.

'There is always, I suppose,' Skelton was saying, 'the danger of legal action in cases such as this?'

Salt tapped his fingers together, brought his heavy head forward once.

'And so to do anything which might seem to be accepting liability . . .'

'Quite.'

Skelton let his glance stray towards the window. After the brave showing of sunshine, today's skies had reverted to an all-over anonymous grey. 'I believe there was an instance, four years ago. An . . . er . . . laparotomy, if I have the term correctly.'

'An exploratory examination of the abdomen,' said Patel.

Salt glared at him with something close to hatred.

'The patient claimed to have been awake throughout the operation,' Skelton continued. 'Damages were sought from the health authority, who settled out of court for an undisclosed sum. You were the surgeon in charge of that operation.'

'The patient,' Patel said, less than comfortable with both of the older men staring at him, 'was in a ward on which Karl Dougherty was working as a nurse.'

Salt shook his head. 'I can only take your word for that.'

'It is true,' said Patel. 'Dougherty himself remembers the incident and, as far as we have been able, we have checked the records.'

'I'm sure you have,' said Salt, a tone neither quite accusation nor patronization. 'And I am sure you have discovered that in November of last year, during an appendicectomy, the anaesthetic was found not to be functioning correctly and the operation was abandoned.'

Skelton looked across at Patel and Patel, who had come across no such information, nodded wisely.

'Only a few months before the operation to remove the gall-bladder,' Skelton said, 'there was considerable adverse publicity around a woman who claimed to have been conscious while giving birth by Caesarian section.'

'Certain newspapers,' Salt said, 'I am sure sold a great many extra copies.'

'Not only were the health authority sued, but also the surgeon in charge and the anaesthetist. I think that is correct?

'In the light of that,' Skelton went on, 'it's reasonable to imagine the authority, the hospital managers, would be very loath to attract similar publicity so soon again. Quite apart from the financial loss, what might seem to the general public like a falling away of professional standards, that would be something to be avoided at all costs.'

'Not at all costs, superintendent. There is no sense of anything having been covered up. And as for this hospital, I can assure you that, cheek by jowl, our record in these cases compares very favourably with others of a similar size.'

'I'm sure it does.'

'The number of operations that are carried out . . .'

'Please' – Skelton spread his hands – 'Mr Salt, even if such issues were my concern, you would not have to convince me that what you say is true.'

Salt cleared his throat and stretched out his legs, drawing them back up again towards his chair.

Skelton glanced over at Patel and nodded.

'The operation to remove Mr Ridgemount's gall-bladder, sir, the anaesthetist was Alan Imrie and his assistant was Amanda Hooson.'

'Correct.'

'At the time of the operation, Tim Fletcher was attached to you as a junior houseman?'

'I believe . . . I should need to check to be . . . Yes, yes. I suppose it's possible.'

'The surgical ward in which Mr Ridgemount was a patient, Karl Dougherty was a staff nurse on that ward.'

'He may have been. I'm sure you know that better than I.'

'Dougherty, Fletcher, Hooson – after the last of these, at least, why didn't you come forward?' Skelton asked.

'I had never drawn the connection you are suggesting.'

'Never?'

'Superintendent, Dougherty may have been one of the nurses who cared for Mr Ridgemount. During his time at the hospital, so would a good many others. And as for Fletcher, I can't imagine that his contact would have been more than peripheral.'

'So you never thought it might be relevant – what happened to Ridgemount?'

'What he alleges happened.'

Skelton looked at the consultant keenly. 'He made it up?'

'An operation, superintendent, it's a traumatic thing. It has been known for patients to hallucinate, for their imaginations to distort what actually happened under the anaesthetic.'

'And you're saying that's what happened in Ridgemount's case?'

'I'm saying it's a possibility.'

'It's also a possibility that he was telling the truth.'

'Yes.'

'Ridgemount,' said Patel, 'he was threatening legal action also.'

Bernard Salt nodded. 'At one time.'

'Against yourself, the senior anaesthetist and the health authority?'

'So I believe.'

'You've no idea, sir,' asked Patel, 'why the action was dropped?'

'None. Although, my supposition at the time was that whoever had been advising him didn't consider his case strong enough to take to court. Either that, or he changed his own mind about what actually happened.' Salt made a point of looking at his watch. 'Gentlemen,' he said, rising to his feet, 'I am in danger of being late for theatre.'

'The anaesthetist in charge that day,' Patel said as they were passing through the door, 'Imrie, wasn't he also involved in the Caesarian section? The case that was settled out of court?'

'I believe he was.'

'If we wanted to speak to him?' Patel said. 'He no longer appears to be on the staff of the hospital.'

'Eight months after the Ridgemount operation,' replied Salt, turning in the corridor to face the two policemen, 'when legal action was still threatened, Alan Imrie committed suicide.'

Instead of going directly to the operating theatre, Bernard Salt went to Helen Minton's ward, where she was just finishing hand-over.

'I assume this is more of your dried-up spite. Dragging this wretched Ridgemount affair back into the open.'

Helen Minton arched her back and stood her ground. 'I thought telling people of your inadequacies as a man was not enough. I thought they should understand how far the same inability to face the truth or to accept your responsibilities is present in your professional life as well.'

While this confrontation was taking place, a zoology student named Ian Bean, fresh back from a field trip to Robin Hood's Bay, walked into Skelton's station and asked to speak to whoever was in charge of the Amanda Hooson murder enquiry.

Less than an hour later, Ian Carew was released from police custody without charge, thirty-two hours after he had been arrested.

Forty-two

'Whatever you do or don't do,' Ridgemount said to his son, 'don't be forgetting the split peas. One thing I don't want, come back out of breath from pedalling up that hill, find the peas have gone to mush, bottom of the pan burned out. Am I understood?'

'Umh,' grunted Calvin, headphones pushed tight inside his ears. 'Um, umh, umf.' What he liked about those old bands like Black Sabbath, when they hit a rhythm it stayed hit.

'Calvin!'

Calvin's eyes widened and he swayed out of his father's reach. Headphones were going to be removed, he'd do it himself.

'You hear what I said?'

'Split peas, watch 'em. Satisfied?' Sound squeaked from the headphones that dangled from one hand.

'Listening to that garbage the whole time, turned up loud as it can go, be deaf this side of twenty-one.'

'Better than being a fool.'

Calvin started down the stairs to his room, his father standing by the front door, pointing his finger. 'Take care, boy. Just you take care.' Whether he was still going on about the peas, or meant Calvin's mouth, Calvin didn't know.

'Whatever else we've done on this one,' Skelton said, 'we've not exactly covered ourselves in glory. The Assistant Chief's already had the Senior Consultant

Anaesthetist on the phone talking about undermining public confidence, asking where the virtue is in unnecessarily tarnishing professional reputations, causing additional distress to the relatives of the dead.'

'Imrie?'

Skelton nodded.

'Not much concern about the poor bloody patient in all that lot.'

'Closing ranks, Charlie. We know about that as well as anyone. A copper stands accused, one of the public brings a complaint, nine cases out of ten, what's the first thing we do? Get the waggons round and form a circle. Keep the buggers out. Doctors, they're no worse than any others.'

'Maybe, sir.'

'All I'm saying, Charlie, if we are close to something, let's not screw it up. Take care. Just take care.'

'Right,' Resnick said. 'Kid gloves.'

David McCarthy had promised Resnick fifteen minutes, no more, a meeting in the brasserie on High Pavement, across from St Mary's Church. Around the corner, in Commerce Square, the first of the old Victorian lace factories was in the hands of the developers and would soon be architect-designed studio apartments, luxury condominiums, a gymnasium, a pool, a sauna.

Resnick had met McCarthy once before and recognized him as he came in, a slightly hunted look, briefcase in one hand, portable telephone in the other. He was finishing a call as he came through the door.

'So,' McCarthy said, carrying his glass of Aqua Libra over to the corner Resnick had staked out, 'why the renewed interest in this old chestnut?'

Briefly, Resnick told him.

McCarthy leaned back and folded his arms across his chest. Cuff links, Resnick thought, noticing the solicitor's pale blue shirt, thought they were a thing of the past. Like those daft suspenders for men's socks.

'You're not, of course, asking for anything that might be considered privileged information?'

'What I want to know,' Resnick said, 'why was the action dropped?'

'Client's wishes.'

'Not your recommendation?'

'Absolutely not. We had every chance of building up a good case.'

'If anything, then, you'd have been encouraging him to stay with it?'

'Financially, it would have served his interests best.'

'But not in other ways?'

McCarthy took a drink, glanced at his phone as if it were about to ring. 'A similar situation to cases of rape, balance out the distress a client is put through reliving the experience in court against the potential gains. Here's a man, held down, physically violated and powerless to do anything about it at the time. How much does he want to talk about it, describe it, have what he believes to be true attacked, even ridiculed? No, he decided enough was enough.'

'Nothing to do, then, with Alan Imrie's death?'

'Imrie?'

'The anaesthetist.'

McCarthy pursed his lips. 'I'd forgotten.'

'You can't remember Ridgemount talking about it at the time?'

'No,' the solicitor replied after some moments' thought, 'he would have been aware of it, I'm pretty sure of that. But, no, I can't recall him mentioning it. As far as I know, it didn't affect his decision.'

Resnick nodded. McCarthy sampled the well-publicized delights of Aqua Libra. Libra, Resnick thought, anything but what it was. 'The other personnel involved in the operation,' he said, 'even though they weren't named in the suit, you'd have determined who they were?'

'Right down to whoever pushed the trolley in and out.'

'You'd have told your client the names?'

McCarthy fidgeted with the mechanism of his briefcase's double lock. Some people used the first digits of their phone number as the combination, others their wife's birthday.

'I can't see why I should. No, I don't think so.'

'Not if he'd asked? Straight out.'

'I don't know.' His telephone rang and he picked it up almost before the sound could register, listened, nodded a couple of times and told the caller he would ring right back. 'I really don't recall his having done so.'

'The names though, they would have been around, committed to paper? It couldn't have been out of the question for him to get a look at them without you realizing. At some point he would have had the chance to write them down, make a photocopy even. What I mean is, he could have known who they were, as you say, even the porter wheeling the trolley.'

'Yes,' said McCarthy. 'That's right. That's reasonable to assume.'

His portable telephone rang and Resnick got to his feet.

'You don't have to rush off,' McCarthy said, one hand over the mouthpiece. 'I'm okay for another few minutes.'

'Enjoy them,' Resnick said. 'Do the concise crossword. Dismantle the phone.' He touched McCarthy lightly on the shoulder in passing. 'Thanks for your help.'

Great thing about the way the house was so high up, built near the crest of a hill, even his own room below stairs, there was no way in which he was overlooked. Except from the garden and who was likely to be standing out there in the garden? His father, maybe, but his father was off somewhere, hopefully getting back into being a fetcher and carrier, bringing home something good for their dinner.

Calvin stretched back on the bed, rearranging the pillows a little, get them really comfortable. This new stuff he'd got, Jamaican, the kid who'd sold it to him had said, but Calvin knew enough to know that didn't mean a thing. It was good, though. Good stuff. Good shit. So good, in fact, he thought he would have another joint. Sometimes, lying there, instead of smoking, he would masturbate, thinking, maybe about the woman who worked in the ice cream van in the park. Sitting inside surrounded by all those Cool Kings and Juicy Fruits and Raspberry Torpedoes. Got the radio tuned to the pirate reggae station. White overalls: he was certain she didn't have anything more than some skimpy kind of stuff underneath. Often, in the park, he would choose a spot where he could see her clearly, sprawl there listening to his music, watching what she did. Never once, she paid him any heed, gave any sign she knew he was even there. But Calvin knew enough to know different.

The tape in the stereo came to an end and Calvin swore and then realized he had his Walkman next to the bed. All he needed now was another tape from his bag and a light and hey! What was that Robert Plant thing? 'Stairway to Heaven'.

Pretty soon, eyes closed, singing along at the top of his voice to Twisted Sister, himself and Dee Snider duetting, except that Calvin kept forgetting the words, getting them wrong, especially in the verses, getting it right for the chorus. Eyes shut tight. Take another hit, that's it, hold it there and suck it down. Arms spread wide. Sing, you crazy bastard, sing! Calvin didn't hear the first tentative taps at the window, only when Divine's fist banged against the frame did Calvin sit up with a jolt and see the man's cock-eyed face grinning in.

Whatever condition he was in, Calvin knew enough to

understand this wasn't the window cleaner, come knocking for payment.

Panicked, he jerked the headphones clear and threw them across the room, pinched out the joint with his fingers and pushed it from sight. Perhaps no one would notice, figure he was resting there enjoying Bensons King Size? Another of them rattling at the back door now, that fool with a plaster the size of a fist stuck to his face, still grinning like he'd woke up and suddenly it was Christmas.

Calvin wafted the air on his way down the room. Quicker to respond, he could have bolted up the stairs and out into the street, made off on foot, but what the hell, what did he have to run for anyhow? Englishman's home was his castle, right?

The underside of a boot struck the door, low by the jamb, and it shook.

'Hey!' Calvin yelled. 'Hey!'

He unlocked and they came in, forcing him back out of the way, not exactly pushing him, never using their hands, the one with the plaster making straight for the bed, easing the last inch and a half of his joint out into the light.

'Home grown?'

'Old Holborn,' Calvin said. 'Cheaper to roll your own.'

'Sure. And I'm Mike Tyson.'

Shit! thought Calvin. You're not even the right colour.

The other one was flashing his card. 'Detective Constable Naylor. This is Detective Constable Divine.'

Divine grinned some more. He was having a good time. The inside of the kid's room smelled like some of the parties he used to go to when he was nineteen, twenty. Wherever he was getting his stuff, it was bloody good.

Naylor had spotted the sports bag on the floor and was making a beeline for it.

'Man,' Calvin said, 'you got a warrant to come busting in here?'

'We didn't bust in,' Divine said. 'You let us in.'

'That or stand there and watch the door kicked in.'

'You didn't invite us on to the property?' said Naylor.

'Damn right!'

'That's okay, because we've got a warrant.'

'Like fuck you do!' said Calvin and wished he hadn't because the bigger of the two looked as if he might be about to belt him one.

Kevin Naylor took the warrant from his pocket and held it in front of Calvin's face.

'What you expect to find anyway?' Calvin asked.

Naylor and Divine were exchanging glances over the bag, lying on the floor between them.

'That's my stuff,' Calvin said. He could hear the whine sneaking into his voice and hated it but there wasn't anything he could do about it. 'That's my personal stuff.'

'Show us,' Divine said.

'Huh?'

'All you have to do,' said Naylor, 'unzip the top, pick it up and turn it out on the bed.'

Calvin didn't see where he had a lot of choice.

He held the bag over the bed and they all watched the contents tumble out. Old rolled-up copies of *Kerrang!*, maybe ten spare sets of batteries for his Walkman, EverReady Gold Seal LR6, must have been twenty to thirty cassettes, most of them pristine, Cellophane-wrapped, stickers still in place, HMV, Virgin, Our Price.

'Kid's a collector,' Divine said.

'Yes,' said Naylor, 'bet he's got the receipts too.'

Two of the T-shirts that now lay on the bed were also in their original wrapping, several others that he'd pulled and worn for a few hours and then rejected. A red-backed exercise book in which Calvin had copied the lyrics of his favourite songs, one day, he'd figured he'd start to write his own. All he wanted was the inspiration. A little more time.

'Shake it,' Divine said.

'Hmm?' Calvin looked back at him blankly.

'The bag. Shake it some more.'

This time it came rolling out of the corner where Calvin had desperately been trying to hold on to it with his thumb. Naylor lifted up the plastic bag, the kind Debbie used to buy in Tesco to keep his sandwiches fresh. He sniffed at the contents and passed it across to Divine, whose attention had been drawn to the bundle of tapes.

'Whatever,' he asked, perplexed, holding up a copy of John Denver's Greatest Hits, 'are you doing with this?'

'That shit,' said Calvin. 'I don't play that shit. I just sell it again.'

'Right,' said Divine, now holding the bag of marijuana, 'to buy shit like this.'

'Hey,' said Kevin Naylor, moving towards the door, looking upwards. 'Does anybody else smell burning?'

Ridgemount had smelt it too, even before he'd eased himself off the saddle and wheeled his bike over the pavement, trailer behind it full with potatoes, onions, ten pounds of bruised Bramleys that he was going to simmer down into apple sauce. Honest to God, Ridgemount thought, I knew it. I just knew it. One thing I asked that boy to do, one thing and he can't even do that. He was sliding the key into the front door lock when Patel came up behind him and spoke his name.

'I don't want to buy anything from you,' Ridgemount said, 'I don't want anything on credit and right now I can't stop to discuss the Bible, because my nose tells me there's a small emergency going on in my house. Now if you'll excuse me.'

But Patel showed him his warrant card instead.

'I'm sorry,' Ridgemount said, 'I have to deal with this first.'

He pushed the door open and left it wide. A man he didn't recognize was standing half-way up the stairs, Calvin two steps from the bottom with another man right behind him, a hand on Calvin's arm. Ridgemount stepped across the hall and into the kitchen; the windows were thick with steam and clouds of it had collected over the ceiling and were beginning slowly to descend the walls. He took a tea towel from its hook and bunched it in his hand, turned out the gas and lifted the pan from the stove. What had been a pound and a half of split peas was now a blackened mass crusted across the pan. Between the stove and the sink, the bottom of the saucepan fell out but the peas clung on, welded to the sides.

'Mr Ridgemount,' said Resnick, who had walked over from his car and followed Patel into the house, 'Detective Inspector Resnick. I'd appreciate it if you'd come with these officers to the police station. There are some questions we'd like to ask you.'

'Dad?' said Calvin from the hallway.

'These questions,' Ridgemount said. 'What are they about?'

'Oh,' Resnick said, 'I think you know.'

Ridgemount looked past Resnick to where Calvin was standing, Divine and Naylor at either side of him, Naylor still holding his arm.

'Let my son go,' Ridgemount said.

Resnick looked questioningly towards Naylor. 'Possession of an illegal substance, sir. Namely, marijuana. Possession of stolen goods.'

'Sweet Jesus!' Ridgemount breathed.

Resnick nodded towards Patel, who went forward and reached his hand towards Ridgemount's shoulder.

'*Nooo*!' Ridgemount screamed and backed clumsily against the stove, cleaving the space between Patel and himself with his fist. 'No! Don't touch me! Don't touch me!'

Patel moved in again but now there was a knife in Ridgemount's hand, a kitchen knife, tears and fear glistening in his eyes.

'Steady!' called Resnick

Behind him, Calvin struggled to be free. 'He won't . . . You can't . . . He won't let you touch him. Not at all. He can't.'

Resnick nodded, understanding.

'Let the boy go,' he said and Naylor, querying the order with his eyes, did exactly that. 'Now, Mr Ridgemount,' said Resnick, moving round Patel, slowly extending one hand, fingers spread. 'Please let me have the knife. You have my word, we won't touch you. Give me the knife and all you have to do is walk to the car and wait with one of the officers. We do have a warrant to search these premises and we'll see that's finished as speedily and with as little disturbance as possible. After we've searched the house, you'll be driven to the station.'

'And Calvin?'

'He'll come with us also. He can ride in the same vehicle as you if you wish.'

Ridgemount reversed the paring knife and placed the handle, carefully, in Resnick's hand.

Forty-three

The postcard was from the island of Mykonos and off beyond the low, white buildings what Lynn presumed to be the Aegean was a dark stain like an ink blot in the monochrome copy on her desk. She imagined how blue it would be and Karen Archer stepping down to it through sand, even this far on in the year, to swim. We thought you would like to see this, Karen's parents had said in their covering letter, we hope it sets your mind to rest.

> Sorry to have been out of touch for so long but felt I just had to get away. Thank God for Thomas Cook and Access!! Think of me in the sun, pigging out on ouzo and olives!!! I'll phone the minute I'm back in England. Take care and try not to worry. I'm fine!
>
> Heaps of love, Karen XXXXXXXXXXXXX

Well, good for you, Lynn thought. Be nice, wouldn't it, if everyone in your position could go swanning off to Greece and pretend it had all been a bad dream. She sat for a moment, resting her head down into her hands. What's the matter with you? Did you really want her to be a body somewhere, just so that you could have another victim, something to trace back to Ian Carew's hand?

'Everything that's said in this room,' Resnick explained, 'everything you say, will be recorded on this machine, afterwards the tapes will be sealed and signed to show that they're a true record.'

Ridgemount nodded to show that he understood.

'What I'd like you to do is say what happened in your own words, exactly as you want. If there's anything that doesn't seem clear, I might interrupt to ask a question, but other than that all I want to do is listen. All right?'

Ridgemount nodded: all right.

Carew hadn't been certain whether to go up to her when she was with other people or wait again until she was alone. He hadn't known whether to wear something not exactly formal but a little less sporty. Suggest that this was serious, not play. Touch and then go. Finally he settled on a faded denim shirt, white slacks, moccasins. Wallet buttoned down in his back pocket in case she said, 'Terrific! Let's go for a drink, celebrate!' Later they could get something to eat, that new place up from the Council House, all white tablecloths and single-stem flowers, Sonny's, he'd been wanting to go there.

In the event, she didn't say a thing. Stood there, staring at him as if not really able to believe it was him. The others that were with her, three of them, nurses, uncertain what to do, whether to walk on or stay, staring from Sarah to Carew and back again. Beneath her long, open coat she was still in her uniform, belted tight at the waist, dark sheen of her hair: perfect.

'Surprise, surprise!' Carew said.

'See you tomorrow, Sarah,' called one of the others, continuing on her way.

'Fine,' Sarah said. 'Bye.'

Then they were alone in the middle of the broad corridor, doors off. Paintings by local primary children on the walls. 'I thought you were in jail,' Sarah said.

Carew smiled. 'I was. It was a mistake.'

'There must have been something. They must have arrested you for something.'

'Is that what you think?'

'Well, yes.'

A doctor, stethoscope around his neck, came into the corridor and walked towards them. He had a squash ball in his hand and he was squeezing it rhythmically, pressing it hard into his palm.

'Well there was something,' Carew said. 'They seemed to think I'd murdered someone. A woman.'

Scarcely missing a beat, the doctor turned through one of the doors and disappeared from sight.

Sarah Leonard was staring at him, unable to work him out. 'And now they've changed their mind,' she said.

Carew smiled. 'The wrong Ian. You see, they found her diary, the woman's, and there was a name there, Ian. They thought it was me.'

'Why would they do that?'

'I don't know. But it was a mistake. The real Ian turned up, the one from the diary and, well, here I am.'

'What for?'

'Um?'

'What for? Why are you here? I don't understand.'

The smile shifted from the mouth to the eyes. 'I thought, you know, we had some unfinished business.'

Sarah waited.

'When we were talking, before, if I remember rightly, we'd just got to the point.'

'Of what?'

'Finalizing the arrangements. Where we were going to go, where we were going to meet. Italian or Chinese. You know the kind of thing.'

'I may do. But what makes you think I'd ever agree to going out with you? Especially now.'

'Exactly my point.'

'What?'

'Especially now. It's not every day the police decide you didn't murder somebody after all. We have to go and celebrate.'

Sarah shook her head. An elderly woman was manoeuvring the length of the corridor on a Zimmer frame, pausing every fifteen feet or so to draw breath.

'We've got to,' Carew said.

'You're the one. It's nothing to do with me. You celebrate.' She began to walk towards him, veering left to go past. As she drew level he caught hold of her hand.

'It's no fun on your own.'

'Tough!'

'I mean it.'

'So do I.'

One of the side doors opened and she pulled herself clear. A porter backed out a trolley bearing a sheet and blankets, nothing else. He was chewing gum and whistling 'When You're Smiling'; recognizing Sarah he winked and grinned and switched the gum from one side of his mouth to the other, all without quite losing the tune.

'Just one drink,' Carew pleaded. 'Half an hour. On your way home.'

'No.'

'But . . .'

'No. How's it spelt?'

Carew hung his lower lip, made a good pass at crossing his legs standing up and stared at her as if she'd asked him to explain the theory of relativity. 'Er,' he stuttered. 'Um . . . er, um . . . the first letter, miss, it's not an M?'

'No.' Willing herself not to find his little-boy act funny, just absurd. Pathetic.

'N? It's an N, isn't it? N for no.'

Unable to stop herself smiling, Sarah nodded. 'Yes.'

'Yes?' Carew was suddenly no longer the timid boy, moving confidently towards her. 'You did say yes.' He'd been saving his best smile for last, the one that never let him down. 'Half an hour,' he said. 'An hour at most.'

'I was lying there,' Ridgemount said, 'I was lying there

with my eyes taped over shut and I couldn't move. They had this tube, see, this tube clamped over my mouth. Taking the air down to my lungs. And they've been saying, before, you know, they give me this shot, put me under, she was saying, this girl, not much more than a girl, just a few seconds and you won't feel a thing. Not till you're back in recovery and it's all over.

'Well, I went spark out all right. Next thing I know, I seem to come to and there I am thinking it's just like sleeping, nights you go to bed and you're so tired you can't as much as remember your head hitting the pillow but the next second you're waking up and it's eight hours or more later. So I'm there thinking, okay what did she say this place was, recovery? All right, I'm in recovery, except my mouth is still covered and my eyes are still taped over and I reason I'm still in the operating room, must be going to wheel me out any minute.

'They don't wheel me out. Nobody's about to wheel me out.

'Even though I've got this tape across my eyes, somehow I can see these bright lights right there above me and it's like, you know when you've been looking up at the sun and you close your eyes and for a while you can see this hot blur, like it's printed on the inside of your eye, that's what it's like. Not only that, I can hear voices. Not too clear what they're saying, not clear at all, so I try and say something, speak to them, what's going on? Only there's no way I can say anything, not a word. I try to move, can't move a muscle. Just stretched out there and I realize, shit, they haven't done this operation, taken out this damn gall-bladder, haven't even started yet. My head's panicking and my body can't move and I can't shout or scream and all I can see is the blur of those lights and I'm thinking, no, it can't be going to happen, no, it can't be going to happen, no, it can't and then it does.

'It's like wire being pulled clear through me. Thin wire.

Only it's hot. It's a piece of red-hot wire and I swear I can hear the flesh tear when he pulls it through. And all I can do is pray for it to stop. Pray to die. 'Cause I know it won't stop ever. Won't stop till it's done.'

Carew was drinking his second single malt, savouring it, the look he gave the stupid little cow behind the bar when she asked him if he wanted ice in it should have made her pee her pants. Where was the point in drinking the good stuff like this, only to water it down with frozen algae out of the Severn-Trent?

'D'you ever come in here?' He looked round at the wide room, stuffed red chairs and shiny black-top tables, like something off a P. & O. cruise ship.

Sarah Leonard shook her head. It was only after he made a fuss about ordering bitter lemon – what kind of a celebratory drink was that? – that she'd relented and had a dry white wine and now she was regretting it.

'We should have gone somewhere a bit livelier. More style.' He leaned forward across the table exactly as she knew he would. 'We still could.'

'Oh, no.'

'Come on. Let's go dancing, for heaven's sake. When was the last time you went dancing? Venus. New York, New York. God, we could even go to the Irish.' He reached for her hand and she pulled it away. 'How about it?'

The wine tasted sour and old, as if the box it had been squeezed out of had been mouldering in a cellar somewhere for years.

'Why don't you ever give up?'

'It's not in my nature,' Carew smiled, 'to accept defeat.'

Sarah put down her glass and stood up.

'Where are you going?'

She pointed towards the door alongside the bar. 'Ladies.'

Carew nodded. 'Sarah,' he called when she was halfway across the room. Swivelling her body, she stopped to look back at him. 'Don't go slipping out the back way now, will you?' And he laughed.

'You could tell from their faces, the way they were all over me, fussing with this, fussing with that, you could tell they knew something had gone wrong. But they never said, never said a thing to me and I couldn't . . . at first, when they pulled the tube away from my mouth, all the time I'd been wanting to shout out and scream and cry and when I could do it I couldn't get a sound to come out.

'Later, yes. Then I would scream and call them barbarians and butchers and they would come running and slide this needle into my arm. Keep me quiet. Take away the pain. That's what they say, make you feel comfortable, take away the pain. It's too late, I say, it's too late for that. And they slide the needle home.'

'What's that?' Sarah asked, pointing at the glass.

'Bitter lemon.'

'And?'

'Ice.'

'And?'

'Gin.'

She picked it up and carried it over to the bar. 'There was a misunderstanding,' she said. 'I didn't want this.'

'I'm sorry,' said the girl behind the counter. 'You can't have your money back.'

'Fine.'

Sarah gave Carew a quick look, see how he was taking that, and headed for the door. A picture in denim, that was how he saw himself. Mr Irresistible. She wondered when a woman had last turned him down and what had happened to her when she had. She had thought he might jump up and come after her, flash another of those practised-in-the-bathroom-mirror smiles, but Carew continued to sit where he was, drinking his malt whisky, looking cool.

A quarter of a mile on, she was less angry about it already, just another bloke trying it on, this one, maybe, a touch more persistent than the rest. Approaching the road that led down towards the old Raleigh factory, Sarah's face opened to a smile. Had he really imagined she was going to go off with him, dancing, dressed like that? The badge on her uniform that spelled out her name and rank. Ridiculous.

And suddenly there he was in front of her, posing at the corner of the side street, having to struggle to control his breathing and pretend he hadn't had to sprint fast to double around that block and get ahead of her in time.

'Now what?' Sarah said, angry again.

'Easy. I walk with you to your door, say good night, turn right around and go home. End of evening. Okay?'

'No.'

Ian Carew didn't say anything; he didn't even smile. He just looked.

Sarah began to walk and he danced into step alongside her, not attempting to talk, simply walking. All right, Sarah thought, five minutes, another five streets and it will be over.

'When I got home from the hospital I could still feel the pain. I didn't go to bed at night, I wouldn't lie down, as soon as I did I'd be waiting for it again, waiting for it to start. The cutting. The wire. I slept sitting up, wherever I was and even then, though I wasn't lying down, I would scream.

'At first my wife, she would come to me and try to calm me down but if she went to touch me I screamed all the more. I couldn't ever bear to have anyone touch me.

'My Marjorie . . . she was little then, she says to her mother, why does daddy shout at me like that, why won't he let me near him, why does he hate me?

'In the end they couldn't take it any more and they left me and Calvin he stayed. No matter what that boy does, I'll always love him for that. He stayed by me when nobody else would.'

Sarah's house was in a short terrace that backed on to a playing field. She had bought it when prices in the city had been lower than almost anywhere aside from Belfast, which was just as well because on her salary it had been all she could afford. She stood with her back to her front door, hands in her coat pockets, fingers of one tight about some loose change, the others round her keys.

'Right,' Sarah said.

'What?'

'Good night.'

The smile was back. 'Good night.'

Sarah didn't budge. 'Let me see you walk away.'

'Just one thing . . .'

'No.'

'Just . . .'

'No!'

'Tim Fletcher, I wanted to ask . . .'

'What about him?'

'You were getting pretty friendly with him, running errands and all that . . .'

'Errands?'

'You were buying books for him, remember?'

'The condition he was in at the time, he wasn't exactly in a position to do that for himself.'

'That's what I wanted to know. How is he? His mobility? I mean, is he ever going to regain that?'

'He's made a lot of progress, yes.'

'I'm sure he has,' said Carew, 'but no matter how hard he tries, however much you do for him, he's never going to get it back fully. Is he?'

Sarah Leonard watching him, Carew was off down the street, not exactly hurrying but gradually lengthening his stride, stepping out, showing his paces.

Forty-four

'Where's Calvin?'

Resnick looked up from changing the tape. 'He's being questioned by detectives.'

'About me?'

'Not directly, no.'

'I want to see him.'

'Afterwards.'

'After what?'

Resnick pressed record and pause simultaneously. 'I think what you were about to tell us was to do with the legal action, why you didn't proceed.'

Sarah Leonard's blue uniform hung down from the handle of the bathroom door, ball-point pens poking from the breast pockets, one side weighed down by a stethoscope, a notebook, her watch still pinned to the front, beneath her badge.

Sarah knelt in the bath, running the water from the mixer shower over her face and hair. She was thinking about Tim Fletcher, how easy he was to talk to, how she might have found him attractive if only he were a little taller. God! Sarah laughed up into the spray of water. If only for Ian Carew's body, Tim Fletcher's personality, his mind. She closed her eyes tight and brought the shower rose closer to her face.

'You can't tell me that man did what he did through anything other than guilt. It had already happened when he was in charge of those machines one time before. And he'd been proved guilty for it. Why else pay all that money out of court? He knew, Imrie, he knew that was his responsibility, same as what happened to me, and he couldn't live with it no better than I could. Except he didn't actually know the pain, he didn't feel the pain, he just knew he caused it and that's why he swallowed all them pills and then took a razor to his wrists on account he didn't want to take any more chances. Risk something going wrong, not when it was his own life he was dealing with. No.'

Ridgemount dampened his bottom lip with his tongue; Resnick signalled to Patel, who poured some more water and left it within reach of Ridgemount's right hand.

'I thought that was some kind of sign. I thought that meant that man had accepted all the blame to himself and now it was going to be over. Except the dreams never left me and I could never get back to sleeping normal like anyone else and all that did leave me was my wife and my little girl. So I knew . . .' looking at Resnick, searching his face, 'I knew that wasn't the end of it. I knew there had to be something more.

'See, it would have been better if they had killed me, there on that operating table, if they had killed me dead, 'cause what I was, what I had become, that was worse than being dead. But God had left me alive and I had to find a way of dealing with that and I knew I couldn't turn round and do what that man had done and take my own life, not after God had sent me through that fire and brought me out on the other side.

'I thought, they are all at fault. What they got to do is accept their blame.

'And I waited and meantime the pains in my head got worse and still they done nothing, so little by little I took it on myself to find out where they were, what they were doing, and they were all, most of them, carrying right on like before as if nothing had ever took place. And I kept watching them, them who'd been in there with me during my operation, I watched them and I waited for something to tell me what I could do that might finally ease my pain.

'Me and Calvin, we lived our life best we could and all the while I was waiting for some kind of sign.'

Sarah watched the pan, waiting until the boiling milk had bubbled almost to the rim before whisking it off the gas and pouring it into the mug, spooning in three heaped teaspoonfuls of hot chocolate and stirring hard. On the way over to the sink she licked the pieces of dark chocolate away from the spoon before dropping it into the bowl. She collected her book and carried book and chocolate up towards the bedroom. She was just settling into bed, wondering if she might get to the end of her chapter before falling asleep when she heard the glass break.

Her first thought, as she sat up in bed, it was someone on the way home from the pub, kids coming out of the Marcus Garvey Centre; once before a neighbour across the street had a brick thrown through her window, some people's idea of fun.

But this had not been at the front, the sound had come from the back.

Sarah stood at the door to the bedroom, eased the door open and held her breath. Nothing moved below: no light save that from the street which filtered through the front room curtains and the pebbled glass above the front door.

Still she waited.

It need not have been her house at all, it could as easily have been next door. It could have been someone throwing stones from the field. If it had been a burglar, it was possible she had already frightened him off; or he could be down there, waiting. For what? Part of her wanted to turn round and get back into bed, pull the covers up over her head. Whatever she had downstairs that was worth taking, let him take it. Not for the first time, she cursed herself for not having a phone point put in the bedroom. Even so, surely that's what she should do, go downstairs and telephone the police.

'What they all still had' – sweat was beading along Ridgemount's lip, running into the corners of his eyes and making them sting – 'was their liberty to do as they chose, have affairs with other women, other men, go off and study, anything they liked and I was trapped by what had happened to me and what had happened to me was their fault.

'So I watched that nurse, the way he would come on laughing and joking all the time with the other nurses and patients, always letting on like there was never a care in the world. No, you're fine, nothing's going to happen to you. Nothing's going to go wrong, you take my word for it, you trust me, this operation's going to be the best thing ever happened to you, put another ten years on your active life.

'And that young woman, the one whose job it was to make sure that anaesthetic machine's working right, she's up to the university making out she's so smart and clever, going to get herself a degree and everything, thinks she's so wonderful, couldn't see the machine going wrong.

'All of them, what I wanted, what I was waiting for, a way to take their liberty away without taking a life, 'cause the taking of a life, that's wrong. That don't help anything.'

'How about Amanda Hooson?' Resnick asked. 'What about her life?'

'Now that,' Ridgemount said, looking straight at him, 'that was never meant to happen. I never knew anyone could struggle so. That was a mistake.'

'Sarah!'

The second she heard the voice, she knew whose it was and she rocked sideways against the door, a single low breath expelled from her mouth.

'Shall I come up to you or are you coming down to me?'

He was leaning against the wall between the front door and the foot of the stairs. In the faint light she could see only his face at all clearly and as she got closer she saw that he was no longer wearing the same clothes as before, but black jeans and a black cotton sweater. Hands in his pockets as he leaned there, nonchalant.

'You see,' he smiled, 'I said it wasn't over.'

'What? What isn't over? What?'

He came towards her and she backed up the stairs, four or five treads, before thinking this is the last thing I have to do, show him I'm afraid. So she went back down, didn't stop until she was face to face with him, more of a sneer than a smile at the corner of his mouth, she could see that now.

'What do you want?'

Before she could react, he grabbed the front of her dressing-gown and pulled hard, throwing her off balance, hard into him. She pushed herself clear, one hand clawing for his face, but he only laughed and pulled again twice with the hand that had never let go and her dressing-gown was wide open, the shirt that she wore in bed with its buttons torn away.

'What I want,' Carew grinned, 'the same as you.'

Sarah kicked out with her bare leg, fast but not quite fast enough, her shin catching him high inside the thigh, and as he hopped back she aimed her elbow at his face, felt it strike something and barged past him towards the front room and the phone.

He caught her below the waist and flung her round, the knuckles at the back of one hand grazed against the iron of the fireplace and her head and shoulder thumped against the side of the easy chair. He jerked her again and lost his grip and she fell heavily on the base of her spine and cried out with the sharpness of the pain.

'Now,' Carew said, not unpleasantly, 'why don't we stop all this silly pretending?'

'When exactly was it,' Resnick asked, 'that you realized what you had to do?'

Ridgemount's gaze lifted from the table. 'When I read it in the paper, what had been done to that young doctor, the way they described how he'd been cut, with a scalpel, cut about the legs so's likely he'd never walk again. That's when I knew. Joseph, I said to myself, that's what you have to do.'

Resnick's pulse was beginning to race. He had to be sure. 'This young doctor, what was his name?'

Ridgemount looked surprised. 'Fletcher. Tim Fletcher.'

'You weren't responsible for that attack?'

Ridgemount glanced over towards Patel, shook his head. 'Haven't I been telling you?'

'Wait,' said Resnick, on his feet, keeping his voice as calm as he was able, 'with Mr Ridgemount. Let him continue with his statement. I'll send someone else along.'

He closed the door firmly and then began to run towards the CID room.

'Now isn't this better,' Carew was saying, 'instead of all that fighting? And over what?'

He was lying next to her, part on top of her, one leg and the weight of his chest pinning her down, pressing her back against the front of the settee. The roughness of the cheap carpet was rubbing against her leg, against her hip, and her other leg was going numb. Carew was playing with her breast, pausing every now and then to kiss her mouth, the side of her face, to slide his tongue inside her ear.

'And just wait,' he smiled, 'it'll get a good deal better.' He lowered his mouth to her face and licked a line from below her ear around towards her chin. 'That's what I could never understand about Karen. Silly little cow!

Didn't know a good thing when she felt one. Dumping me for Fletcher. Pathetic!' Carew slid his tongue inside Sarah's ear and slowly out again. 'Still,' he grinned, 'soon cut him down to size.'

The two cars cornered too quickly, almost colliding with one another as they swung into Carew's street. A third was pulling up in the road at the rear, not wanting to get caught out the same way a second time. Divine hammered hard at the door and when a sleepy medical student opened it warily, he barged him aside and went in, Naylor close behind.

Sitting in the second car next to Lynn Kellogg, Resnick thought, he isn't going to be there, eating a take-away and watching television, it isn't going to be that easy.

'When we picked Carew up,' Resnick said, 'he was chatting up one of the nurses, Sarah Leonard . . .'

'You think he might be out with her?'

'I don't think we should wait around on the off chance they come wandering back, hand in hand. Get through to the station, see if her address is on file. If not, check with the hospital. Don't let them give you no for an answer.'

Resnick got out of the car and walked along the pavement to where Divine and Naylor were now standing.

Carew readjusted his weight, used his knees to ease Sarah's legs further apart.

'Aah,' he breathed, closing his eyes. 'This is going to be beautiful.' Opening them again, face so close to hers, 'Don't you think?'

'Yes,' Sarah said.

Ian Carew smiled and sank himself down.

Sarah braced the fingers of both hands against his forehead, found his eyes with her thumbs and pressed as hard as she could. Carew screamed and arched back and she continued to squeeze her thumbs into the sockets, rocking him off balance without slackening her grip and managing, almost, to roll him over, till he punched her in the stomach and she couldn't prevent one of her hands from jerking away and then the other. He screamed at her and this time she hooked her thumbs into the corners of his mouth and pulled. Carew swung up and knocked her clear, forcing her away with his legs; stumbling to his feet then, jeans around his thighs, unable to keep his hands from rubbing at his eyes.

Sarah pushed at him hard, stiff-armed, and as he fell backwards she raced for the door. She had the top bolt back and was working on the second, the one that always stuck, when Carew staggered into the hall. For a moment she froze, thinking he was going to come for her, but instead he went in the other direction, towards the scullery where he had broken in; a wave of relief swept through her and she ran back into the front room for the phone.

He hadn't gone away: he had gone to the kitchen for a knife.

His words came with difficulty, jagged spaces in between.

'You bitch . . . fucking stupid . . . bitch . . . I'm going to . . . kill you for that.'

Sarah screamed.

She grabbed at a cushion and held it out in front of herself as Carew closed in with the knife. She continued to scream, loud enough to be heard in the street.

Resnick charged the front door with his shoulder and very little happened. He and Lynn barged it together and it shifted against its hinges but wasn't about to give. Resnick lifted the green dustbin from the front yard and yelled a warning just before putting it through the glass of the front window.

The screaming stopped.

Lynn Kellogg was in the room first, in and racing towards the back of the house, following Carew. 'Lynn!'

Resnick called. 'Let him go!' He knew Divine and Naylor were out there somewhere, covering the back alley. To his right, Sarah Leonard swayed and Resnick moved swiftly to her, fearing she might fall. 'Are you all right?' he asked, sensing the emptiness of the words as he spoke them. Sarah nodded once and shivered as she pulled the cushion close against herself and hugged it tight. Resnick picked up the phone to call for a doctor, the ambulance.

As he ran, Carew clawed at the jeans that were slipping back down his legs. He couldn't properly see where he was going and he was rocking from side to side, scraping himself against the chain-link fence, grazing his leg against the brickwork of the wall.

Lynn saw the discarded pram in time and hurdled over it, cursing herself for being so unfit, aware that by rights Divine and Naylor were waiting to pick Carew up but knowing how much she wanted him herself.

Thirty yards ahead of her, Carew's toe caught the edge of a sodden mattress and he lost his footing and that was all she needed. When she took hold of him, one arm in a choke hold round his neck, her free hand tightening on his right wrist, Carew still had the kitchen knife gripped tight. Lynn shifted her balance so that one of her knees was pressing hard into the small of Carew's back and then, as she would say later in her report, she applied the necessary pressure to the prisoner's arm to make him drop the weapon he was carrying.

The flicker of light came from Divine's torch as he and Naylor hurried towards her.

'Are you sure you're okay?'

'Yes. Yes. Thank you. I'll be fine.'

Resnick stood over her, hesitating. The sound of the ambulance siren could be heard as it approached along the main road heading into the city.

Sarah Leonard had refastened her dressing-gown and sat

the cushion in her lap; she had only looked at Resnick once in the past few moments. She looked up again now as Kevin Naylor came into the room from the rear of the house. 'We've got him, sir. Lynn got him. And a knife. He's on his way back to the station.'

'Good work.'

Sarah started to shake then, cry tears of relief. Resnick knelt alongside her and held her until the ambulance arrived and the paramedics helped her away.

'Make sure nothing gets moved till forensic are through. Just in case we can't prove what he did to Fletcher, I want to make this one stick.'

'The woman, sir. No danger she won't, like, give evidence?'

'No danger at all.'

Resnick unbolted the front door and let himself out on to the street as the ambulance pulled clear. In the space before the next police vehicles arrived it was quiet. Neighbours had retreated back into their own lives, the *News at Ten*. Above the upward slope of houses he could see the amber light that hung over the centre of the city. He thought about Ridgemount about to spend his first night in a police cell and the things he'd felt driven to do to find peace. He thought about Sarah Leonard, the next time she was in her house alone, the response to every unfamiliar sound, each opening of the door. And somewhere, in some small hotel or rented room, Elaine. He left the car where it was and began to walk, hands in his pockets, wanting something to clear the air, wanting rain.